Books by B. V. Larson:

IMPERIUM SERIES
Mech Zero: The Dominant
Mech 1: The Parent
Mech 2: The Savant
Mech 3: The Empress
The Black Ship (Novella)

STAR FORCE SERIES
Swarm
Extinction
Rebellion
Conquest
Battle Station

Other Books by B. V. Larson
Technomancer
Velocity
Shifting

Visit BVLarson.com for more information.

ISBN-13: 978-1477694008
ISBN-10: 1477694005
BISAC: Fiction / Science Fiction / Adventure

MECH 1: The Parent

(Imperium Series)
by
B. V. Larson

IMPERIUM SERIES
Mech Zero: The Dominant
Mech 1: The Parent
Mech 2: The Savant
Mech 3: The Empress
The Black Ship (Novella)

"And if you gaze for long into an abyss, the abyss gazes also into you." - Friedrich Nietzsche

One

Out along the rim of the galaxy hung a loose configuration of some sixty stars known as the *Faustian Chain*. From Old Earth, the cluster presented a colorful display of plasma-streams, luminous nebulae and brilliant pinpoints of light. Sparkling suns in relative proximity to one another shone down on numerous, rocky planets.

One such planet was Garm, a backwater colony world in the northern section of the Chain. It was an unimportant world to humanity—but as was often the case, the local population felt otherwise. Today, the arrival of a great tradeship caused countless eyes on Garm to turn upward and gaze at the dark structure, which was visible from the surface in the clear, gray sky.

The tradeship *Gladius* slid into a stationary orbit over Garm's southern continent. Originally built in vast orbital docks over Old Earth, the vessel was a marvel of technology which local colonists could not hope to replicate. A thousand modules swung majestically around the ship's central torus like a spinning constellation of stars.

Sitting inside one of the more luxurious modules was the Captain of *Gladius*. Dining with him was none other than the new Planetary Governor of Garm: Lucas Droad. The captain knew who Droad was, but most of the crew thought of him as a reclusive passenger. Garm was a turbulent world, and new Nexus officials often had short lifespans.

"You've been in this system on several occasions, Captain," Droad said. "Can you tell me something of Garm?"

"There's not much to say about this planet," said the overweight Captain with a shrug. He stirred the cup of tea that sat on his belly. "Garm was colonized some four centuries ago by

1

German and Chinese separatists from Old Earth. A watermoon named Gopus orbits Garm and is inhabited, although very sparsely. If anything, Gopus is even more inhospitable and uninviting than Garm. On both planets the climate is exceedingly hot and the people exceedingly primitive."

Droad tried not to let his disappointment show. He'd expected more than an entry posted by tourist agent. Both men knew the walls were full of listening AIs, and neither wanted to trigger the generation of a report, but the captain seemed more than just circumspect. Did the man fear to speak plainly aboard his own ship? Droad was uncertain what to make of the situation. Suspecting the Captain did not yet trust him enough to divulge real information, he decided to probe delicately. "I take it you prefer the more sterile and civilized environment of the habitats? The brochures say that Garm is a wild planet with unspoiled natural beauty. Aren't you looking forward to a few months of shore leave?"

The captain pursed his thick lips. "Any thinking man would prefer the high ground. Cheap holo-fabric stretched over a wall can simulate more stunning vistas than nature can provide. The greatest dream of most dirt-huggers is to scrape enough cash together to retire to a luxury hab."

"But there are no large habitats in this system."

"Certainly not, there is precious little luxury of any kind. Garm is greatly isolated and hence technologically and culturally backward. In short, I find the planet repulsive."

"I see."

The conversation lagged until the Captain cleared his throat. "I've noticed you're wearing the drab native clothing."

"No sense in being overly conspicuous," Droad said with a smile. He glanced down at his black gauzy smock and tight pantaloons. An overcoat of dark fur with a matching double-peaked hat hung near the doors. "I find that bankers feel more at ease when facing an inspector from the Cluster Nexus if he at least dresses as they do."

The Captain chuckled, causing the teacup on his belly to bounce. "A bank inspector? Is that what you're supposed to be?"

"For as long as necessary."

"The only place on Garm a man needs such heavy clothing

2

would be near the pole," commented the Captain. "More tea?"

"No, thank you."

Droad frowned into the cooling liquid in his cup, then glanced up and noticed the Captain watched him. They were both pumping one another for information, and coming up dry. He took a tiny sip, then put the cup down on the table. "I find the attire suitable," he said. "It's midwinter now and it's quite cold this season all the way down to the Slipape Counties, I'm told."

"I see, you don't wish to say where you're headed," said the Captain, nodding. "Of course—I understand. Well, I won't keep you any longer."

"Perhaps we'll meet on the surface at a later date."

The Captain blew out his thick cheeks, setting down his tea as well. "It's unlikely that I will get down to the surface during this trip. My duties are up here with the ship."

Droad stood up. "I'll be on my way then."

They clasped hands briefly. The two men smiled cordially while Droad slipped credit vouchers into the Captain's sweating palm. The Captain's smile broadened. He nodded, and in return he tucked a flimsy molecular datastrip into Droad's hand.

Then Droad left, heading straight for the docking tube. As soon as the captain was out of sight he unobtrusively wiped the other man's sweat onto his pantaloons. He suspected the material on the datastrip was worthless. He also wondered if his bribe would help matters, or make them worse.

Droad told himself it didn't matter. He'd known from the outset this entire mission was a gamble. Nevertheless, he had to try to turn the colony into a law-abiding community. The common people of Garm had lived without a proper government for too long now.

* * *

Droad glided down the miles-long jet-tube from orbit with the other passengers and arrived without fanfare. There was no one at Grunstein Interplanetary to meet the new Planetary Governor, as no one officially knew he was coming. His typical Garmish clothing made him resemble the local populace and in-system

3

traffic more than the new immigrants who had been his travel companions on the journey out from Neu Schweitz. He blended easily, only his greater than average height and weight distinguishing him from the crowd. A flood of traders swept by, tycoons from the Slipape Counties and the foodstuffs people from Gopus.

He pulled his Garmish hat down over his head more snugly, enjoying the unaccustomed feel of the fur against his skin. He moved with the crowd that flowed from the jet-tube gates down to the customs area. Once there, he separated from the crowd and approached the exit for official personnel. He ran his ID card through the machine, touched his thumbprint to a lit-up pad and focused his gaze on the optical sensor so that his retina could be scanned. Instantly recognized and catalogued, the steel doors shunted open and he was allowed to pass by the customs area without the routine body search. Tourists and businessmen from around the system gave him speculative appraisals as he passed them by, his single bag rubbing against his legs as he walked. The other immigrants from the *Gladius* shuffled along dazedly, ignoring him.

He stepped out of the foot-traffic that flowed relentlessly toward the exits to put on his coat. While he stood there he watched a very large man bypass the security just as he had. This man was a giant from Mendelia, one of the more common forms of genetic specialization they practiced on that strange world. The giant approached and stood next to him. Standing just over eight feet tall, he also wore furs and carried his luggage with him.

"Any problems, Jarmo?" Droad asked the giant.

"No sir."

Droad stretched his aching shoulders. "It's good to feel the solid pull of a planet under my feet again after three years of cryo-sleep. I know we only aged a few months on board the *Gladius* during the long flight out from Neu Schweitz, but I'm convinced that I still feel those years somehow, deep down in my bones."

Jarmo's eyes never stopped scanning the crowd. One by one, he located the security devices and appraised them expertly. "We are under surveillance, but I see no reason why we shouldn't move to the hotel immediately."

The Governor nodded and rode his way up the slider to the

4

nearest waiting cab. As he climbed in, the giant appeared at the exit, smoothly folding his body into the cab immediately behind him.

* * *

"There he is," said Militia General Ari Steinbach in a hushed voice.

Mai Lee inclined her head a fraction, the equivalent of a nod. Linked directly to the security feed from the spaceport, Mai Lee of New Manchuria stared at Lucas Droad speculatively. "I'm an excellent judge of character, General."

"Naturally."

"I don't like this man. There is no softness in him, no weak button to push."

"Well, it certainly hasn't shown up in his classified files, or in our psychological simulations, or even in the darkest secrets of his past, which are few and far between," said Steinbach.

"Most importantly, it doesn't show up in his face."

Steinbach said nothing.

"Will you be able to guide him?"

He hesitated a moment before answering. "He doesn't appear to be a weak man. However, enough money..."

"Blur dust and amp-rods speak louder," purred the lady of New Manchuria. "You will persuade him somehow." She watched with a knowing smirk as Droad breezed through security, then paused at the door for his giant to catch up a bit before going outside.

"Should I, ah—alert Governor Zimmerman that his replacement has arrived?"

"I'll do it myself. I'll enjoy the worm's terror."

"The presence of the bodyguard shows that he isn't completely ignorant of the situation here," said Steinbach. He broke off at Mai Lee's gasp of surprise and followed her gaze back to the security screens.

When the new Governor and his bodyguard left the spaceport, more giants made their appearance. They waltzed through security and waded through the throng near the luggage claim section. Each of them wore a black jacket with silver trim and carried long cases

5

like those used by rayball players. Mai Lee judged that they were all close to, or over, eight feet in height. They touched the delivery cubicles and grabbed up huge packs as they were dispensed.

"One, two, three, four, five... He's not kidding," muttered Steinbach.

"Count silently," hissed Mai Lee. "Pay the Captain half the agreed amount, since he withheld half of the information."

"He will not be pleased."

"He is either double-dealing us or incompetent. I have no time for him in either case."

Mai Lee noted one of the other passengers had touched a giant on the sleeve. She pressed the audio focus button immediately, and the computer-controlled parabolic microphones homed in and picked up the man's words.

"Go Rangers!" the passenger said, and laughed.

The Giant stared at him for a moment, frowning in suspicion, then gave a wintry smile.

"Obviously, the man thinks he's one of the new rayball players," said Steinbach, chuckling. "They're often giants. I doubt that they intended such a reaction."

Mai Lee ignored him. She squinted a bit, examining the giants closely.

"They are wearing black and silver, the Rangers' colors. Could they be players?" asked Steinbach.

"Of course not," snapped Mai Lee. "If you looked carefully, you can see that their cases aren't quite long enough to hold rayball sticks. Besides which, there are only flares for catch-baskets at one end, not at both ends. Viewed objectively, they looked suspiciously like weapons cases."

Then the giant that she had focused in on turned an eye to the optical probe. His eyes challenged hers. Staring into the giant's somber face Mai Lee blinked and for a split second felt a quaver of... not fear exactly, but what did the fool Germans call it? *Angst.* This emotion was followed immediately by rage.

"Damned Captain! Pay him nothing!" she screeched.

"He probably sold them as much information as we got out of him," said Steinbach. "More perhaps, since it would be easier to get, I wouldn't be surprised if the new governor was carrying a load of files in that bag of his on both of us."

6

"Cease your prattle!" Mai Lee was becoming increasingly agitated.

Steinbach glowered and pursed his lips. "I take it you want me to do something about this rather large team of problems."

"Ignore them for now. Kill the new Governor. Give him just enough time to let his guard drop a bit, but not enough for his flashy little escort to get organized."

"Direct," said Steinbach with an amused nod. "Quite a tall order milady. Might take a good deal of credit."

"Do it."

With a cordial nod, but not the bow that she demanded from her staff, the General turned on his heel and left.

She snapped off six months worth of nail-growth from her fingertip as she jabbed the cut-off button. The scene of the spaceport faded. She walked to the north side of the room, where a wall of one-way glass looked out over the city and into the forest of red hork trees beyond. The fruit on the tallest of the giant trees glittered in the sunlight.

She thoughtfully tapped her chin with the remaining inch of her broken nail, then called the Governor.

* * *

Governor Rodney Zimmerman was sitting naked in his bath, sipping from a glass of green hork-fruit wine when Mai Lee's call came through. He was quite irritated. It was time for his afternoon sex, which he liked to have while relaxing in his ten-thousand gallon tub, to be followed immediately by his afternoon nap. To his mind, there was no room in this scheme for a rude call from the dried up old prune that had helped appoint him. Accordingly, he let the phone chime six times, flashing Mai Lee's ID and stern image on the screen each time, lest he forget who it was that was calling, before he gulped his wine and opened the connection.

"Working hard as usual I see, Governor," she said, making no attempt at pleasantries. She stared rudely at his exposed fatty pink abdomen and stick-figure arms.

"I'm on vacation," he said stiffly.

"Naturally," she purred, a dangerous sound.

7

"Of course, it's always nice to hear from you, Empress," he smiled, using the title he knew she liked best. There hadn't been an official Emperor or Empress of New Manchuria since the earliest years of the colony, but Mai Lee had the proper blood and the power to fit the title.

"I've got some unpleasant news for you," she said, pausing to ponder her broken nail. Governor Zimmerman knew she was playing with him, but couldn't help responding with a groan. He so hated bad news. Bad news usually meant work at the capital, or worse, a field trip away from his beautiful villa on the rim of the famous Stardrop Cliffs to some squalid corner of Garm.

"Do you recall how you got your post, Governor?"

"Why... why, of course," stammered Zimmerman, spilling a dollop of his green wine into his steaming bathwater. He had refilled his glass, having sensed he might need bolstering. "I was appointed by the Planetary Senate."

"After the unfortunate demise of the duly commissioned Governor Riedman sent out from Neu Schweitz by the Cluster Nexus."

"Yes, the shuttle accident over the Desolation, a black day for the colony," said Zimmerman, really beginning to hate Mai Lee all over again. She had swung her clan's votes in his favor unanimously, which when added to the block from the Zimmerman's made him a shoo-in for the appointment. She all-too-often made a point of recalling this to his attention.

"Yes. I recall your presence at the funeral. You can fake tears like a holo-actor."

"Could you get to the point, Mai Lee?" he asked with uncharacteristic bluntness. Her prodding was beginning to get under his skin, which was pruning up badly in the churning waters. His paygirl stepped out onto the terrace wearing a terrycloth skirt and slippers. He waved her back into the house. She left with her lower-lip protruding in an exaggerated pout.

Mai Lee appeared to be enjoying herself. "Ah, how strange are these coincidences of fate that change the faces of power."

Feeling the first pang of real worry, Zimmerman leaned toward the phone, pressing his flabby side against the cool lip of his tub. "What's happened?"

Mai Lee's eyes ceased wandering and focused back on his

face, her black-eyed gaze hardening. "The new Governor has just arrived on the *Gladius*. He will be claiming your title shortly, I suggest you prepare a reception for him."

"What!" cried the Governor, horror-struck. He sunk back into the warm waters, eyes bulging like a heart-attack victim. "But it's only been eight years! How could this happen? What will I do?"

"It was bound to, sooner or later. The Cluster people aren't total idiots, you know," said Mai Lee with an off-handed gesture.

"What are we going to do?"

"I'll do what I can, and you do what you can. That means get your heavily-invested crowd of uncles and aunts to back you and slow down any kind of action in the Senate, in case he announces before we can move."

"But what will you do?"

Here Mai Lee grinned and showed all her ancient teeth— unnaturally preserved enamel that should have rotted out of her head one hundred and eighty years ago. Somehow that grin shined through all the make-up and the operations, showing her true, fantastic age. She leered at him, a skeleton clothed in flesh that hung on her bones like limp putty. "I'll do what I do best. I'll kill him."

After the connection cut off, Zimmerman was left to stew in his warm gurgling bath. He swam to the far side of his bath and looked out over the edge of the Stardrop Cliffs. Fluffy clouds scudded along far below him, brushing up against the great rock walls. Ten thousand feet down, air-swimmers wheeled over an endless stretch of white sand and black rocks. The sea pounded against the cliffs with huge waves churned up by the powerful gravity of Gopus overhead. It was a scene unchanged for millennia.

But it would change for Hans Zimmerman. If this new usurper were allowed to take his place, he would no longer be allowed to enjoy his villa, nor the jungle house, nor his saber-reed plantation on Gopus. He wouldn't be able to afford them without the tens of thousands of credits in graft he received weekly for his lax police services and general rubber-stamping of the Senate's every bill. Roasted air-swimmers and even green hork-leaf wine, his favorite, would be things of the past.

With a knot of cold fear in his belly that he had not known for almost a decade, Hans Zimmerman gulped down the last of his wine and swam back to his phone. He began tapping wet fingers on his contacts-list like a man possessed.

Two

Three shadows slid through the interstellar oceans at fantastic speeds. As silent as space itself, the Imperium seedships glided toward a bright, G-class star. They were bound for their Homeworld, the fifth planet in the system. Unfortunately, that planet had long ago been blasted to rubble. A dense asteroid belt now orbited in its place.

A few million kilometers from disaster, the ancient navigational organics finally came online and discovered that communications were out with the Homeworld's long dead traffic-control. After many millennia in the void the organics had grown slipshod in following procedures. Rather than engaging the emergency subroutines, a stored virtual model of the Homeworld was used to set the course. At a leisurely pace, the ships began thawing the crews.

Unaware of their doom, the Parents twitched feebly within their icy chambers, slowly reanimating. On full automatic, all three seedships sailed into the asteroid belt, decelerating and maneuvering to orbit a planet that no longer existed.

The youngest of the three Parents was the first to awaken. She knew immediately that something had gone wrong. The task force had passed the designated revival point, and now the ships were rapidly closing on the Homeworld unchallenged. She rose painfully out of her encasement, extended a pod for the first time after eons of cryo-sleep, and attempted to alert her sisters. Soon, more of her sensory organs began functioning and she was able to comprehend the data the ship was trying to feed her.

Despair bubbled through the Parent. The entire task force was doomed. They were about to collide with a mammoth, rapidly spinning asteroid and none of the others were awake enough to avoid destruction. With great effort, she engaged the override and commanded the ship to evade, to ignore its navigational software and switch to auto-defense. Immediately, the vessel swerved and jerked, wrenching the young Parent's delicate birth-chambers and half-thawed ovaries. Hideous agony ripped through her, but it was nothing compared to the pain she felt for the others as their ships sailed serenely onward.

Twin white pinpoints blossomed upon the surface of the asteroid. Mountain peaks twirled by her ship and barreled away into the void. She was alone.

Assuming she was in hostile territory, the Parent suppressed the ship's energy emissions and reflections to avoid detection. She let the ship coast through the asteroid belt and on toward the inner planets without applying further thrust. Her swollen organs shuddered with relief as she dumped liberal doses of hormones into her bloodstream. Feeling less stressed she began analyzing the data from the passive sensors and played back stored records from the datapods.

Within minutes she had a new objective. The fourth planet out from the home star had a hotter climate than the destroyed Homeworld, but was still inhabitable. It had been used by the Skaintz Imperium as a breeding ground for livestock in the past. Now however, the sensors reported that it was in the hands of unrecognized aliens. Judging by their space vehicles and radio emissions, these aliens seemed technologically advanced, and possibly were the minions of the hated ancient enemy: the Tulk.

Incredibly, the Homeworld itself was gone. She could detect no sign in the modern universe that the Imperium had ever existed. It was possible that she was the only survivor, the last in the universe capable of bearing offspring, the final hope of her race. She thought of the Homeworld, once the center of a vast interstellar empire. Thousands of black starships, the gloaming skyreefs, the air-swimmers soaring over the cliffs of the Grand Abyss—all were gone.

Watching and listening to the nearby aliens, she knew hate.

12

Despite the calming effect of the hormones, she quivered with emotion. Here were the destroyers! Applying only the most minute and undetectable jets of thrust, she guided her ship toward the fourth planet. The key to the success of her mission would be absolute surprise combined with blinding speed of attack.

Her mission was clear. The Imperium would be avenged.

* * *

On the surface of the fourth planet in the system, renamed Garm by the human colonists, a skald known as Garth huddled close to a tiny campfire that sputtered and popped, greedily eating the sparse fuel of spiny weeds he fed it. The weeds were all that grew on the sifting red sands.

Garth squatted beside his fire in the depths of the region known as the Equatorial Desolation. In this region of the planet, the days were blazing hot, but the nights were bitterly cold. An hour went by and his fuel dwindled until he was forced to hunt for more scrub brush to burn. Shortly after midnight he spotted an unknown figure approaching along the highway.

Garth was surprised. He had followed the perfectly straight ribbon of highway through the wastelands for days. He'd seen a few vehicles, but there had never been another person on foot. As the stranger drew near, Garth's surprise was compounded when he realized the stranger was a fellow wandering skald.

Garth hurried to place what wood he had managed to gather onto his fire. He added it all at once, rather than feeding it one stick at a time. The tiny flames flared up and brightened the scene.

"Your rider is the great Fryx?" the stranger asked as he came into the firelight.

"Yes," said Garth. "Come and sit with me."

"I'm Zeke," the stranger said.

"I am known as Garth."

Zeke, a small skald with large ears and long fingers, sat beside him. "You are indeed blessed to carry one so exalted as Fryx."

Garth smiled slightly, trying to quell his pride. He added another twig to the campfire and in so doing moved slightly so that the red scarring that slashed across his face was more visible in the

13

firelight. The stain was dramatic, and much more visible than scars most skalds bore. "The dictates tell us that it's not proper for a skald to feel prideful."

"Ah!" Zeke exclaimed, beaming. "I see now the mark of a great rider. The way it encompasses your eyes with livid red is truly striking," Zeke leaned forward so that he could better examine the red stain in the flickering light of the campfire. "Only the oldest and the largest of the riders leave such a blaze of glory upon mounting their skalds. Now I understand why my rider has driven me to find you. Surely, I have much to learn from the skald who bears Fryx."

"It was more good fortune than anything else that brought Fryx to me," said Garth, trying to sound humble.

"But tell me, communication must be easier for you than I, how does it go with Fryx?"

"True connectivity with one's rider always takes time. Today I started playing at sunset, and still I continue to play and listen, hours later in the depths of night."

Zeke nodded. "It goes much the same with my rider. Tell me, brother Garth, why did you come out here to this forgotten corner of this uninteresting planet?"

"I seek what all skalds seek: truth through communion with my rider. I have wandered over much of this star system."

"You are young yet."

"Yes, I'm still serving my pilgrimage. I've visited many of the works of man and nature, and recently entered the Desolation seeking solitude. The Desolation at night allows the closest intimacy and communication with one's rider."

"I beg your forgiveness for disturbing you," said Zeke seriously.

Garth waved his hand in a dismissive gesture.

"So you follow the great crossing highway northward," Zeke said, "while I follow it southward. I came here for no reason of pilgrimage, however. My rider drove me here with the express purpose of finding you and Fryx."

Garth stared into his fire for a moment, watching the tiny yellow tongues of light. He produced his skire. "Perhaps it's time we let our riders have free rein with us."

Zeke nodded and solemnly produced his skire as well.

14

Together, they began to play.

Soon Garth was in complete harmony with his rider. His fingers danced over the reed instrument with fluttering bird-like motions. He heard only the warbling music and felt only the cold night air. The desert climate gave his skire an excellent clarity of tone. Each thin note seemed to last for an eternity.

After a time there came a welcome scratching in his brain, indicating that Fryx was active and willing to commune. Garth opened his eyes long enough to glance over at Zeke. The man played his skire fervently; his fingers danced madly over the tiny holes and his cheeks puffed out. Sweat bathed them both despite the cool night breezes.

Zeke stopped playing his skire and made a croaking sound, as if trying to speak.

Garth looked at him in surprise.

"We must. We must perform the dance. Our riders must communicate. Micyn wishes to commune with the great Fryx."

Garth felt a stab of pain in his skull. His jaw locked up, then loosened slowly. He groaned and whispered, "Fryx agrees to the communion."

Setting aside their skires, the two men rose up and clasped hands. Together they let go the reins of their minds and their riders took over. Their sandaled feet shuffled in the red sands.

An unknowable time passed. Garth was so deep in communion that he didn't notice the roadtrain until it was almost too late. In their trance state the two men had danced right out onto the highway. What finally impinged on Garth's consciousness wasn't the thunder of the roadtrain's man-sized tires, or the glaring brilliance of its headlamps, or the vibrating ground that tingled his legs. What awakened him was the *sense* of it. The roadtrain had a presence, a malevolent spirit of its own. A spirit of combustion, rubber, steel and glass. A spirit of noise, speed, heat and grinding metal. It was a legendary behemoth with burning hydrogen in its belly and hot machine oil for blood.

The roadtrain was making its run from Space City on the east coast of New Amazonia to the Slipape Counties on the northern tip of the continent. It had crested the mountains early this afternoon and the driver had spent all evening making good time on the endless stretch of flat desert.

The headlights searched for Garth. Clear plastic lenses focused brilliant halogen suns and burnt purple stains into the back of his eyeballs. They stabbed through the crisp Desolation night like lasers cutting paper.

Garth threw his arm up to defend his gaping pupils and drew in a ragged breath. The roadtrain wasn't on him yet, but it was close, less than a kilometer off and coming very fast. Out here the only speed limits were in the guts of the driver and the number of squeeze-bottles of beer he had set between his legs along the way. He stepped back from Zeke, who was still lurching and shambling in an odd, inhuman fashion. He scrambled away and ran until he felt the reddish sand splash over his feet. He had taken to camping near the arrow-straight rolling carpet of tarmac because it retained heat better than the sand did. Traffic was a rare event this deep in the Desolation, and usually didn't pose a problem.

His intimacy with his rider broken, he suddenly felt the discomforts of his weary body. The desert night had stolen the heat from his bones. The void between the big shimmering stars overhead had leeched through the insulation of his heavy cloak and sucked the warmth from his thin sunburned body underneath. The nights in the Desolation were as cold and dark as the days were broiling hot and bright.

His eyes could focus a bit now in the glare the gargantuan truck was putting out from its six headlights. He realized that Zeke was about to be pulverized by a stampede of thundering black tires. Snaking out his tongue to slide over cracked lips he took a step back toward him.

NO! His rider shouted in their shared mind, a command that physically stopped the skald in his tracks. His leg muscles spasmed and went rigid.

Then the roadtrain was on top of them, and he realized that his rider had been right. He hadn't judged the speed of the oncoming monster of metal correctly. It moved too fast, and he would have been killed. As it bore down on him, the driver gave a single deafening blast on the horn, then for a moment the behemoth was right there, close enough to touch. Far, far up in the lofty cab sat the dim outline of the driver, and Garth thought he could feel the man's curious eyes on him for a blurred fraction of a second. Then a powerful wall of air hit him and knocked him flat upon the sands.

16

A hundred huge black tires thundered by, roaring as they greedily pulverized Zeke, grinding him into the tarmac and coating his corpse with black rubber and grease.

Instantly the blinding apparition was gone, shrinking to a set of glowing red trailer lights in seconds.

Garth grieved briefly over the rider Micyn and the skald Zeke. He performed what ceremony he could over the cooling mess on the highway.

Troubled, Garth spent the rest of the night trying to regain communion with his rider, but it was no use. Only the threat of death seen through Garth's eyes had gotten such an extreme emotion through loud and clear into Garth's consciousness. The frightening encounter with the roadtrain had caused Fryx to withdraw again. He played his skire for a while anyway, hoping to coax Fryx out of his mood, but to no avail. His rider refused to respond, remaining an inert cool presence hugging the nerves at the base of his skull. After a time he gave up on his music— without his rider's participation, there was no magic in it.

Sighing, the skald wrapped himself tightly in his cloak and settled down on his bedroll. He wondered about the strangeness of the night and grieved for Micyn and Zeke. What had Micyn come so far to communicate to Fryx? He doubted that he would ever know. He recalled the instant of direct communication he had experienced. Fryx had actually spoken to him, commanding him to halt. Few skalds could boast of such a moment. If the night had not turned into such a horror, he might have felt exalted at the interference of his rider.

Lying with his hands behind his head, Garth gazed at the heavens. Spread out above him were the nearby stars of the Listak Cluster. Gopus was below the horizon, but due to rise in the next hour or so. Hanging over the South Pole were the twin stars Thor and Loki, Thor a red giant that fed an endless stream of super-heated plasma to the vampirical white dwarf Loki. Down low on the eastern horizon, half-blocked by the Parched Spikes, was a liquid waver of stars that formed the constellation Taurus, seen at an oblique angle. Garth knew that Sol and Old Earth lay somewhere beyond, too dim for the naked eye to pick out.

He stared up at the brilliant Desolation stars, seemingly closer and brighter than anywhere else on Garm. As he fell asleep, it occurred to him that the riders had been discussing something about the stars. He recalled the sensation of fear and dread, he had associated it with the roadtrain before, but now he wasn't so sure. The two riders had been discussing a danger from the beyond Garm, of that much he was certain.

* * *

With a lurch, Fryx forced Garth's body to sit straight up. His legs were wrapped in a dusty bedroll. Everywhere stretched the sands of the Desolation. The rising sun was a lurid red glow on the horizon and the heat of it was already in the moistureless air. Standing in an awkward, stiff-kneed fashion and clumsily fixing sun-goggles on Garth's face, Fryx scanned the landscape through Garth's bloodshot eyes.

The nothingness of the Desolation met the optical organs, sending impulses down the optical nerves and into Fryx's worm-like tangle of interrupting tendrils. A flat stretch of slightly reddish sand reached up to meet the horizon in all directions, fringed with the hazy images of barren mountains. Those mountains were the Parched Spikes, the wardens that kept this vast wasteland a prisoner. Beyond were the steamy jungles and the oceans of Garm.

Gathering up Garth's meager belongings, Fryx rammed a wad of salty meat into the skald's mouth and added two mouthfuls of body-warm water from the tube-like waterskin that encircled his hips. Chewing mechanically, he set the body into a lurching march, heading back the way they had come. Fryx was in luck; the nearest settlement was only forty miles away.

Long legs swung forward, striding fast, eating up the ground. Wide eyes stared ahead, almost unblinking in the blinding morning sun and the wind-whipped sand.

Driving Garth's body like an ailing power-walker until it all but collapsed, Fryx managed to hitch a ride up into the Parched Spikes, entering the section of the range that formed the southern border of the Desolation. Soon he reached the summit of the high passes among the sheer cliffs and precipitous spires of the Parched Spikes. Here, the man he was driving with stopped at what was apparently the sole service-station between the Desolation and

18

New Amazonia to fill the car's tanks with hydrogen.

The man who had picked him up claimed to be an archaeologist on an extended sabbatical leave from Bauru University. He was an aging man with a sparse growth of gray facial hair that didn't quite fall into the category of a beard. Frequently during the trip, he drank from a canteen filled with an odorous alcoholic beverage that he kept on a chain that hung around his neck.

Fryx took a moment to feel an overwhelming wave of self-pity. He had thoroughly enjoyed his life as Garth's silent rider, peeking out from his quiet meditations only occasionally for variety. Physically, his kind consisted of little more than two pounds of grayish ooze and prickly spines. All riders preferred the inner solitude of a chosen skald's brain and nervous system to the harsh crude world of open elements. The interior of a human's body was a shrine of purity compared to the external world of oxygen-breathing creatures.

"As an archaeologist, these people intrigue me," said the driver, indicating the service man with a discrete gesture.

With an effort of concentration on the motor functions, Fryx swiveled Garth's eyes and focused on the man servicing the car. As gross and unclean as all of the beings that inhabited the open world were, this man stood apart as a figure of unrelenting filth. A tallish man in the loose bags of the desolation peoples, he was broad only around the middle, where he had tied a brown sash smeared with black grease. His pink face was clearly diseased, eroded and scabbed like wood that has been randomly carved by the worm. His eyes were mercifully hidden beneath heavy, dust-coated goggles.

"Oh, but I'm forgetting," said the driver, tugging at his scraggly beard and taking another swig from his canteen. "You've taken a vow of silence, haven't you? I'm a proper star-fearing man, but I'm afraid I'm just not used to having a fellow like you around. I mean, skalds just don't make it down into the Parched Spikes that often."

Fryx ignored the prattling of the driver and scrutinized the service man who moved about the front of the car, poking and prodding at the exposed machinery. Slipping something from his sash that flashed metallically in the brilliant sunlight, the man

19

leaned forward into the power compartment. Fryx directed Garth's body to hunker forward. Uncaring, he allowed the eyes to stare protrudingly and let the jaw hang slack. A white thread of saliva slipped from his lips and turned instantly cold as it adhered to his chin.

The driver frowned a bit, then returned to his indulgent smile. "Of course, I know I've got you at a bit of a disadvantage with you being silent and all, but a man in the desert doesn't get many chances to talk with anyone but himself, so please don't be annoyed."

He took a moment to fiddle with his low-brimmed desert hat, smoothing an imaginary crease while giving the skald a perplexed, sidelong glance. "Now take this fellow here, for instance. You'd think he'd be dying to talk to someone, but no—he's all business even though there can't be another customer within fifty miles or more. It's just his way, I guess."

Suddenly, the service man stood erect, triumphantly holding aloft a long narrow tube of some kind. He appeared at the window, dangling it in front of them for inspection. "This hose broke in your engine," he explained simply. A fetid odor tainted the interior of the car. Green liquid dripped lazily from the open end of the hose.

"Oh dear," said the driver, kneading his hairy chin with dusty fingers. "That's from the front stabilizers, isn't it? It wouldn't be safe to drive any further until we have a new one. You don't happen to have any hoses in stock, do you?"

The man leered in amusement at the concept and shook his diseased head. Fryx was suddenly alarmed. The dangling end of the hose was clean-edged and showed no sign of fraying. It had been cut, obviously. Then the service man spoke, and the fetid odor grew stronger. "We could send away for one. The next delivery flitter is due tomorrow morning."

"Well, let's order it then," said the driver resignedly. He turned to the skald, taking another swig from the canteen. "Looks like we could be stuck here for a bit. Perhaps we should go inside with him and take the opportunity to get out of the heat while we wait."

Behind his sun-goggles the skald's eyes were even wider now, although this would have seemed an impossibility a minute before. Fryx worked Garth's muscles, jerkily raising one hand to point at the hose. Was it not obvious that the man was a bandit? His throat made a rumbling croak, but he couldn't afford to release the vocal cords. If he activated enough of Garth's mind to permit speech, the human would have to be conscious and aware. If he allowed that, his control over the nervous system would be in jeopardy.

Fryx felt fear wash through him. He was facing the unimaginable indignity of exposure—possibly, and even more unthinkable: death. The stimuli of the outside world after so many years of quiet inner peace were too much. The urgency of his mission regarding the demons that stalked the heavens combined with these filthy thieving creatures of the hellish exterior world, and the final effect was simply overwhelming. His gelatinous mind shivered, causing his spines, planted deeply in the cerebral cortex, to jolt various neurons.

Garth's body wheeled to the passenger door, fumbling with the levers. He thrashed convulsively, a wild bucking horse with a mad rider. Desperately Fryx tried to get out of the car, but he couldn't control Garth's motor responses closely enough to open the door. Lurching back the opposite direction he found that the driver had produced a gun and pointed it at him.

"You've got to be the craziest bastard I've ever robbed in this godforsaken desert!" He whistled in amazement at Garth's alien demeanor. "Rolf, open the door for him, will you? Before he does something disgusting in my car."

Fryx was beyond hearing and interpreting the primitive grunts and warblings of human speech. The world had narrowed to that black-barreled weapon that confronted him and the oblivion it represented. Contemplating his possible exposure to the open air and radiation, sensing the nearness of death, Fryx loosed a terrible scream, a long chilling shriek of mindless fear. The sound was inhuman in nature, and its passage made the skald's throat rattle eerily, as though he was indeed already dead.

* * *

Garth was dreaming. Deep in the ocean of the subconscious, the glowing ember of his personality still glimmered, trapped in twisted memories and imagined fantasies. He dreamed that he was

21

at his confirmation again, the ceremony that had elevated him from the lowly position of a shrine-sweep to the exalted status of a skald.

What he remembered best about the experience was the odd combination of terrible pain mixed with a sense of ultimate fulfillment. The rider had been extracted from the skull of a dying skald and placed into his shortly after completing his manhood rites. Although he was a bit young for the process, his mentors had decided he was the most fit of the current candidates to bear Fryx. He was very fortunate indeed to gain such an aged and wise rider, who was of great size for his kind. Fryx performed expertly, this being his fifth such mounting over nearly three centuries of life. The skalds marveled at the rider's clean style. There was no hesitation, no shivering in the unfamiliar cold air of the external world, nor did he have to hunt for the appropriate opening.

With startling rapidity, a dollop of spiny gray jelly slid into young Garth's nostrils. Quickly burrowing through the thin lining of the sinuses, Fryx took up residence in Garth's cranium in less than a minute. Wrapping itself around the base of the brain, Fryx slipped thread-like nerves into the brainstem and tapped into an artery to feed.

For Garth it was the lancing of his nerves that hurt the most, even more than the bloody rip in his nasal passages. In fact, the pain had driven him into a frenzy, during which the hard, ready hands of his fellow skalds had firmly gripped him, lest he injure himself or the venerable Fryx.

Before the involuntary reactions had lessened and finally subsided all together as Fryx released chemicals through his spines to ease the young skald, Garth had been in a state of total panic. Thrashing wildly, eyes rolling and tongue gripped in bloody teeth, he had wanted nothing but to get away from the horrible pain in his head.

That feeling of mortal terror gripped him again now, reaching down deep into his dream and pulling him up to the distant surface of his mind.

The scream that Fryx had allowed to bubble up through Garth's dry throat had been half-human.

Garth came awake with a lurch, finding a gun with an alarmed-looking man pointing it at him. The man had a round belly, a bald pate and a scraggly gray beard. Without thought he grabbed at the gun, trying to wrest it away from the shocked bandit. The gun fired, the windshield starred and tinted safety glass sprayed the interior. With the wild scream that had awakened him still echoing in Garth's throat, the two wrestled for control of the weapon. The filthy service man outside the car had his blade in clear evidence now. He swiftly stepped around to Garth's side of the car. Murderous intent was evident in his stance.

Fryx made a play to regain control of Garth's brain, sinking his spines deeper into the nerve tissues. The attempt was unsuccessful, but managed to goad Garth into a frenzy of activity. Maniacal strength powered the skald's slim arms. Ripping the weapon away from his opponent's grasp, he tossed it to the floor and reached for the man with sunburned, claw-like hands outstretched.

Then the self-proclaimed archaeologist lost his nerve, popped open the door and tumbled out of the car onto the hot sand. Garth had enough of his mind left intact to engage the car's transmission and slam the power rod down. The car lurched forward, engine coughing then roaring as the great balloon tires churned up an enormous cloud of dust. He soon found that the car was far more delicate to drive than the power-sweeps he had rode about the monasteries as a boy. He careened through the desert, barely able to steer the wildly accelerating car with sudden twists of the wheel that vastly overcorrected. Eventually, he got the hang of it and eased off the power rod to the half-thrust point. The door and the hood closed themselves automatically, and the bandits were left dumbfounded in front of their shack.

Behind him the two men argued, one waving the severed belt he had pretended to pull from the car's engine, the other gesticulating with his canteen, which spilled liquid into the red blowing dust.

Garth was free of his rider's reins at last. He brayed wild laughter, spittle flying from his quivering lips. Freedom tasted delicious, like cool sweetmeats set on a catered platter. Grit swirled into the hole in the windshield and pelted his exposed tongue and formed a thin dusty film over his teeth, but he ignored it all and went on laughing.

Three

The Parent spent the days before planetfall analyzing incoming data from the passive sensors and planning her strategy. Studying the planet with enhanced optics, she decided to invade the larger of the two continents. The majority of the aliens were concentrated near the southern pole, indicating that the high temperature of the surface was generally not to their liking. This helped her decisions in designing the genetic make-up of her offspring.

Breaking out the feeding tubes, she stimulated her ovaries and prepared her birthing chambers for use. In less than a day, she would internally hatch and then birth several larvae. Using the ship's precious supply of protoplasm judiciously, the larvae would grow to adult offspring by the time the invasion began.

Laying back in a bath of simmering mud and earth salts, the Parent felt her body quake with excitement. The combination of the hormonal stimulation of the conception process and the mud bath was most pleasurable. Ovulation after so long was a real treat. It would be good to have offspring about again.

In this state of near-bliss, with her ovaries working and her glands producing a steady stream of delicious secretions, she recalled the long war with the Tulk. At first the Tulk, an ancient and powerful race of fading glory, had fallen easily to the hot aggression of the young Imperium. They were a shy race of philosophers, seemingly evolved beyond the crude machinations of warfare. They still retained vast wisdom from their past, however, and cleverly used other beings to fight for them. Eventually the tide had turned and despite all their early victories the Imperium had been driven back.

The seedships were part of the last effort of the dying Imperium to perpetuate itself. Sent out into the unknown to start new colonies at the end of the losing war with the Tulk, the seedships had slipped quietly through the interstellar void for millennia, dropping into any inhabitable system. Sadly, she was the only Parent in this system, possibly the only Parent of her kind currently alive and active anywhere. She had to assume that the future of her race had been left to her alone.

With intense interest, the Parent studied the datastream coming in from her long-range optics. It appeared that the enemy was quite well entrenched on the hot water-world. Within hours, she had located all the major spaceports open to local system traffic and identified the largest one at the southern pole where the huge ship orbited.

Ah, the ship! What a fantastic vessel she was. Her incredible size could only mean she was built for interstellar travel. The ship was a great blot that must have shadowed a significant portion of the gleaming watery surface a thousand miles below her. The Parent considered the capture and control of the ship to be one of her primary strategic goals. What was more incredible than her size, suitable for transporting hundreds of thousands of offspring, was her apparent lack of weaponry. In a way, this was a sad note on the disintegration of the Imperium. Surely, if the Skaintz Imperium had still been a viable military force in the region then no such ship would be without escort. The Parent's dim hopes of support from her own kind were all but extinguished by this one logical conclusion.

But not all the data was bad, not by any means. For one thing there was no sign that her presence was suspected. Equally important, there seemed to be a simple method by which she could secretly pilot the ship down to the planet surface. By studying the traffic patterns, it seemed clear that small ships the size of her own seedship were regularly landing and departing without official sanction. As many as one in twenty landings were accompanied by tiny shadows, the small ship riding close in the slipstream of the larger, merging their radar signatures. The ground controllers and almost certainly the captains of the shadowed ships should have

26

been able to detect some of the activity, but never were any of the perpetrators apprehended. These actions and other elaborate efforts to escape detection by a veritable fleet of small ships that flittered about the system baffled the Parent. Her ship's sensory enhancement systems were excellent, but it was difficult to believe that these obviously advanced aliens couldn't match it. She had no real concept of graft and corruption, at least not on such a broad scale. She briefly entertained the idea that the aliens were already being invaded by a third party, or perhaps that they were staging wargames to train their pilots.

Shuffling her sensory fronds in a gesture equivalent to a shrug, the Parent decided that the rationale behind the comings and goings was of trivial importance to her plans. What was important was that this practice represented a path for her to make her landing undetected.

She sat back from the optics interface and slurped a liquid refreshment into her digesters. Inside her fourth birthing chamber she felt the stirrings of an offspring. It was an umulk, the largest of the offspring she was currently gestating. Very soon, the larvae would break out of its capsule and be born, soft wet spines hardening, mouth open and mewling with ravenous hunger. The prospect of having a shipload of suckling larvae gave the Parent a deep sense of satisfaction.

She slurped more refreshment before returning to the optics. She enjoyed the slippery, slightly bloated feeling of having the offspring inside her. It would be good to see her larvae grow and mature into fine Imperial warriors.

* * *

Sergeant Borshe, out of uniform and off-duty, sat outside the Renaldo Hotel with two New Manchurian gunmen. Inside the hotel his plants pretended to clean the lobby, their weapons stashed in the utility carts which had been provided by the intimidated hotel management.

Ari Steinbach had quickly tracked the Governor down to the Renaldo and sent Sergeant Borshe out to take care of things. The Renaldo was a very nice, but not quite elegant hotel along Black

Beak Avenue. The Governor had checked in about an hour ago and then left alone, either to make contacts or to eat, as it was dinnertime.

"This will be an easy one," said one of the gunmen. He wore a suit of the most elegant style with neck ruffles of indigo silk. He fidgeted with a Wu rattler, keeping the sleek black barrel pointed at the car door.

"Don't count you're swimmers yet," said Sergeant Borshe, checking his watch and thumbing the safety off of his Wu hand-cannon. He was a big man with heavy jowls and hands the size of rayball gloves. He looked all wrong in his clothes, like one of the great bald apes yanked out of Garm's southern jungles and shoved into a suit. "They're due any second now, boys."

The New Manchurian toughs looked at him in disgust. Borshe was always finding a way to call them *boys* or *monkeys*. Borshe noticed their expressions, but didn't bother to acknowledge them.

"Just because they're giants doesn't mean crap," spoke up the younger one in back. He also wore a sharp-cut suit so as to pass for a hotel guest, but had kept his cloth headband. He put the barrel of his rattler on the driver's seat headrest, inches from Borshe's ear. "This gun will cut any giant in half, no matter how big."

Borshe didn't bother to reply. He pulled a second hand-cannon from his rucksack and checked it thoroughly. Then he glanced in the rearview mirror. "Governor is coming in."

The two toughs wheeled in their seats and they all watched as the cab slid up to the lobby doors and sank down on its skids. Borshe hit the dimmer and the windows went dark, shading the inside and hiding their faces and weapons. Goosing the power rod, he followed the cab up the drive.

* * *

Governor Droad wasn't pleased with what he learned from the files he had purchased from the Captain of the *Gladius*. Nexus Cluster Command's worst fears concerning the progress of Garm toward corruption and decay had apparently been surpassed since he had left Neu Schweitz three years before. Graft, smuggling and factionalism amongst the ruling elite had the colony teetering close

28

to anarchy.

Equally disturbing, the previous governor had lasted only a few weeks into his term before experiencing a deadly accident over the red hork jungles in New Amazonia. The new governor was of the worst sort. Hans Zimmerman was a self-serving inbred crony of the ruling families. Spineless and unconcerned, he apparently left the job of rulership completely up to the aristocratic Senate, coming out of his permanent vacation only long enough to perform the most perfunctory duties of state.

As he climbed out of the cab, Lucas Droad saw the car coming up the drive out of the corner of his eye. The car was coming a bit too fast, but he wasn't really ready for an attack yet, so he didn't respond. He paid the driver and mounted the steps into the hotel lobby. The car pulled up behind the cab and the doors slammed shut behind the three men who piled out. Droad looked back and noticed that the car had the windows dimmed even though the sky was entirely overcast. Then he saw the shape of a sleek black weapon and threw himself at the glass hotel doors.

Tossing the confused bellhop out of his way, he plowed into the lobby, drawing a slim-barreled pulse-laser. Bullets shattered the glass behind him and the bellhop was cut down, blood welling up from a dozen holes in his blue vest and staining his silver epaulets. Surprised to find himself still breathing, Droad sprinted into the marble-walled lobby.

Tapio Kuosa, one of his giant bodyguards, sat in the lobby reading a newsfax and sipping hot caf. He looked up as Governor Droad came running in. With one moment of eye contact the giant was up and drawing his weapon, but it was already too late. The Manchurian janitor behind him fired thirty rounds into the back of his huge head. The Mendelian giant toppled forward. His body destroyed a rich horkwood table while the red ruin of his head crashed between two shouting guests on a silk divan.

Another assassin came out of the restroom with his weapon raised. Droad dove over the front desk, flattening a clerk. The clerk's hairpiece skittered across the floor. Bullets streamed over the desk and a woman screamed.

From outside there was a heavy *crump* of a high-powered weapon. The car the assassins had come in exploded into melting fragments. Droad darted up over the counter and burnt away the throat of the man who had come out of the restroom while he hesitated, looking at the burning get-away car.

Then a big Anglo man pushed through the glass doors, holding a hand-cannon in each of his beefy fists. Droad threw himself to one side behind the desk, taking a spray of plastic splinters in the face and arms as the hand-cannons barked in unison.

The assassin approached the desk, blasting head-sized holes in it as he came. Then the glass doors behind him simply disintegrated. His hand-cannons barked once more before he was seared by a direct hit of plasma from behind. As soon as the echoes of the plasma blast had died down, the sounds of the street outside could be heard through the opening. Charging into the breach came Jarmo Niska carrying a recoilless plasma rifle big enough to mount on an armored personal carrier. Two more black and silver dressed giants backed him up. More giants sprinted from the elevators and gunned down the last of the assassins in the hotel.

The remainder of the governor's bodyguards thundered down the stairs and into the smoke-filled lobby. Jarmo made a quick inspection, then whistled and gave a quick hand-signal. Droad still crouched behind the front desk with his pistol in his hands while the terrified clerk eyed him with dread.

"Do you think they've gone?" asked the clerk.

"Only until the next time," said Droad, giving the man a grim smile. He tried to get up and found that his leg had been injured.

"Are you hurt, sir?" asked the huge, moon-like face of Jarmo Niska as he loomed over the desk.

"Yes, my leg caught a few splinters, I think. Pull me up, will you?" While the hotel clerk gaped, Jarmo bent over the desk and gently lifted Lucas Droad into the air.

"I think that our location and identities have been compromised, sir," said Jarmo stiffly. His yellow-blond brow furrowed deeply as he examined Droad's injuries.

"Obviously. So much for posing as a bank inspector, eh? Could you hand me a med-kit?" asked Droad, tearing apart his left pantsleg and exposing a bleeding wound. He sighed, they had no time to pick out the red horkwood splinters and buckshot now. He simply sprayed on a double layer of pink nu-skin and tossed the empty canister. Meanwhile, Jarmo marshaled his team and placed them about the lobby in a defensive arrangement. Sirens sounded out on Black Beak Avenue as police cars and an ambulance rushed toward the hotel.

"What's our situation?" he asked Jarmo.

"One of our men dead, plus seven civilians. We put down all of the assassins. We're running an ID check on them with the police computers now. Several more of the civilians were badly injured. I took the liberty of calling the emergency services on my phone."

"You did excellently, Jarmo, as usual. Once again, I owe you my life. I hope we all live long enough for me to repay the debt," said Droad, struggling to stand. The anesthetic in the nu-skin was taking hold, easing the pain and stiffness temporarily. He looked over toward the fallen giant, his ruined head still face down on the silk divan. "That's Tapio Kuosa, isn't it? Damn."

"Yes sir, a good man," replied Jarmo. His eyes never stopped roaming over the lobby and the street outside. His phone beeped and he touched the device embedded in his huge ear. After listening for a few seconds, his expression changed to one of alarm. He shouted curt orders to his men who jumped to obey. Outside, the police vehicles and the ambulance had pulled up. The police were forming up behind their cars, readying their weapons.

"Sir!" boomed Jarmo, his voice deafening at close quarters. "The Caucasian was a police sergeant, off-duty!"

Droad's head jerked up at this, looking out the blown out doors toward the gathering police forces. He nodded. "So that's how it's going to be." He turned back to Jarmo. "Emergency exit. Let's move it."

Without bothering to acknowledge the command, Jarmo shouted again to his men. They withdrew instantly from their posts, retreating from the policemen outside. Droad hobbled painfully after them into the corridor, and then suddenly he was swept up in a pair of massive arms. He was carried off at a sprinter's pace into the hotel. Feeling slightly embarrassed, he looked up into the blue eyes of Jun, a man with a nose the size of Droad's fist. All around him the other Finns clustered, ducking down as they ran so as not to ram their heads into the ornate overhead lighting fixtures. Behind them, the police cautiously approached the smoldering hotel lobby.

"Everyone in the hotel is under arrest," said a sergeant with a bullhorn from the safety of his vehicle. "Lay down your weapons

31

and come out."

They ignored the corrupt police and carried Droad swiftly to a location they had scouted out immediately after checking into the hotel. Jun turned to shield the Governor with his body as two other giants unlimbered their plasma rifles and simultaneously fired at the back wall of the hotel. Masonry vaporized and fragmented, blasting a hole out into the open air. Moving as a smooth team, the men rushed through the breach and climbed into the rented hover-limos that waited in the parking lot beside a row of trash consumers.

"We have a safe hiding spot nearby, sir," Jarmo said as they climbed into the car. "We've lost our pursuers for now, but we should take cover until things cool down."

"Right, we'll duck low for tonight," Droad sat on the floor of the limo, surrounded by the huge hunched-over forms of his bodyguards.

"And tomorrow?"

"We'll head back to the spaceport," said Droad grimly. He noted Jarmo's upraised eyebrows. "They aren't going to let us just walk in and take their power from them, that much is clear, but I'm not going to just hide, either. Grunstein Interplanetary is owned by the Cluster Nexus itself. We'll make our stand there."

Jarmo dipped his head slightly: a nod. He gave a small shrug and then went back to the business of keeping the Governor alive.

Four

"Imbecile!" hissed Mai Lee into the video unit. The luxurious hanging tapestries of the Planetary Senate Chambers lined the walls behind her. She was wearing the blue velvet robes of her office, and held a portable video unit in the palm of her hand. Her tense, harsh face was a wild network of lines that no surgery could completely erase. "Everyone is outraged! How could you fail at so simple a task?"

Ari Steinbach made a wry face, raising his eyebrows until they disappeared beneath his hanging blonde bangs. Out of sight of the video pick-up, he silently drummed his horkwood desk with his fingers.

"My operatives—"

"Your operatives are cheap, ineffective thugs," she said from between her clenched teeth, trying to keep other nearby Senators from hearing. She poked her pen-shaped note-recorder at the video pick-up so that it seemed to lunge out of the screen at his end. "All you did was put him on his guard and get the damned Senate stirred up with headlines. The media is playing shots of the wrecked lobby and the bodies at every commercial break! The crazy Zimmermans have mobilized their estate armies in Grunstein and Slipape County."

Ari nodded his head gloomily. After the failed assassination attempt, he had spent all night at militia headquarters, trying to cover his involvement and fend off the newsmen. Sergeant Borshe's bloody corpse had done nothing to help matters, as his close relationship with Ari was known to the media. After a night of being run ragged by hungry newshounds, he had spent the day trying to calm the excitable aristocracy of the colony. All day reports of the powerful elite families pulling together their 'security forces', some of which had air assault and light grav-armor units, had flooded his desk.

He sighed and glanced out his window briefly, eyeing the heavy cobalt waves of the polar sea. So near to the pole the days were only four hours long during the winter and darkness was closing in fast. The skies were dark and pregnant; it looked as if they were in for a storm tonight. It might even snow if it lasted until morning.

"General!" she snapped, rapping her note-recorder on the audio pick-up so that a loud clacking noise sounded at the other end. Ari jumped and grimaced.

"Sorry, your Excellency," said Ari distractedly. He made a dismissive gesture with his hand, then rubbed his eyes and sipped his hot caf. "I've been here all night trying to clean up this mess. I might point out that you suggested this course of action."

"And I might point out that you are on the edge of losing your lucrative office, General," said Mai Lee with a flash of her merciless eyes. They were the eyes of a reptile, cold and devoid of compassion. "Listen, you just find where Droad is hiding this time. You just find him and call me. I will have my personal assets take care of matters after that."

Ari heard his own involuntary sharp intake of breath. The old battleaxe was talking about committing her personal guard. Known as the Reavers, they were also giants, monstrous Korean men that normally guarded her hilltop palace in the Counties. Ari had seen them often on her estate, and he feared them. With under-sized heads, long gorilla-like arms and incredibly wide barrel chests they seemed only marginally human. As a group, they were mysterious, legendary for their cruelty and brutal professionalism. He was surprised that she would allow them to stray from her stronghold. It was obvious that Mai Lee was under terrific pressure from the Zimmermans and probably the Manchurians in the Senate as well.

"Recall that you are my creature, General. You can be destroyed as easily as you were created."

Ari narrowed his eyes, feeling deep hate surging through him

34

for this evil wraith-like woman. "Recall, Senator, that we're in this together, and that you need me. In fact, I seem to be one of the few friends you have at the moment."

Mai Lee seemed overcome with fury and Ari worried that he had overstepped himself. Her face was a rictus of hard-lined hatred. Then her eyes seemed to bulge less. Her face softened and sagged back into its normal shape.

"So," she said, her voice becoming soft and silky, the way it must have been centuries before in the flower of her youth and beauty. "The puppet has teeth."

The screen went blank, and Ari was left with a feeling of dread in the pit of his stomach. Unlike Zimmerman, he had no powerful family of his own to turn to in times of need. The Steinbachs owned a successful software publishing company in town, but they controlled no land or vast amounts of capital.

He decided it was time to put into action his emergency plans for the worst. Things were going poorly, he needed to move quickly before events took an even darker course.

Ari rose and drew an anti-snooper device from his desk. He turned the jammer on and set his windows to a metallic opaque setting. After securing the inside lock on his office door, he dragged a heavy pseudo-marble reproduction of a skald sculpture to one side. Using a knife from his desk, he cut a squarish hole in the thick carpet. Underneath was revealed a locked safe. He proceeded to disarm six security systems and type in the lock's ten-digit hexadecimal code. The safe opened and he withdrew a satchel, identical to the one he used at the office. Switching the two satchels, he resealed the safe and reset the devices. Working with nervous speed, he replaced the carpet and the sculpture, eyeing it from many angles to make sure that the placement was identical. Satisfied, he rubbed his hands together as he donned his thick fur-lined coat and left the office.

Striding briskly, but not quite trotting, he took the elevator to the underground garage and climbed into his waiting limo. He directed the driver to head for the cross-colony autobahn, rather than toward his home in the hills overlooking the old colony domes. He settled into the backseat, holding his satchel on his lap like a sleeping child.

It was dark outside now and the wind was a growing, low-

35

pitched howl. The first heavy raindrops splattered the limo's windows as it reached the gates of the spaceport.

* * *

When Mai Lee returned to the main conference chambers located on the floor directly below the Senate floor, most of the faces that meant anything in the power structure of Garm were waiting there for her. They were like a panicked herd of jaxes, she thought. Then she amended the thought, seeing the dangerous look in many of their eyes. No, they were more like a panicked lynch-mob, and they smelled their witch.

Most knew that something big had hit, many of them knew that the new governor had arrived, and a few even knew that the militia had made a stab at assassination and cut their own fingers. What everyone knew was that it was all Mai Lee's fault.

"You told us you had planned for this eventuality," said the formidable figure of Johan Zimmerman, gripping his robes at his chest and giving her a look of utter contempt.

"You said they wouldn't come for years yet," whined a thin-faced Senator from New Manchuria with six-inch long rat-tail mustaches. He dropped his eyes as her glare swept over him.

"The Cluster Nexus will drop troops when they hear of it!" shouted the Thane of the Slipape Territories, the bright florescent lights reflecting from his shiny bald scalp. He was one of the few individuals in the group who truly owed no fealty to either the Zimmermans or the Manchurians. He valued nothing more than his political independence, and thus had only enough power to prove annoying to the others. "You crazy southern bastards have tried to kill the legitimate governor twice in a row and this time you missed!"

"Shut your hole, you old fool!" shouted back Mertrude Evans, a staunch supporter of the powerful Zimmermans. Mertrude was an immensely fat woman with protruding eyes. She was at least as colorful in personality as was the Thane himself. She was an environmentalist, he an exploiter, both were fanatical in their cause. Their long-standing mutual hatred was well known and generally tiresome for the others.

Johan Zimmerman raised his hands overhead in a dramatic gesture for calm. Due to his political clout, he soon got it. With a sweeping motion of his arms, he gestured toward Mai Lee, who still stood in the entryway, reviewing them all coldly. "Let's hear what the Lady has to say."

Acknowledging her greatest competitor with a curt nod, Mai Lee addressed the assembly. "Senators, we are all on the same side. Let's not forget where our profits come from, regardless of our political differences concerning the management of our planet. Nexus influence constitutes the removal of power from this body, and is to be avoided at all costs. On this I hope we all agree."

There were several heads nodding and a general murmur of agreement rose from the Senators. The Thane, however, saw fit to interrupt her. "Of course we all want the Nexus to keep their noses away from our arse. That's not the point, woman!"

"What is the point, you old goat?" demanded Mertrude, unable to restrain herself, so great was her dislike for the Thane. Johan Zimmerman quieted her with a blunt stare of disapproval.

"The point is," boomed the Thane, ignoring Mertrude. "That you could do all this in a much more subtle fashion, rather than trying to kill the man and his retinue on his first day planetside! A hand-cannon to the head, that's all you Manchurians understand, isn't it? Your political objectives for personal power have caused you to put us all in jeopardy. I vote that we remove you as our protectorate and find a new man to run the militia. Ari Steinbach is a coward and a cretin!"

For a moment, Mai Lee marveled at the man's bravery. Perhaps he was unaware of the danger he was placing himself in. As an unaligned member of the Senate, he had no faction sworn to avenge any sudden accidents that might befall him. Indeed, the stunned silence and furtive glances that followed his speech seemed to unnerve him just a bit. He looked flustered for a moment, then raised up his eyes and locked them with Mai Lee's.

"The problem will be taken care of." Mentally, she marked the Thane for a dead man, when she could find the time to dispose of him properly.

"When?" asked Johan Zimmerman.

"When I see fit," she said, baring her ancient teeth just a fraction. Spinning around in a whirl of blue fabric, she left the chambers and mounted the steps to the flitter pad. She boarded her private flitter and directed the pilot to her home estate, which sprawled over thousands of square miles, half in New Manchuria and half in the aristocratic Slipape Counties. On the way she cursed the governor, cursed the Thane, and cursed Ari Steinbach.

* * *

Mai Lee had returned to her estate to meditate after the debacle in the Senate Chambers. She levitated near the ceiling, while a panorama of Old Earth played on the holo-plate.

The communications module disguised as an arrangement of orchids chimed three times before she responded. "What is it? I am highly stressed this evening."

"There has been a crime in the estate village, Empress," said a soft voice. "The people require your judgment."

"Ah," said Mai Lee, rising into a sitting position. "Just the thing I need to relax."

The holo-plate images of Old Earth evaporated to be replaced by the wooded hills around her estate. The speaker hidden in the flowers narrated. "This very day a serious crime was committed by the second son of a power-cart driver. Instead of delivering his jaxes to the tax collectors at the gates of the marketplace for proper accounting, he drove his load of livestock off the road and into the forests."

Following along with the narration, the holo-plate played a computer simulation of the crime. The jaxes shrilled and stamped as the cart bumped through the trees.

"There he staged a crude robbery, in which the power-cart was rammed into a tree and emptied of its valuable cargo. After killing the jaxes and stashing them for later illegal sale, he tore his own clothes in a conspicuous manner and rolled through a muddy thicket to appear as if he had been beaten. Staggering back to the village, he was horrified to find his story was not believed."

"How was the crime discovered?" asked Mai Lee. Her shoulders were relaxed and she even sported a grim smile. Passing judgment on criminals always agreed with her.

"The village's chief enforcer deserves considerable credit for discovering the critical flaw in the man's story: he still retained the code-card for operating the power-cart, which although damaged, could have been driven away. Allowing the man to retain the code-card seemed an unlikely oversight on the part of these otherwise intelligent and ruthless thieves. Launching a full investigation, the enforcer soon learned the truth. Due to the flagrant nature of the crime, we recommend no leniency under estate law."

"Of course not," snapped Mai Lee. "The man attempted to steal from me."

"What punishment shall be delivered, Empress?"

Mai Lee sat back and floated for a minute or so, entertaining various ideas. "Have him drawn and quartered in the town square," she said finally. "That always makes a good show. I need a good show right now."

"It shall be done," said the orchids, then fell silent.

Mai Lee meditated while the punishment was prepared. When it finally came, she was all but quivering in anticipation. Depicted in stark 3D perfection she watched as the four hydro-powered engines chugged into life in the town square.

Soon the cables running to the man's limbs drew tight and lifted his body from the ground. The engines, normally used to generate power for the village, coughed steam and revved up the scale. They were placed into their lowest gears and the throttles were opened. As a tug-of-war, the contest between man and machine was uneven. With a horrible ripping noise, first one arm gave, then the other. The two remaining contestant engines dragged their victim across the compound. Each held one leg and rapidly took up the slack in the cable. He flopped about in a frenzy of motion. This quickly subsided into a feeble quivering as the cables again went taunt and the left leg gave out with a distinct popping sound. The engines were stopped and the enforcer directed the tearful family members to clean up the mess.

The Great Lady herself watched the entire enterprise on live holo. It seemed to be over with too soon. She sighed as the man expired. She needed more intense relief from the stresses represented by Lucas Droad and the bumbling General Steinbach. She needed relaxation, a diversion, and a release of tension. The execution had not quenched her thirst for sensation. She tapped her nails on the control console thoughtfully, watching as the dismembered corpse was dragged away leaving a pink trail in the sand. Her penciled-on eyebrows jerked up, and would have risen above her hairline had she not gone completely bald over a century ago. She smiled for the first time in a week as she thought of her battlesuit hidden beneath the castle. This scandal in the village might be just the thing for a little sport. She would have to clip all her nails down to the quick in order to drive the suit again, but it would be worth it. She believed, as her father had before her, that peasants were best dealt with in a heavy-handed fashion. Occasionally, a reminder of their status was in order.

* * *

Long after darkness had fallen over the village that huddled beneath the castle walls and the cookfires had died down for the night, a team of four barrel-chested brutes from the palace guard stalked through the narrow mud-splattered alleys. The gorilla-like men were unarmed, but as they weighed over three hundred pounds each and were exquisitely combat-trained, they needed no weapons. At the house of the criminal family, almost everyone slept except for a young boy that couldn't so easily forget his big brother. He lay huddled at the foot of the family shrine, breathing the last of the incense.

Because he was still awake, he caught sight of the men outside the hut and tried to climb out a window, shrieking in alarm. He surprised one of the small-brained brutes that struck him with a bit too much force, snapping the thin neck and killing him instantly. The boy's body was tossed back through the window, landing on a mat with his three sisters. Then the giants forced the doors and immediately the beatings began in earnest.

Mai Lee drove her battlesuit out from under the castle and up into the courtyard via a secret tunnel that slanted down into the deeps. The tunnel opened at the base of the fountain that dominated the mosaic gardens in front of the main keep. Anyone who might have witnessed her appearance would have seen a black monster in the shape of an ancient, terrestrial allosaurus materialize in the gardens. Standing over seven feet high and weighing several tons, the collapsium-armored battlesuit indeed resembled a reptile.

40

It had huge rear legs, stubby gun barrels that thrust from the chest like foreclaws and a computer-controlled rear tail that moved incessantly to balance the machine. With a heavy stride that crushed vegetation and cracked flagstones, she set off down the hill toward the village.

The battlesuit had been custom-made for her on the distant Nexus, back before such things had been rigorously recorded. She had ordered it partly for protection against assassination and partly for sport. The proud technicians that had brought it with them over so many light-years had trained her in its use and helped her set up special security codes so that no other could operate it. As a precaution, she had turned the chest-guns on them at the end of the final operator's lesson. Since then, countless murders had been performed in the guise of the estate dragon, which had become something of a folk legend in the region over the years.

Hearing the terror-stricken cries of pain coming from the hut of the criminal family, the villagers had reacted by extinguishing all fires and artificial lights and bolting their pathetically thin doors. When the first rasping, crashing footfalls of the dragon were heard and recognized, however, the mood changed to one of panic.

"Gi!" they cried, voicing the local name for the legendary monster. Many of the villagers fled for their lives into the fields, others buried themselves in makeshift hiding places, trembling in fright. Only the bravest and the most foolhardy snuck to their darkened windows to catch a glimpse of Gi.

The monster walked directly through the town square itself. The foreclaws thrust into the empty windows of the shops with vicious swipes, its tail whipped about, striking down tent poles and smashing trade goods. From the great head a blue glow was visible where the eyes and mouth should be, and a faint blue radiance could be seen outlining the major plates in its armored body.

Purposefully and unerringly, it strode directly to the alleyway where the family of criminals lived and struck down the front door of the hut by simply walking through it. Inside the huts, the cries of woe took on an even more chilling note, the note of people faced with imminent death.

Mai Lee was enjoying herself more than she had in years. For too long, she realized now, she had been willing to content herself with watching the video-feed of her bumbling minions artlessly

41

executing her will. Tonight was different. Now the blood was on her hands directly, now the victims looked directly at her as they screamed in mortal terror. Inside the suit, her eyes were wide and staring, her heart pounded with true excitement, her lips were pulled back from her teeth in a death's head grin.

First, she killed the oldest male by shoving one of the chest-mounted gun barrels into his belly and ramming him against the wall of the hut. The gun barrel ran through him like a spear. He was already dying but she loosed a burst of forty rounds into his chest cavity anyway, blowing a hole through the back wall of the hut.

She turned the machine around and reached with one foot to crush the life from a boy that lay supine on the floor, but halted. From the impossible angle of the boy's neck, it was clear that he was already dead. A rush of wild rage swept over her.

"My instructions were quite clear," her amplified voice boomed inside the hut. "I was to perform all the actual executions myself. Who is responsible for this?"

"Oh great Gi, forgive him, but Jin killed the boy," one of the brutes ratted quickly, gesturing toward a giant who held aloft a young woman by her hair. The other giants, a worried look in their eyes, quickly agreed, pointing to the slack-jawed Jin.

"They lie—" he began.

He got no further as the dragon's mouth opened and the blue glow inside grew in intensity. With a sudden gush of burning superheated gas, Jin, the girl, and two other peasants were engulfed in searing blue vapor. The surviving palace guards vaulted out of the windows and through the ruined door, running through the mud toward the castle.

Mai Lee, enjoying herself thoroughly again, continued her work in the hut until it was leveled. The sound of the chest guns ripped the air; the flares of livid blue ignited the horizon. Before she marched Gi back up the flagstones to reenter the garden, three huts had been burned and twelve people lay dead.

42

Five

The hot little water-world with its swampy sister planet had grown from a speck to a fat blue-white disk over the last two days. Less than a million kilometers out and coming in fast, the Parent began a hard three-gee braking to bring it into a safe descent pattern. Landfall was only hours away. The larvae had been hatched and birthed and now crowded the tiny ship with their humping, glistening bodies. They ate liberally of the protoplasm supplies, and the Parent estimated that soon the tanks would be sucked dry. At that point they would enter the pupae stage. They would transform and awaken as adult offspring less than an hour before the invasion began.

The Parent herself ate sparingly, taking in only enough to keep her ovaries working. Her external egg sacs were already distended with the seeds for more offspring, and every hour they swelled further.

The Parent heard a rustling back in the cryogenics chamber. Extending a pseudopod to investigate, she found two of the larvae had climbed through the hatch and had gotten into a death struggle inside. One of them had killed and half eaten the other, to her chagrin. She could not, of course, blame the surviving youngster. It was quite possible that the dead larvae had been defective genetically in some way. It shouldn't have been so easily bested. Yet it was vexing to have to birth another so soon.

Reaching out with her tentacles, she herded the surviving

43

youngster out of the chamber and sealed it. The others romped about in the control room and chased one another up to the ceiling on their sticky-padded feet. One of the larvae had bitten a chunk of sticky flesh from the other, causing it to run a little faster.

The Parent sucked up the carcass of the dead larvae with her foodtube and ruffled her tentacles in amusement at the antics of her offspring. Then she turned back to the ship's data-interface. She shifted the ship's approach path to bring it in directly behind the smaller planet, interposing the satellite between the planet and her ship. Orbiting the moon were many of the small ships that seemed to sneak down to the planet's surface so easily. She targeted one that was just picking up speed and falling out of orbit toward the planet. Her dark, silent ship locked onto the target and rapidly closed the distance between them.

Once this was done, there wasn't much left to do other than to enjoy the last frolicking of the larvae before they settled down and spun their fleshy, egg-shaped cocoons.

* * *

"Come on, come on, you poor wretches," muttered Sarah Engstrom under her breath, sitting in the cockpit of her flitter.

Sarah's flitter sat in the middle of the vast swamps of Gopus on an illegal saber-reed farm. Daddy and his son Mudface lived on the huge triangular-shaped island, a lump of mush called Sharkstooth. Their huge moldy stockade was visible through the trees, built out of tough mangrove-like timber. At each of the seven guard towers that lined the walls of the stockade bearded thugs slumped over their rattler turrets. Sarah eyed the walls with trepidation, although it looked primitive, she knew the electronics and weaponry employed by the drug kingpins were unsurpassed. They maintained a facade of simple-mindedness because they liked it that way. Several hundred swamp-folk lived with them in and around the stockade, doing all the work and getting off-handedly abused for it whenever Daddy had a little too much reed-whiskey.

Sarah pushed her dark hair back from her face and wiped sweat on her jumpsuit. She wanted to move fast because Mudface was showing signs of getting amorous again, and worse, Daddy would be back any minute.

"You sure are pretty today, Sarah. You sure you don't want another hit off the reed-juice?" asked Mudface, leering at her.

Sarah was used to men who leered, it usually didn't bother her. But Mudface was different, because he was a mech. He'd died some years ago and his brain had been revived by Daddy, who was rich enough to afford the expensive procedure to save his son. Sarah privately believed Daddy had killed Mudface personally, and felt bad about it afterward. Unlike most mechs, Mudface hadn't had his personality scrubbed during the process. His brain was still human and now stewed inside a bubbling tank in the center of the artificial body. His body had been rebuilt with artificial nano-tube muscles and titanium bones. Unlike most mechs, he was built to look like a normal human, or at least to look as Mudface had in life. He didn't resemble a robot, he looked more like a store manikin—the kind that modeled the clothes in an automated loop. He was rail-thin, with a permanent, stupid-looking grin built onto his plastic face that belied the malevolent cunning behind it.

"No time for it, but thanks," Sarah said, managing to smile back at the mech. She knew that it was best to keep on the good side of Mudface and Daddy, especially when visiting their island. "Your people have gotten almost all the cargo aboard now."

Mudface nodded, watching the swamp-folk load Sarah's flitter with bales of dried, bluish saber-reeds. "Ground up into blur dust, this load will make a lot of people happy down there," Mudface said, his impossible grin seeming to widen a fraction. "We grow the best here on Sharkstooth, you know."

"No rot-eye, right?"

"This is the good stuff. Our customers rarely go blind," said Mudface proudly.

Sarah wasn't so sure it was 'the good stuff'. Her stomach twisted at the thought. Blur dust induced euphoria with the usual vicious side effects such drugs had on the chronic user. The drug was named for the side effect of temporary blindness, which sometimes became permanent. She told herself that every spacer in the system did it. Smuggling was almost required to keep afloat as independent these days. The graft alone to keep flying inflated every year.

Mudface turned a sharp eye back to the swamp-folk, who were carrying heavy wicker cases to the flitter on their permanently crooked backs. One man, even thinner and less healthy-looking than the rest, stumbled and sagged down beneath the weight of his burden. He struggled desperately to get up, his feet slipping in the loose mud. Despite the generously low gravity on Gopus, he couldn't stand. There was a wild look in his black-circled eyes. An old woman and a boy came forward to help him up, but Mudface waved them back.

"Leave him," said Mudface.

The old woman reached out a hand. Mudface pulled his short-barreled shotgun out of his belt and hit her with it. It was a Wu hand-cannon semi-automatic, loaded with high-velocity shells. She staggered away with blood running out of her bedraggled hair.

"I said leave him be! You people never listen!" shouted Mudface. Then he bent down beside the fallen man, prodding him with the barrel of his hand-cannon. The man struggled harder, and got one corner of the wicker case off the ground. "You sick or something, boy? You got the fever, don't you?"

Sarah squirmed in her cockpit, biting her lip.

"Can't have you spreading no fevers," said Mudface, cocking his hand-cannon.

"I've changed my mind about that drink, Mudface," Sarah called from the cockpit of the flitter. "It's quite hot out here."

Mudface turned away from the man struggling in the mud and beamed his idiot's grin at her. "Now, you've got that right, girl," he said and sent the bleeding old woman into the stockade to fetch a fresh bottle of chilled reed-whiskey. As soon as his attention had shifted, the other swamp-folk helped the sick man to his feet and finished loading the flitter.

Then Daddy showed up, riding his sagging, one-man flyer over the tops of the Red Hork trees and landing in the glade next to the flitter. Daddy was hugely fat, with a belly that protruded over the rim of his stained greasy workpants. His mean eyes protruded from their sockets, matching his belly. He had a trailer behind the flyer with a load of dead waterfowl in the cradle. Feathers, beaks and claws stuck out here and there between the slats.

"Looks like a nice catch," said Mudface.

"Must be fifty, sixty black-beaks in there, plus a good dozen of those noisy gronk birds," rumbled Daddy as he climbed off the flyer's saddle. The flyer buoyed up a few feet in obvious relief, then the roaring engine shut itself off and the vehicle sank to the muddy surface. A group of bearded thugs gathered around the craft, slinging their weapons over their backs and whistling at the kills.

"Gronks are crap to eat."

"Yeah, what do you care? You don't eat anymore, anyway," laughed Daddy, slapping his flabby thigh.

Mudface's optics locked onto Daddy. Mudface stared at him for a moment. Sarah wondered how much he still hated his father. She'd heard Daddy had drown Mudface in this very swamp one dark night after too much blur-laced whiskey.

Daddy pulled out his hand-cannon, the twin to Mudface's, and began reloading it with shells. He walked up to Sarah, still loading the gun. A trickle of sweat ran down from his huge hands onto the hot barrel, producing a wisp of steam.

"What's taking so long with the crates?" demanded Daddy.

"One of the swampers came down sick," said Mudface.

"Sick? Has the fever, does he?"

Mudface nodded. He swatted a buzzing insect that chewed at the tough, false skin of his neck. Sarah shuddered slightly. Could he actually *feel* a bug biting him? What did the bug get out of it?

"Can't have him giving it to the others," said Daddy grimly. He headed toward the huts.

"Can't you just give them all some antibiotics?" asked Sarah in concern.

"Nope," said Mudface. "It's viral. No easy cures. There's only one sure fix for a bad case of swamper fever."

From inside the hut a shotgun boomed. Sarah felt sick. She told herself it had nothing to do with her. If she had never come today, it would have happened anyway. But somehow, she still felt sick. Daddy came out again, looking satisfied. Sullen-looking people dragged the flopping body out and deposited it in the swamp.

"Now, you have our deal real straight, don't you girly?" rumbled Daddy. He kept his eyes on his gun, shoving another shell into the magazine with a fat thumb.

"No question about it, I'll transport this stuff down, hide it in the caves, then you deposit my share of the cash at First Stellar."

"Nice and simple," said Daddy. He raised his head and bored into her with hard little eyes like glass chips. "Let's keep it that way."

Sarah nodded.

"We've got friends with ways of fixing people who screw us," said Mudface, his optics swung to stare at her. "I like you, Sarah. Wouldn't want to see you get messed up."

"That's right," added Daddy. He finished loading his hand-cannon and the breech snicked shut automatically. "I don't like coming into town to do business. It'd be a shame to have that kind of business with you."

"I assure you, gentlemen," Sarah told them with her hands raised and open. She spoke with deep sincerity. "I have absolutely no intention of screwing up this deal."

They both nodded, and the tension eased. Later, after they all had a cool glass of reed-whiskey, in a surprisingly clean glass, Sarah made ready for lift-off.

"Awe now, look at that. That damned swamper got mud all over your flitter with that last crate," complained Mudface. "I'll have him beat for you, girly. Beat real good!"

Sarah's mouth opened and she found herself about to say thanks automatically. Her tongue caught in her teeth and she said nothing.

Mudface just waved at her, grinning his permanent, idiot's grin. Sarah pressed the automatic return button on the flitter's control screen and soon his face was lost in the glade around the stockade. Then the glade was lost on the mold-green carpet of Sharkstooth and finally even the triangular island slipped away beneath the fluffy white clouds of Gopus. The flitter slid up into orbit and docked with her ship.

As she made her way through the airlock and climbed into the rotating shower to wash the sweat from her body, she thought about Mudface's words *beat real good*, and shuddered in the warm water.

"Hello mom," Bili Engstrom shouted into intercom. The sound startled her.

"Hello Bili," she replied, "how's your arm, any change?"

"Nope, the heal-bag's still brown and just a little cloudy. How's old Mudface? Still a pervert?"

48

"Bili, let's not talk like that."

The connection was cutoff for a minute or so while she removed her spacer suit and made her way in Zero-G up to the passenger section of the boat. Bili, who sat in the tiny galley section working on a model of Garm's star system and getting glue everywhere in the process, took the time to examine his injured arm. He poked and prodded at the limb through the tough clear plastic bag that encased it in liquids until he could feel the pressure with his new, tingling nerves. His right arm had been crushed just above the elbow in the same accident that had killed his father out in the asteroid belt six months ago. His mother had gotten him to a clinic in time and they had amputated the mutilated arm. Without full medical, they couldn't afford a really professional regrow, just one of those kits you could buy at the survival supplies department, alongside the jungle ape venom kits and the do-it-yourself amputation packages. It just wasn't coming out right, though. The bag was supposed to remain clear and colorless, but had turned a nasty, hazy brown over the last two weeks. Bili gave it another hard poke and winced.

"Mom, we don't have to do this job, you know," Bili said as his mother emerged from an opening in the ceiling and did a summersault to a standing position.

She wordlessly examined his arm in the healing bag. "It's worse," she announced tonelessly.

"We don't need this job," repeated Bili. "This regrow will work okay, and even if it doesn't, I can get along with one arm. I'm left-handed, anyway."

"Don't worry about it, kid, we're going to get you on full medical," she said with false bravado. "It's a done deal." She ruffled his hair and used the handrails to pull herself forward to check the screens.

"Not much out there," Bili said. "Not much on the scopes, either."

Sarah did find one thing on the scopes however, a small ship of unknown configuration. It was coming in fast from the asteroid belts, approaching Garm from behind Gopus. She shrugged mentally; probably just another smuggler like herself, coming in to make a rendezvous with a freighter headed down to Garm. She pressed her fingers against her temples, feeling the sickness of despair gnawing at her guts. Every time she looked at Bili's arm now, she wanted to retch.

* * *

Back in the galley, Bili poked his withered-looking new arm through the tough plastic again. It looked like a bunch of rotting sausages strung along a white plastic pipe, which was about what it was. He looked at the swirling brown liquids, circulating through the tiny pump and filter with a soft gurgling sound. He bet it stank in there. He bet it stank real bad.

Turning back to his project, he found the glue tube and began to glue the dark little pebble-shaped asteroids into place.

Six

Bili was right next to Sarah, strapped into his crash-seat and eating a bluish hork-apple. "We're going to meet the freighter now, Bili. Time to close your visor and pressurize your suit."

"I know, Mom."

Bili took two more quick bites of his apple and tossed the rest into a zip-bag to keep it fresh and anchored until later. Snapping his helmet visor down, he struggled with the wrist controls for a moment, finally getting the air flowing. It was hard for him to use the wrist controls on the suit since his right arm was rammed into the suit's tight sleeve, still in the heal-bag and still useless. Unfortunately, the controls were located on his left wrist. The only way he could work them was to push them against the edge of his belt buckle, half the time nudging the wrong button. He looked sidelong at his mother, making sure that she had not noticed that he had done things out of sequence. He was supposed to get the air pump working first, people had suffocated that way in the past, but he liked to think he was saving a little oxygen by closing the visor first. Space on a shoestring budget could be a scary place; you never knew when you might need that last little gasp of air.

Fortunately, his mother was far too preoccupied with making her rendezvous on time and without incident to notice what he was doing. "See it? The *Yeti* is right there above Garm's crescent."

Bili squinted and thought he could make out a tiny speck, gray-white, hanging above the curved sickle-like shape of Garm sun-side below. "Yup."

51

"Hang on now, we're coming in hot, and we'll have to brake hard for just a few seconds when we get in too close for anyone to tell down on the dirt that it wasn't just an attitude jet from the *Yeti*."

To the great, and preplanned, fortune of Sarah and all the smugglers in the system, the orbital traffic radar net was regularly sabotaged and operated improperly. This created large holes in the planet's coverage and left many regions only partially covered. Cashing huge checks weekly, the communications staff at the spaceport routinely reported major malfunctions as *calibration and adjustment*, blaming equipment damage too serious to ignore on Grunstein's harsh weather.

All this kept operations like Sarah's running night and day, and kept a long receiving line of greased officials fat and happy.

"What's that Mom?" asked Bili, seeing a new contact on the sensors, closing in fast on a converging angle.

"I—" said Sarah, focusing a sensor array and setting it to track the contact. "It's that ship that's been following us."

Bili sat back, his eyes wide. He didn't like this at all. Things were supposed to go exactly as planned when you were in space. They had to otherwise you could end up dead, just as his father had. *Or armless*, his mind countered.

"What ship?"

"It must be another smuggler, from farther out. Maybe he's running in some illegal fissionables from the asteroids," Sarah said, stress making her voice raise up in volume and pitch.

"It's not a Nexus patrolship, is it?" whispered Bili, fearing the worst. The new ropy muscles on his regrowing arm constricted in tension and the pain was sickening. He closed his eyes and sucked his lower lip.

"No. It's another smuggler, he's going to beat us, he's coming in to steal my ride," Sarah said with sudden conviction, putting the pieces together. "He's planning to beat me to the *Yeti* and go down with her! Damn it!" Sarah smashed her gloved fists down on the armrests of her crash-seat and growled inarticulately.

Bili waited, relaxing a bit. As long as it wasn't a Nexus patrol ship. He didn't want his Mom doing time over this. He wondered, not for the first time, what they would do to him if his Mom went to prison and his Dad was dead. It was an unpleasant idea, so he pushed it from his mind.

Sarah looked at Bili, her face deadly serious behind her faceplate. "Bili, we've got all our money tied up in this run. We paid for this ticket down and we can't let them steal it."

"We can go back down, Mom. Just drop the cargo. We can sell the ship and hide in the West Annex, or Amazonia."

"No, Mudface and Daddy would find us, they'd have us killed." She glared back down at the ship coming in. "No, no way. Nobody is going to just steal this ticket from us."

With a quick friendly slap of her glove on Bili's helmet, Sarah fired up the jets and increased her speed of approach. Together, the two small ships converged on the big freighter as it began its arcing descent into the atmosphere.

It quickly became apparent that the intruder wasn't going to just give up and run away. Pressing in hard with the intruder on their heels, Sarah swung underneath the looming freighter and hit the brakes hard. Multiple forward jets flared into brilliant life all around the viewports, which automatically darkened to filter the glare. Even so, Bili blinked as purple splotches stained his vision.

The intruder was braking too, expertly following her right between the huge steel ribs of the freighter and rising up toward the massive central spine that held the framework of engines and cargo pods together. Following her example, the intruder found a slot between the massive bulbous sacks of cargo and secured itself to the spine like a leech. Up close, the other craft appeared to be fractionally larger than theirs and of a strange design unknown to her.

"If I didn't know better, I would have thought it was a small warship." she said, perplexed and angry. How could this be happening? "Fortunately, its sensor profile doesn't match any of the Nexus warship designs."

They all descended together, a mothership coming in on grav drive with two delinquent children hiding in her skirts. Just over five miles above the surface before the ship cleared the slopes of the forested hills around the spaceport, Sarah was supposed to let her ship freefall down into a valley and then land undetected. Unfortunately, at a ridiculous altitude of seventeen miles the stowaway ship suddenly disconnected and dropped from sight into the cloud cover.

Sarah cursed volubly, something she rarely did in front of her son, heaping abuse upon the second ship. "I only wish we had a gun mount, I'd blast him."

Bili giggled uncontrollably at his mother's bad language. What his mother said next made him swallow his amusement.

"He's flagged us. We have to follow him now, the traffic-control diagnostics couldn't have missed that stunt, and they will dispatch atmospheric patrol craft to find him. We can't stay here, either. They're sure to go over this ship with a pipe wrench when we land after that," said Sarah, speaking half to Bili and half to herself. Bili saw in her eyes how scared she was, and that scared him more than anything.

With a gulping breath, Sarah pulled a hand-lever and the ship was instantly freefalling into the clouds. Blind, not daring to use the active scanners to look at the terrain below, she nosed the craft directly toward the ground and applied the thrust. They screamed down through the clouds in a powered dive directly toward the surface.

The ship jerked and jinked wildly, caught like a bird in a man's hand by the storm winds. They were thrown side to side violently against the restraints of their crash-seats. The storm screamed and howled, clawing at the ship. Bili thought he was screaming too, but it was hard to tell.

* * *

When the invasion of the colony began the spaceport commissioner had left early for the day. It was Wednesday after all, and the rayball games would begin down at the Zimmerman Colonial Stadium by 4:00 PM. It was an important match; KXUT would be netting the video live. The Jinzhou Dragons were facing off against Bauru, the surprise champions from the jungles of Amazonia. The spaceport commissioner always managed to leave by 3:30 on Wednesdays.

That left a bored Major Drick Lee in charge of the spaceport. From Drick's point of view, he was left with most of the responsibility for the spaceport, but with little of the authority and only a niggardly share of the graft profits. If there indeed existed a clearer example of the sort of injustices that were heaped upon him daily by his superior than his Wednesday afternoon trips to the rayball stadium, he was at a loss to come up with it. While the commissioner and several of his shuttle captain cronies rode an airbus to the stadium, doubtless already half sloshed on brimming pitchers of hork-leaf wine, Drick had to content himself with the small portable holo-set which he kept stashed in the bottom drawer of his desk.

To further darken his mood, before the players had finished warming up and set their treads to the highwires, the intercom commenced beeping. He glanced at it with immense dissatisfaction. It was on the emergency channel, so he couldn't ignore it forever. If, on the other hand, he let it beep for a time, the caller might well give up if it were not a real emergency. Content to wait, Drick poured himself a shot of swamp-reed distillate, illegally imported from Gopus. He kept the moonshine hidden in a very flat flask under his drawer along with the holo-set. Sighing as he took a mouth-numbing sip, he watched the fat-tired motorcycles of the Bauru team thunder through the entry gate and circle the arena. The cheers became deafening at their appearance, proof of their popularity with the crowds. Drick himself was a Dragons fan, but couldn't help but admire the style of the Amazonians.

Unfortunately, the beeping continued. With heavy disappointment, he answered the call. "Who is this?"

"Harrington, sir. I—"

"This had better be good, Harrington. What is it?"

"Smugglers sir, they came down from Gopus with the *Yeti*."

"For this you used the emergency channel?"

"Something went wrong, sir. Two ships dropped out, and at much too high an altitude. The diagnostics picked it up sir, there's nothing we can do, it's been recorded."

"Oh fine! On my watch, too. Who's responsible? Who arranged for two tickets on that freighter?"

"No sir, you don't understand. There was only one ah, legitimate guest on that trip. Should we send the interceptors after them, sir?"

"Eh? What? Are you insane man?"

"It's regulations, sir."

"Fine, fine. Make an entry into the log that we scrambled the interceptors and shot them down or something. You know my password, take care of it," said Drick, bored with the entire affair already. The game was about to start.

"Well, sir. Things have gone a bit beyond that now."

"What are you prattling about?"

"Captain Dorman has taken up two interceptors and is chasing them now, sir."

That got the Major into action. He stabbed the cut-off and paused only long enough to sweep his holo-set and flask out of sight, then headed for the door. Vaporous distillate dribbled from the seams of his top drawer after he left, as he had forgotten to stopper it. Smoking blue drops splattered his chair and the carpet beneath his desk.

* * *

The interceptors were Stormbringers, shipped out from the Nexus just two years ago, they were the latest in colonial-class atmospheric gunships. Built like a missile with short stubby wings and high-thrust lifters, the ship had an excellent feel in the air and was instantly responsive to the controls. Captain Dorman had loved the ships since the first time he saw them and they had always been a real pleasure to fly. Two hundred yards to his right was his wingman, a trusted flyer that he felt he could take with him on this mission without fear of treachery.

"Dorman to central, we are overhauling the slower of the two unauthorized craft now."

"Dorman, this is Major Lee," said a hurried voice, cutting in.

"Please get off the channel, Major, this is a combat mission and the situation is under Nexus Cluster jurisdiction now. Come in, Harrington."

"You are ordered to return to base immediately. You do not, repeat do not have authorization to pursue."

"We don't need your authorization now, Major," replied Dorman, grinning inside his helmet. "The situation has been recorded and relayed to Nexus Cluster Command. The NCC will handle this. Dorman out."

Still grinning, he closed in and easily sat on the first of the smugglers. Although the pilot maneuvered with considerable skill, the bulky spacecraft wasn't really designed with atmospheric flight in mind. The two Stormbringers paced the ship with absurd ease. Dorman was in fact more worried for their safety than about keeping up with them.

"Captain, the other target is escaping to the north at a very high speed. We won't be able to catch him if we don't go to full acceleration in about two minutes," said his wingman.

That decided it for Dorman. There was no time for a lengthy effort on his part to talk the pilot down. He dropped down quickly and slid beneath the smuggler's jetwash. "I'm engaging the target. It's probably a decoy to keep us busy while the other slips away."

"Dorman!" screamed Major Lee. He had been listening in on their intercom circuit, and now interrupted. "Under no circumstances are you to engage that ship! Answer me!"

Dorman flicked a switch, arming his forward cannons. "There seems to be some interference, sir. Could you repeat that last?"

"Listen to me, Captain—" said Major Lee, his voice shaking with rage.

"Unidentified craft is attempting to evade," said Dorman breaking in on Major Lee. He knew he was covered on this one. With the diagnostics records black-boxed and relayed to the NCC, they couldn't court-martial him for disobeying orders. If they tried, he could bring counter-charges that they didn't dare to face in the Nexus courts. Without hesitation he set the mission selector to disable then depressed the attack studs, letting the microprocessors take over. Instantly, a quick burst of explosive pellets neatly removed the lifters from underneath the target. It stuttered, then dropped like a rock. Two parachutes opened as the crew ejected before impact.

"Target has been disabled. Hope they all made it," said Dorman, calling in a rescue-lifter. After one spiraling pass over the wreck, he lifted the nose back up and the two Stormbringers poured on the thrust. In ninety seconds they achieved low orbit, where they could use max thrust in order to catch up with the second ship, which was half-way to New Chad by now.

Seven

The front doors of the arrivals section blew in with roar. Partly by luck, partly by design, no one was injured. Giants carrying heavy weapons and one normal man jogged into Grunstein Interplanetary. The giants all wore silver and black. Their huge jaws were grimly set, their boots crunched on broken glass fragments, grinding them to dust. Although he was quite tall, the single normal human was dwarfed by his massive companions. They took no notice of the screaming, scrambling people and moved smartly to a stainless steel door located underneath the escalators that led up to departures.

Jarmo leveled his long-barreled weapon, taking aim at the steel doors. Droad pushed the weapon aside, shaking his head while he pulled out his ID card. The card slid through the lock smoothly and he passed the optical and thumbprint tests as cleanly as when he had first arrived on Garm. With his giants behind him, he strode into the spaceport control center.

In the front office, there were cries of *terrorist attack* from the staff. When Droad burst into the operations room with Jarmo at his heels Major Drick Lee was already on the phone to security.

"How in the hell did you get in here?" Major Lee demanded in disgust. His eyebrows went shot up at the sight of the armed giants that were marching into the room. "Are you the manager of some new rayball team?"

With something of a flourish, Droad produced his ID card. He plunged it into the slot under the view-screen beside the door. He

58

pressed the ID verify button and his identity along with frontal and profile holo shots were instantly displayed.

In the stunned silence that followed, Droad got himself a cup of hot caf. While he poured, he demanded a report of the current status of the spaceport.

"Well sir, there was a slight security breach just about half an hour ago," replied Lieutenant Harrison, breaking the shocked pause.

"What kind of security breach?" said Droad, focusing on the lieutenant.

"It was nothing, we filed a routine report," snapped Drick, glowering at the lieutenant, who averted his eyes. He wheeled to face the intruders, his hands behind his back. "We can't accept the data of one probably tampered with terminal as proof of your identity, sir. In any case, even if you are who you say you are, until you are properly inaugurated and recognized, you have no authority here. Now, I suggest you leave the premises and turn yourself in to the militia authorities, who will sort all this out. We have work to do here."

"What security breach?" Droad repeated, more sharply. He completely ignored Major Lee.

The lieutenant flicked his eyes back and forth between Major Lee and Droad, clearly ambivalent.

"If you would please leave," repeated Major Lee, his teeth clenched.

"Major, you're relieved of your duties. Jarmo, escort this civilian to the security doors and remove all of his identification passes," ordered Droad, taking a drink from his hot caf. The staff all watched wide-eyed as the heatedly protesting Major Lee was half-carried to the doors by the hulking, scowling giant. "Now, who is next in command?"

"I am," said the lieutenant. He stood at attention. "Sir."

"What's your name?"

"Lieutenant Harrington, sir."

"Good. You are now acting commissioner of this spaceport. Deliver your report concerning the security breach," he said, stirring his drink. "No carload of criminal types was involved?"

"Sir?" said Harrington, blinking.

"Nothing like the little assassination crew that shot up the

Renaldo hotel yesterday?"

"Oh no, sir. It was a smuggler sighting sir, two of them dropped out of the *Yeti* during her descent. They dropped out early, and we were able to detect them."

"Good work. Naturally you activated the SAM batteries and shot them down," said the Governor, feeling relieved. His enemies hadn't gotten here ahead of him. His hot caf was a bit too hot and he slurped it noisily.

"Ah no, we didn't shoot them down," said Harrington uncomfortably. "Captain Dorman took up two Stormbringers in pursuit. He forced one down and I believe he is about to engage the other now."

* * *

When Major Drick Lee was tossed staggering out of the security door, which immediately snicked shut behind him, there was a general shout of alarm. The spaceport security squads had gathered about the locked door in response to Drick's calls for aid. Believing that a terrorist action was in progress, they had begun clearing the spaceport and setting up barricades made of planters, benches and even cartloads of unclaimed baggage. Surprised by Drick's appearance, they mistook him for one of the terrorists and opened fire. Only the fact that Drick had pitched forward on his face saved him from the storm of small arms fire that crackled and spanged off the steel security door.

"Hold your fire! Stop shooting, idiots!" screamed Drick, sprawling with his arms wrapped around his head. Eventually, someone recognized his uniform and called a cease-fire. Many of them stopped simply because they had run out of ammunition.

Miraculously uninjured, Drick made his way to the nearest overturned planter, fear giving way to rage. The security people looked sheepish and avoided his gaze. "Fools! I'm not a terrorist!" he screamed at them.

"Well, how were we supposed to know that?" questioned a man behind the barricade, summing up all of their feelings. Major Lee was not the most popular Nexus officer at the spaceport.

Shaking off his experience, the Major realized that he was

standing in the open in front of the security door, while everyone else was on the other side of their flimsy barricade. With as much dignity as he could muster, he scrambled over a pair of overturned benches and crouched beside the duty Sergeant. "Have you evacuated everyone?"

"Down here at arrivals the place is empty, but we haven't had time to clear everyone out of departures," said Sergeant Manstein, a balding man with deep-set eyes and large hands. "The militia say they're on their way."

"Why haven't you cleared the spaceport?" demanded Drick, fury creeping back into his voice. "Can't you people follow a single regulation today?"

"Come on Major, give us a break," said the Sergeant, his eyes dark and unfriendly. "We aren't prepared to handle this kind of thing."

"I'll do it myself then," said Drick, standing and waving for two of the guards to follow him. Together they headed for the escalators. With each rapid step they took away from the security door, Drick relaxed a bit inside. He didn't want to admit it, but between the rough handling of the giants and being shot at he had had quite a bad scare. He felt an urgent need to visit the restroom, but forced himself to wait.

It was when they reached the departure lounge and began herding people toward the exits that Drick got his first big break of the day. He saw a man wearing a close-fitting hat and a pair of auto-shades set curiously dark for the interior of a building. He was at the ticket counter, arguing with an attendant and holding a handsome leather satchel with both hands. He squinted at this man, sure that he had seen his likeness before... and then he had it. That satchel, that sharp-pointed chin, it could only be General Ari Steinbach, whom he recognized from the militia's bimonthly security inspections.

The General represented everything he wanted just now, which was absolution of responsibility for the entire affair. Unable to believe his luck, he rushed up to the man, who pulled his satchel up in a defensive gesture. Drick reached out his hand, grinning broadly. When the General hesitatingly took his hand, he pumped it and rapidly described the situation.

"And I hereby turn the matter over to the militia, sir. We have no way of handling this sort of thing here with just our security team," he said. He gave the Sergeant at his side a wry glance.

* * *

When the two Stormbringers managed to overhaul the second craft, they were over the steaming jungles of southern New Chad, almost down to the borders of Amazonia. A thousand miles farther south loomed the rocky cliffs that separated the jungles from the barren Desolation.

Dropping out of orbit, they descended rapidly toward the target, a darting black speck that skimmed so low over the treetops that it seemed to almost fly between the monstrous leafy horkwoods. Swooping down on the craft, they punched through the cloud layer and screamed toward the uneven green surface of leaves. Captain Dorman netted in his position and waited for acknowledgment from the spaceport.

"Captain Dorman, this is Lucas Droad, duly appointed Planetary Governor of Garm. I want to commend you on downing that last smuggler, and I order you to disable the craft you are pursuing now," said a new voice, interrupting the traffic controllers.

Dorman raised his eyebrows and grunted at this unexpected turn of events. "So, the Nexus sent out an early replacement. About time."

"Thank you for your support, Captain," said the new voice, sounding amused.

Dorman didn't hesitate to exercise his new orders. To his surprise however, the craft didn't attempt evasive action, but instead rose up from the treetops, coming up aggressively to meet them. "The target is turning to attack," reported Dorman, shocked. Nothing in the system could stand up to the Stormbringers in atmospheric combat. The pilot had to be insane.

"Missile incoming!" squawked his wingman. That was all he managed before being engulfed in a fireball. Seeing the red burst that had been his wingman's Stormbringer out of the corner of his eye, Dorman thumbed the emergency kill switch, releasing all the warship's offensive capacity to the computers. On full automatic, the Stormbringer rolled over and did a streaking dive toward the surface. Close to blacking out, Dorman felt the ship shudder as a dozen missiles were loosed to speed toward the target. The cannons were all firing now, the controls working themselves furiously to evade incoming fire that was beyond human capacity for response.

There was an explosion the next second and the starboard wing disintegrated into flaming debris. The ship went into a spin, and Captain Dorman lost consciousness as the computers ejected his crash-seat through the bottom skin of the craft.

He came to again less than a thousand feet above the surface. Locked in a sitting position in his crash-seat, he floated down into the green treetops. Blinking away the haze that clung to his vision, he righted his head and saw three black plumes of smoke rising up from the jungle. All three of the combatants had been destroyed.

"Least we got him," Dorman muttered before the blood pressure in his brain ebbed and he lost consciousness again.

* * *

"Uh, yes of course," stumbled Ari. Inwardly he groaned. He had hoped his auto-shades would be enough of a disguise.

Major Lee, too pleased to notice the General's unenthusiastic response, led the way back toward the security door. "Perhaps you would like to take stock of the situation? Or do you want to call in your tactical squad immediately, sir?"

Ari balked, refusing to move from his spot near the ticket counters. He gave the flight-departure gates a wistful glance, then flicked his eyes nervously over the security video pick-ups hidden about the spaceport. Mai Lee could be watching even now. "Who exactly is this terrorist group?"

"A madman, sir. He has a gang of giants, either they're rayball players, or just hired killers. The man claimed to be the new Governor, of all the crazy things. Imagine that!"

Ari jumped involuntarily. "Giants with him, you say?" he asked, his tongue wetting his lips. He took up his satchel with both hands, pulling it close against his chest.

"Yes sir," replied Major Lee, frowning at the General's odd

manner.

Ari eyed the security door in concern. Suddenly, his eyes narrowed in speculation. "The situation has possibilities." he muttered aloud.

"Sir?"

"I'll handle this, Major. You and your men just take up positions around the center. Clear the building, I have some phone calls to make."

Beaming, Major Lee jogged off with his men and began shouting. Ari frowned after him, envying him his newfound freedom from responsibility. He turned to eye the departure gates again. The elevator up to the orbital platform was so close. He could even take the flitter that went up every fifteen minutes, that would be faster. Before he could move, however, the clerks began to close the ticket counters and the loudspeakers announced that all flights were canceled due to an unspecified emergency. With a sigh, Ari turned toward the line-up of public paylinks. He had left his own unit at his office to make himself harder to trace. He dropped a credit coin into the first paylink he found that was operable.

Eight

"What I don't quite understand, General," said Mai Lee, her eyes narrowed in a habitual expression of suspicion. "Is exactly what you are doing at the spaceport."

"A hunch, your Excellency. Call it the intuition of an experienced militia officer," Ari answered crisply. "I've been studying this man carefully, and I predicted his return to the spaceport. Stationed here is the largest organization of forces loyal to the Nexus that he could draw on for support."

"But why didn't you bring your tactical squad with you?"

"They're on the way here now. I didn't want to remove them from their alert status at the militia headquarters until I was sure. Besides, your instructions were to locate him and call for your aid," Ari said, again with convincing certainty. He had anticipated these questions, but hoped that she didn't probe any further into his motivations concerning coming to the spaceport. It was time to deflect her onto another course. "So, now that we've got him here and he has holed himself up, how do you wish to handle the situation?"

"Your effectiveness in this instance astounds me. It isn't like you to take to the field yourself, General."

"This is a most serious matter, Empress. Both of our futures are at stake and I felt I couldn't afford to trust the matter to my operatives. Although I have great faith in them," he added hastily. The itching sensation of erupting sweat grew in his armpits.

"If you want something done, you have to do it yourself, eh?

65

Very well. While you're waiting for your tactical squad to come and destroy them, I want you to go in and parlay. Tell Governor Droad that you're on his side. You could be useful as a mole."

"Begging your Excellency's pardon, but are you serious? Why not simply bring in the militia and kill them? We could even hit the entire spaceport, reduce it to rubble with attack lifters and mortar fire if necessary."

"We will not level the spaceport without need, General. You will enter and lull the Governor, perhaps you can even coax him out of his lair. My forces are fast moving into position, even as we speak," she said, her ancient eyes boring into his head. "No one is going to escape the planet from that spaceport, let me assure you, General."

Halfheartedly, Ari tried a few more arguments to avoid the dangerous task that Mai Lee had in mind for him, but she was adamant. It was clear that she suspected his loyalty, even suspected that he had been about to flee Garm. Her command to parlay with Droad was clearly a test. The problem was that Ari suddenly seemed out of options. He could wait for his tactical team, the majority of which were at the rayball arena for the afternoon, not at militia headquarters, but Mai Lee's palace guard might arrive first.

Thinking hard, Ari took his satchel over to a rack of rentable lockers next to the restrooms, popped a two-credit piece into one of them, deposited the satchel and pocketed the key. Heading back down the escalators, he joined Drick and his ragtag army behind their laughable barricade.

"I think we could take them out," said the General conversationally. "We have the manpower, I could use my security card to bypass the locks. We would have the advantage of surprise."

"Yeah?" snorted Sergeant Manstein. "You first, General."

"If I order it, you will obey!" shouted Ari, losing his composure under the pressure of the moment. A tremendous headache throbbed at his temples now.

Major Lee looked dubious, but Manstein exhibited nothing but contempt. "Look, General. I was in the regular infantry once, but even then, I wasn't fool enough to assault a steel door with a crack squad of giants behind it. Especially not when they've got heavy weapons and we've got pea-shooters."

Ari glared at the Sergeant, but held his tongue. Mentally, he weighed his chances at sending in the security detail against Droad and his giants. Although he had little doubt that the giants, who were obviously professionals, would win the confrontation, the possibility remained that Droad would get killed or at least injured in the fighting. He rubbed his chin in deep thought.

No, it wouldn't work. Mostly because of the abject cowardice of the security personnel. If they had been a bit more willing to risk their lives, the attack might have a chance of success. Unfortunately, the only way he could think of to get them to go in hard would be with him going in with them, and that of course was out of the question.

His thoughts were interrupted by the spaceport's public address system, which had apparently been taken over by Droad and his giants. "Loyal soldiers of the Nexus. It is time that I explain this aggression against your base. I am Lucas Droad, the newly appointed Governor of Garm," said Droad, his face flashing up on public holo-plates throughout the spaceport. Ari and the security detail stared at the holo-plates, fixated.

"I was about to publicly announce my arrival, but certain factions in your government, opposing my appointment, attempted to take matters into their own hands," said Droad. Then the image switched to a scene of the Renaldo hotel, apparently videoed by Droad's giants during the action. Seen from outside the hotel, the assassins chased Droad into the hotel, firing as they ran. Inside more firing erupted as three men ran into the hotel after Droad. The hulking figure of Sergeant Borshe lumbered through the doors, his Wu hand-cannons making their unmistakable barking noises. Apparently at that point the giants got their weapons out and the glass doors vaporized. The camera, jostling and lurching sickeningly at Jarmo's hip, ran with the bodyguards into the ruined lobby.

It was the talkative Sergeant Manstein who said, "Hey, isn't that big thug a militia man?"

Ari rose quietly from his place at the barricade and walked quickly for the nearest exit. One look at the expressions of the security people told him where their loyalties were going to fall after this damning video had run its course. If there was one aspect of conflict that Ari had mastered, it was the strategic withdrawal.

"Where are you going, General?" came a booming voice from behind him.

Ari made a dismissive gesture with one hand, not bothering to turn around or slow down. In fact, he walked even faster. "The tactical squad is arriving out front," he lied glibly. "I'm going to meet them."

His back burning with the anticipation of a bullet, his ears straining to catch the sounds of pursuit, Ari reached the doors—and froze.

His eyes squeezed shut and his teeth clenched in a grimace of sudden indecision. He had left his satchel in the lockers near the restrooms. His eyes slid that way, and he wavered for an instant, his fear of the Nexus-loyal security people almost outweighed by his anxiety about the satchel. Then there was a shout behind him, a guttural sound without words, the sound of a Gopus lynch-mob that has just caught up with a reed-rustler in the deep swamps. The sound raised the hair on his neck and lifted the heels of his boots, goading him through the door and out onto the sidewalk. He stepped out of their sight and broke into an all out run for the parking lot.

* * *

"There's no militia van out there," spoke up a security woman. There was deep suspicion in her voice. She, like all the spaceport personnel, was loyal to the Nexus first, rather than the militia and the colonial Senate.

Manstein's eyes followed hers to the General's retreating back. "Right you are," he said, rising up from his crouched position behind the barricade. He dusted off his pants as the others stood with him. "He's running out on us. Remember that crash that killed the last governor that the Nexus sent out? I recall Steinbach getting promoted from Colonel to General right after that."

"Well, let's demote him this time," suggested another man, waving his pistol at the ceiling.

Manstein raised his big hands, quelling their urge to chase the General down. "Let's have a vote right now."

That got their attention. The tape of the failed assassination tape ended and Droad's ID shots came up, proving his claim to the governor's seat. The simple silver star and black background, the seal of the Nexus, glittered under his serious face.

"Our new governor has gotten himself in a jam. If we join him, we could be killed by those personal armies out in the Slipape Counties, or even the militia themselves. This could even mean civil war. So the question is, do we play it safe and slink home like the General, or do we stand by the Nexus?"

There was a brief moment of hesitation, but only a brief one. Unanimously, they voted to join Governor Droad.

* * *

When Sarah and Bili came floating down into the horkwoods, Sarah had at first been crazy with worry that Bili would be hurt. After finally extricating themselves from their harnesses and finding one another in the deep shade beneath the green canopy, she began to feel despair. They had lost everything.

"We can't let them catch us, Bili," she told her boy, gathering their survival kits from their crash-seats and heading uphill, deeper into the forests.

"I know. If they put you in jail, Mudface and Daddy will kill you for sure," Bili finished for her gloomily.

"We have to head away from the wreck. If we go deeper into the mountains, we might get away from the search lifters," she told him. Silently, she added to herself the fact that going uphill should take them farther from the landsharks which infested the wet valleys of this region.

"I hope they blast that other pirate," said Bili darkly. "I hope he goes down with his ship, too."

Sarah said nothing. She couldn't approve of her son's wishing someone dead, but she felt the same way herself. Blind chance had reached out and dealt her family another bad hand. Bad luck seemed to follow the Engstroms. It seemed to shadow their lives. Right after they had gotten married, her husband Daniel had lost an eye in a pressure accident. The injury hadn't kept him from working, but had put his commercial piloting days behind him. She had gotten pregnant soon after the accident, and although she loved

Bili more than anything in the world, he had not made life any easier. When they had finally gotten things together and seemed to be making some headway, the second accident had come. With her husband dead and her son injured, finding the credit to make ends meet had become a daily struggle. Now, here they were in the cold mountains of Grunstein with nothing, chased by the law and soon the criminals as well.

With an effort, she pushed aside such depressing thoughts and tried to come up with an escape plan. It was Bili, however, who gave them the direction they needed.

"Mom, look over there," he said, pointing into the forest.

Following his gesture, Sarah frowned at a path cut into the trees. Perhaps a dozen of the great trees in a row seemed to be down, their thick trunks lying like tumbled matchsticks. They stepped closer, cautiously.

"Looks like they just went down today," said Bili, looking up and down an open alleyway in the forest that had been cut by some mysterious force. A ruler-straight clearing had been slashed through the trees. Murky light fell down upon the dank recesses of the forest, touching plants that had perhaps not been struck by such radiation in centuries. Examining the scene more closely, they could see that the trees had indeed been recently knocked down. The leaves of the giant horkwoods were still green and fresh-looking. The exposed dirt craters around their roots were fresh wounds in the black ground, like the bleeding gums of pulled teeth.

"I know what it is!" said Bili out loud, and at the same moment Sarah knew too.

"The other ship dropped its payload," she said, finishing Bili's sentence for him. She understood it all now, the other smuggler had dropped his goods out as soon as he came out of the *Yeti*. This made the fact that he had jumped out so early more reasonable. After a slanting fall of perhaps ten miles or more, the payload had landed here, cutting a swath through the forest and probably burying itself in the hillside.

She was just considering the idea of pilfering the payload, and the counter idea that someone would soon be along to pick it up, when she thought she heard a sound. It was more of a vibration really, beneath her feet.

With a premonition of great fear, Sarah grabbed Bili by the

70

shoulders before he could step out under the open sky. She hunkered down with him, hiding in the undergrowth. Bili glanced over his shoulder at her as if she was crazy, but at the look in her eyes he was silent. Together they watched the strange clearing closely; breathing through their open mouths so their nostrils would make no whistling noises.

Then, just as Sarah was beginning to think she had gone mad, there was another sound. It was an odd, scraping sound, muffled somewhat as if someone didn't want to be overheard. The scraping sound continued for a time, then stopped. Hardly daring to breathe, Sarah pulled the pistol out of her survival kit with fantastic care.

As she thumbed off the safety, making a tiny click, a new sound erupted. It was the sound of dirt being tossed about. It grew in intensity, and suddenly a large creature nosed its way out of the ground at the far end of the clearing. Together, Sarah and Bili put their hands to their mouths to stifle an involuntary scream. The creature was huge and hideous. With a streamlined snout and a rippled, leathery surface, it swam through the black forest dirt like a fish in water. Dozens of curved claws protruded from its walrus-shaped body. As they watched these claws scooped and churned at the dirt, tossing a hail of debris behind the monster. In essence it swam through the dirt, tearing and splashing through the ground like thick black liquid. Heavy clods with green crusts sailed about the clearing.

It churned around in a circle, showing itself to be over thirty feet in length and perhaps eight feet thick. Then the gigantic walrus-like monster finally dove back into the ground, disappearing from sight. Sarah and Bili took this opportunity to run from the scene, back into the cool gloom of the forest.

What kept them running a long time, despite their great fatigue, was the certainty that the creature they had seen was not natural to Garm. The Engstroms were nothing if not well-traveled, and they had never encountered or even heard of such a monster before. Nowhere in the great forests of Grunstein, nor down south in the steamy jungles of Amazonia and New Chad, nor even on the remote archipelago of the skalds did such a creature exist.

* * *

71

Sarah and Bili emerged from the horkwoods as evening fell. They had reached a small jax-raising farm outside of Hofstetten. After negotiating the electrified landshark fences, they met up with a boy about Bili's age.

"Hi, I'm Jimmy Herkart," he said, as if this was enough to explain anything and everything to two total strangers.

Bili did most of the talking. In an act of diplomacy far beyond his years, he gave his father's spacers watch to Jimmy. They approached the farmhouse and safety with only occasional glances back to the dark edge of the forest.

Nine

Garth took another sip of his hork-berry spritzer. The red liquid cooled his parched throat.

"You look like you could use some sleep, skald," said the barkeep, a man with reddish-bronze skin. He had immense hairy arms and a bald head. His speech revealed the lilting accent of New Amazonia. "I've got a few cots in the back if you've got the credits. Be an honor to have you."

Garth shook his head, not meeting the man's eyes. The ice in his drink tinkled as he set down the glass.

"All right, but you look like you're going to drive right into a ravine if you keep going."

Garth took up his drink again. His hands shook. He was a rogue now; he had shunned his rider two days ago. Sleep was unthinkable.

As he finished his drink and coded a tip into the barkeep's account, another skald came into the tavern. A wave of greenhouse heat and humidity gusted in the open door with her. The fetid smells of the jungle outside eluded the thrumming air conditioners for a time.

Garth sensed her before he turned, feeling the increased agitation of Fryx. The rider, trapped in the skull of a rogue, desperately wanted to communicate with another of its kind. Garth screwed up his eyes and bared his teeth as nerves flared with red pain. Garth knew that Fryx would never kill or seriously damage his host, but he could freely use pain as a goad.

73

The skald stepped up to the bar and took a stool beside him. Garth turned away, pulling the wide-brimmed hat he had bought lower over his forehead.

"You're the one," said the skald quietly. Her voice was soft and melodious. "You're the one my rider brought me here to find."

Garth whirled. His sweating face and haunted, sunken eyes leered at her. "I want solitude."

The woman was tall and thin in the way of the skalds. Her long limp hair hung to her waist. It was white and very fine. "No skald can ever have that," she said with a slow shake of her head.

Garth grabbed up his drink and tossed it down. He sucked up a sphere of ice and rattled it about against teeth. With the relish of a man recently come from the desert he chewed it and swallowed. The cold explosion in his mouth helped ease the agony up higher in his head.

The skald's eyes widened as she watched him. "You're so—so uncontrolled, so unreserved—" suddenly, she gasped in understanding. "You're a rogue."

Garth grinned at her, his eyes doing a wild fluttering roll before refocusing on her face. He removed his hat with an almost drunken flourish. "Yes, meet Garth the rogue, pretty one."

She drew back, aghast and fascinated. "I am Kris and I bear Tuux. What is your rider's name? I see by the mounting stripe on your face that you bear a great rider."

"My rider's identity is unimportant," slurred Garth. His shoulders rolled and his fingers writhed seemingly of their own accord. "What is significant," he hissed out in agony, "is that he plays on my nerves like a player plucking at a harp just now. I must ask you to leave me, he seems bent on torturing me in your presence."

"He wants only to communicate with another rider, I'm sure. Let Tuux contact him," she pleaded. She placed her hand on his. "He must feel so alone, so isolated. Your conduct is most disrespectful."

"No," Garth hissed, pulling back from her touch as he would the fanged mouth of a leaf serpent. The skin of his hand burned and tingled. Standing, he reeled toward the exit.

"If the militia pull you over, don't tell them you came from here," shouted the barkeep, shaking his head.

Kris quietly followed him, biting her lip.

* * *

Garth drove the lurching ground vehicle further into the jungles of New Amazonia. He passed by several settlements on the way, ignoring the reclusive inhabitants who gaped at him as they did all outsiders. Beneath the dark green canopy of the tropical hork-trees fantastic creatures hooted, howled, trumpeted and screeched. Howlers dented his vehicle with heavy seedpods. Leaf serpents dropped into the roadway, attacking the car in the belief that they were defending their territory. Garth crushed the seedpods and the serpents with equal disregard, his overriding concern being the need to stay awake.

Over a hundred miles out from the settlement where he had met Kris and rested, a large vehicle normally used for hauling timber approached from behind. The stabbing sensations in his mind let him know instantly that Fryx sensed the nearness of another rider. He had been expecting this, clearly Kris and Tuux had gathered what help they could to hunt him down.

He shoved the power rod upward, braking sharply. The car shuddered, became difficult to control. Stabilizers whined in protest. He swerved off the road and into the undergrowth. The car bucked and lurched, steering became almost impossible. Fighting the controls, he managed to guide the car into a narrow gully. Fronds lashed the car, probing into the broken windshield like green fingers.

Out of the greenery stepped a monster. Standing erect, directly in front of him, stood a male bald jungle ape of terrific size. In panic, he swerved the car wildly and hit the rocky wall of the gully. The front end crushed inward and he was ejected into the leafy undergrowth. Inside his head Fryx screamed in mortal terror.

Stunned, he lay on a bed of moss. A trickle of water dribbled over his back from somewhere high above in the forest canopy. Whining insects crawled on his skin and tasted his sweat. Out on the road the hauler stopped where he had entered the jungle and there was the sound of heavy boots on the pavement. Men shouted to one another as they entered the forest to pursue him. He shifted his head a fraction, but could see no sign of the jungle ape.

"He's back here somewhere, see the path he's carved through the jungle?"

Shouts came from his pursuers as they followed his trail and found the mouth of the gully. Garth remained prone, fearing the dark form of the jungle ape more than any group of men. Men might be reasoned with.

"Over here!" cried the melodious voice of Kris. "I've found the car. It appears to be wrecked."

The men appeared now on the fringe of Garth's vision. They were strong-looking men of the forest, not the thin pallid forms of skalds. Two held rifles while the third toted a hand-cannon. Soon the man with the hand-cannon, seemingly the leader, discovered Garth where he lay in the undergrowth.

"Is this the man who raped you?" he demanded, prodding Garth's inert form with the barrel of his hand-cannon.

Garth listened with only half an ear. He thought to see the flickering of a dark shape along the edge of the gully.

"Well—he," began Kris in a troubled voice. Garth knew that she battled against her rider to tell the truth. "He needs help."

"Come now, girl," said the man with the hand-cannon. "You can't be soft with him now."

Even as they spoke, Garth felt a huge soft shadow fall over them. He cringed involuntarily, unable to play dead any longer.

"Hey, he's waking up—" began the leader, then broke off into a hoarse shout of surprise. Incoherent shouting erupted from all of them. A heavy wash of foul air swept over Garth.

He glanced over his shoulder to see the leader being lifted up into the trees in a great black fist. His jungle boots dangled, dribbling moist earth. The hand-cannon barked twice, then there was a crunching sound. The body dropped down into the undergrowth beside Garth, flopping unnaturally like a crushed doll.

Running back toward the road, the other men fired their rifles in panic. Garth had to fight an overwhelming urge to join them in their flight. His rider helped him lay still; sending soothing, numbing sensations down his spine to his legs.

The men were caught up in massive fists and borne aloft into the red hork treetops. The incredibly thick trunks shuddered and swayed with the passage of a huge shadowy form. The foliage thrashed and branches snapped. A single heavy grunt sounded from far above.

Silence reigned over the jungle for several minutes. Not even the most brazen of the cackle-grouse dared to cry out. During this entire time, Garth continued to lay supine on the moss-bed, trying to ignore the stream of marcher-bugs that had decided to use his back as a shortcut.

"Is it gone?" came a whisper.

Garth shifted his head a fraction in surprise. His eyes slid upward as far as they could and he made out the pallid bare feet of Kris only a few feet away across the jungle floor. She too, lay motionless, feigning death.

"It watches us," he whispered back. "It's somewhere above, crouching in the treetops."

Both of them were silent for a time, listening to the wild sounds of the jungle. Evening was coming and the howlers were beginning their twilight serenade. Talking became more feasible with the covering cacophony of sound.

"I'm sorry to have led these men to chase you. It seemed so imperative that I told them anything to gain their aid."

"Now you have gained only their deaths and perhaps ours as well," replied Garth, unable to keep the bitterness from his voice.

"Tuux and I apologize to you and Fryx."

Garth's lips curled back in disgust. "It was Tuux that coerced you into following me. I accept nothing from any of his kind."

"You are indeed a rogue."

"Yes," replied Garth, blinking back exhaustion. "For so long as I can remain awake."

They were both silent for a time, listening for movement in the distant treetops. The light that filtered down to the jungle floor dwindled somewhat with the approach of nightfall, but the heat continued, relentless.

Suddenly, something occurred to Garth. He half-turned to face Kris before checking himself. He noted that she was only partially covered by her torn clothing and quite attractive, even in her disheveled state. "How did you know I carry Fryx?" he demanded.

"The greatness of your stripe," Kris said with the tiniest of shrugs.

"No, no," he said, laying his head back down in the moss.

77

"Many riders are as large. You reported me back to the greatest of the skalds, back in their shrines. From my description and whereabouts they identified me. I have no doubt that you told the Jarl himself."

Kris made no attempt to answer.

"Soon, they will hunt for me, and due to your proximity, they will expunge you as well. Consorting with a rogue can be infectious. We will both be handled roughly."

Kris, knowing the truth of his words, wept quietly for a time.

Garth chided himself not to soften. He refused to even look at her. Lying on the jungle floor, listening to the howlers and feeling the steady tread of the marcher-bugs, Garth slid helplessly into the oblivion of sleep for the first time in days.

* * *

Fryx awoke when Kris cried out. It was still dark, but the howlers had fallen silent. Near at hand, he caught a glimpse of Kris' pallid form rising up swiftly into the air. Fryx goaded Garth's exhausted body into flight, but he too was snatched up in a hairy black fist. Moving with sickening speed, the jungle ape bore them hundreds of feet up into the hork trees. Sure-footedly, it trotted along branches as wide as highways, leaping from tree to tree.

The constricting fingers held him so tightly and the beast's stench was so foul that Fryx had difficulty forcing Garth to retain consciousness. His terror of the crude outer creatures had never been greater. Soon, he felt sure, he would have to abandon the crushed husk of Garth's body. A rider feared little more than being exposed to the open air and unknowable dangers of breathing creatures. He would most assuredly wither and perish, an ignoble ending to a magnificent life span filled with philosophical achievement. It was enough to set his spines to quivering.

In desperation, Fryx did his utmost to reach out to the monster, to touch its brutish mind and perhaps nudge it in the proper fashion. He did his best to generate an aura of curiosity about Garth, suggesting that perhaps this creature was fascinating and worthy of study.

Whether due to his feeble efforts at telepathy or to some other dark motive of its own, the ape didn't kill them out of hand. Instead it deposited the two humans in its nest, a stinking bowl of mud, leaves, half-eaten carcasses and feces.

Gasping, Fryx sought Kris and led her up to a more wholesome spot in the nest, presumably the spot where the animal slept. Under the scrutiny of a shadowy mound of flesh, they curled up together, massaging their bruised ribs. After a minute or two, during which they could only listen to and smell the bellowing breath of the giant simian, it made its decision. Leaping backward smoothly, it fell out into open space. They heard branches below creak and swish as the creature caught itself and moved away through the treetops.

Kris rolled apart from him and sighed in relief. "I believed myself dead. How will we ever get down?"

Fryx allowed Garth to say nothing. His hold on his host had disintegrated greatly of late. Allowing the rogue's speech centers to operate was out of the question. Even interpreting her words was an unwelcome strain. Eyes bulging in the darkness, he reached out and grasped her wrists.

"What are you doing?" she demanded, squirming to get away.

Fryx drove Garth to climb on top of her, ignoring her efforts to escape. Their touch allowed him to communicate with Tuux, and Kris immediately quieted. Her rider allowed Kris to shed her human inhibitions and she quickly became amorous. In the way of communion between skalds of opposite sexes, they mated most vigorously on the crude bed of moldering hork-leaves and black animal hair.

* * *

The next morning found them entwined together with the cackle-grouse making a great deal of noise in the treetops around them. The bald ape, to the best of their knowledge, had not returned.

Garth was surprised to find that he was in command of himself. He suspected that Fryx had been over-taxed by the previous evening's activities and had receded somewhat to recover. Maintaining control of the skald's body was a constant mental battle for both of them.

"Look, there's blood here," he pointed out to Kris. "Fresh blood, and yet no signs of a recent kill."

Kris shrugged disinterestedly. She kept her eyes lowered. Her limp white hair hung in her face.

"Maybe the beast was badly wounded yesterday," said Garth with fresh hope. "Perhaps it could even have died during the night."

"Or perhaps it is only the blood of the men I led to their deaths."

"Ah, disregard that," Garth chided her gently. He turned to her and noticed her sullen appearance. "You were goaded by your rider—as we both were last night."

She turned away from him further.

"You're upset about our communion?" asked Garth quietly. He felt a small knot of guilt. He had enjoyed the activities, but not the way they had come about.

"I am embarrassed."

Garth nodded. "Put it out of your mind. Or better yet, use it to turn rogue against your rider."

She whirled on him. Her white hair shone in the sun. "That's why I'm upset. This whole thing has got me thinking like you. The philosophies of my rider now seem like nothing but idle platitudes. It is clear that association with a rogue is indeed dangerous."

Garth shrugged and climbed to stand on the rim of the nest. "It makes no difference to those who will now seek us whether you've turned rogue or not. Certainly, you realize you are to be expunged."

"Then I must leave you, we must part ways."

Garth shook his head. "If you believe that then you don't know the inquisitors as I do. Have you ever seen them in pursuit of a rogue?"

"No," she admitted.

"They are ruthless and thorough. They will have full accountings from all skalds involved, coerced by their riders into giving exact testimony. Your current feelings combined with my influence will be your undoing."

After this Kris fell silent and moody, while Garth searched for a way down from the jungle ape's nest. The equatorial variety of

80

the great horks was the largest. They dominated the plant growth in the ecosystem, and were in fact ecosystems unto themselves. Whole species of animals had evolved that relied particularly upon a given stratum of the great horks, which often towered over five hundred feet into the air. Every branch and leaf of these living islands teemed with insects and parasitic plants. Garth kept a sharp eye out for the deadly leaf-snakes, but none seemed interested in approaching the nest.

A careful search of the nest revealed the badly mangled corpse of a forester. One of his power-boots still remained, rekindling hope in both of them.

"We can use this to drop down from the trees safely," she said, excitedly testing the slid controls on the top of the boot. Although bent and scored they were operable.

"There's only one boot and two of us," he said doubtfully. "How will we balance well enough to get down without destabilizing and falling to our deaths?"

Kris made an impatient gesture, already strapping the boot to the belt around her midsection. "I live in this region. I have passed all the basic survival courses, don't worry."

Worrying strongly, Garth followed her directions, lying on top of her while she lay on the boot. Delicately, she adjusted the angle of the boot and pushed the power control slider to the maximum. Giving a desperate groan of fear, he allowed himself to fall from the side of the nest, clinging to Kris and the power-boot.

They fell together in slow motion. Even set to maximum power, the boot couldn't force them to rise, although it did manage to turn their fall into a gentle drifting descent.

"You certainly are heavy for a skald," she said, gasping for breath.

To Garth's relief, Kris didn't attempt to drop all the way to the forest floor, but rather made short trips from one major branch to another. Howlers pelted them with debris and leaf-serpents hissed as they passed. Cackle-grouse, resplendent in their yellow and crimson plumage, sought to bomb them with guano. Their odd, laughter-like cries soon became tiresome.

After perhaps half an hour of drifting in the humid air of the jungle, they reached the ground. Garth stamped about in pleasure, enjoying the feel of solid land against his feet. They made their

81

way toward the highway, which they had caught a glimpse of during the long flight downward.

Not far from the base of the great hork tree, they found the body of the great ape. A vast mound of furred flesh it was, already being eaten away by scavengers. Long black hair covered the creature from head to foot, save for its leathery face and the white-skinned bald spot on the peak of its pointed head.

"I guessed right," whispered Garth in a hushed voice. "The gunshot wounds finally took their toll."

"Well, I'm glad it's dead. It killed three good men."

Massive wounds showed in the creature's head and neck. Part of its cheek was blown away, revealing a mouthful of gleaming white teeth.

"Such an impressive creature. We seem so puny in comparison," said Garth. Gingerly, he climbed up onto the broad chest and stood there, rubbing his chin. "It seems such a waste."

Kris snorted. "It would have eaten us before the night was out if it had survived. These beasts relish live food and often store prey in their nests for later. I'm surprised that it didn't snap our legs to prevent escape, that is what they usually do, or so I'm told."

"Probably, it was distracted by its injuries," said Garth. He climbed down from the hairy mountain of death. "Come, let's get back to the road before other less pleasant things begin to stalk us."

"What could be less pleasant?"

"There are more horrid things about on Garm, even now," said Garth. "My rider has intimated this to me over the last few days, mostly in dreams, or during our most intense battle for control. This is what Fryx fears as much as death itself, I believe. The threat from the skies has driven him and I into disharmony."

"You don't seem to battle Fryx now as you did earlier."

"No. I believe this is due to the fact that I've decided to listen to his desperate warnings. I won't relinquish my body completely again without a struggle, but I will head for the South Pole, as he wants me to. As long as I travel this way, I think he will restrain his desire to control me."

Scrambling over a tree root the size of a flitter, Kris asked, "Do you not miss the philosophical heights to which only a rider can take a human?"

"Yes, at times, although I've had precious little time to

82

consider it."

They reached the gully and Garth's wrecked air car. Hunting about, they managed to find the hand-cannon and one of the rifles. Taking up the unfamiliar weapons, they found the hauler still sitting beside the road. They climbed in and soon were winding deeper into the jungle toward New Chad.

Garth took the time to tell Kris of the horrors that Fryx had intimated to him. Both parties tactfully avoided all discussion of the previous evening's activities, although Garth noted that he was treating her differently and he thought to notice a similar change in her manner. As he sat in the hauler's cab with her for long hours, free for the first time in days of his rider's constant abuses, he took the time to study her face sidelong. She was indeed attractive.

* * *

It was the following evening at camp deep in the jungles that Fryx began to trouble him again. A stabbing pain seemed to exist directly behind his left eye, causing him to blink and twitch in an unnatural fashion. Itching spasms traversed his spine at regular intervals, making it almost impossible to eat or sleep.

"What does Fryx want now?" asked Kris in concern.

"He would like to commune again with Tuux," slurred Garth, leering. The left half of his face clenched up in an unnatural manner.

Kris looked away.

"I'm sorry," sighed Garth, trying to regain all of his mind. "I think he wants to commune with me." With shaking hands he produced his skire, which he hadn't had the heart to destroy. Placing the reed to his lips he began to play.

Fryx was right there, aiding with every note. Clear beautiful tones sounded in the humid night. A group of howlers somewhere in the forest hooted a contemptuous response.

For a time it was as it had been before with Fryx. Garth exalted in close communion, the music of his skire filling everything with rose-colored joy. While Kris looked on happily, he pranced about the fire they had lit, playing his skire as a satyr would play his pipes. His rider intimated further details concerning the Imperium and their fantastic aggressions of the past. Images of entire worlds enslaved and burning filled his mind. Dark ships sailed out of the void to devastate unsuspecting worlds, exterminating spindly bipedal creatures that bore riders in their skulls, as did skalds. Garth learned that these ancient hosts of the riders had perished in a fantastic war with the Imperium that had lasted for a thousand years.

So entranced was he, that at first he didn't hear Kris' cries of distress. Shots rang out from the forest and he saw her frail body collapse in upon itself, folding up like a holo-image when the power is cut off. Blood pumped between her fingers. She looked into his eyes with horror and agony. Some dim part of his mind realized with cold logic that they had gut-shot her so that she would take a long time to die.

Making an odd, croaking noise, Garth stumbled away from the campfire. Fryx goaded him to stay put, to wait for the inquisitors to join them and perform the necessary extractions. Bucking like a wild horse, he lurched and shambled into the trees. He crashed through black-green walls of vegetation.

The shadowy jungle night swallowed him up whole. There was no possibility of immediate pursuit. Taking up refuge in the hollow bole of a fallen tree, he pressed the barrel of his hand-cannon to his forehead and wept profusely.

Inside his skull, the spiny gelatin that was Fryx writhed in fear. Half of Garth's face sneered in grim delight while the other half sagged in grief.

Ten

The farmer had a loud rolling laugh that boomed out over the fields and was audible among the smooth dark trunks of the horkwoods. It was the loud laugh that killed him. Thinking that the sound was a warning, that perhaps the vertebrates had somehow detected it, the killbeast altered course toward the farm. Normally, it wouldn't have bothered with this farm, as there was a relatively small herd of food-animals huddled in the barn. Its orders, however, were clear on the subject of detection: there could be none. Any enemy attempting to sound the alarm had to be silenced.

Reaching the edge of the trees, the killbeast paused to investigate a crude electric fence. Clearly, it had been designed to keep unintelligent animals in and out. With a single, contemptuous spasm of its powerful hind legs, it vaulted the ten-foot barrier and landed in the moonlit fields. Slinking toward the unknown and misunderstood sounds of laughter, it slid from shadow to shadow, nothing but another ripple in the waving fields of grain. Using the radio crystals grown in its thorax, it sent a single burst transmission. The chirp of data signaled the trachs waiting back in the forest to advance, there would be much protoplasm to carry back to the Parent's digesters very soon.

The jax herd in the barn lowed mournfully at the strange and frightening smells that came from the woods. Inside the shelter of their barn, they shoved and grunted their way into a huge circle of tightly packed animals, forming a single mass of woolly bodies.

85

The ones in the center were soon crushed near to death and bucked up above their comrades, scarring the others with their stone-sharpened hooves and trying to walk on the lumpy, woolly sea of jax backs.

* * *

"The jaxes are balling up again!" cried little Jimmy Herkart, trotting into the harvester garage where his father and Uncle Rolf were smoking a bit of swamp-reed in their long-stemmed pipes. "Daddy, they'll kill themselves this time, it's real bad. They'll be deaders in the middle for sure!"

The two men stopped laughing abruptly at the news. "Damned morons," muttered Jimmy's Uncle Rolf as they set aside their pipes and followed Jimmy out of the garage. They were a bit unsteady on their feet, and Dev Herkart, Jimmy's father, almost fell into the old dried-up well shaft as he staggered across the yard.

"Where the hell are the dogs?" Dev demanded, rubbing bleary eyes. He shook his head to clear it, and seemed to stand straighter.

"They ran off into the fields, barking at something out there. They haven't come back yet," explained Jimmy, pointing toward the shadowy treeline. The silvery wires of the electric fence glimmered in the bluish light of Gopus.

"Probably after a tree-yeckler, or maybe a landshark pup that the patrols missed. If the herd's been harmed, I'll take the lot of them to the auction tomorrow," said Dev with a growl. As the two men and the excited boy approached the barn, the frightened lowing turned to a terrific screaming. The scream of a Jax, despite its great size, had a disturbingly human sound to it, and all three of them recoiled.

"Sounds like a slaughter!" shouted Uncle Rolf, clapping his hands over his ears.

Dev broke into a run, and the others followed. As they passed the toolshed, the farmer stopped to throw open the door and pull out a long-barreled Wu shotgun and a box of shells. He shoved shells into the breach as they all trotted up to the barn door, cursing his absent dogs with each step.

"It's a landshark, sure as shit." said Uncle Rolf with just a hint of nervous fear in his voice. "It's got to be."

Inside the barn, the unmistakable sounds of a slaughter in progress continued. If anything, they had heightened. The very walls of the barn shuddered with the impact of heavy bodies charging about in blind panic. The leaves of the doors buckled, and the chain across the opening went taunt with a rattling sound. Human-sounding shrieks, wild grunts and the heavy thumping of hooves filled the night air.

Dev didn't bother with the chains; he simply blew the lock and the chain apart with his shotgun. Inside, a jax buckled against the doors and the body rolled out into the yard, forcing the doors open wide. The leaves opened with such force that they smacked against the wooden walls. The jax was dead, its head half-blown away by the shotgun blast.

Then the herd charged for freedom, but fortunately they had been expecting this and had stepped out of the way. Eyes rolling with terror, tusks wet with blood from chewing their own tongues, the jaxes poured out of the barn in an avalanche of woolly bodies.

"Only forty?" howled Dev as the last of the jaxes able to move staggered out. "I have ninety head in there!"

Rage took over and drowned out all caution. Dev rushed into the barn, finding and snapping on the overhead lights. They flickered into life and illuminated a scene of dreadful carnage. More than half the herd lay twitching, all obviously victims of violent death. Throats had been ripped out and left exposed, entrails had been pulled from soft bellies and splattered on the walls. One nearby jax, its front legs both severed at the midpoint, tried repeatedly to stand on its remaining stumps. Blood covered the walls and ran in rivers on the concrete floor. There was an overpowering odor of excrement and death.

The humans were speechless for a moment. Then they all choked on their dinners, near to vomiting. Dev held back the urge, however, too angry to give in to retching. Instead he walked into the ruin of his barn and his livelihood, shouting inarticulately for whatever had done this to come out.

Uncle Rolf put his hand on Jimmy's shoulder. "You go back to the house now, boy," he said. "You tell your mom to get the militia on the net and bring them out here."

Jimmy nodded and stumbled back toward the light and safety

of the house. On the way, he vomited into the well shaft.

The two men squinted up at the roof and examined the loft carefully. "There," said Uncle Rolf, pointed toward a patch of black sky visible through a hole in the roof. He wiped acidic bile from his mouth with the back of his sleeve. "Whatever it was, it probably entered and left through that hole."

"Not big enough for a landshark, not even a small one," said Dev doubtfully. "Besides, a 'shark couldn't climb up there."

"Oh, I don't know," said Uncle Rolf while the two men warily approached the hole and stood beneath it. "I've seen 'em scuttle right up a hork tree after a howler. Anyway, it must have jumped down into the orchard on that side of the barn. Probably, used one of the trees to get up there."

Uncle Rolf would have said more, but Dev held up his hand for silence. Both of them listened. There came a sound from the trees outside the barn, the sound of crackling branches. Walking quickly and quietly, the two men left the barn. Uncle Rolf paused to grab up a heavy wrecking bar that hung near the entrance. He hefted it experimentally, feeling the weight of it.

Outside it was cold and a fresh breeze had come up. The cool air blowing in their faces helped lift the drug-induced fog from their minds. They stalked the source of the sound, following it into the orchard. Gopus was just coming over the peaks of the Polar Range to the north, and it provided a bluish light that filtered through the finger-like branches. A tree creaked with the weight of a moving body, the sound coming from deeper in the orchard. Perspiring despite the cold, they followed it.

Dev saw something ahead, a shadowy form that flittered from behind one tree trunk to another, crossing their path. He halted, raising his gun.

"What is it?" whispered his brother.

Dev didn't answer. Above them a branch creaked, then snapped. A few twigs fluttered down from above, swirling about in the wind.

"It's above us!" shouted Rolf, holding his wrecking bar over his head.

Dev' shotgun boomed, more twigs showered down and a dark shape fell out of the tree and landed with a heavy thump.

They jogged forward to the fallen body. "It's one of your

dogs."

"The head's missing," Rolf pointed out unnecessarily. "Where's the head?"

They found it laying a few feet away. The lips were curled back in a permanent snarl.

"It's Shaker, dammit," said Dev, "a good dog."

Rolf was examining the tree above them. "Look," he said, pointing to more shapes up in the tree. "They're all hanging by wires. The same wire you use to run the fences, I'd warrant."

For the first time they knew real fear. Above them hung Dev's whole pack of seven dogs, minus Shaker who lay at their feet. Dev swung the shotgun barrel about in wide arcs, aiming into the trees and cursing.

There were more sounds of creaking branches directly ahead of them. Almost immediately afterward, a gray shape moved through the shadows off to the left. Another rustling sound came from the trees to the right a moment later. "There must be more than one, I just saw something up ahead a second ago. Nothing could move back up into the trees so fast."

"They're stalking us," said Rolf with mild surprise in his voice.

Without thinking, the two men stood back to back, their boots buried in wet grass. They breathed in visible gushes of white mist. Their heads swiveled rapidly, trying to pick up any significant movement in the dim light.

Suddenly, a shape dropped down from a nearby tree and ran toward them for a moment before darting behind another tree trunk.

"What the hell—" Dev said, swinging his shotgun into line. He fired, scarring the tree trunk with a gash of white wood in the dark pool of bark. They advanced on the tree the creature had gone behind, wrecking bar and shotgun upraised. Dev jerked his head, indicating that Rolf should go forward and flush the creature from behind the tree trunk with his wrecking bar. Rolf hesitated for a moment, but as he was the younger of the two and accustomed to following Dev's lead, he did it. He moved through the grass with the wrecking bar cocked over his shoulder like a rayball player swinging for a double.

He came around the far side of the tree with a growl, swinging the wrecking bar with killing force. It struck the bark with a dull thunk, stinging his hands. There was nothing there.

"Did you get it?" asked Dev.

"It's gone."

"Gone?" Dev said in amazement, stepping around the tree with the shotgun leveled. While Rolf sagged against the trunk and waited for his heart to slow down, Dev examined the bark and the dirt at the foot of the tree. "It was here, see these claw marks? And they go up the tree, too. The thing just ran up this tree like a goddamn howler."

Rolf snapped erect and backed away from the tree quickly. "Do you see it up there?"

Both of them stared up into the treetops, but saw nothing. Rolf heard a swishing sound off to his right, behind Dev. Dev stiffened, making a strange sound. A gray blade-like object protruded from his belly for a moment, and then it was withdrawn. Slumping against the tree trunk, he sagged down to his knees. Behind him stood the creature.

It resembled a giant lizard of some kind, with gray reptilian skin. There was no visible hair, horns or claws except for the blades of hard black material that sheathed the feet. It had run Dev through with one of these machete-like blades. The creature stood at least seven feet high on long powerful hind legs. Two short, wiry forelimbs each ended in three opposing fingers that had a sinuous, rubbery look to them. It had no head, but rather from the top of its torso sprouted several ropy-looking stalks and a cluster of mandibles above an open maw for eating. The stalks floated about and appeared to direct themselves in unison. Their behavior immediately suggested that the bulbs terminating the stalks were eyes or at least that they were sensory organs.

Rolf swung his wrecking bar for the creature's head-area, for the spot where the waving stalks sprouted. The creature danced away and disappeared into the trees.

Snatching up his shotgun, Rolf took a moment to check on his brother.

Still hugging the rough black bark, pressing his cheek against it, Dev was dying. He choked on blood, then stopped breathing altogether. The light of Gopus glinted in his dead eyes.

Too scared to feel grief, Rolf snatched up Dev's shotgun. He began to run for the house. Something came up behind him, and

90

then it paced him, running through the trees to his right. Then it vanished again, and appeared over to the left. With sudden clarity of thought, he realized it was playing with him, that it had been simply probing—testing for reaction the whole time.

He fired a wild blast at the dark shape, hoping for luck. He got it. The creature was bowled off its odd feet. It rolled through the wet grass that carpeted the orchard. Showing a horrible vitality, it sprang back up again, like a tumbler at the end of a run.

Rolf stopped and tried to take advantage of his lucky shot. He fired again, but this time he missed. Black dirt and grass fountained behind the creature. It charged him. Even as he heard the click of the next shell being automatically spring-loaded into the firing chamber, he realized he would never get off another shot. Perhaps if he hadn't smoked the second pipeful of swamp-reed, or if he had been less surprised, he wouldn't have missed so badly. But he had and now the thing was on him.

The thing snatched the shotgun from his grasp as effortlessly as Rolf himself had snatched a jax-goad from Jimmy's hands earlier that very day. In almost the same fluid motion, the thing made a flying kick for his head. The bladed foot swept up, caught Rolf under the chin, and cleanly decapitated him. His head and body fell in separate directions.

Showing its lack of familiarity with the human anatomy, the killbeast pointed the shotgun at the headless corpse, found the trigger with its odd rubbery fingers, and fired several times in rapid succession.

* * *

Jimmy, hearing the shots in the orchard, reached the house at a dead run. He entered the backdoor and was swept up in the welcoming arms of his mother.

"Sarah! Bili! There's some kinda monster out there!" he sobbed into his mother's dress. "It killed the jaxes!"

Sarah and Bili exchanged terrified glances. Sarah wrapped her arms around her Bili's neck and shoulders, squeezing him tight.

"You two know what he's on about, don't you?" demanded Sasha Herkart. Her eyes squinted with suspicion; her otherwise

91

comely face went taunt with dark lines. "You know about this. You came out of the forest like something was chasing you. Now you've brought it here!"

Outside, there was a renewed screaming from the jaxes milling about the yard. Something was among them, something was killing them. Sarah listened but there were no human sounds. There were no more shots, no more shouts, and the men didn't come back.

"Where's the cellar?" Sarah asked, heading for the kitchen. On the way past the home public-net terminal, she pressed the emergency call button three times and kept going. The woman followed, not seeming to hear the question.

"My man is out there fighting that thing. You should be out there. Those jaxes are all we have," her voice wavered and she was trembling.

Sarah found the door to the cellar and she took Bili down the steps with her. Sasha and Jimmy stood at the top of the steps, uncertain. Jimmy rubbed at the spacer's watch that Bili had given him as a present. His eyes were big and wet looking.

"Come down, we must hide," called Sarah. She and Bili moved crates of wine away from the walls to make room for them to hide beneath the stairway. Sarah had her gun out and the safety was off.

"No," said Sasha. "I'm going to get Dev."

"Don't do it," said Sarah. The two locked eyes for a moment. Sarah could see the battle of emotions running through the woman. Jimmy, two years younger than Bili, began to cry. Suddenly, he turned and raced through the kitchen and out the backdoor. Sasha ran after him.

Sarah sprinted up the stairs after them, but hesitated at the top of the steps. The door had shut itself, so she opened it a crack, her pistol leveled. Bili waited behind her, panting in the dark. In the kitchen she could see the net terminal's screen flare into life, it was the militia duty-sergeant, wanting to know what the trouble was. There was no one to answer him.

Sarah screwed up her courage and readied a simple plan of action. She would order the woman and her child back into the cellar at gunpoint and they would all wait for the militia. The militia could handle this. They had to handle it.

Two shotgun blasts rang out in the yard. Sarah's plans crumbled. She and her son just stood there in the dark at the top of

92

the cellar steps. Although she wanted to go further, a deep dread stopped her. It was as if an invisible wall, a barrier had sprung up at the top of the stairway. She couldn't will herself to go further. After what she had seen in the forest, that creature, swimming through tough roots and stony soil like a walrus swimming through dirt, somehow she couldn't bring herself to follow. She didn't want to see any more aliens. She wanted to forget that she had seen anything at all.

When sounds finally did come, they were the stealthy, furtive sounds of something coming in from the night outside, quietly opening the backdoor. Taking great care lest the stairs creak, and cursing silently every time they did, they made their way back down into the black cellar on wobbly legs. Crawling into the alcove they had made beneath the stairway, Sarah and Bili pulled sacks over their bodies and rested their backs against a lumpy wall of preserved tubers.

Overhead, they could hear the creature as it roamed the house. The timbers creaked beneath its heavy tread, giving away its otherwise silent movements. After a quick survey of the house, the killbeast left, as yet not familiar enough with human dwellings to realize that there was probably a cellar worth investigating.

Outside, under the shining eye of Gopus, a pair of trachs moved among the dead. The trachs were table-like creatures with four powerful legs and a single, massive claw that they used to load the carcasses on their wide, flat backs. Their squat bodies were slow-moving, but fantastically strong, able to carry or drag thirty times their own weight. They were very thorough, preferring to head back to the nest only when they could carry no greater a load up the mountain. They picked the place clean of protoplasm, including the gibbets on the walls of the barn and the shorn limbs in the yard that glistened in the moonlight.

At last they made their final trip back to the tunnel entrances, stumping away toward the breach in the electric fence with the killbeast protectively hovering near, sensory organs quivering. Behind them the bodies of the jaxes, dogs and humans were gone. Only the bloodstains were left behind as evidence of the slaughter.

* * *

93

Deep beneath the polar mountains near New Grunstein, the Parent received her first nife commander while ensconced on her birthing throne. Approximately every two minutes she shifted her uncomfortably bloated body to a new position and released another larva from her birthing chambers. She was in full production now, with all four chambers working around the clock. Her birthing orifices had already grown quite sore.

The nife commander, fresh from the cocoon, was overconfident, overzealous and talkative. He was the first of his kind on Garm. The only true males of the Imperium, the nife leaders were the field commanders of the race. The Parents themselves ruled over them, of course, but often accepted the judgment of a trusted nife in military matters.

The nife swaggered up to the birthing throne, his exo-skin still glistening with the slimes of his cocoon. The Parent's orbs tracked him carefully. Just to see him, after so long with no companionship other than the boring killbeasts and the nearly mindless trachs, sent a shiver through the Parent's digesters. Here was stimulation of an entirely different sort.

"Welcome, offspring."

"My birth was long in coming, but none the less glorious for it," replied the nife with a flourish. "You are a welcome sight to my orbs as well, my Parent. Clearly, you are no loose-fleshed immaculate at the end of an over-stretched life span. You glisten with youth and beauty."

The Parent ruffled her tentacles, affected by the nife's words in spite of herself. It was good to hear praise again; especially when she felt it was true. She was, after all, still quite young physically. She felt that the years spent in cyro-sleep couldn't truly be counted. "You flatter me in good taste, I am proud to have birthed you," she replied formally.

"I will go further," declared the nife, immediately growing exuberant at her approval. "I intend to capture this world and bear it back to this historic nest-site on the backs of ten thousand trachs. My glories shall outshine those of the Imperium's Ancients, and lastly,"—he paused dramatically and extended his stalks so far toward the roof of the throne chamber that the Parent half-expected to see his orbs to pop out of their cusps, "I will win the right to meld with you and conceive the Imperium's next generation of Parents!"

The Parent made a shocked sucking noise with her food-tube. "You overstep yourself! You are beyond the boundaries of decorum!"

"But my ambitions are boundless!"

"Your ambitions are the foolish dreams of the inexperienced," the Parent snapped back severely. "Only I will choose whom I am melded with."

"Of course, I meant only to state my goals."

"You are fortunate that you are the first of your kind," continued the Parent, her frontal clump of tentacles lashing the air in idle irritation. "There is no one for me to promote over you for your impropriety."

Crestfallen, the nife seemed to shrink somewhat. His stalks drooped, and his orbs retreated again into his cusps. "I beg forgiveness."

"I grant my forgiveness. Don't presume upon my good favor again, however. Now, we must have a tasting of the fresh flesh the trachs are bringing in. Some of it may not be fit for the larvae to eat."

"And some of it may be good enough to set apart for us," amended the nife. His spirits and his stalks were on the rise again, seemingly he had already put the recent rebuke out of his mind.

While they were eating, delicately selecting chunks from the back of a patient trach, the Parent continued to gestate new offspring. With great regularity, more offspring larvae were unceremoniously birthed, coming out squirming and hungry into the chute behind the birthing throne. As soon as they appeared a small spider-like creature known as a hest trotted up on numerous churning feet and carried it away to its own individual supply of food, safely away from other ravenously hungry larvae. Located beneath the Parent's four dripping orifices, the birthing chute was slick with amber resins. The resins produced a vile pungency that permeated the throne chamber.

"Exactly what are our strengths?" asked the nife professionally, in military matters his genetics took over and he functioned well, despite his incredibly young age. "How many effective killbeasts, juggers and umulks do we have?"

95

"The initial complement upon landing was only six effectives."

"Six?" asked the nife, incredulous. He almost dropped the shaggy jax haunch he had been gnawing on.

The Parent took a moment to slip her food tube into the skull of a jax and slurp out a good portion of the brain before continuing. "Of the task force only our one ship made it through. Fortunately, we have yet to encounter serious resistance. Our original complement included an arl, a killbeast, two trachs, an umulk and a culus with her ingrown shrade. Of that group, we lost only the arl in a planned diversionary maneuver."

"Ah yes, I picked that up from the datastream briefing in my cocoon. A nice maneuver, sending off the majority of the ship with the arl to lead away the enemy's atmospheric fighters. The umulk, of course, was a requirement for digging the nest. The culus and shrade, however," the nife paused and made a gesture indicating perplexity. "I don't understand your reasoning there, given how limited our defenses were. What if it had come down to an immediate fight?"

"Then the plan would have failed and we would all have died," replied the Parent with an unconcerned shrug. "I deduce that you are thinking I should have birthed a second killbeast for security?"

The nife bobbed his stalks in assent, too busy with a mouthful of slippery intestines to vocalize a reply.

"You could be right, but I reasoned that if the landing ruse had failed, if it had come down to an immediate fight, then the whole invasion would have been a failure anyway. One killbeast wouldn't have made the difference in such a battle. On the other hand, planning for the best case, getting the valuable military intelligence that the culus and shrade can provide is very helpful. Without them, we would be virtually blind right now. Proper reconnaissance is critical at this early stage.

"Your decision shows cunning and foresight."

"Thank you. To answer your original question as to our strength, I can say that with your hatching we now have one nife, a battlegroup of killbeasts, a squad of umulks, three culus and shrade teams, two teams of trachs and six hests. In another forty-eight hours, we will have another four more battlegroups of killbeasts and more of each of the other types. At that time too, I will have to consider melding to conceive more daughters. One Parent can't populate a whole planet alone."

"What about juggers?" asked the nife immediately.

"I have jugger zygotes in the birthing chambers now, but have halted their gestation until we formulate our attack plans. They simply eat too much and can do no useful work other than in battle. It would be bad logistic practice to birth them too soon."

At this the nife waved his claws briskly, signaling an emphatic negative. "I must differ with you and urge you to produce as many juggers as you can immediately. They take a longer time than most in the cocoon stage anyway, and we simply must have them for security purposes. For serious defense or offense, the killbeasts alone aren't enough."

The Parent ruminated on this a moment, mashing raw flesh with slow movements of her mandibles. "I bow to your greater genetic prowess in warfare. I am by nature conservative, perhaps too much so in an offensive campaign."

"Secondly," continued the nife. "There is the lack of arls to contend with."

Again, the Parent shrugged. "We have no more need of pilots. There is no means of manufacturing imperial battlecraft on this planet, probably not for the duration of the campaign."

The nife waved away her argument impatiently. "Of course not, but the enemy have such craft. We must be prepared to make use of their equipment, as we have no mass-transport technology of our own. For this reason maintaining a cadre of arls is essential."

Again the Parent ruminated and assented to his judgment. Once the production goals were set, their attentions turned to the flesh they were consuming. Both found that they preferred the flesh of the humans slightly over that of the jaxes. Although it was more spare on the bone, it tended to have more flavor, probably due to greater variety in the diet. Both of them agreed after careful tasting of the limbs and abdomens of various specimens, that the female probably tasted the best. The flesh was soft and generally had a higher fat-content.

Rasping upon something hard in her mandibles, the Parent indelicately picked at her serrated grinding spikes with her tentacles and pulled loose a metal object. It was a spacer's watch that had once belonged to Jimmy Herkart and to Bili Engstrom before him. Tossing it aside, she went back to chewing.

One of the Hests scuttled out of a gloomy tunnel and snatched up the gleaming piece of metal. To the creature's vast disappointment, she found the watch to be inedible. She carried the ruined watch away and deposited it down one of the rubbish tunnels where most of the bones from the endless feast in the throne chamber were going.

Eleven

Captain Dorman returned to the spaceport aboard a rescue-lifter. He was set down on top of the parking garage and managed to walk unaided into the terminal building. His head was ringing and his left shoulder was sore from the ride down into the jungle canopy strapped unconscious to the ejector seat. He refused the medical team, however, and headed directly into the security center to meet the new governor. Jarmo met him at the door, and after a cursory inspection allowed him through. Another intimidating giant named Jun followed him wherever he went in the center.

"Hello Captain," the Governor greeted him warmly, clasping his hand. "I hope you're all right, quite a hairy mission as it turned out. Frankly, I'm amazed that a pirate spacecraft could do battle with two Stormbringers on equal footing. I'm anxious to hear your report on the matter."

"That wasn't just a smuggler, sir," replied Dorman, marveling a bit at how easy it was to fall into the subordinate role with this man. It was clear he was used to giving orders and seeing them obeyed. "It was a combat ship, as good as anything the Nexus fleet has."

The Governor nodded. Dorman believed that he had already reached these conclusions.

"Jun, could you bring up the current scene on the holo-plate?" asked the Governor.

Jun worked a keyboard with over-sized fingers, punching up an image on the holo-plate that dominated the conference table. The image was a fuzzy, military-spec holo of the jungle where the smuggler had first appeared. A line of trees was down where the ship had ditched its cargo. "This is where they dropped their load and ran for it," said the Governor.

"What were they carrying? Did we recover the cargo?"

"No," the Governor said, shaking his head and frowning. "There was nothing there but a tunnel leading into the mountain. The lifter we sent out to investigate put in a recon team, but they found that the tunnel dead-ended into solid rock half a mile into the Polar Range."

"A tunnel?" said Dorman perplexedly, rubbing his sore temples.

The holo-plate image shimmered as the camera landed in the newly made clearing. Floating just above the heads of the recon team, it followed them to the mouth of a huge black hole in the fresh earth.

"A very large tunnel, big enough for men to stand upright in. The payload landed right in the middle of it."

"It would take a week to dig such a thing," marveled Dorman. "Seems amazing that they could land the payload that precisely under combat conditions."

The image on the holo-plate dimmed then flickered out.

The Governor shrugged. "A mystery. I'm very new to my office, and was hoping you could shed some light on it."

"I also wanted to speak to you about that, sir," said Dorman, straightening in his chair. "About your new office, that is."

"Proceed."

"As a Nexus officer, I offer my support to you, sir, provided you can produce proof of your identity."

Without a word the Governor ran his ID card through the terminal embedded in the conference table and waited as Dorman convinced himself that the data was genuine.

Dorman sighed at the end of it. "It seems that your claims are legitimate."

"You disapprove?"

"This planet is my home sir, and I'm don't relish the idea of a civil war."

"In your view the Colonial Senate will oppose my

100

inauguration, then."

"Yes, most vehemently, Governor. I will assist you in gathering what forces we can that will stand loyal to the Nexus. We must mobilize before they do."

The Governor nodded, and together they began to place a series of scrambled calls. Sergeant Manstein joined them, and soon they had a working defense strategy sketched out.

* * *

The culus emerged from the black treeline flying very low. The blue-green disk of Gopus had sunk beneath the horizon, leaving the cloudy night skies overhead pitch-black. Heading toward the sparkling streetlights the culus entered the city in the hilly residential section of Hofstetten. She glided silently among the houses, passing over fences and hedges, swooping down unlit streets and winding lanes.

The offspring flittered down into the center of town, where the tallest buildings on the planet stood. She passed the sixteen-story First Colonial Bank and she skirted the low, old-fashioned masonry walls that surrounded Fort Zimmerman, the militia headquarters. After that she entered the river district and ducked down between the moored barges that plied the river, hugging to the surface of the water like a seafloater skimming for jump-fish. Following the river down to where the spaceport edged up against it, the culus reached the cyclone fence around the compound and alighted atop a cement pipe.

The pipe was a sewer outlet that disgorged its steamy contents into the waterway. With a controlled vomiting action, the culus brought up the contents of her stomach, which consisted of the indigestible shrade. The long snake-like body of the shrade wriggled out of her mouth and slid immediately and stealthily up the pipe. The culus then rose up into the air, soaring back up the river on its leathery wings as silently as a giant hork-forest owl in search of prey.

A full six feet in length, the shrade was as thick around as a man's arm. She slithered up the pipe encountering relatively few obstacles. Little more than a long narrow piece of muscle, the shrade compressed her body and wriggled through holes in grates smaller in diameter than a five-credit piece and slid underneath the edge of barely open valves. Swimming against the steady flood of raw sewage she encountered a colony of large rodents, which scrambled out of her path while emitting high-pitched cries of alarm. The shrade was tempted, but passed them by, ignoring the possible food source, as she needed all of her stealth and speed to achieve her objectives. She did, however, mentally mark their location as a resource for later nourishment.

Finally reaching the main buried tank beneath the spaceport, the shrade encountered a maze of pipes leading up to the surface. After a few exploratory efforts, the shrade found a convenient exit.

In the men's public restroom on the arrivals floor, the toilet in the third stall suddenly seemed to flush itself. Water erupted, bubbling and splashing the tiled floors. Whipping her head about, the shrade struggled to extricate herself from the tight confines of the sewer pipe. The toilet seat clattered and walls of the stall were sprayed with soiled water. The shrade paused her thrashing for a moment to listen. Sensing nothing, she continued her efforts, finally managing to grip the base of the toilet and pull herself through, escaping from the cold depths of the sewers. Sliding out underneath the door of the stall, she determined that the restroom was indeed empty.

With a ripple of sucking, popping sounds, she extruded twelve short stumpy legs on each side of her body. From beneath her large single eye a spreading array of tentacles blossomed. With a peculiar humping gait, she moved rapidly to the restroom door. Using her tentacles, the shrade opened the door and surveyed the scene in the terminal with her single optical orb. She peered out into the baggage-claim area, immediately noting the presence of numerous active vertebrates.

The spaceport was in fact a scene of furious activity. Armed vertebrates marched back and forth about the building, gesticulating and making loud sound modulations. This immediately confirmed that the vertebrates communicated primarily through sound and visually detectable movements. Even as she took in this information, the shrade transmitted the scene using the radio crystals located in her tail-section, thus forming a living video pick-up for the open receptors of the Parent.

From the nature of the activities of the vertebrates, it seemed clear that they were preparing for a defensive military operation. Logically then, the offspring could only deduce that the vertebrates were now aware of the invasion and their impending peril. Worse, they had obviously predicted that the spaceport was strategically a key target and therefore would be one of the first objectives of the attack. Further, the fact that the rest of the city appeared so tranquil suggested that the vertebrates were quite capable of subtlety themselves and were perhaps laying a trap for the forces of the Imperium.

Heavy disappointment came to the offspring and was relayed to the Parent at this news. They had greatly hoped to take the spaceport by surprise as easily as they had the outlying food production zones. Somehow, they had been inefficient, incomplete, in their efforts to close down all information of the invasion. It was obvious that the vertebrates were preparing to do battle. Surface observations wouldn't be enough to counter this enemy's operations. All major targets had to be penetrated and compromised by shrades if reconnaissance was to be relied upon.

This changed the objectives of the shrade's mission. No longer was it so mission-critical that the shrade's presence go undetected. Having completed her check upon the enemy state of readiness, the shrade propelled her wet body at a slapping gait toward the janitor's door to the left of the stalls. Flattening herself and squeezing beneath the door, she found a ventilation duct in the janitor's closet and removed the wire grate. She slithered into the open duct, vanishing into the depths of the terminal building.

Finding a bank of tentacle-thick glowing tubes, the shrade delicately wrapped her snake-like body around them. The tubes carried the spaceport's data-net, one of the old-fashioned optical liquid networks that had gone out of use in most colonies. Due to budgetary restrictions imposed by the Colonial Senate, however, the system was still in place here. With an oily sucking sound the shrade exuded one egg shaped pod onto each of the slick-surfaced tubes. The moment they were in place, the glistening pods flattened themselves a bit and then punctured the tubes with their eight-tined data-forks. A few droplets of milky fluid dribbled into the darkness before the pods sealed the holes they had created and began soaking in data.

Transmitting at a very low frequency, the pods were quickly monitoring and relaying virtually all transmissions over the spaceport's datanet. A steady information dump fed the Parent's newly grown computers. It would take a considerable amount of time for all the information to be compiled, digested, cross-referenced and analyzed by the computers, they were really a bit young for this, but once the job was finished the Parent would have a diverse wealth of information concerning the enemy.

* * *

Late Friday morning Militia Dispatch finally got around to investigating the reports from Hofstetten of gunfire and screaming jaxes. A ground car pulled up at Dev's place with militia officers Kwok and her partner Friedrich. The cruiser rolled up the gravel drive, engine idling softly.

"I don't see anything," said Friedrich, "let's just call in and get back to town."

Officer Kwok glanced over at her partner in disdain. She was the senior officer and Friedrich's lack of respect for procedure often rubbed her the wrong way. "We'll check it out, then go back."

She stopped the cruiser in front of the house and they both got out. Friedrich climbed out with a grunt, grumbling, "damned waste of time."

It was when they rounded the side of the house and saw the mess in the yard that they both became fully alert. Bloody tracks and the few bits of meat left by the trachs covered everything. An empty shoe lay on the porch steps.

"What happened?" demanded Kwok, dragging out her pistol.

Friedrich pulled his weapon out smoothly and stepped into the open, eyes sweeping the scene. "Can't be just an early slaughter, too close to the breeding season. See the barn door? It's wide open."

"But where are all the jaxes?"

"Dev wouldn't have sent his jaxes into the high pastures this time of year, not with all the landsharks hatching in the woods."

Kwok nodded, heading toward the shoe on the porch. "The

screen door's been crashed in. It looks like the boy's shoe, here. Call in and report. Request a backup cruiser."

Friedrich tapped his earphone and called headquarters.

"Could be someone hurt in there. We have to go into the house—now," said Kwok. She looked Friedrich in the eye; both were scared.

Together they entered the house, following the odd trail left by the killbeast the night before. The three-clawed holes in the kitchen tiles were particularly disturbing.

Neither of them saw the culus that had flattened itself out against the roof of the barn, camouflaged to match the color of the shingles. When they moved out of sight, the culus rose up and dived from the roof, disappearing into the forest.

Down in the cellar, the two officers and Sarah came within seconds of shooting one another in the dark.

* * *

Daddy ordered a second platter of roasted air-swimmers while Mudface sipped a slurry of glucose mixed with light mineral oils. The waiter took the order with a forced smile, tactfully waiting until he had turned away from the two before putting a perfumed hanky to his nose.

"I won't have this kind of thing. I don't like coming down here and there's going to be hell to pay," said Daddy. Bits of roasted meat coated his fingers.

"Yeah," said Mudface. "Looks like she ran out on us."

"At the very least she screwed up and lost our shipment," expounded Daddy, shaking a large forkful of meat at his son. "We can't let people get the idea that we're soft. Nobody pulls one over on the boys from Sharkstooth."

"I kinda liked her though," complained Mudface. "A young man has plans, Daddy."

Anger brewed on Daddy's face. His fatty jowls pulled down in deep folds. "Young *man?* Plans? What are you going to do, leak oil on her?"

Mudface ignored the gibe. "So, we're gonna kill her?"

"No, we're gonna do more than that," said Daddy, his mood

lifting. He munched another forkful of air-swimmer, then grinned. Dark flecks showed on his teeth. "We need plenty of pictures to hand around to people who might be getting funny ideas."

After dinner the two men moved into the bar and once the maitre'd told the bartender who they were, they were served two foaming mugs of beer. Mudface barely sipped the foam from his. He had to be careful as the alcohol went straight to his brain. They selected the sports net on the bar holo-plate. After a few minutes, a news update from Nexus News Network interrupted the rayball highlights.

"Hey, that's the witch now," exclaimed Daddy, blowing beer all over the bar. The holo-plate wavered, then made automatic adjustments to clarify the image.

Sarah and Bili were both shown in a news snippet concerning the mysterious disappearance of an entire farming family. The announcer explained that they had been connected with the failed smuggling attempt on Wednesday and were being held at the Hofstetten detention center for questioning. The cameras did a slow pan of the house, the yard and the bloody mess in the barn. Militia officer Choy came on for about three seconds, saying that a rogue landshark was probably responsible, that perhaps the family had tried to harbor landshark hatchlings and had paid the ultimate price.

Mudface whistled and focused his optics on the holo-plate. "What the hell did she get herself into? They said something about another smuggler. Could we have some competition horning in on us here?"

"We'll find out," said Daddy, blowing the top off another mug of beer. "We'll find out everything."

* * *

A long low limo pulled off the cross-colony highway and slid into Hofstetten's main street. Governor Hans Zimmerman himself rode in the back, fuming. The limo floated up to the gates of the militia detention center and was quickly admitted.

Irritably, Zimmerman brushed past the guard at the door, shoving his ID card at the duty Sergeant. Surprised, the Sergeant

106

ran the card through the checker and nodded him through to the Captain's office. The Captain, having only just gotten word of Zimmerman's visit, was still busy shoving papers, holo-disks and bottles into his desk.

"What a pleasant surprise this visit is, Governor," he said, rubbing his hands together and snapping the top buttons of his uniform.

"Cut the crap," Zimmerman commanded, making a sweeping gesture. "I'm here to take custody of that woman and her kid."

"The ones from Dev's farm?" asked the Captain, surprised.

"Yes, yes, be quick about it, man."

"I must say, Governor, this comes as a shock."

"Yes," sighed the Governor. "It's a bit of a surprise for me, too."

"But our magistrate hasn't even set bail yet, sir. They haven't even been charged, although it looks like they'll at least get smuggling and resisting arrest. We haven't figured out what they had to do with the murders of the family of farmers."

"Murders? I thought the family had simply disappeared."

"Yes, well, the evidence shows that the family members were indeed killed, along with much of their jax herd."

"I'm too busy for such nonsense just now, Captain."

"But we haven't even set bail yet, sir," repeated the Captain with emphasis.

Zimmerman glared at the man for several seconds. "So you want money, is that it?" He stifled the man's protests with upraised hands, pulling out a checkbook. He keyed in his code and the device instantly spit out a five thousand credit voucher. "This will have to take care of it."

The Captain eyed the amount critically.

"Well? Are you going to get them or do I have to order my deputies into your cellblock?" demanded Zimmerman.

"I will get them, Governor," said the Captain stiffly. "I must point out, however, that the amount is certainly less than what the magistrate would set for charges of such gravity. I assume, of course, that your office will be good for the difference in case anything, ah—unexpected should happen."

"Of course," said Zimmerman. He made a dismissive gesture. "I must say that I find your demeanor less than cordial, Captain."

Tucking the credit voucher into his breast pocket, the Captain manufactured a smile. "If you would be so good as to wait in the outer office, I will have the prisoners delivered to you. The duty Sergeant will handle the required processing of codes. Oh, and by the way, do you wish them to be under restraints?"

"Yes, certainly. Magnetic cuffs should be sufficient."

Sarah and Bili were hustled up the stairs and through the security gate. There they were greatly surprised to meet Governor Zimmerman, whose face they recognized from the holo-plate news snippets. He had with him three burly men wearing autoshades set to extra dark.

Governor Zimmerman flagged a second limo, which pulled up behind the first. "If you two will excuse me," he said, "I'm late for a dinner engagement." He gave Bili an absent pat on the head and graced Sarah with a smile and a nod before climbing into his limo.

The deputies still gripped Sarah's elbow. She twisted her hands, but the magnetic cuffs held as if welded. "Where are you taking us?" she demanded. Loose strands of hair hung down into her face, matted with sweat.

"Right this way, madam," said one of the deputies, his eyes invisible behind his midnight-black shades. They were escorted to the second limousine and shoved into the back. The deputies popped the magnetic cuffs off and slammed the limo doors.

Seated comfortably in the plush interior was the unmistakable fat form of Daddy. Mudface was driving, wearing a peaked driver's cap. His idiot grin spread wider at Sarah's expression of despair. He touched his cap to greet them.

The two limos floated away in opposite directions. The culus that had followed Sarah and Bili from Dev's farm detached itself from an exhaust chimney and slid through the air in silent pursuit.

Twelve

Outside the spaceport compound, Ari Steinbach was beside himself with frustration. He had assembled an army consisting of numerous squad cars, two heavy lifters, a crowd of militiamen with pistols and Wu hand-cannons, plus 1st tactical squad. His tactical team had taken the longest to gather, and a third of them were still unaccounted for. Most likely they were attending the militia officer's banquet being held up at Fort Zimmerman tonight. They were probably not ignoring their beeping phones completely, but just taking their time in answering the summons. It was enough to make Steinbach grit his teeth in frustration. How had discipline become so lax? Why should they be enjoying good food and dancing while he sat out in the bitter cold, besieging a madmán and gnawing on dried jax meat?

Higher in priority than any of these things, of course, was the disposition of his satchel sitting in the lockers in the baggage claim section. It was too exposed there, he knew. If this whole thing got out of hand and heavy weapons were used, the satchel could easily be destroyed or lost. It was unnerving.

He wanted to strike now, before the enemy got any stronger or more organized. With his tactical squad in full body armor and toting waist-mounted Wu automatic rifles, plus the militia back-up, he felt confident that they could wipe out the giants and the undisciplined security people. The problem was with Mai Lee's instructions to wait for her support. To disobey her now, just before the arrival of her troops, could easily be a suicidal act.

"Why don't you move?" asked Major Drick Lee, smacking his small fist into his palm. "Send them in, before they call in Nexus-loyal Stormbringers from Fort Zimmerman."

"The pilots are preoccupied with the banquet tonight. Besides, our own loyal pilots outnumber the Nexus Tories," Ari snapped back, not looking up from his field glasses. He studied the glass doors of the terminal building with interest. There was definitely a lot of activity in there. Benches, potted plants and luggage were being thrown up as barricades. He tried to get a glimpse of the lockers, but the angle wasn't right.

"Every minute they get more prepared." Major Lee crossed his arms and huffed.

"Maybe you want to lead the charge, eh?" shouted Ari. "I don't want to hear any more whining! We wait!"

Rolling his eyes, Major Lee leaned up against the hull of a lifter and said nothing.

Ari seethed. Where was that ancient witch and her army of simians?

* * *

Sitting like a spider at the center of a great web of glittering datastreams, Mai Lee was one of the first humans on the planet to see a culus. It overflew her estate during her afternoon meditation, skirting the village and slipping over the moat and the flame-pits to peruse the outer battlements. Although her palace and the surrounding fortifications had the appearance of being a primitive place, built along the lines of ancient earth fortresses, its defenses were far from outdated. The culus was detected even as it circled the village. While it glided up to the outer walls a camera tracked its every movement.

"I beg your Excellency's pardon," whispered a speaker hidden in the center of a new and exquisite flower arrangement crafted that very morning by the skalds of the palace.

"I am meditating," said Mai Lee, floating in free fall over a gravity repeller. The mere fact that she didn't screech at the disruptive voice emanating from the clustered orchids indicated her good mood. Ever since the activities of the castle's legendary dragon the night before, she had felt a rare inner calm. A smile played over her lips at the memory of last night's excesses. "I don't wish to be disturbed."

"May I explain the request, Excellency?" the orchids begged.

Mai Lee cracked one eye and sighed. "Speak."

"The security drones have sighted a very odd intruder. It is currently examining the estate."

Mai Lee frowned slightly. "Send out a detachment of the guard to capture the spy. I will witness the interrogation and execution at my leisure. Must I give every instruction personally?"

"Certainly not, Empress, but the situation is difficult. The intruder is not a man, but some form of living being that can fly."

Mai Lee snapped erect, the gravity repeller easing her down to the floor automatically. "Put it through on the holo-plate."

The chamber contained a large holo-plate, which dominated much of the floor space. Instantly, the decorative image of a tinkling waterfall and the three persimmon-colored hummingbirds that hovered over it vanished, replaced by a very different kind of flyer. The creature was shaped like a skate from the distant sea: it resembled an air-swimmer, but more flattened out and streamlined. It was a milky mottled brown in color with flapping wings and a hook-knife tail. A single orb on a flexible stalk roved over the landscape. While she watched it expertly wove its way through a copse of delicate gauzepines, soared over the flame-pits unconcernedly and then rose up to crest the outer walls.

"What are its dimensions?" Mai Lee demanded. Her heart accelerated in her chest, already she was thinking of a prelude to assassination. Could this be some kind of new scout from her Zimmerman enemies?

"The wingspan is something less than six feet. From the frontal eyestalk to the tip of its tail is just over four feet."

She frowned; observing the creature as it slid around the courtyard, a dim shadow against the walls. "Wasn't it brown a moment before? It looks like gray stone now."

"Yes, it seems to automatically camouflage itself in flight, blending in with its surroundings. As a scout, it excels at its task. We only picked it up by accident."

She felt sure these things had been watching her for months.

111

Mai Lee felt her tension return, all the work of her lengthy meditation had been undone. Irritably, she ordered the beast stunned and brought to her council chambers beneath the castle. It appeared that she would have to begin sleeping in the bunkers beneath the castle again. As she watched the creature investigated the fountain, the very fountain from under which she had driven her battlesuit the night before. There was an intelligence evident in the thing's manner, a sense of direction and purpose. She was sure that it was alien to Garm and to her experience. Utterly alien.

"Order the compliment of guards to return," she said coming to a sudden decision. She had many enemies and consciously maintained a heavy tendency toward paranoia that had played a great role in keeping her alive for the past two centuries.

"They have almost reached the spaceport, your Excellency. General Steinbach has repeatedly signaled his impatience concerning their arrival."

"The safety of the estate and my person overrides the importance of their current mission. Instruct him to proceed alone."

The orchids acknowledged the commands and fell silent.

In the high atmosphere over the polar range, two heavy lifters each bearing a large compliment of ape-like shock troops reversed course and headed back to Slipape County.

In the courtyard of Mai Lee's palace, three stunners fired, catching the culus and dropping it into the fountain. It plunged into the cold water and sank to the bottom. Moments later the underbelly of the culus exploded from the inside outward. In a flurry of motion a shrade appeared, birthed into the cold water from her partner's digestive system. Swimming away from the billowing clouds of fluids that stained the clear water, the shrade was free. She popped her head above the water's surface for just a split second to look around, and then quickly dove to the bottom of the pool. Finding a drain entrance, she wriggled inside and vanished.

Sometime later the shrade reappeared, popping out of a drainage pipe in the lower levels deep beneath the castle. Slapping unnoticed in the forgotten corners of the lower labyrinths, the shrade investigated the varied garbage of the vertebrates' technological society. She spent only a few minutes indulging her genetic compulsions, rummaging about in heaps of burnt out memory modules, acid-leaking energy cells and ruptured data-liquid cabling. Soon, she managed to slip beneath a few doorways and entered the more frequented areas of the dungeons.

When she found the war machine, she knew she had made an important discovery. Standing two-thirds the height of a jugger, the gleaming hi-tech weapon stood out from the primitive feel of the dungeon itself. That the machine was no discard was clearly evidenced. Not a millimeter of its surface contained tarnish and the walls were festooned with tools and diagnostics equipment. The machine itself was open hatched and undergoing maintenance service by a squad of vertebrates, clearly technicians.

The shrade knew exultation. Here, at long last, was a clear example of the enemy's greatest powers of war. To study the machine was worth the deaths of ten shrades.

The shrade reported her findings with a short blip of data to the Parent. Though she fairly quivered with curiosity, she contained her violent need to know. Fantasies of attacking the three service vertebrates and expunging them ran through her tactical brain, but she managed to restrain herself. Built into every successful scout was a good dose of caution and patience. Hiding herself among a stack of fuel cells, she bided her time.

Hours passed before the vertebrates finally left the fantastic machine unattended. Quickly humping forward, the shrade mounted one of the metal monster's great legs. Nosing about inside, she discovered a myriad of wonders, all of which she catalogued and reported in coded transmissions.

A sound of approaching vertebrates warned her. She popped an optical organ just out of the hatch, eyeing their noisy approach. There were many of the vertebrates approaching, some of them armed and armored. It was too late, the shrade had over indulged herself—there was no way to slip out. She coiled herself inside the war machine, preparing to kill as many of the soft technicians as she could.

Another idea occurred though, concerning the numerous open hatches inside the war machine. Could she possibly hide inside the thing? Wriggling and scraping herself severely, she managed to slip into one of the hatches and seal herself in. Waiting inside to be discovered, she began to regret her hasty decision. How could the enemy's diagnostics not discover her immediately? She chided herself for being overly concerned with her own survival.

Outside, the sounds of the vertebrates rose in level, and then dropped away again. The shrade inside knew great relief. Soon, she judged that they had all left her alone again with the great machine.

Surprised at her own good fortune, she made to stealthily exit, but couldn't. Try as she might, the hatch wouldn't open. She was jammed in tight.

* * *

Scampering larvae simply thronged the nest. The Parent grunted and heaved, depositing another egg into the waiting arms of a clittering hest. Three large, cavorting killbeast larvae chased a smaller one, probably a hest or a culus—it was difficult to tell them apart in the larvae stage—up onto her birthing throne, across her painfully swollen chambers and down the other side. An involuntary hissing sound of discomfort and exasperation escaped from her food tube. It was simply too much for one Parent, all this birthing. Already she had laid an estimated five thousand eight hundred eggs since arriving on the target world. Developmentally, the offspring were now broken roughly into thirds, one third as eggs, one-third larvae and one-third adults.

...Suddenly, a cramp gripped her fatigued fourth birthing orifice. The fourth chamber was currently at the end of its cycle in producing a jugger. The fourth orifice cinched up tight, puckering at the worst possible moment during the cycle. The jugger egg was of course the biggest variety, requiring the greatest dilation of the birthing orifice in order to pass. Powerful muscles involuntarily contracted, bearing down on the rubbery egg and attempting to force it out. The results were inevitable, and exceedingly painful. A great wet ripping noise filled the birthing chambers. Her fourth chamber ruptured, releasing a gout of fluids. The Parent set up a tremendous fluting howl that turned the orbs of every hest and larvae in the nest. The hest came scrambling to her aid, while the larvae, fearing discipline, stampeded away toward the farthest reaches of the tunnel-complex.

When the Parent had regained some of her composure, she reprimanded herself sternly. She lacked experience and had made the classic error of a young Parent, thinking she could do the whole job herself. Enough was enough. She had to have help: she had to have daughters.

Leaning her vast bulk heavily on her left-side clump of tentacles, she raised her drooping orb-stalks to call for the eldest nife. It was time to meld.

To her vague surprise, she found he was already swaggering into the chamber. His manner was that of barely concealed triumph. His stalks stood excitedly at full extension, his orbs all but popping from their cusps. "I heard you cry out, and knew I should rush to your side. Are you damaged?"

"Yes," she said weakly, past being offended by his obvious excitement. "You are chosen. We must meld immediately."

The nife's frontal tentacles slapped together in an exaggerated and enthusiastic affirmative. He swaggered forward and began climbing the birthing throne.

* * *

After discovering the culus, Mai Lee moved to her command bunker immediately, sealing it off except for the datastreams which came from every sector of Garm. Her ancestral computers were legendary in technical circles, and nowhere else on the planet did such a comprehensive and intelligent nerve center exist. Every city on the continent was wired in for sound, many of them providing full holo-plate feed. The computers served to perform the gargantuan job of assimilating this continuous mountain of data, finding interesting tidbits in the vast ocean of insignificant events.

She ordered the culus dissected by her medical team, a group of seven middle-aged Manchurian women. They wore white smocks and thin paper slippers. They worked at the task efficiently, only their dark eyes visible over their masks. Every step of the operation was carefully recorded. Small hands wielded flashing scalpels; the culus was quickly dismembered.

While she awaited their report, Mai Lee riffled through the incoming intelligence reports. She paused over a transcript from the spaceport.

* * *

Grunstein Colony Spaceport, aboard militia command lifter: *Salient*. Governor Hans Zimmerman has a private discussion with General Ari Steinbach.

Transmitting Agent: Major Drick Lee. *Imperial grand nephew.*

Agent Reliability Index: 84%.

ZIMMERMAN: I see you have yet to rid us of this man. I fail to understand your hesitation in this matter. Note the full media team that has now arrived. KXUT will be broadcasting the whole thing live if you turn it into a bloodbath now.

STEINBACH: We lack the firepower, sir.

ZIMMERMAN: You have an army here!

STEINBACH: Since the renegade Colonel Dorman brought in a squadron of Stormbringers, deluded into thinking they support the legitimate Governor, they have held the decisive edge.

ZIMMERMAN: You should have moved immediately! If you had attacked when the tactical squad first arrived you could have wiped them out.

STEINBACH: Your point is well taken. Please excuse me now, sir, while I return to my duties.

ZIMMERMAN: *Growing hostile.* Not so fast you little weasel. This is my political life we are talking about, here. Who do you want running this colony, anyway? Are you some kind of Nexus-loyal plant? What do we pay you for, man?

STEINBACH: Governor, with all due respect I don't really have the time.

ZIMMERMAN: You'll make the time for me, General! I am a Zimmerman, if I must state the obvious.

STEINBACH: Give my regards to your family, sir.

A tense silence ensues.

ZIMMERMAN: *Speaking in a low voice.* You don't know who your screwing with. I know you work for that witch, but she's not the only one with assassins in this town. Now, I'm going to lay out what's going to happen, and you're going to follow orders like a good little soldier. First, I'm going to go in myself and try to talk to

116

the bastard—

STEINBACH: You're bravery surprises me.

ZIMMERMAN: I'm going in with plenty of cameras. He won't do anything. How would it look if the new Governor shot the old one coming in to welcome him? What kind of a civil war could he put together after that was splashed all over the evening news? Who would rally to the call of an exposed murderer? Second, if I can get him to come out, we will have a much better chance at him later, at a phony inauguration ceremony, for example.

STEINBACH: *Thoughtfully.* Your plan has merit, but I can't help but think that Droad would be too smart to fall for it.

ZIMMERMAN: And if you hadn't jumped right in with an unplanned assassination attempt and warned him off, we could be on good ground right now. You and your Manchurian cronies panicked, that's all there is to it.

STEINBACH: *Shrugging.* So, what if he doesn't bite?

ZIMMERMAN: Then I call him a criminal and order you to retake the spaceport. Now I know you have instructions from 'Her Excellency', but don't worry about her. Whatever she's paying you we'll cover it, and she won't dare bitch about it because the whole Senate's howling for her blood right now. The Zimmermans are taking their rightful place as the leaders of this colony, Steinbach. It's time you put yourself on the winning side.

STEINBACH: *Both men stand up.* Your logic is unassailable, Governor.

ZIMMERMAN: I thought you might see it that way.

* * *

Lucas Droad was reviewing Manstein's defense plans with Jarmo when Governor Zimmerman came calling. Tapping timidly on the front glass of the terminal building with a three-man media crew in tow, Zimmerman was allowed in by several astonished security people.

"He has more balls than I figured," said Manstein, watching him as he was escorted across the terminal by two suspicious giants. "He's been putting on a little weight since the last fixed election, too."

117

"Indeed," agreed Governor Droad.

Zimmerman was patted down along with the media crew, and then they were all led into the security center. He joked with the giants and with the media people, insisting on a publicity-shot of he and Jarmo standing close together to allow size-comparison. Jarmo refused to smile for the cameras, but rather maintained a stony, unpleasant expression throughout the affair.

Droad met them in the conference room. "This visit is an unexpected pleasure, Governor."

"Mr. Droad, I'm afraid things have gotten out of control, and I apologize," said Zimmerman, shaking Droad's hand warmly. Droad rubbed his hand on his pants afterward.

"I'm glad you came here in such a timely fashion. It's critical that I am instated as the Nexus-appointed Colonial Governor of Garm immediately. I am here to replace the last Governor, whom I understand is now deceased."

Zimmerman looked pained. He glanced sidelong at the humming holo-cameras, and then his eyes slid back to Droad. "Now Droad, you must understand how things are here. I'm the rightful Governor of this Colony, by senatorial appointment. Your claim hasn't been validated as yet, but let me assure you that if you are who you say you are, you will of course become the head of state here, after your official inauguration."

"The protocol you suggest would be adequate under normal circumstances. However, your appointment is not valid since only the Nexus can appoint a colonial governor, therefore it is not in your power to require such a protocol, nor do you have the authority to inaugurate me in any case. As an additional factor to my judgment, there has been an attempt on my life by assassins, at least one of whom was a member of the militia. Given the near-anarchy I've witnessed here, I am unwilling to allow such a gross delay."

Zimmerman was clearly unhappy. He made an irritated gesture. "Look, you can't just come out here, hop off a three-year sleeper ship from the cluster and expect us to all hail you as Governor without even checking it out. Listen, I'm offering you the benefit of the doubt to prove yourself. You've committed numerous criminal acts, but in deference to the Nexus we are willing to consider the possibility your claim is legitimate. What more can you ask for?"

"Immediate compliance with Nexus Cluster Law."

"The Colonial Senate will never accept it."

"Nevertheless, this is my position. Nexus Law supersedes local authority. I hereby order you to accept me as the rightful Colonial Governor of Garm."

"That's the best you can do?" asked Zimmerman, obviously surprised.

"I am inflexible in this regard."

On the way back out of the terminal building the Governor was far less outgoing with the media people. His joking, smiling politician's mantle had been discarded. Instead he sulked, answering their questions only with monosyllabic grunts. This made for bad video, but the media people only voiced their complaints in low mutterings.

* * *

When Zimmerman returned to the militia lines stretched across the tarmac, he was livid with fury. Gray-coated militiamen hustled away the protesting KXUT news team and Zimmerman confronted Ari Steinbach in his command lifter for a second time. Outside, Major Drick Lee carefully focused his handheld laser-snooper on the lifter's side windows. He adjusted the gain until he had a good clear signal-feed into the speakers implanted in his ear canals.

* * *

Back in the command bunker beneath Mai Lee's palace the transmission was received and the AI software began printing a hardcopy of the transcript even as the words were spoken.

ZIMMERMAN: Okay, you're going in now, and I don't want to hear any more excuses. I want you to wipe them out, I want you to kill them, you understand me?

STEINBACH: Of course, sir. The operation will begin at once.

ZIMMERMAN: Good. What will you do first?

STEINBACH: *Sounding irritated.* Please Governor, let me run this affair without the burden of micro-management. Let the

119

experts handle it.

ZIMMERMAN: *Snorting.* The experts have been as shy as newborn air-swimmers so far! I want to know what your plans are!

STEINBACH: Very well. I have men moving to encircle the terminal. Even now they are out on the tarmac runways. No large aircraft will be able to land and give them support.

ZIMMERMAN: What about the Stormbringers you so stupidly allowed them to gather?

STEINBACH: They have landed on the roof. The plan is to send our own aloft and force them to scramble up to the challenge.

ZIMMERMAN: Why not just blast them? Why don't we just forget all this pussyfooting around and blow up the whole terminal?

STEINBACH: *Speaking quickly and urgently.* That really isn't an option, sir. There may be innocent hostages involved, which would make for bad video. Besides, why waste the taxpayers money rebuilding the spaceport?

ZIMMERMAN: Okay, okay, so you fool around and try to draw off the fighters. What about the assault?

STEINBACH: After a period of sniper-fire to suppress the enemy while we maneuver into position, we simply send in the tactical squad, using the rest of the men for backup.

ZIMMERMAN: All right, General. You get a few hours to pull this off, then I call up Fort Zimmerman and order them to ready the missile batteries. If you can't take them out by then I'll level the terminal building.

STEINBACH: *Speaking with great certainty.* I assure you, sir, that will not be necessary.

* * *

At precisely 10:00 PM the power went out at the spaceport. Emergency generators in the basement kicked in, and some of the lights flickered back into life. Outside the rain showers had abated for the moment, but the wind had freshened and the temperature had taken a sharp plunge. Shivering a bit as they squeezed off their laser rifles, the militia snipers managed to hit one of the female security personnel with the first volley. Struck in the shoulder, she

120

spun around, gushing blood. A second burning red hole blossomed in her vest and she went down. Everyone else ducked behind their barricades and began firing blindly out into the darkened parking lot.

"Jarmo, dial up the *Gladius* and transfer it to my phone," said Droad. He felt he had no choice but to call in his reinforcements.

"Priority signal to the cargo deck, sir?" asked Jarmo, guessing his intentions. He was already tapping his earphone.

"Right. It's time to call for the Mechs." The Governor sighed with disappointment. "I had hoped against all rationality that things would somehow turn away from bloodshed. But like so many rulers throughout the ages, I am faced with the harsh requirement of using force or losing the right to rule. I suppose the Nexus aristocracy wouldn't have chosen me for the job if I would have made any other decision."

Jarmo was listening with sudden intensity to his headset. "Another attack sir, inside the building."

"Militia?" demanded Droad, eyes locking on the giant's huge face. "If they're inside already, we'll have to order an immediate pull back to the inner security zone, damn it."

"No sir—" he paused, and barked a command for clarification. "No sir, someone has killed one of the traffic-controllers in the lavatory. He was just found, strangled to death."

Droad's eyebrows shot up into his hairline. Did they have a traitor in their midst?

"Sir, I would like to examine the scene personally, right now."

"Now? We're in the middle of a battle, here."

"Immediately. There are details to the report that I don't understand or like. As for the militiamen, given the tactical situation they probably won't undertake a serious assault until they are fully in position and have done something about our aircraft. This sniper fire is to keep us pinned down while they maneuver."

"What if they just rush us? I'd like to have my best field commander on the front line."

"Historically speaking, corrupt police forces fight little better than would hired thugs. They lack dedication, and will use extreme caution while attacking a determined adversary. What I don't understand is why they haven't yet bombarded the spaceport from Fort Zimmerman."

121

"Maybe Dorman and his buddies aren't the only Nexus loyal officers on this mudball," suggested Droad hopefully.

"Maybe," agreed Jarmo without conviction.

"Go ahead, find out who strangled the techie and get back up here."

With a crisp nod of his great head, Jarmo turned and made his way back to the stairs in a running crouch. Reaching the lavatories on the lowest level of the terminal, he met with Jun, who was staring and frowning fiercely into the lavatory. He held his weapon at chest-level, the odd cone-shaped muzzle directed at the wall of stalls.

"Where's the body?"

Jun just nodded toward the stalls, keeping his weapon at the ready. Drawing his own plasma handgun, Jarmo squeezed past him and into the lavatory. He noticed that the floor near the stalls was coated with an odd liquid that was both slippery and sticky at the same time. He assumed it was liquid soap. He found the body in the third stall, and immediately realized why Jun had been so cautious.

The strangled man lay sprawled in an undignified pose with his head shoved down into the toilet. His neck had been squeezed with such great force, that it had been all but removed from his torso.

"A giant did that," said Jun at the door. He and Jarmo shot each other worried looks. "Had to be a giant to crush his neck like that."

Jarmo nodded, the killer had to have fantastic strength to squeeze the flesh off of a man's neck, right down to separating the vertebrae. The neck looked like the remains of a ripe banana squished in a pair of vise grips. "Could have been a giant," he agreed.

He began a closer inspection, and discovered more of the slimy fluids that puddled the floor of the lavatory. There was an odd stink as well, that of a sewer, mixed with something else. It was an acrid, fishy smell.

He searched the rest of the stalls, finding nothing of note. When he finally returned to the body, he was frowning intensely. He wasn't a man who enjoyed mysteries. Reaching down into the mess in the toilet bowl, he pulled the head out by the hair as gently as possible under the circumstances. Laying the corpse face up on the floor he examined it and the bloody interior of the bowl.

122

"Very interesting," he muttered. "Come, what do you make of this, Jun?"

Jun moved to his side with only the slightest hint of hesitation. They were not normally squeamish men, but these were extraordinary circumstances. "What do you see?"

Jarmo indicated a circle of puncture wounds around the base of the neck and a matching circle under the chin. He then pointed out the gouges in the toilet bowl.

"Do you suggest that the man wore rings, or perhaps a clawed glove of some kind?"

"Perhaps," said Jarmo, rubbing his chin. He wondered if perhaps a mechanical hand would have the strength to perform such a feat. A hand like that of a mech, for example. That still would not explain the slimy jelly-like liquid, but it was a start.

Still, though, he couldn't help but feel that there was more to this, that he was missing something. Something about the bizarre murder triggered off a tingle of danger in his mind, a primitive fear of the unknown.

Walking over to the utility closet, he forced the lock with a twist of his huge wrist and looked inside. With the long barrel of his weapon, he poked around inside the closet.

"What are you looking for?" asked Jun curiously. He had come forward, but wasn't quite looking over Jarmo's shoulder.

"I don't know. Something strange. Ah, more slime!" he said discovering a damaged vent and more of the glistening, jelly-like substance. "Some kind of animal has been in here, it must have gotten into the air ducts. I don't remember reading about anything like this in the file-tapes, though."

"Maybe it's some kind of snake," said Jun, peering into the closet that was more than filled by Jarmo's great bulk.

Both men froze as they heard an odd splashing sound coming from the stalls. It was as if the toilets were gargling. Soon after, there was a wet, slapping sound. Jarmo put a big finger to his lips and the two of them bent down to look under the doors.

The sounds suddenly stopped. The giants exchanged glances and leveled their weapons. Whatever it was, it had heard them.

Baring his teeth in an unconscious snarl, Jarmo leapt forward and threw open the stall door from which the sounds had been coming. A ghastly creature sat there, half-in and half-out of the

123

toilet, at their approached it reared its ugly head. The sucker-like mouth was bloodied. It had been feeding on the dead man's corpse.

Jarmo fired and the thing sprang at the same time. The plasma burst missed, but took out the rear wall of the restroom. The shrade landed on Jarmo's chest, sticky sucker-feet gripping his clothes and the flesh of his neck. He was yanked forward into the stall as it struggled to pull the rest of its body out of the plumbing.

Four giant hands grabbed the thing immediately, and a struggle of unnatural strength began. Grunting and heaving, the two men managed to rip it loose from Jarmo's chest, although it was like pulling apart welded steel. With a final, mighty thrust, they threw it to the floor of the restroom and blew its head off as it humped for the utility closet.

Breathing hard, the two giants knelt over the twitching body.

"Incredible," breathed Jarmo. "If this is an indigenous life-form, it's something they left out of the briefings."

Jun wiped his face with the back of his sleeve. "Almost had you."

Jarmo nodded, "I don't know if I could have pulled it off alone. I want you to take this thing back to the security center. See if the medical center people can identify it."

Jun looked disgusted for a moment, then pulled off his jacket and wrapped the thing in it. Jarmo accompanied him out into the terminal, waving off the security people who had come to investigate the plasma burst.

Before he was halfway back to the security center, Jarmo heard the crackle of gunfire outside. He was already trotting when his phone beeped. Beginning to run, he snapped, "I'm on my way."

Thirteen

At about ten o'clock Thursday night, the battle for the spaceport began in earnest. The first steps went according to plan for Steinbach, as he succeeded in drawing off the enemy Stormbringers with his own. Steinbach followed up by sending in his tactical squad, almost fully accounted for now, with the militia men backing them up.

The tactical squad moved through the parking lot at a brisk trot. Captain Qing at the point felt invulnerable in his full body-shell armor. The men behind him cheered as they broke from cover and charged the remaining distance to the doors. A wild volley of covering fire from the militia lashed the building in front of them.

Inside, the front line of security people pulled back to the escalators, leaving their dead behind. A group of giants let them pass, then opened up with plasma rifles as the tactical squad tackled the barricades. Despite their body-shell armor, several men went down. The rest took cover and opened up with automatic rifles and exploding slugs. A vicious firefight at close range began.

"Pull them back, Jarmo," insisted the Governor.

"They have to hold until the Mechs arrive, sir," replied the giant.

"Pull them back! We can't let them get slaughtered. We can hold the security center, let them have the rest."

Jarmo swiveled his great head. "If we give up the rest of the terminal now, they will gain a great morale boost. We need to hold until either they break, or the Mechs arrive."

The Governor paced back and forth in the security center reception area, fuming. Sergeant Manstein, Jun and Jarmo all watched him. Finally, he gestured impatiently. "All right, all of you go up, but keep your heads down! Just hold them until the Mechs land."

The tactical squad had carried the fight down to the second floor and now the fighting was desk to desk, door to door. A gigantic leg, blown clean off, was draped over the escalator handrail. A headless suit of body-shell lay nearby.

When Jarmo committed himself and the last of his reserves, it was too much for Captain Qing. He had already lost half his men and there seemed to be no sign of a break in the enemy defenses. The security center in particular, should he even manage to get that far, looked impregnable.

He called an orderly retreat, which combined with Jarmo's last ditch charge to turn into a rout. Men danced in their body-shell armor as countless rounds struck them. Upstairs, the militiamen had just triumphantly entered the terminal, expecting little resistance. The sight of the tactical squad in full retreat, dragging their wounded, set up a panic. Jarmo, with the handful of giants and security men still standing, chased them from the building and back into the relative safety of the parking lot.

Jarmo sat halfway up the escalator, his great chest heaving. Through a bullet-shattered skylight overhead he examined the night sky. The mechs should have arrived by now. What could have stopped them?

* * *

The first flakes of snow fell as Steinbach stood behind a lifter with his field glasses leveled on the terminal. Every militia trooper was engaged in the assault, except for Steinbach himself, who preferred to survey the battle from a more comfortable angle.

He startled when Major Drick Lee appeared at his side. He grimaced, turning slowly to face the man, whom he was rapidly coming to despise.

"What are you doing here?" he demanded. "I thought I ordered

126

everyone into the attack."

Major Lee snorted and said nothing.

Steinbach returned his eyes to his field glasses. He ground his teeth. "Just because you're related to a senator doesn't make you God, Major. You're a soldier out here, just like the rest of us."

"Look, General," began Major Lee, "I don't want trouble with you, but if you think I'm charging through that parking lot just to save a building, you're out of your mind."

"We aren't fighting for a building, Major."

"Then let's just blow the place up! Unlimber the big batteries and have done with this little fiasco. Then we'll have another eight to ten years of profits before the Nexus bothers to ship the next fool out here."

Steinbach jumped a bit at the mention of the missile batteries. He swiveled to examine the walls of Fort Zimmerman, just visible on the horizon. He looked for smoke trails, but as yet there were none. It was only a matter of time, however. Whatever had possessed him to put his satchel into that locker?

"We'll do this my way," Steinbach told him.

Major Lee shrugged disinterestedly. "Suit yourself, but count me out of the heroics."

Fifteen minutes later, the tactical squad was repulsed and came staggering back to the lifters. Medical corpsmen shouted and rushed about. Steinbach slumped down in the seat of his limo, defeated. The missiles would have to come now.

They waited, regrouping and applying first aid, until midnight. Steinbach kept a sharp lookout on Fort Zimmerman, and tried to get a hold of someone over there on his phone several times without success. He kept waiting for the batteries to wind up and snap off their missiles, but nothing happened. Hours passed and Steinbach became increasingly apprehensive. He had just sent a cruiser up to the fort to see what was going on when Major Lee sauntered over to his car.

"Reports of fighting up at the fort are coming in over KXUT," remarked Major Lee. He had been sitting in one of the lifters, idling the engine to run the heater. "They say some kind of riot is going on. Maybe the banquet got seriously out of hand."

Steinbach looked up the hill to the fort, noting for the first time that the floodlights on the guardtowers were out.

127

What was going on up there?

* * *

One of the few official events that Governor Zimmerman truly enjoyed attending was New Grunstein's annual militiamen's banquet and ball. Held in the central hall of Fort Zimmerman, he always found the food excellent and the entertainment reasonable. Moreover, each year he was asked to make a speech, which was always well-received by the agreeable crowd. Sitting at the high table mounted on the stage, he argued good-naturedly with a militia officer, his mouth full of Garmish polar cod.

"Females are best in their teens, I tell you, and I speak from vast experience," expounded Zimmerman. His face was florid from too much hork-leaf wine. "These days I will have nothing to do with a paygirl who is over sixteen. After that, it seems to me that something of the glow of youth begins to fade from them. It's difficult to put your finger on, but it's there."

The officer made a polite gesture of agreement. "Isn't it about time for you to address the assembly, Governor?"

"Quite right, quite right," said Zimmerman. He stood ponderously, his ample belly brushing the table edge as he heaved himself erect.

"The stairs are right there, Governor," said a deputy, taking his elbow. "I'll just help you put on this throat-mike."

The Governor and the deputy fumbled with the microphone for several seconds before it was in place. Zimmerman pushed the larger man away in irritation and mounted the steps on unsteady legs. The deputy followed to stand beside the podium, his thick arms crossed and his autoshades in place.

Zimmerman rattled the hardcopy of his speech for several seconds. "Ah, yes. At last we meet again, and I am honored to thank you all for another year of exemplary service to the colony. And I do mean all of you: wives, husbands and children of the officers present are included. The families of militia officers are just as worthy of praise as are the officers themselves."

He paused for the applause that must surely come. It did, right on cue. How could it not, after he had complimented their

128

families? Get your audience applauding early and often, that was his motto.

"Among the notable accomplishments of militia officers this year I must include..." he went on for several minutes, listing the names of each officer awarded a major certification of achievement. A line formed at the steps, where the honored officers were given ribbon-bound hardcopies of their citations and a warm handshake from the red-faced Governor. The deputies critically eyed each of the officers in turn, inspecting each as a possible assassin.

Before the line-up had gone through half its length, however, there was an interruption. A commotion began at the back of the hall, where the corridor led out to the restrooms. A woman burst through the doors, screaming with terrific force. In hot pursuit, a bizarre creature like a giant caterpillar humped into the hall after her. Too surprised to react instantly, the officers at the door simply watched with gaping mouths as the six-foot long thing caught up with the woman and sprang onto her back, bearing her down to the floor. With startling speed, the shrade wrapped itself around her torso and convulsed with all its fantastic strength, crushing the ribcage. Ribs and vertebrae crackled and popped loudly. The woman's eyes bulged and she wheezed a final cry of agony.

By this time the nearest armed officers managed to drag their guns out and get to the fallen woman. Although it was obvious that the woman wouldn't survive, they made an effort to avoid shooting her, firing at the head of the thing that rode her still-jerking body. Shots rang out and people the length of the hall began to scream and duck. The shrade was hit in the head three times, but still it managed to disengage itself from the woman and rear up, as would a snake preparing to strike. The guns sounded again and the shrade finally slumped down, pumping dark ichor onto the dead woman and the carpeting.

Governor Zimmerman stood on the stage; his hand still outstretched to provide yet another congratulatory handshake. He gaped at the confusion at the back of the hall, unable to see exactly what had happened. He waved the line of officers back and returned to the podium. "There seems to be some kind of interruption, but I'm sure that the officers on duty can handle it. Will everyone please take their seats."

129

One of his deputies moved to his side and whispered harshly in his ear, "It could be a terrorist attack, sir."

Zimmerman's eyes showed fear. He pursed his lips, then waved his deputies forward to stand in front of the podium, presumably between him and any assassin's bullet. Standing with knees bent slightly, so that less of his form showed over the podium, he spoke to the nervous crowd again.

"If we can continue with the program now, please," he said, tapping his stylus on the mike to get their attention. Why did something like this always have to happen when he was really enjoying himself? He hated nothing more than unexpected interruptions.

Before he could utter another word, however, more shrades chose that moment to drop from their hiding places in the hall's great chandeliers. Falling onto the circular tables stacked high with polar cod and roasted air-swimmers, the things tackled the nearest armed humans and wrapped them in deadly embraces. One man's head was squeezed cleanly off his body to thump and roll down the main aisle. Horror-struck, people leapt to their feet and scrambled for the exits. An amazing level of noise arose.

Even as the shrade attack began the flooring directly in front of each of the major exits heaved upward. Violent tremors shook the hall. Then there was a quiet moment, a lull, during which the crowd milled in fearful anticipation. The swelling numbers at the exits hesitated, uncertain. What might lurk in the darkened corridors? Even Zimmerman found himself crouching down behind his podium, listening to the floor, watching the swaying chandeliers. Everyone waited with pounding hearts for whatever new form this bizarre attack might take.

Finally, the moment came. Like surfacing whales, the heads of the great umulks burst through the maroon carpet, spraying plumes of dirt and dust. Tables were overturned, tossing their contents and the people sitting at them about like toys. With earth and bricks rolling from their huge heads the umulks took the opportunity to snap up fallen men, women and children where they lay. The crowd surged forward then realized the exits were blocked by these new monsters and fell back. In their midst more wriggling shrades dropped, tackling anyone they could catch. Utter panic swept the hall.

To their credit, the militia officers were somewhat faster to react to the unexpected attack than perhaps your typical group of humans might have done. Working in teams, they counterattacked the shrades, pulling them from victims, stabbing them with forks and table knives. Many had brought weapons; pistol shots and the booming of Wu hand-cannons reverberated from the walls. Many of the shrades were destroyed, but only after leaving dozens of crushed corpses in their wake.

Then the great umulks withdrew their fantastic snouts, sliding back down into the earth like worms slipping into their burrows. For a few seconds there was a pause, during which an enterprising few undertook to escape through the exits. Only a handful managed to dash into the kitchens or reach the corridor leading to the visitors lobby before squads of killbeasts boiled up from the great black holes. Moving with terrifying speed, teams of killbeasts shredded everyone near the holes then stood guard while more squads climbed up into the hall and formed up ranks.

The humans took this time to maneuver. The officers armed themselves as they could and moved to the front, forming a circle around the spouses and children. Here and there a militia officer shouted orders; crude incomplete barricades were thrown up using the long banquet tables. Several marksmen, getting over their shock, put their pistols to good use by squeezing off round after round into the growing mass of killbeasts.

Then a different sort of alien appeared at the mouth of one of the holes. Strange bulbous pods, assumably optical organs, extended up from his misshapen head, waving about disconcertingly in their cusps.

* * *

The nife surveyed the scene with neural thrills coursing through his frontal lobes. Here was a glorious victory for the Imperium in the making. The human fortress had been breached and the core of leaders taken almost without a fight. The nife felt sure that his brain would experience chemical euphoria later tonight due to this great military coup. His genes would see to it that he was rewarded for masterminding this bold stroke.

He hesitated only a moment before sending the amassed killbeast squadrons to slaughter the enemy. Something about the aliens and their variations in preparedness concerned him. He could understand why they had virtually no defenses against underground invasion, as they were clearly arboreal descendants. But why had the spaceport been so obviously gearing for combat while the central defense fortress itself was apparently engaging in festivities? The unpredictable vertebrates seemed astoundingly clever one moment and pathetically idiotic the next.

Unable to answer the riddles inherent in the actions of the enemy, the nife decided it was time to finish the taking of the fortress. With a single chirrup of code, he signaled the killbeasts to perform their prime function. The gray leaping forms moved to their tasks with relish. The crude barricades were bounded over or simply plowed through. The reptilian killbeasts kicked out with their deadly bladed feet, neatly decapitating and disemboweling anyone that resisted their advance.

The vertebrates, to their credit, fought savagely. The nife noted with detached interest that the ones protecting their offspring tended to fight with greater energy. Certain relationships soon became evident. A lone vertebrate or a pair of them stood no chance against a killbeast, but working as a pack, three or four of them could usually win if they fought together. The most common approach was to hack and shoot at the armored knees, then knock them back with repeated blows from makeshift clubs fashioned from table legs and the like. Once down and unable to leap back up, the vertebrates would swarm forward, fighting past the deadly sweeping foot-blades. They would then tear, cut or shoot away the optical sensory fronds, rendering the killbeast blind and crippled. More often, however, the killbeasts were simply too fast, too strong and too vicious. Ignoring injury, they fought with amazing skill, speed and daring. Pistol shots boomed, blood splashed the floors as bellies and throats were ripped out. Dark ichor spilled from wounded killbeasts to join the growing slicks on the carpeting.

After several minutes of wild melee, the battle moved toward its inevitable conclusion. All vertebrates that had any fight in them were soon exterminated by the bounding horde of killbeasts. Here and there a culus soared over the tangle of struggling forms.

Several shrades worked the crowd in the wake of the killbeasts, riding about on panicked vertebrates. Umulks, disinterested in the battle, nosed about amongst the corpses near enough to their burrows to reach without excessive effort. They sought and ate the youngest and the fattest vertebrates, chewing methodically.

Soon, the fight was beaten out of the enemy. They crouched down in a quaking, lowing mass and awaited death. Once they were subdued the killbeasts had to be urged back from them, so that enough would be alive to provide the livestock that the Parent desired. The nife ran about the hall, commanding individual killbeasts to halt the slaughter. So caught up were they in their bloodlust, their genetic purpose and greatest desire being sated, many had to be clubbed to their senses.

Finally, the nife had achieved some sense of order and began classifying the livestock according to the quality of their meat, culling out those too old or muscular and stringy to make a good meal. Out of the burrows trundled an army of trachs to bear away corpses back to the nests. Killbeasts rounded up satisfactory livestock and herded them down into the ground. The nife thrilled at the idea of fresh tender meat in the nest. The larders would be filled for days.

During this process, which took several minutes, gunfire broke out in the kitchens. The nife had expected a counterattack and responded instantly. He ordered three squadrons of killbeasts into the kitchens, with a fourth stationed at the entrance.

In the darkened chambers a tremendous roar of gunfire began.

* * *

Although it took several minutes to put on their body-shells, Captain Bergen of 2nd tactical squad insisted on it before they went to the rescue. He had not expected so many people to be slaughtered in so short a time, and was sickened as he watched on the security video. The men shoved ammo into their waist-mounted automatics feverishly, casting frequent wide-eyed glances at the horror on the holo-plate.

"Here's the plan," boomed Bergen's voice in their helmets. "Ruble, Fung and Lee, I want you down in the kitchens. Shoot up the place and get the attention of these monsters. Set up a fire zone right in front of the door and blast everything that comes through."

The men acknowledged and ran for the stairs. Bergen turned to the remainder of his troops. "The rest of you follow me. Switch to infrared, no suit-lights, and move as silently as you can."

* * *

The nife's elation with the promise of quick victory faded as the killbeasts met up with organized heavy firepower. A dozen gray forms lay in the entrance to the kitchen, bodies blasted apart by armor-piercing exploding rounds. The three squads of killbeasts had been forced to pull back, leaving behind half their number. The effectiveness of the enemy's ballistic weaponry was unexpected. He had sent in a humping swarm of shrades through the drainpipes and air ducts, but as yet they had been unable to reach the enemy holed up in the kitchens. The nife's stalks lowered somewhat in concentrated thought. His cusps were closed to mere slits over his orbs.

Then a small girl came running into the hall from the main entrance. She halted upon seeing the Imperial forces and screamed shrilly. Running after her, a female militia officer darted out, snatched her up and disappeared back into the corridors.

The nife's cusps snapped open wide. He chirruped rapidly to a culus that soared about the hall with a flock of her sisters. A group of them broke off and headed into the corridor to reconnoiter. Trotting behind them came more squadrons of killbeasts, fresh from the nests. Several more squadrons were sent off in pairs through all the other exits. The nife moved to speak with an umulk who was in the act of chewing the legs from a particularly fat vertebrate.

* * *

Bergen crouched in the main corridor, congratulating the efforts of officer Sung and her daughter. He ordered them both out of the building, explaining that little could be done without heavy armor and weaponry.

They didn't have long to wait. Almost immediately, a group of bizarre-looking flying creatures swooped into the corridor. The men held their fire until the creatures were almost upon them before blasting them out of the air. By that time, the first of the killbeasts was springing toward them. The ripping sound of automatic fire was amplified in the enclosed space. The killbeasts kept coming, a new pair appearing as the last were blown to bits.

While the killbeasts gave their lives for a distraction, the shrades burst forth from their transport forms. A culus at Bergen's feet exploded, and the shrade was wrapped around his legs in an instant. Armor compressed, crushing the flesh underneath. Bergen cried out in agony.

Falling into confusion, 2nd tactical squad resorted to firing at their own men, hoping the body-shell would protect them while blasting away the vile shrades. This allowed a killbeast to reach their lines and attack. Several more sprang up from behind, having successfully encircled them. Both sides quickly realized that the body-shells were impenetrable for foot-blades, but when wrestling in hand-to-hand, the killbeasts were much stronger. Guns were ripped from their waist-mounts and the members of 2nd tactical squad were killed by continuous streams of fire from their own weapons.

* * *

Governor Zimmerman was among the last to be found as he masterfully played dead beneath the corpse of a gutted deputy. After a cursory glance from the nife commander, he was judged suitable livestock due to his body-fat content and hustled off into the burrows of the umulks. After what seemed like hours of travel through muddy tunnels he joined the rest of the human herd and soon learned the horrors of the Imperium nest.

Fourteen

Mudface pulled the limo over to the side of a dark street that led down into a cluster of quiet estates and summer homes. They were high up in the hills surrounding New Grunstein now, on the edge of the Polar Range itself.

"What about the kid?" asked Mudface, waving his shotgun in Bili's face.

"We're almost there. We'll kill them as soon as we get to the house," said Daddy, grunting as he heaved his bulk out of the limo and slammed the door shut. He went to relieve himself on a road sign.

"You can't kill a little boy," Sarah pleaded.

Mudface shrugged disinterestedly.

Bili said nothing. He gazed out the window into the forests and seemed absorbed.

"You can't, Mudface," hissed Sarah urgently. "I'll make it worth your while if you just let him go. What can he do?"

"Little ones grow up. Maybe one day he'll come looking for poor Mudface."

Sarah reached out and touched his plastic skin. She forced herself to caress him. "Please."

Mudface tracked her carefully with the barrel of his hand-cannon. Never did she have a moment to make a move on him. Not that she thought it would do her any good. All mechs were stronger than normal people. He was very small for a mech, but not that small.

136

Mudface fidgeted indecisively. "Oh, all right," he said finally, opening the car door and giving Bili a shove. "Off with you."

"I don't want to leave you," said Bili seriously. He tried to catch his mother's eyes. "Not yet."

"Go on now. Go," his mother insisted, pushing him away.

Bili turned and ran into the night, hot tears burning his cheeks. Mudface fired a few wild shots into the woods after him to convince Daddy, then turned back to Sarah. "You know I've got a soft spot, don't you missy? You're gonna have to pay for this favor, don't you know."

Sarah said nothing.

Daddy came back to the limo, fumbling with his fly and cussing at Mudface.

Sarah searched the fringe of dark trees for some sign of her son, she thought she saw a dark shape flittering through the trees, but she couldn't be sure.

* * *

The drive through the forest to the secluded vacation house Mudface and Daddy kept there seemed to take forever, although it only lasted a few minutes. The entire time, Mudface grinned silently and ran his cold plastic fingers over Sarah's legs.

At times, as the limo wound its way up into the mountains, they came upon open vistas beneath which all of Grunstein was visible. As they passed one of them, they could see the flashes and hear the distant rattling of gunfire coming from the spaceport. Daddy slowed the limo and rolled down the windows to watch.

"That's a squadron of Stormbringers up there," he said, rubbing his stubbly chin. "I don't like this at all."

"So what if the dirt-huggers are getting a new Governor? Let them fight it out," said Mudface.

Sarah could tell he was anxious to get the car moving again so he could continue his fantasies and his gropings.

"Nope, don't like it at all," repeated Daddy. He cleaned a long triangular fingernail with his teeth. "Big changes in who's who won't help our business. I've paid a lot of money for Zimmerman's rubberstamp. What if this new Droad guy out from the Nexus is

137

uncontrollable?"

Mudface rolled his eyes and bared his teeth in impatience. Sarah braced herself as Daddy rolled the window up on the distant battleground and drove onward. Mudface's ministrations began again immediately and in earnest. He leaned close to kiss her and she forced herself to respond. It was still possible for them to go back and try to find Bili. She had to give him as much time as possible to get away.

The smell of the man, up close and personal, was enough to gag her. His fake skin had a burnt smell to it, probably the effects of long exposure to the elements. His breath was indescribably powerful.

Breathing through her mouth, Sarah endured this silently. She wondered if anyone would have cared even if she had been screaming her head off. Mudface started on her knees next, squeezing hard enough to bruise her. Sarah steeled herself and stared out the windows into the forest.

"What's that?" she gasped. A dark shape glided across the road ahead. For a moment the headlights caught an image of a stingray-like creature with mottled brown skin. The creature vanished into the forest.

"Shut up!" barked Daddy. "Just some kinda bird."

Sarah fell silent again, but inside her a numbing block of icy fear began to form. She knew the creatures of Garm well, and she had seen too many odd monsters lately to count this one as normal. What was happening? It seemed as if she were caught up in several nightmares at once.

Shortly after that they pulled into a driveway that curved downward at a sharp angle. After one more switchback they reached the house, and the floodlights came on, sensing their approach. A subsection of the house slid away and the limo glided inside.

An elevator took them from the garage up to the main floor. Daddy sent Mudface to the security center to check all the systems out. The moment he was gone, Daddy advanced on her, grabbing up a handful of her hair and placing the barrel of his hand-cannon to her temple.

"Come on, girly," he rumbled in her ear. "Quiet now."

He dragged her out to the indoor pool area and shut the door

138

behind them. The walls and the domed roof reflected wavering lines of light from the pool. Sarah's breathing became short and desperate. Her heart pounded in her chest.

"Sorry, but I just don't think we have time to do this little bit of business properly," said Daddy. With that, he unceremoniously gripped her throat in both hands and began squeezing. She struggled, kicking his blubbery body and scratching at his face. He cursed a bit, but was otherwise unaffected. He forced her down on her back and slid her head toward the edge of the pool.

* * *

The frenzied sounds of splashing echoed around the indoor pool. Daddy held Sarah's head under the water, trying not to let her scratch his face and hands. The barrel of his hand-cannon, shoved into his waistband, gleamed in the wavering pool lights. After a time the splashing stopped.

"What are you doing?" demanded Mudface. He returned from the security center and rushed up to father's side.

"Shut up."

Mudface reached out with two thin hands. He grabbed his father's flabby arms and lifted. His unnatural muscles were narrow, but they were stronger than a normal man's. Daddy went flying into the pool, howling. He splashed down. Both Daddy's arms were bleeding. The skin had parted where Mudface's titanium-boned hands had gripped them.

There was a lot of cursing and splashing as Daddy climbed out of the pool.

"I should have left you at the bottom of the swamp, boy."

"I'm sorry Daddy," said Mudface. "But you killed Sarah."

"We haven't got time for her tonight, boy. Strange things are happening around the colony. Lots of reported riots and disappearances. I think that new Nexus Governor is making a play to start a civil war down here and I don't want to hang around for it."

"I had big plans," said Mudface, looking at Sarah's blue cheeks longingly.

Daddy sighed and rolled his eyes. He looked at the ceiling of his luxurious summer home. He rarely came down from Gopus these days to visit—except to do a little business like tonight. Publicly he held that he couldn't stand the crowds of Garm. In truth he didn't like the gravity, which made his vast bulk twice as hard to move around.

"Okay, boy, I know I promised and I don't like to go back on promises. Look, we both know CPR. Let's give it a try," suggested Daddy, moved to a rare attempt at pleasing his son. He grabbed Sarah's arms and jerked her out of the pool. Chlorine-smelling water dribbled from her broken fingernails.

"What are you talking about? She's dead."

"We've got one of those reviver kits in the poolhouse. Go get it."

Mudface left at a trot and soon returned with a shrink-wrapped package. He pulled off the wrapper and popped the safety-seal cap. Beneath the cap were two copper prongs and a long steel needle. Daddy grabbed them from him saying, "Get back."

Mudface shuffled backward and Daddy jabbed the instrument into Sarah's chest. There was a jolt of electricity and the body lurched in a grotesque parody of life. The bulb at the end of the needle pumped automatically.

The two performed CPR for nearly a minute before Sarah coughed and vomited. Her chest heaved and her eyes rolled loosely in her head, but she was breathing again.

"It worked," marveled Daddy.

Mudface was peering outside, past the windows. "I don't know, but I think something's out there."

Daddy heaved himself up off his knees with a grunt. At their feet Sarah shivered, barely conscious. Her toes and lips were blue with cold.

"Now you don't want her? Ah, to hell with it," he said, pulling his hand-cannon from his waistband. "I'm not up for drowning her again. Nobody will care about one more blasted smuggler with a civil war going on."

"What was that?" asked Mudface, turning. Another clattering sound came from the poolhouse, near the back gate.

"You go and see, I'm gonna finish matters here," said Daddy, prodding Sarah with his boot. "Again," he added. He raised his hand-cannon.

140

Mudface frowned, opened his mouth to complain, but the words never came out. At that moment the poolhouse door burst open. Into the open ran Bili, followed by a grotesque caterpillar-like monster. The shrade humped after him eagerly, making ready to spring onto the boy's back. It halted and reared up when it saw the others. It stared at them, quivering.

Bili dashed past them, his breath coming in ragged sobs. Without ceremony he flung himself into the swimming pool. Mudface and Daddy grunted in disgust at the shrade and lifted their weapons. Mudface's first shot only grazed the creature, but Daddy managed to blow off two of its stumpy, sticky-padded feet. Then the shrade jumped onto Mudface. Grappling with the monster, Mudface sought the thing's biting head and tried to pull it away, as he had sometimes done with swamp-kinks on Gopus. Far stronger than any kink, however, the shrade constricted on him. His thin arms heaved it away. It was a struggle between two beings of uncommon strength.

"I think I've got this thing," said Mudface.

"Good boy, tear it up."

Two more shrades ran into the room then and after a fraction of a second, they all hopped onto Mudface. Working together, squeezing inexorably, they crushed his arms down to his sides. One of the mech's optics popped out and clanked onto the concrete patio.

Aghast, Daddy reached to help pull the monsters off his son, but quickly realized it was useless. "Sorry, boy," he rumbled. He repeatedly fired his hand-cannon, point-blank. Chunks of flesh flew away from both Mudface and the shrades indiscriminately. Soon they sagged down together, still struggling. Life fluids ran slickly into the pool, staining the water with dark clouds.

Another sound came from the poolhouse, and Daddy whirled. He brought up his hand-cannon. His eyes were wide and his bulky sides heaved. The gray shapes of three killbeasts charged him. He fired once, staggering the leader. Then the other two closed with him. Daddy threw himself back into the pool where Bili was still treading water. Maybe the kid knew something.

One of the deadly foot-knives was already sweeping up for his neck, however. Seeing that it wouldn't reach, the killbeast diverted its kick and neatly knocked the hand-cannon from Daddy's grasp.

Three severed fingers dropped with the gun.

Daddy splashed into the water and came back up sputtering and howling. He gripped his damaged hand and watched with his mouth gaping as the killbeasts flitted about the rest of the pool area and disappeared into the house. More of them soon appeared at the door of the poolhouse and this time there was another type with them. This alien was clearly a leader. He bore two striking stalks that protruded from his head and blinked like eyes.

Daddy realized with a start that he was already thinking of these things as aliens, *intelligent* aliens. There simply was no question about it. That was what they were.

The leader alien had the killbeasts march them all out of the pool and lined them up. Sarah leaned on Bili heavily. He walked up and down in front of them, clearly inspecting them with his waving sensory stalks. In particular, he seemed taken with Daddy. His mandibles drooled noticeably as he examined Daddy's vast belly. This filled Daddy with a great unease.

Finally, the leader stood erect and the three of them were hustled out of the house by the killbeasts. Sarah and the remains of Mudface were borne away on trachs, while Daddy and Bili were forced to march. Daddy had to be forced to enter the open mouth of the tunnel. Stumbling along in the darkness, he was soon heaving and puffing with exertion. The way back to the nest was long.

* * *

"Great Lady," the Captain of the Gladius greeted Mai Lee, bowing slightly toward the video pick-up. The glare of the ships running lights reflected from his shiny bald pate. "To what do I owe the honor of the call?"

"Your word choice is most accurate," said Mai Lee dryly.

"Excuse me?"

"You do indeed owe me," she said with sudden vehemence. Her lined face broke through the pancake make-up in a fine network of a thousand wrinkles.

"I—I do not understand," quailed the Captain, taking an involuntary step backward from the leering holo image of Mai

142

Lee's horrific face.

"Let me explain," hissed the ancient mask of powdered leather. "First, you withheld the fact that Droad had a bodyguard of combat-trained giants. Second, you delivered information concerning myself and my assets to Droad, for a liberal gratuity, I have no doubt. Third, you have failed to mention the cargo of mechs in your hold that you have transported for Droad, with the express purpose of removing me from power."

A sudden change overcame the Captain. He no longer crouched and simpered. Instead his stance became erect, almost swaggering. A hint of a smile tugged at his lips. "Ah, it seems you have become acquainted with the subtler points of our arrangement. I beg to differ on one point, however, milady. The mechs are to the best of my knowledge charged only with the protection of Lucas Droad, not with your destruction."

Mai Lee became agitated. Her claw-like hands gripped her seat and she leaned forward, snarling. "It amounts to the same thing. You owe me."

"What do you suggest?" asked the Captain, a bit ill-at-ease again. His eyes wandered away from the holo-plate and he frowned.

"You will destroy the mechs in their cargo pods. You will provide me with full holo-video of the event so that I may feel confident in your actions."

"Your plan has merit... For you, anyway," he said, drumming his fingers on his generous belly. "There is the small matter of increased payment, of course. Just enough to reward me for my efforts."

"You will be paid the stipulated amount, nothing more," said Mai Lee emphatically. "You owe me."

"Hmm. Yes," said the Captain, appearing to be in deep thought. "I must say that I find your attitude less than endearing. What if I simply let them go, perhaps with the financial blessings of the new Governor?"

"Then I'll have you killed and be done with it," said Mai Lee with absolute certainty.

The Captain blinked and made an alarmed, gasping sound.

"My agents left with you from Neu Schweitz and more have infiltrated the *Gladius* since you arrived. Don't believe for a

143

moment that I can't do it, or that I won't."

"But such an action amounts to nothing more than petty revenge," sputtered the Captain. He smoothed his nonexistent hair with a sweaty palm. "There would be no profit in it for anyone."

Mai Lee shrugged. "My reputation is based on such actions. I find that my reputation is worth much in business dealings and I am therefore quite willing to take something of a loss here to enhance the aura of cooperation my name engenders. You have forfeited your life to a good cause at least, Captain. Let that be of some small comfort to you during your last seconds. Now, if you would excuse me," she said, reaching for the cut-off button.

"Wait," cried the Captain, his voice rising up and cracking. "I will comply!"

Mai Lee let him stew a moment, looking down as if she hadn't heard, pretending to fondle the cut-off button. Finally, she looked up in disgust. "You agree to halt the exodus of the cargo?"

"Yes, immediately," gushed the Captain. He wrung his reddened hands and attempted a sickly smile. "Your Excellency," he added.

Mai Lee let play a long moment of indecision. "Very well. Your assassination is stayed," she said and moved again to cut-off the connection.

"But wait, we haven't yet discussed our new terms."

Mai Lee made a gesture of exasperation. Her lips curled back in a grotesque snarl. "There are no terms, worm. You will stop them or die."

She pounded her fist on the cut-off button and the screen went dark.

* * *

Inside the aft hold of the *Gladius* a twelve-foot tall shipping polygon of gray foam suddenly ruptured. A massive bio-mechanical hand, called a gripper, extruded from the breach. The gripper swiftly tore away the top of the foam, like a spoon topping a boiled egg. The mech lieutenant stepped out of the cocoon, swiveling his optics. As the hold was pitch-dark, he switched to infrared mode and quickly moved to activate his platoon.

This was the moment that the security forces had been waiting for tensely. The Captain had been emphatic about waiting for the leader of the mechs to reveal himself before taking him out. The others would then never be activated and that meant they could be salvaged. The salvage value of the combat-ready mechs would be much greater if they were still intact.

Unfortunately for the security team, however, they had failed to consider the fantastic sensory apparatus of a mech manufactured for combat. The mech lieutenant heard the ambushers breathing and sensed the heat of the sighting lasers playing on his head encasement. Instantly, he bounded away behind an immense carton containing a power-dozer.

Shouting to one another in alarm, the security team broke cover and tumbled forward in pursuit, snapping off shots at every flickering shadow. A sergeant roared in alarm and fired wildly into another of the gray cocoons, which had also extruded a bio-mechanical arm. The mech's second gripper shot out to grasp the Sergeant's shoulder, which was instantly crushed to jelly.

"Turn on the floods!" screamed a green-suited security woman. She ripped off her night-goggles and opened up on the cocoons as well, as many of them were now popping open.

A hailstorm of exploding bullets and lancing laser beams turned the gray foam coverings into a disintegrating cloud of particles. One mech's arm was blown off. Unconcernedly, he reached out with his remaining gripper and squeezed the head off the nearest rifleman.

The floods went on, removing the mechs' advantage of superior night-vision. The lights also revealed the dark towering form of the mech lieutenant who now stood in the midst of the humans.

Moving with berserk speed, the mech lieutenant yanked a rifle away from a man, his claw-like steel gripper taking a good portion of the man's arm with it. Wielding the rifle first as a club, he swept it around at head-level, dropping three more security personnel. With fantastic dexterity he flipped the weapon into his cradling arms, found the trigger and fired into the fleeing pack of humans.

After that it was a rout. Leaving most of their people behind, the security forces escaped through the huge pressure doors into the ship. They hit the emergency pressure-loss toggles, shutting the doors with explosive force in the faces of the pursuing mechs.

A hurried meeting was held in the Captain's briefing room.

"The aft hold is over six miles long and is an absolute maze of cargo," began the Security Chief. He had been involved personally in the attack on the mechs and his right hand was damaged, crusty with dried blood and coated thickly with nu-skin. "I suggest we open the primary bay doors and space the entire hold. We can then recover most of the cargo with the tug fleet. Even mechs can't operate in vacuum for long."

"I won't hear of it," rumbled the Captain. "Your team's incompetence has already cost me dearly. I certainly will not dump a billion credits worth of trade goods into orbit to rid the ship of a handful of crazy robots. This trip has too slim of a profit margin to suit me already."

"Sir, these aren't crazed robots," explained the Chief with a hint of exasperation in his voice. "They're highly intelligent and ruthless beings built for warfare. All we've managed to do is get them to classify the crew of this ship as hostiles."

"What are our other options then?"

"Well, we should remember that the mech lieutenant doesn't really care about us. I mean, he has a mission to do, to get down to the planet surface, I assume. We disabled their jump-flitters before they woke up, so he can't get down without improvising."

"What exactly are you suggesting?"

"Why don't we just let them go? Give them the flitters they need, and let them out one of the airlocks."

The Captain rubbed his chins and glared at the Chief. He puffed out his cheeks and threw his arms up in a gesture of exasperation. "I positively fail to understand your cowardice in this. We have a full combat-ready company of marines and several hundred security people on this ship. There are only sixteen of these pests in the hold and some of them are damaged. What you're going to do is go in there and hunt them down and blow them apart."

146

Fifteen

After hunting the rogue for three days, the inquisitors were exhausted, and even their riders grew tired of the chase. Fryx had given them no further telepathic hints and Garth was leaving behind him precious little in the way of spoor. They had tracked him back to the highway where he had apparently caught a ride to the next village, then proceeded on foot. In the muddy jungles of the river basins they lost him again.

The man whose turn it was to watch fell asleep in the bole of a stink-vine tree. In the night, with Gopus only a dim sliver of light barely discernible through the jungle canopy, an odd figure entered the camp. Wearing a black hat with a wide low brim and a black cape, the figure moved with infinite care lest he awaken the men or in some way alert their wary riders. After a few minutes of slinking in their midst, the dark figure discovered the man in the stink-vine tree. With a delighted fluttering of the fingertips, the figure stalked the sleeping man, coming up behind him.

Gathering up a handful of pebbles, the figure flicked them, one by one, onto the sleeper's back. After the third such attack, the man snorted and half rose up. Suddenly, he lurched upright, his rider goading him to wakefulness. The figure behind him pranced forward, cape swirling. A length of steel glittered and the inquisitor slumped back down.

The commotion awakened another of the men, however, who

147

climbed from his bedroll. Not aware that anything was amiss, the tall, slender man wearily opened the tent flaps and rummaged in the cooler for a squeeze-bag of refreshment.

There was movement in the back of the tent. The man startled, then peered more closely. "Jed?" he mumbled, still half-asleep. His rider, withdrawn into unknowable private thoughts of its own, did nothing to warn him.

The shadowy figure loomed up. Beneath its low-brimmed hat blue eyes blazed with insanity. The figure pounced.

This time the kill wasn't a clean one. Staggering from the supply tent with his throat bubbling fresh blood, the inquisitor fell dead on top of his companions.

The others leapt up, drawing their guns and turning on the floodlights. The jungle was illuminated by a harsh glare. There was a ripping sound at the back of the supply tent. Rushing to the spot they saw a gaunt figure dive into the underbrush. A storm of gunfire broke out. Howlers protested their loss of sleep from the treetops, pelting the inquisitors with sticks, fruit, feces and other offal.

As they reached the edge of the jungle, knee-deep in ferns and sucker-plants, their quarry rose up before them. Clearly visible in the harsh glare of the floodlights, Garth stood in full view. The eyes of a murderer burned from within the broad red stripe his rider had left when mounting him. In one hand he gripped a hand-cannon, in the other he brandished a bloody knife. His lips formed a ghastly rictus for a grin. Only a few feet from this apparition, the three men halted and raised their weapons.

Fryx chose that moment to loose a desperate, pleading howl for mercy. A keening wail, not of sound, but rather of thought, washed over all the men and their riders. The cry caused the other riders to pull back on the reins of their skalds, digging in spiny nerve-spurs to halt them. For a full second the inquisitors, intent on killing, slackened. Their arms drooped, their muscles rubbery, their weapons suddenly too heavy to aim.

As the figure advanced the riders realized their error: the keening was desperation on Fryx's part, even treachery. Incredible though it seemed, the revered one wasn't in control, the rogue was. With great urgency, the riders goaded their skalds forward again, demanding that they kill the rogue quickly.

148

But it was already too late. The hesitation had been enough, Garth leapt forward and stood among them. He blew the skald on the left's head from his body. Closing to an arms-length, he planted the gun against the second man's chest and fired again. With his other hand, he drove his knife into the throat of the third inquisitor.

After they had slumped down in the ungraceful postures of death, he waited a tense few moments. From the nasal passages of two of the skalds rose quivering liquid jellies. Wet spines shivered in the night air. With cold precision, Garth blasted the riders repeatedly. Scraps of spiny jelly and white skull fragments showered the jungle floor.

* * *

Weary to the bone, Garth spent a long night at the camp with only stiffening corpses for companions. Corpses, and the vile presence of Fryx in his head. Overall, he thought he preferred the dead men.

While facing the inquisitors he had felt a wild strength run through him, had taken maniacal glee in killing them. He seriously questioned his sanity in these matters. It seemed that whenever he was acting in direct conflict with the desires of Fryx, he could do so only as a madman.

Upon reflection, he decided that if insanity was the only path through which he could control his own destiny, then so be it.

He shuffled around the camp aimlessly, his desire for revenge sated. He had no further immediate purpose, as Kris' killers and his own hunters were dead. More may follow, but they would most likely be a long time in coming. It was quite possible that he would be allowed to move about now with greater freedom, as long as he avoided the strongholds of the skalds. Riders, he knew, were more akin to emotionless accountants than vengeful demons. A rogue that could dominate Fryx and kill five of their inquisitors was probably best left alone.

Listlessly, he chewed a wad of dried howler meat and drank the juice of a goy-goy pod. The meal tasted uncommonly good, being the first relaxed, halfway civilized meal he had had in days. Fryx was silent in his mind, probably mourning his fate and the deaths of his fellow riders.

Something did nag at his mind, something dark worried at him, doubtless the tickling of Fryx. But it seemed as though he had forgotten something....

Then he had it. The threat from the skies. The horrid aliens that danced through his nightmares. The very reason that Fryx had gone to incredible lengths to take over his body and direct his every action personally, an unthinkable abasement for one of his kind except in situations of grave danger.

Standing erect and removing his hat, Garth drew his hand-cannon. Placing the barrel to his head, not at his temple, but rather at the base toward the back, where he knew Fryx resided, he spoke aloud: "Fryx, it is time we talked."

He shut his eyes and concentrated. Beneath his forefinger, he felt the cold hard surface of the trigger.

"I have nothing to lose anymore," he said, speaking to the chirruping jungle creatures. Somewhere in the distance a great ape grunted heavily. "At least my death will bring about yours as well. To be free of you, even in death, would be a great pleasure."

His mind was silent.

"Come now, there will be no skires tonight, no self-hypnosis, nor dancing, nor mating. Exert yourself! Come forward and speak with me directly, or be forever silent."

There was a tickling sensation in his head. At first, he thought it was only perspiration, or perhaps the coldness of the gun barrel pressing his hair against the thin skin of his head. Then it became more pronounced. Soon, it seemed to him that he heard words.

You must repent.

Garth laughed. He laughed long and loud, the wild mirth of an unbalanced man. It was all he could do to keep the gun barrel against his skull. A howler hooted and tossed a hail of sticks down, protesting the noise. Garth said, "You are indeed arrogant, jellyfish."

It is you who are arrogant, rogue.

"Ah such petulance! You are a sore-loser, as well as arrogant. But I would suspect such traits go together," said Garth. As he spoke, he pranced across the campsite and sprang up onto a lump of granite that protruded up from the jungle floor. Hardly aware of

150

his body's actions, he danced an odd jig without rhythm.

You waste my energies. You are a foolish and uncontrolled thing, a host-being without the comforting guidance of its rider. In short, a pitiful rogue.

Garth grew impatient. He tapped the barrel of his hand-cannon against his skull. "Let's recall that I'm in charge here. Dispense with trying to regain the reins to my mind. They are forever out of your grasp. Should you regain them again, even for a few moments, I assure you I will kill us both. I have no desire to live further as a slave."

His mind was silent.

"Good," Garth said, "now we can discuss your warnings of death from the skies. Why have you repeatedly tried to convey images of alien invasion to me? Was this simply another failed control technique?"

It is absurd that you should question me. Interrogation of a rider by a lowly skald is an unheard of insult. You will refrain from further questions or I will induce great pain in your extremities. Even as Fryx communicated, Garth became aware of an excruciating sensation in the arm and hand that held the hand-cannon. It was as if flames engulfed his arm. He struggled to retain his grasp of the gun.

"You bastard! I can see that you don't yet take me seriously. Doubtless, this is due to the fact that your kind could never contemplate suicide, such is the depth of your cowardly natures," said Garth. He gritted his teeth against the pain in his hand and slowly began to increase the pressure his finger was putting on the trigger. When the trigger was depressed halfway to its firing point, the pain eased.

Stop mad-thing! You must not damage me! wailed Fryx. A wave of fear and rage swept over Garth, emotional spillover from his rider. He eased his grip on the trigger.

"Will there be further attempts to coerce me?" he asked. His feet had slowed from an odd jig to a slow shuffle. To stop his idle movements, he sat cross-legged on the granite boulder.

His mind was silent.

He again applied pressure to the trigger.

Halt! How can you so easily play with your life? demanded Fryx, in a frenzied state. *What if the gun were to go off with*

151

fractionally less pressure this time than the last? What if the manufacture of the weapon wasn't up to the specifications? How can you bet our lives upon the assumed competence of some unknown other? Do you realize what would happen if anything went wrong?

"Then we would die, here in the jungle, together," said Garth with remarkable disinterest.

You are indeed a mad-thing. I can't believe my fantastic misfortune in finding a host of your quality.

"Self-pity will gain you nothing."

You must halt this game of death-threats. You are playing with higher stakes than you know.

"What stakes?" demanded Garth with sudden interest. He stood up again and jumped down from the boulder. He began to pace about the darkened camp, absently stepping over the cooling bodies of the dead skalds. "What is it that caused you to break our trust, to come forward from your meditations and take up the reins of my mind in such an intrusive manner? I know that this is not a pleasant thing for you."

Indeed not. Unless it is in conjunction with communing with another rider, I find it most repulsive to expose my nervous system to your outer world of filth and pestilence. I came forward only out of the greatest need.

Fryx proceeded to explain at length that he had sensed a presence from the dark past, that of the Imperium. Seedships must have come home to Garm. Parents had landed and the Imperium had begun to pacify the world as had been done here a thousand years ago, he was sure of it. Only he and perhaps a handful of other riders were both old enough to remember the old wars with the Imperium and sensitive enough to detect the presence of the enemy.

In the end, as dawn broke over the steamy jungle campsite, the two came to an odd pact. Convinced that his rider was really heading for Grunstein, the capital of the colony, with vital news concerning the Imperium, Garth decided to travel that way. The huge effort that Fryx had gone to, so unlike he and his kind, made him believe. In any case, he had nowhere else to go, nothing better to do.

At the very least, the endless painful battles for dominance

152

with Fryx would stop for a time.

* * *

Driving the inquisitors' vehicle non-stop to Bauru, the skald and the rider worked together for the first time in days. Each of them slept in shifts while the mind of the other drove Garth's body and the vehicle.

As evening closed over the jungles, a haunting figure arrived at the Bauru Colonial Shuttleport and purchased a one-way ticket to Grunstein Interplanetary. Wearing a black hat and matching black cape, both coated with dried stinking slime from the jungles, the man strode down the jetway and climbed aboard the shuttle. His neighboring passengers moved away with expressions of distaste, many asking the stewards for a seat in another section of the cabin.

Unconcernedly, Garth leered at them with wild, staring eyes. Settling back into the sparse cushions of the economy class, both the minds in his skull fell asleep, exhausted.

Sixteen

"The war is going badly, Chamberlain," Mai Lee told the orchids. It was a nicer arrangement than usual today, full of crimson blossoms with accents of lavender. "The planet is being overrun."

Mai Lee seemed calm enough, but beneath her placid surface raged a torrent of anger. The orchids wisely chose to remain silent.

On the huge holo-stage that dominated the room were displayed multiple battle scenes. All around the Slipape Counties other estates were in flames. Images of slaughter dominated the broken ruins of Castle Zimmerman in particular.

"All so quickly, my most pressing concern has shifted from Droad to this new assault," she lamented. "With amazing speed, these aliens are destroying hundreds of years of history. They're so easily wiping out enemies that I've struggled with for centuries. I find it all somewhat annoying. I've come to loathe most of my fellow aristocrats, but still, they were mine to loathe, if you catch my meaning."

"Certainly, Empress," said the orchids hesitantly. "Ah—there is another urgent call from the Zimmerman High Command."

Mai Lee waved her hand imperially. "Display it."

A red-faced older man wavered into being just to the left of the hummingbirds. His hair was in disarray and he carried a gun in his hand. "Mai Lee, I've retreated to the forests just north of your lands. You must come to our aid. Most of the kindred are dead.

The Castle of my ancestors has fallen, but we can retake it with your troops, I'm sure of it."

"Ah, so the great Zimmermans finally swallow their pride," she said with an obscenely girlish giggle. She placed her fingertips together in a butterfly pattern and leaned back to bask in the moment.

"We must join forces! No one will be spared! They come right up from the ground, drop from the skies, hundreds of monsters," Zimmerman looked down, shaken, reliving a recent memory. "They're so fast!"

"But my fortress is stronger than yours."

Zimmerman shook his head emphatically. "It doesn't matter. You haven't really prepared for an attack from beneath. Even though the hill you're on is mostly rock, it won't matter. They'll come, they have good weapons now, and there are more of them every time. They'll come and wipe you out as they did the rest of us."

Mai Lee tilted back further, the picture of happy relaxation. It seemed that his every gloomy word gave her greater pleasure. Finally, she snapped upright. "I'll take to the field, but not to save your precious plot of miniature forests and family treasures. I'll take to the field if you'll join me, if you'll place your remaining vehicles and knights under my banner."

Zimmerman glowered and blustered for a moment, his bushy white brows stormy with indecision. "Why would you leave your stronghold?"

"A painful decision, let me assure you," said Mai Lee. "But a necessary one. I've studied these creatures and their tactics. Just as you pointed out, our fortresses were never built to defend against the kind of attacks they launch. They are serving only as traps for our forces, convenient concentration points for the aliens to destroy us."

"All the same, what will you do in the field? Wait for them to come out and attack you? Before I commit my forces I must know how you plan to fight them."

"My science staff has studied these aliens and concluded that they are a fast-growing, short-lived species. Genetically, all the different types are very similar, whether they fly, dig or march. It is my belief that they have a small number of queens, as would

155

ants or termites. If we kill these queens, they will stop multiplying. We must carry our attack to the enemy, destroy whatever is generating all these appalling creatures. Just defending our lands is a losing proposition."

"That's all very well, but how do we find this queen?"

"Some days ago I captured one of these creatures and discovered that they use in-grown quartz crystals to communicate via radio waves. Triangulating carefully, we have located one of their nests, and I wish to assault it."

"You'll attack the nest, with our help? No hanging back at the last moment and using my knights as cannon fodder?"

Mai Lee snorted. "Your weaponeers are best used in ranged combat, where their plasma cannons would be put to good use. I myself will lead my troops down into the nest."

"Ah, so you will be marching in your battlesuit, I presume?"

Mai Lee looked startled, but only for a moment before regaining her aplomb.

Zimmerman laughed unpleasantly. "You aren't the only one with spies in the field."

She waved away his words irritably. "Is it a deal?"

"I'll not relinquish all command, but I will comply with your strategies. You will be in overall command."

"Done," she said, smiling. "Meet me on the Moonbreak Heights at dawn."

After she had cut off the connection, she sat brooding for a time, watching alien monsters ravage her neighbors' lands. One of the sections of the holo-stage showed a detachment of several hundred aliens moving swiftly into position to the south of her fortress. She would have to move soon.

Disturbed by Zimmerman's words about spies in her midst, she headed down into the darkest levels beneath her fortress and there found the battlesuit, parked in its cubical. Climbing inside, she curled up into the womb-like pilot's webbing to sleep until it was time to march, two hours before dawn.

No assassin would find her easy prey tonight.

* * *

156

"Gi!" cried out the peasants in terror as the lumbering battlesuit marched swiftly onto a lifter in the great courtyard. Running for the shelter of the village, the peasants scattered. No one had bothered to tell them that a war was in progress. The predawn light was a pleasant pink tinge in the air. Sounds of heavy equipment filled the last minutes of the night.

Surrounded by six squadrons of her heavy troops in full battlegear, Mai Lee's lifter rose up to join the others. In unison, the flotilla moved off, surrounded by a flock of escorting helicopter gunships.

Reaching Moonbreak Heights and meeting the Zimmermans, Mai Lee drove her battlesuit down the ramp and onto the granite mountaintop. She was thrilling inside, this entire experience was turning into a fantasy for her. Over the years of her incredibly long, dull existence she had come to enjoy nothing more than battle, but was too wise to put herself into most of them. Life had become extremely boring of late. Now, however, simply sitting back would no longer do. It was no longer the wisest, safest course. The aliens had forced her hand. She almost felt thankful to them for this rare opportunity to indulge herself. She looked forward to witnessing and participating in a great deal of carnage. Like a child in a sweetshop, she relished every moment of the experience.

"ZIMMERMAN!" boomed the amplified voice of the battlesuit. Mai Lee grinned as she watched the man take an involuntary step back from the blast of sound.

"Turn that damned thing down!" Zimmerman growled back, not easily intimidated even by a madwoman driving several tons of high-tech weaponry.

Mai Lee modulated the volume somewhat, but still left it turned up to a domineering level. "Report your strength, commander," she demanded.

Zimmerman stood in battlegear with his aides and bodyguards surrounding him in a nervous knot. "Now wait," he said, upraising his forefinger. "We have to get some things arranged. First—"

"There will be no further arrangements," barked the giant figure of Mai Lee. The suit took a half-step forward, powerful claws gouging the mountainside. "Place yourself under my command, at least strategically, and report your strength immediately. There is no time for dickering. We must move at

157

once."

"I plan to comply, but—" began Zimmerman again, his lips lifting from his teeth. His knights were snarling among themselves. One man threw his computer slate aside and drew his sidearm.

"Comply immediately or I will withdraw," came the booming response.

"Sir, we have no need of this witch," the young man who had drawn his weapon hissed in his ear. With her amplified hearing, Mai Lee caught every word. She recognized the youth as Zeel, one of the new hotheaded generation of the Zimmerman clan.

For a moment neither of the leaders spoke. Around them gathered the simian-like giants of Mai Lee's palace guard and the expertly trained blue-suited knights of the Zimmerman clan. Both sides eyed the other with distaste and an eagerness to fight.

"We will comply," said Zimmerman. A wave of emotion swept the Zimmermans. "But, we will keep a separate unit command, and my men will not follow your orders without my approval."

Hidden from view, Mai Lee grinned inside her battlesuit. The grin soon turned into a cackle of mirth. She calmed herself enough to activate the exterior voice circuit and accept his offer.

Things moved more smoothly after the issue of command control was settled. The group set up the battle computers under a dome on one of Mai Lee's lifters and gathered there to organize their forces. Although the Zimmermans had taken casualties, several other related clans had also bolstered their numbers. All in all, their combined armies represented a formidable, fast-moving force.

"We have mobility on them, and air-power. Additionally, they have lost the element of surprise," boomed Mai Lee. Still wearing her battlesuit, she ignored the jibes of the officers concerning her personal cowardice. Let them see in battle who would be counted as a coward. She swept a powerful mechanical claw to the south, toward the Polar Range. "There, in the mountains around Grunstein, resides the nest of our enemies. After some careful maneuvering and a diversionary attack, we will strike it hard."

"Where will we strike?" demanded a cadet out of turn.

Mai Lee wheeled on him. She let him ponder the blue radiance in the mouth of Gi long enough to turn pale before answering. "Right here. The enemy is coming to us, even now. And we shall be waiting for them."

She brought her titanium fists together with a resounding clang.

* * *

Before noon they mounted their first counterattack. Tunneling had been discovered beneath the Arden, a huge tract of forestland that separated the Slipape Counties from the polar range. The aliens were, in fact, building an underground highway between their strongholds in the Polar Range and the counties.

But the Moonbreak Heights, a natural formation of solid granite thrust up from the planet's interior, formed a barrier to the tunneling. Too deep to dig beneath, they would have to either dig around the obstacle, or take the position and cross it in the open before tunneling on the other side. Mai Lee thought they would try the latter, more daring approach.

Shortly before noon the aliens proved her right by boiling up out of the ground at the foot of the heights. Culus and shrade teams discovered their positions, and were quickly eliminated by sniper fire. Simultaneously, Mai Lee ordered a heavy barrage of artillery fire to suppress the enemy pouring out of the tunnels. The tunnel mouths were quickly turned into a mass of molten craters, and then smoke hid the scene from view.

There was a lull in the fighting.

"Looks like we gave them something to think about," said Zimmerman, staring into a holo-image enhancing set of lenses. "I can't make out anything moving, just a lot of bodies."

"We surprised them, but we haven't stopped them," rumbled Mai Lee. "Do you see any of the whale-like digging creatures?"

"Yes," said Zimmerman. He paused to adjust his goggles. "At least two of them, or what's left of them."

"Good."

"What we should do now is head for their nest immediately. We can hit them by surprise before they get any stronger," said Zimmerman. "Let them dig their tunnels. Before they're done we could take their nest. Our lifters move much faster than anything they've got."

Mai Lee grimaced. The man had been whining about this for

over an hour now. "That's why I'm in command," she stated bluntly.

Biting his tongue, Zimmerman returned his attention to the foot of the heights. "You were right. They're down there, forming up ranks just inside the treeline to rush the slopes. They must have opened up more tunnels further back in the trees."

Almost immediately, exhibiting the blinding speed of attack that was characteristic of their tactics, a dark line of killbeasts rushed out from the treeline and began to climb the slopes. Without orders, the men along the ridge opened fire. Before they could reach cover, the alien line thinned and finally became ragged.

"We're slaughtering them!" whooped the officers.

Then a wave of counter fire came up from the trees and the slopes. Rifles, plasma-weapons and laser carbines swept the crest of the ridge. Men screamed and were shorn in half. One of Mai Lee's troopers, his helmet blown off and his head on fire, toppled from the ridgeline and rolled down the slope into the face of the enemy.

Covered by this hail of weapons fire, a new cloud of flying creatures rose up from the trees and zoomed toward the ridgeline. Mai Lee stabbed the intercom button, ordering her helicopters out of hiding. The gunships rose up from the heights and met the airborne enemy with heavy fire. Several culus squadrons diverted to attack the helicopters while others drove on to close with the men on the ridgeline. A great number of them were blasted from the sky to fall on the advancing line of killbeasts below in a rain of pulpy fragments.

Reaching the helicopters and attacking them directly, the crews found themselves in desperate hand-to-hand battles on board their own aircraft. Spiraling crazily, several of the gunships went down in roiling flames.

A handful of the flying demons reached the ridgeline and loosed their shrades. Men fought with knives and handguns. Screams echoed out over the Heights.

"Damn suicidal bastards," cursed Mai Lee. She dented a battle-computer with a heavy blow from her fist. Fortunately, the machine was built to take such punishment and only flickered once before returning to accurate service.

"Look, they're moving to flank us," said Zimmerman, directing

160

her attention to another screen. During the confusion of the culus and shrade attack, the killbeasts had taken the opportunity to rush further up the slopes. More and more dark knots of troops raced out of the treeline and took cover on the slopes. Fanning out, they maneuvered to gain the ridgeline on either flank of the humans.

"Focus your fire on the ones nearing the ridgeline," ordered Mai Lee. Even she was a bit appalled with the strength and speed of the enemy, and with the eagerness with which they faced death. She was soon forced to spread her lines out more thinly on the ridge.

"Why don't we just pull out?" demanded Zimmerman.

"You don't understand. We have to repel their initial assault."

Their conversation was halted when a spray of earth fountained up from the ridge alarmingly close to them in the command center. Like a surfacing whale, an umulk burst up right on top of the ridge and in the midst of their forces.

"It's one of their digging monsters!" shouted Zimmerman, drawing his sidearm. "They'll be coming up any second for a close assault."

"But how could they get to the top of this rock?" demanded Mai Lee. "My geological surveys show it to be solid granite."

"Probably there's a fault like a well-shaft in the mountains. They move through earth like fish do in the sea. I've fought them before, remember."

Mai Lee unlimbered the suit's chest cannons, making ready to join the fight, but her troops reacted with surprising speed, managing to kill the umulk with an overwhelming storm of gunfire before it could pull back into the tunnel. It sagged down and blocked the passage to the surface, but it left open the question of other such faults in the rock, allowing the monsters to burrow their way up and burst out behind the troops on the ridge.

The attack up the slopes was stepped up to a further level of ferocity. Bounding with great energy in a general wave assault, the killbeasts came on like sprinters, ignoring the uphill climb. More culus squadrons were among them, zooming from bush, to tree, to rock on the way up, instead of simply flying straight at the men.

"We've done our bit to surprise them and bloody their noses, why should we lose men over this lump of rock?" complained Zimmerman. "Let's pull out."

"SHUT UP!" roared Mai Lee, dialing for maximum volume. She wheeled her battlesuit to face him. Chest cannons swiveled and locked-on, targeting his head. "I WILL NOT TOLERATE YOUR CRETINOUS COMPLAINTS."

Zimmerman staggered back, clamping his hands to his ears.

As the echoes of Mai Lee's shout died away, the dead umulk's body, not more than a hundred meters from the command center, twitched in an unnatural fashion. With a sudden jerk it was pulled downward and it vanished from sight. A gaping black hole was left in its wake. Mai Lee tossed over a table, scattering a group of aides, and simply walked through the fabric wall of the command center and out onto the ridge. With swift liquid strides she drove the battlesuit toward the hole. She signaled for a detachment of her heavy troops to join her. She looked forward to a release of tension.

There was a moment of relative quiet while they encircled the hole and waited. She could hear her men breathing, panting really in unaccustomed fear. The aliens were unnerving, unlike anything they had ever faced. She reflected that they had become somewhat soft after years of sitting around the fortress doing little more than playing escort and abusing insubordinate peasants.

Thinking to see a flicker of movement far down the hole, one man opened up with his automatic. Everyone joined in, hailing gunfire down the black hole. Mai Lee had to shout at maximum volume again to get them back under control. Grabbing the man who had fired early, she tossed him into the pit where he disappeared, screaming.

Then she grew a bit unsteady on her feet. The battlesuit lurched alarmingly, the balance systems screaming. Hastily, she caused the suit to leap backward. The suit's great clawed feet gouged deep wounds in the earth and stone. The ground where she had stood opened beneath several of the men and they fell in, waist-deep, struggling to climb out of the soil which seemed to have liquefied. Then they stiffened and blood gushed from their mouths. When they were dragged up, it was discovered they had been bitten in half.

Even as they dragged the corpses from the dirt a full culus squadron burst out of the hole, flying straight up. Arcing fire after them they were quickly shot down, but not before a rain of shrades

162

had dropped amongst the men.

Mai Lee ignored it all, knowing it to be a ruse. These aliens fought well, her respect for their warcraft was rising by the minute. She let her men deal with the shrades and kept her focus on the mouth of the hole. She was rewarded when a large number of killbeasts sprang up to attack. With a mighty blast of blue flame she burnt them, firing her chest cannons in a sweeping spray. More and more killbeasts essayed the breach, but they all fell back, blackened and fragmented. Soon the attack halted. She ordered high explosives to be dropped into the breach and set off.

Striding back to the command center, she learned that the rest of the battle was going better as well. The killbeasts had been repelled from the heights with light losses on the human side except one or two spots where they had actually gotten into close range. The resulting desperate hand-to-hand battles had been fantastically bloody, the aliens selling their lives dearly.

"They are pulling back, withdrawing," said Zimmerman. He was white-faced and exhausted. Mai Lee noted that his lips curled back from his teeth at the sight of her, but he still managed to sound calm. "Perhaps you were right to keep the position, but won't they just gather a larger force and attack again?"

Mai Lee snorted. "Of course they will. We only stayed to attract an even bigger force here. Now that they have pulled back to wait for reinforcements from the nest, we will move out. While their main forces are stalking us on Moonbreak Heights, we will storm their nest. This entire exercise was nothing but a feint, Zimmerman."

* * *

Garth and Fryx awoke together when the shuttle seat bucked beneath them. Instantly, with no clear reason why, they knew the ship was going down. Canting forward at an alarming angle, they rapidly lost altitude. Garth released his seatbelt, slid over to the window seat that had been vacated by a passenger that couldn't abide his company, and buckled in again. He stared downward.

Below them, the flitter was just coming down into the cloud layer. In an instant, the window went opaque white, then cleared again. The snowy peaks of the Polar Range appeared below the shuttle. They were on the approach to Grunstein Interplanetary, but they were descending much too rapidly.

Garth sat back, thinking about what he knew of shuttle flights. They would have touched orbit on the long leg out from Bauru, but only for a few minutes before the boosters cut out and let them coast back down again on stubby wings. The drop should be steep, but not hellish.

The other passengers were becoming alarmed around him. Several shouted for the stewards, demanding to know what was happening. A child was crying somewhere.

Garth turned his attention to the window again. He examined the stubby delta wing just behind his row of seats when he saw something flash by. It was an odd dark shape, a flying thing that zoomed past the window like a hurtling rock. The shuttle shuddered from another impact, and suddenly the bulkheads separating the passenger compartment from the cockpit slammed shut with a hiss of escaping gas.

"They've got a breach in the nose!" shouted a tourist wearing a fur hat with blinking, holographic novelty buttons all over it.

Indeed, it seemed that they were still losing pressure. Garth felt his ears ache, then pop. Hearing became difficult.

"Someone's throwing rocks at us," said a voice from behind Garth's seat. It sounded like a child.

Garth could feel Fryx in his skull now, like a lead weight embedded there, fused to the bone. There was a familiar tickling sensation.

It was a culus! What a cruel cosmos this is that I should die locked in the mind of a balking imbecile! moaned Fryx in his head.

"What's happening?" asked Garth aloud. His fingers began uncontrollably drumming on the armrests of his seat. To his surprise, he realized he was humming quite loudly as well.

They're bringing down this primitive thin-skinned vehicle, you fool!

Garth looked outside and saw that indeed, more of the dark hurtling shapes were hitting the wings and doubtlessly the nose of the craft. He wondered worriedly what would happen if one of them went into the air intakes for the engines.

That's precisely their plan, Fryx interjected into his thoughts.

164

Even as the two considered the possibilities, there came a great sound of tearing metal from the rear of the cabin. The shuttle lurched sickeningly, then nosed toward the mountaintops at an even steeper angle.

Get away from the windows! Move to a center seat in the rear section of the cabin! commanded Fryx.

"What about the crew? Can't they control it?"

They're all dead, if not from the bodies of the enemy coming through their windshields then from the lack of oxygen. Now, get away from the windows before I am exposed!

Before Garth knew what he was doing, he was out of his seat and moving back up the aisle. He knew this to be the coercion of his rider, but for once he didn't object. The shuttle was now canted at such an angle that it was as if he was climbing stairs. Ignoring the other passengers, who in their fear were also ignoring him, he found a seat in the rear of the cabin and buckled himself in.

Then the automatic braking kicked in and he was wrenched against the seatbelt. He had gotten it into place just in time.

The rest of the crash was a blur. Although it only took a few seconds, perhaps less than a minute, to Garth it seemed to go on forever.

Upon impact, he blacked out. He had the faintest impression of seeing water splashing against the windows before he lost consciousness.

He awoke a short time later to see that the shuttle had indeed struck a mountain lake, whether from sheer chance or the excellent programming of the auto-pilot, he couldn't be sure. Designed not to sink immediately, the shuttle groaned and creaked like a sailboat in a storm. Icy water lapped at his ankles.

The emergency hatch in the roof of the cabin was the first one to be opened. Surprisingly, none of the passengers had yet managed to get to it when it swung up and outward, letting in welcome sunlight and a biting cold breeze of fresh air.

Garth's seat was just below it so he was among the first of the humans to see the monster that peered in at them. Unlike the other passengers around him, Garth didn't cry out in terror. He merely stared.

A killbeast! screeched Fryx in his mind. A wash of numbing horror swept over them both.

165

Seventeen

"Lieutenant Ferguson, main doors, are you ready?"

"Affirmative, Chief."

"Team A, aft doors?"

"Check."

"Auxiliary portals?"

"We're ready, sir."

"All right, let's take back our hold," said the Security Chief, moving down a steep service shaft behind a squadron of his green-suited troops. Beads of sweat matted his hair inside his helmet and made his face and neck itch intolerably. It was with great trepidation that he led his men into the hold in search of the mech platoon. His right hand, healed over with nu-skin, still pained him, but it wouldn't keep him from pulling the trigger.

On close-range intercom, one of his sergeants tapped his shoulder and said, "I've got a full load of grenade-launchers right behind us, sir. The Lieutenant Ferguson's Marine weaponeers are packing their mortars as well, just in case."

"I hope we won't need them."

"So do I, Chief."

The Chief hoped they wouldn't have to use explosives even more than his men did. The Captain had used the direst threats in conjunction with even carrying such things near his precious cargo. The Chief had ignored his orders and brought them along. He wasn't about to send his troops against combat mechs without

166

everything available in their hands.

For the first hour or so, the hunt in the great hold was relatively uneventful. Except for pre-arranged, tightly-beamed communications between the teams, communications were kept to a minimum. Closing on the mechs was extremely difficult in the miles of equipment. Tracking them with sensors, the original plan, was impossible, as the mechs had immediately destroyed them all.

Crouching beneath a giant packing crate containing a construction crane, the Chief activated his phone. It was time to find out how the other teams were doing.

"Main doors? How's it going, Lieutenant?"

"Check, we've moved in about a mile, nothing to report."

"Aft doors?"

"No contact, sir. Are we sure they're still in here?"

"Auxiliary portals?"

Silence.

"Auxiliary portals? Report your status."

Due to the perfection of the technology, there wasn't even the hiss of static to entice him. The Chief began to sweat profusely.

"All teams, head for the Auxiliary portals. Back-up teams head for the flitter bays. We may have a breach."

* * *

The mech lieutenant slid his optics carefully over the corpses, looking for signs of resistance. There was none. Silently, he ordered his platoon forward. Padding past the dead men and through the auxiliary portals and into the service shafts, the mechs moved with unnatural speed. They were little more than a pack of massive gray shadows, nightmares of flesh and metal.

They didn't head for the flitter bays, however. Instead, they ran through the dim-lit shafts of the *Gladius* to the engine rooms. Brushing aside the panicked engineers who fled for their lives, they took a few hostages, trained their weapons on them, and dictated their terms.

* * *

A white-faced comm officer signaled desperately, trying to get the Captain's attention. Sitting comfortably in his quarters, the Captain ignored his efforts for several minutes. He was viewing a particularly good erotic holo and grew angrier by the second as the damned intercom kept chiming. Finally, he paused the holo and activated the intercom.

"What? What is it now, man?"

"Sir, we have an emergency."

The Captain groaned, heaving his great bulk erect. Even the half-standard gravity, provided by centrifugal forces as the *Gladius* rotated, was becoming an annoyance. He would have to consider lowering it to one-third standard, and damn the health regulations.

"What's the problem?" he barked.

"It's from the engineering room, sir—"

"Just put it on the holo, will you?" he said, slamming down the handset.

The comm-officer clittered at his keyboard. A shocking image flickered into life in front of the Captain's easy chair. It was the mech lieutenant. Implanted in the steel head-encasement in the midst of a face of waxen flesh, the thing's optics slid about disconcertingly.

"What is THIS?" demanded the Captain. Thinking that a horror-holo from the ship's library had somehow been patched into his personal system, he hammered his fist on the control console.

"If this is some cadet's idea of a joke, I'll have him doing radiation inspections of the aft exhaust ports until he's nothing but a mass of tumors," he vowed.

"We do not require the surrender of your ship," said the apparition on the holo-plate, "but you will give us four flitters suitable for a combat descent."

Slowly, the reality of the situation dawned on the Captain. "What are you talking about? Are you one of those mad-dog machines?"

"I am Lieutenant Rem-9. I am assigned to Lucas Droad, Planetary Governor of Garm. My mission is to—"

"I don't give a frig what your mission is!" shouted the Captain. "What are you doing in my engine room?"

With an air of tried patience, Rem-9 repeated the end of his statement. "My mission is to locate Lucas Droad and defend him

168

from an unspecified emergency situation. You will provide me with four flitters, or we will perforate the stern engine cupola. The resulting lack of lift will cause the *Gladius* to sink into the atmosphere."

"You're mad! The ship would tear apart! It isn't built for atmospheric pressures. We would all be crushed!"

The mech gave no sign of concern. "We will encapsulate ourselves in packing foam and eject during the reentry. Some of us may survive to achieve our mission."

The Captain argued further, but the Rem-9 was adamant. He provided video feed proving his claims. High explosives taken from the dead security men were already wired into place. Remote control detonators were ready for use. The heavy blast shielding that surrounded the engine rooms had been lowered and sealed; there was no safe way to get at them in there.

Within minutes stark fear replaced outrage on the Captain's face. If they wanted to, these crazy machines could bring down his ship. For the first time in many centuries of cyro-sleeping between star-systems, he saw the possible end of his career, even his life.

"I should never have come to this miserable system," he lamented into his phone. "Give them the flitters."

As soon as the order had been given, his fears redoubled. He sealed off his quarters and refused entry to everyone, including his Security Chief, although he dearly would have loved to discuss the high explosives with him. Foremost in his thoughts was Mai Lee's reaction to all this. Vengeful and cruel, she had long arms and her agents were renown for showing up at the crucial moment. He put nothing beyond the reach of that cold witch.

* * *

"The Militia reservists are here, sir," the orderly repeated for the third time.

General Ari Steinbach snorted, then rose up blearily. The coat he had been using as a blanket slipped off his chest and onto the floor of the limo. With a heavy sigh he blinked red-rimmed eyes at the setting sun outside.

After the abortive attack on the spaceport last night, things had

169

reduced to the level of a slow siege. Neither side had made any serious moves toward resolving the issue. Ari had spent much of the night and the early morning calling up the militia commanders he could find, ordering them to mobilize every unit in the province. His alarm had increased steadily as he realized that most of the officers could not be found. In fact, every officer who had attended the Militiaman's banquet last night was absent.

"Have any scouts returned from the Fort? What's the situation up there?"

"Still unknown, sir. The earliest scouts we sent out last night disappeared, as you know," said the lieutenant, absently sipping a cup of steaming hot caf. A light blanket of slushy snow coated the limo. Overhead the skies were still dark and pregnant, although there hadn't been any snowfall in hours. "The most recent reports indicated that no one can get into the gates. Sniper fire has killed everyone attempting to enter the compound. KXUT claims the Fort, like the spaceport, is in the hands of Lucas Droad the 'Pirate Governor'."

"Well, it isn't," snapped Ari irritably. He took a proffered cup of hot caf and tossed it down. Donning his coat and stretching he marched for the lifters.

"Major Lee!" he shouted, cupping his hands over his mouth to increase his volume. "Come out of there."

Major Drick Lee slowly opened the pilot's cupola and eyed the General with distaste. It appeared that he too, had been asleep.

"I need you to call that witch of an Aunt of yours and get some answers."

Major Lee appeared disinterested. "Why don't you call her?"

"Because she isn't responding to my attempts. I know you have special methods."

Major Lee gave him a dark look. "Are you accusing me of spying, sir?"

"Forget the semantics. We're in a serious and incomprehensible situation. Who is in control of Fort Zimmerman? What are all these reports of animal attacks and alien invaders? What is going on out in the Slipape counties? Who is fighting whom, Major? I want answers."

A tall man with severely short red hair and cold blue eyes crunched up through the snow to join them. An antiquated pipe

170

stuck out of his mouth, inside it a stimulant burned, producing a cloud of bluish smoke.

Ari regarded him with little enthusiasm. "Yes?"

"Are we planning to assault the new Governor, sir? Because if we are, I can't say that my men and I much like the idea."

"No, we're planning to take out one terrorist and self-proclaimed dictator," replied Ari with sudden fury. Why was it that no one showed him the respect his uniform deserved? "And just exactly who are you?"

"Madison, sir. Militia reservist Captain, Company C, Group Five reporting sir," answered the man in an unhurried fashion. "I've just come in from Hofstetten, and I couldn't help overhearing that you don't grasp the situation."

Ari and Drick both looked at him in askance.

"They're aliens, sirs," the man said simply. He sucked on his pipe for a moment then relit it before continuing. "Aliens are all over Hofstetten, that's why we were already mobilizing and why we got here ahead of most of the other units. Killed a lot of good people last night and today, cut off all our communications, too. The nets are down all over the colony."

"And what do these aliens look like, commander?" asked Drick contemptuously.

"Sort of like fast air-swimmers, mostly, but they can drop snake-like things out of their bodies. There are other kinds, too, but the worst are the dinosaur-types. They run like ostriches and carry weapons like a man."

Drick laughed.

"I must say that is a rather amazing story," said Ari. "It seems remarkable that KXUT hasn't reported any of these sightings, doesn't it?"

The man pulled out his pipe, examined it closely, then placed it back in his mouth. "Not really. KXUT's been off the net for hours. All they are playing now is pre-recorded stuff. It's not even the right stuff, just yesterday's daytime programming. No news reports, no live stuff at all." The man turned and crunched back through the snow to his unit.

The officers frowned after him.

"Whatever is happening, we need to get this business with Droad over with so we can go handle it," said Ari, rubbing his

171

hands together. "Damn, I'm beginning to wish I'd called in sick this week."

Major Lee nodded in agreement. "I'll try to contact the senator. She may know something."

"If she doesn't, then no one does. I'll gather up the men. We have an army of militia troops now and the 1st tactical squad is up to full strength, although God only knows where the 2nd squad is. Let's finish this thing with Droad."

He moved off and soon had two ragged lines of six full militia companies formed up. He ordered them to attack in waves, the first leading the second by two minutes. Ahead of the first wave was the 1st tactical squad, eager for a rematch with Droad's giants.

Hundreds of men moved through the parking lots, firing as they came. The fresh white snow was trampled to gray slush, then splattered red in places as return fire found targets.

"We have overwhelming numbers. We can't lose," whispered Ari, half to himself. He eagerly trained his goggles on the area of the baggage lockers in the arrivals section. Already he was planning how to get back his satchel in a smooth manner that would arouse no undue suspicion.

Drick, standing at his side, commented, "You seem unusually eager to see this battle through, General."

"It's my job," answered Ari.

"Yes, but it just doesn't seem like you—"

He broke off at the screaming sound of missiles in flight.

"The missile batteries have finally opened up!" shouted Drick exuberantly.

"No, damn it, no!" hissed Ari through clenched teeth. He hunkered down and focused his goggles on the front walls of the terminal building, fully expecting to see them disintegrate in a fireball. But instead of falling on the spaceport, sounds of explosions erupted from downtown Grunstein. He looked that way and his mouth gaped in amazement. The top third of the KXUT building, including the dish and the transmitter had been blown completely away.

His surprise increased into shock as he saw a squadron of Stormbringers lift off vertically from the Zimmerman field on the fort grounds and turned northward. Two of them broke off and zoomed over the city, where they began methodically bombing the

172

commercial district. The rest headed off in the direction of the Slipape counties.

Then, explosions rocked the heavy struts of the lifter he was leaning on, causing him to jerk his gaping head around the other way. The cars in the parking lot were blossoming into red flowers. The leading militia riflemen of the first wave dissolved, like insects caught by the sudden gushing of a blowtorch.

* * *

With a flourish, the doctor removed the sheet covering the thing on the table. "Quite a monster, eh?" said Doctor Risi with something akin to pride. He watched their reactions while tapping his right forefinger against his teeth.

Governor Droad grunted and Jarmo wrinkled his great nose.

"So, it is your belief that this creature is alien to Garm?" asked Droad. His eyes moved up and down the disgusting mess that covered the stainless steel table. At the damaged head section, an incision began that ran the length of the thing's brown, fleshy belly. Bizarre organs and thick rubbery muscles lay exposed to the harsh glare of the doctor's surgical lamp. He was reminded distinctly of the parasitic worms and sea slugs he had dissected in college.

"Absolutely. There is no record of anything like this organism in the colony files, nor in the Nexus Cluster records," replied the doctor. He was short, wiry little man with odd fingers that seemed overly long and delicate even for his small hands. The tips of these fingers tapered to elfin points and each of his fingernails was precisely cut.

"What is it then?"

"I haven't come up with a name for it yet, but when I do I'll let you know," said the doctor, smiling. Droad shot him questioning side-glance, but he seemed not to notice. "I can tell you what it isn't. It isn't a snake, nor any kind of reptile. It's more like a hot-blooded caterpillar with an extremely large brain and a lot of organs that I've yet to analyze."

"What about the radio emissions?" demanded Jarmo, intrusively leaning over the mound of twisted flesh on the table.

"That's what interests me most. Have you discovered yet how they do it?"

The doctor raised one fingertip between himself and Jarmo's looming face. He was clearly not intimidated. "I was just getting to that. The thing definitely has a built-in organic radio, just as we surmised from the security system records."

The finger dived downward like a pointer, aiming into the damaged head area. "I found it here, near the brain, just below where the ear would be on most earth species. Fortunately, the crude methods used to kill the creature didn't destroy it."

"And so Jarmo was right? This thing can use radio waves to communicate the way we use sound waves?" asked Droad, shaking his head in amazement.

"An assumption, but probably a safe one. With only the crudest of lab equipment available here at the spaceport, I can't tell you much more. Certainly it can receive such transmissions, and it would only make sense that it should be able to transmit them as well."

Droad stepped back from the table and urged the doctor to continue his research. Together, he and Jarmo headed back toward the security center. "What do you think Jarmo?"

"I don't like it. I don't like it at all. It would seem most likely that our opponents set this thing to spy on us or to assassinate you. We know little about how powerful the elite on Garm really are. Do they have a source of bio-weapons like this? I would give a lot to know where it came from."

"There is another possibility," said Droad. "Recall the earlier declarations made by the newsies. All that talk about an alien invasion up in the hills."

"That sort of thing makes good video," replied Jarmo.

"Yes, but that thing on the table is quite real."

The two of them reached the security center and settled down to rest a bit. Soon it would be nightfall again, and as the militia units outside were growing in strength, they expected an attack soon after dark. The primary topic of conversation, even more vital than the alien from the restrooms, was the disposition of the mechs in the hold of the *Gladius*.

"We have to assume they aren't coming," said Droad, sitting with his boots on Major Lee's desk and sipping another mug of hot

174

caf. There was a special flavor in the Garmish variety that he couldn't quite identify, but which he was beginning to appreciate.

"Although I am generally the conservative one here," said Jarmo, "I wouldn't count them out by any means. Rem-9 is intelligent, experienced and more than competent. More importantly, they're mechs. A bunch of security men and sleeper agents on the ship should not be able to take them out."

Droad frowned into his steamy mug. "One well-placed explosive on each of those shipping capsules would do it, though. We checked them right before we came down, but it's obvious now that the rulers here were onto us from the start."

Jarmo opened his mouth to comment further but was stopped by an echoing explosion from the front of the terminal. The men leapt to their feet and went out into the main room. Sergeant Manstein was there, looking over the shoulders of an operator.

"They're coming back for more, sir," he said as Droad entered the room.

On the main screens a wave of riflemen, led by a knot of men in black body-shell charged through the parking lot. Gun muzzles flashed and plasma bursts blossomed.

"They're serious this time. Sergeant, take everyone you can gather and head for the arrivals level. Jarmo and I will take over here," said Droad. "Jarmo?"

Jarmo was working with the radar techs. He turned around at the Governor's call. "I don't know for sure, sir, but I think the mechs may finally be coming down."

For the first time in hours, Droad felt himself smile. It felt good.

"You see their jump-flitters?"

"No, but we have picked up four flitters, coming right on us from the *Gladius*. Unless the Captain has decided to join the battle, I think it's a safe bet that the mechs will add their weight shortly."

Droad nodded. "How long until they get here?"

"About ten minutes."

Droad returned his attention to the monitors. The men in body-shell had reached the terminal entrance already. Behind them, the line of riflemen was even more ragged, but still moving forward. One of the monitors went dark as a security camera was hit and rendered inoperable.

"I don't think we have ten minutes. They're going to overrun us."

"Governor—ah, there's something else, sir. Something is coming up the river."

"What?"

"The river borders the spaceport, sir. There's nothing down there but some reeds and a chain link fence, but the security system is monitoring a fault of some kind, a violation."

"Are they coming at us in boats, too?" demanded Droad with a hint of exasperation in his voice. He felt himself losing control of the situation. It was slipping from his grasp like a handful of water. What an ignoble way to end his short term in office, hunted down and slaughtered by a pack of jax herders with laser rifles, hiding beneath a desk. At least the previous Governor had lasted nearly a month.

"Not boats, sir. Here, I'll patch it through to the main holo-plate."

The riflemen vanished and an image of the riverfront shimmered into existence. It zoomed into focus. Wide and sluggish, the river was cold-looking and littered with floating debris. Droad squinted. No, not debris—upside-down boats, that was his first impression. Then one of the boats raised up out of the water, turning into a gigantic head. One mammoth dark eye swiveled about, and then the head sank back down. From another of the submerged heads fountained a fine white mist. Droad was reminded of an extinct earth species, what were they called? Whales?

"What the hell are those?"

But Jarmo was too busy bringing up more strange images to answer him. Set beside the riverfront view, the angles of other cameras shifted and focused automatically, panning with sickening speed. To the left of the giant heads in the river was now a flock of odd, stingray-like things in the air, flying out of the cover of the trees. To the right of the river scene, and most alarming, a column of humanoid creatures where depicted running up, no *bounding* up the colonial highway toward the spaceport's front gates.

"What the hell are all these things?" demanded the Governor. He slammed his fists against the console. This was intolerable. The situation was getting completely out of control. "What in the hell is going on?"

"There's more sir, Fort Zimmerman is firing its missile batteries on the city. Stormbringers are joining in the attack, bombing the downtown section," said Jarmo. He looked at Droad, waiting for orders.

"Unbelievable. No time to think about it." Droad paused, thinking despite his words. Were the aliens with Steinbach or against him? If they were with them, they had little hope of survival. If they were against him, they were in such numbers that he needed all Steinbach's men plus his men and the mechs to face this new threat. It occurred to him that leading the militia and his own men in a joint effort to stop an alien attack was an excellent way to cement his position as the new governor.

"Jarmo, you said that the column of humanoid creatures were coming from Fort Zimmerman? And that the Fort is firing on the city?"

"Yes sir."

"It seems clear then that the aliens are attacking both sides. Set off all the car-bombs immediately."

"But sir, the enemy aren't in optimal position yet."

"I don't want to kill them all, just to slow down their attack. If I'm right about these aliens, we're going to need all those men out there alive."

Outside, the bombs that Jarmo's demolition team had spent much of the night planting in the cars nearest the terminal went off. The resulting firestorm erupted between 1st tactical squad and the leading elements of the militia. The tactical squad, invulnerable in their body-shell, were knocked to the pavement and tossed about like leaves in a thunderstorm. Behind them the first wave of riflemen fell back, many of them screaming and rolling in the slush between the vehicles.

Deciding not to face the terminal's defenders alone, 1st tactical squad pulled back amongst the burning vehicles, firing their waist-cannons to cover their retreat.

"Tell the front line not to use their plasma cannon against the men in body-shell. Just use small arms to keep them retreating," ordered Droad. Sitting down again and leaning close to the flickering holo-images, he felt he had regained some of his composure. No new threats had materialized for nearly two minutes. He put his hand to his earphone and said to Jarmo, "It's time to get in touch with Steinbach."

* * *

"They're pulling back!" screeched Ari in frustration. "They were right there at the doors and they're pulling back. Those bombs only singed them! I don't believe this!"

Literally hopping mad, Ari had to struggle to not destroy his field goggles against the steel side of the lifter. So close! He could almost feel the weight of his satchel in his hands, the way an amputee could feel the ghostly presence of the absent limb.

Major Drick Lee came up, smirking. "Looks like we'll have to use the mortars after all."

Ignoring him, Ari wheeled to direct his goggles toward Fort Zimmerman and the city beyond. The missile batteries continued to snap and whine, smoke now obscured the entire downtown area. Stormbringers burst from the roiling white clouds of smoke, then wheeled and vanished into them again, beginning another strafing run.

"And what about that?" screeched Ari, pointing toward Grunstein with a trembling finger. Major Lee's smirk faltered as he followed Ari's gesture.

A lieutenant appeared beside them. He cleared his throat apprehensively, but with an air of determination. "Sir, begging your pardon, but what are we doing fighting men in the spaceport while aliens are destroying the colony?"

Ari looked at him in confusion, as if he had spoken in a foreign dialect. Then all at once it hit him. The boy was right. He had been so intent on regaining his satchel that the vile realities of the situation had failed to dawn on him.

There came an odd hissing sound from the snow near Ari's left boot. He looked down, seeing a widening black streak of asphalt materialize from a patch of snow that had vaporized into steam.

"Laser fire!" he shouted, throwing himself onto his belly. Major Lee followed suit, almost as fast. The young lieutenant, however, didn't drop reflexively. There was another flash of heat and a hissing sound, and the lieutenant did join them on the

178

ground, thrashing with a hole blasted in his chest.

More shots hissed into the snow. A blackened gouge appeared in the steel hull of the lifter overhead. Ari exchanged glances with Major Lee. Plumes of white mist billowed from Lee's clenched teeth.

"We're being hit from behind," grunted Major Lee.

Nodding, Ari scrambled to his feet and threw himself into the open door of the lifter pilot's cupola. Major Lee was right behind him. Together they climbed into the glove-like seats and hunkered down away from the exposed windshield.

Up about ten feet now, they could easily see their attackers. Bounding along the snowy road, a large number of bizarre animals poured in among the vehicles. Almost everyone was looking at the battle for the terminal; most were taken completely by surprise. A newsie man, speaking into a holo-camera, was gutted even as he paused to sip some hot caf. The man with the camera ran, but was quickly overtaken and decapitated by one of the things as it bounded high over his head.

The *things*. Running like ostriches, looking like small gray dinosaurs with hands and no heads, they immediately brought cold numbing terror into Ari's gut. Handling weapons expertly in their three-fingered hands, they seemed as efficient at killing with their bladed feet as with guns.

The lifter whined and lurched. Ari looked over at Major Lee, who was flipping switches and pulling at slide-controls. The engines screamed into life and Ari felt his seat vibrate beneath him. "You know how to fly this thing?"

"No, but I can get us into the air on autopilot," said Major Lee, his face pulled in a tight snarl.

Even as he spoke the lifter rose up and became airborne. Ari, finally getting his wits about him now that the immediate threat of death seemed more remote, ordered the waves of troops in the parking lot to pull back and attack the monsters pouring through the gates. Below them, he saw the fabric walls of the medical dome fall in shreds before three of the aliens. It was obvious that a terrific slaughter had begun inside. Holes from laser fire burned through the walls and dome. Wounded men staggered out the exits, falling and dying in the snow.

Another channel on his phone beeped insistently. With infinite

179

irritation, he opened the link. "What do you want?"

"General Steinbach? This is Governor Droad."

Major Lee, fighting the controls to keep the lifter hovering about a hundred feet over the battle, shot him a glance of surprise.

"What do you want?" repeated Ari, frowning. He had finally recalled his sidearm and pulled it out, releasing the safety.

"General Steinbach, you must listen to me. We must talk. Aliens are attacking both of us. It is ridiculous to proceed with fighting among ourselves," said Droad.

"So, you think we should let you out of that terminal, do you?" began Ari, snarling. Then his face changed—became speculative. His thoughts turned to his satchel in the upper row of lockers in the arrivals section. "Perhaps you are right..."

"I suggest we fight together. There are more of them than just the ones hitting you from the rear. There are flocks of flying aliens coming at you—at us—from the trees, and more gigantic ones from the riverfront."

"Hold on a moment," said Ari. He pulled his field goggles over his eyes and gazed east, sure enough a lumbering horde of creatures, gigantic creatures, were moving up from the swampy shores of the river. To the west, tiny dark specks flitted toward them from the trees.

"What do you suggest?" asked Ari, deflated. Things were completely out of his hands. His first instinct was to run, but not without his satchel. Ari envisioned Droad as a cruel school bully, dangling his satchel just out of reach.

"Order your first wave and the troops in body-shell to enter the terminal, we won't fire. Then land your lifter, load it with all the men you can from your second wave and bring them into the terminal, too. We need walls between us and the enemy immediately."

Ari pursed his lips. He and Major Lee exchanged knowing smiles. Into the phone he said, "I agree, Governor Droad. You have my word that my troops will cease firing on you, at least for the duration of this much more significant situation."

"Excellent. Move now," replied Droad. Ari frowned in annoyance at the clipped tone of command that had entered Droad's voice so quickly.

"Steinbach's scared. I think he'll join us, at least for now," said Governor Droad. "Tell me what we should do with these aliens. They seem to be forming up ranks before they attack. At least that gives us a few minutes."

"I detected the alien maneuvers that are up on the holo-plates now with the radio-scanner initially," explained Jarmo. "For the last day or so the communications officer and I have noticed unusual traffic on several rarely used frequencies. After learning from Doctor Risi that the aliens used built-in radios to communicate, I simply set the air-traffic control computer to search for emissions in the proper frequency range and report them as traffic contacts. Here's what I got," he said, manipulating a keyboard with his stubby fingers. The holo-plate changed to a normal topographical view of the immediate spaceport, but on it were an incredible number of contacts. Hanging beside each contact were ghostly identification letters. There were a number of them moving up from the riverbank, larger groups coming from the trees and the main entrance to the spaceport. "They're all classified as unknown, of course."

"So, we can at least track their movements," said Droad, nodding. "That's quite an advantage."

They watched as the flying aliens joined up with the ostrich-like ones at the main entrance. Together they advanced into the parking lots, while the giants from the river swung around to approach the terminal from the rear.

"Can we recall the Stormbringers? The aliens should be easy targets for them."

Jarmo shook his head. "Captain Dorman has already scrambled his planes and has engaged the enemy attacking Grunstein."

Droad nodded. "Well, we can't very well call them back to save us while a whole city full of civilians is under attack. If he disengages, tell him to come back and give us a hand."

Jarmo worked his phone.

"Put those river-things on the main plate," Droad ordered the operator.

Instantly, massive creatures seemed to be running in place on the plate. They were huge, lizard-like things on four legs. Their backs and head were encased with what appeared to be natural scaly armor. Their broad, triangular heads weaved from side to side as they walked. Sprouting from the center of each triangular head was a long black horn of some kind.

"These things are so large that they were actually walking on the bottom of the river to sneak up on us," said Jarmo, shaking his head. "Dorman says he'll return as soon as he can. He also says that there are definitely aliens flying the rogue Stormbringers."

Droad looked at him in amazement. Still looking amazed, he turned back to the main holo-plate. Whatever these things were, they were definitely intelligent. "It seems that they are preparing for a major attack. What about General Steinbach and my greatly delayed mechs?"

"General Steinbach appears to be complying with your directions. He's using his lifter to transport his troops here. The mechs are also close, they will land in about two minutes."

The image on the holo-plate changed again, this time depicting a militia lifter wobbling unevenly as it landed hundreds of troops onto the roof of the terminal building.

Droad nodded, then stood up. "It's time we greeted our reinforcements."

Leaving Jun and some of the security men on duty, Jarmo and Droad headed for the arrivals section. There they greeted General Steinbach and Major Lee, just coming down the steps into the building. There was a pause as the two sides met. Hundreds of militia riflemen were right there, facing a handful of Nexus-loyal security people, giants and Stormbringer pilots. Weapons were held in white-knuckled hands.

"My good Governor," said Steinbach coming forward with a falsely warm smile. "Let's put aside our differences. Men should not fight men while these monsters destroy us all with indifference."

"Do you swear your allegiance to the Nexus?" asked Droad severely.

Steinbach took a step back in shock. "Certainly, sir. I take pride in my loyalty to the Nexus."

Jarmo snorted rudely.

"Do you swear allegiance to me as your duly appointed

Governor?"

Steinbach turned white. His hands shook. For some reason, he kept looking over the Governor's shoulder at the alcoves containing the restrooms and the rentable luggage lockers.

"Ah... I'm not closed to such a consideration, but this isn't the time to debate your legitimacy. Let us fight together, and then decide matters of authority and legality at a later time."

All eyes were upon Droad and Steinbach. Droad finally smiled. "Good enough, they're almost upon us."

Together, the men rushed to the barricades.

"For once they're all pointing their weapons in the same direction," said Droad, smiling at the sight.

"Let's see what they do when it's over, assuming we're alive then," said Jarmo.

Once inside of accurate rifle range, the aliens charged the terminal building with frightening speed. A horde of gray shapes came on, sailing over parked vehicles in single bounds. Zooming around and among them came the flying things, spreading their odd bodies into perfectly aerodynamic gliding shapes.

The men in the terminal building screamed and pulled their triggers until their fingers bled. Thousands of explosive rounds and lancing laser pulses ripped the air and the aliens. The fantastic bodies of the aliens flew apart. Some of them, blown nearly to fragments, continued to crawl, hop or creep forward, ignoring their missing body parts.

The flocks of flying things arrived first, immediately dropping shrades into the ranks of militiamen. Even less disciplined than the rank and file militia thugs that guarded the streets and gave out traffic tickets, the reservists were quick to rout. Ragged holes were torn in the line even before the headless killing machines with their deadly bladed feet could arrive.

"Sir, they're hitting us from the rear!"

"What's that?" shouted Droad motioning forward 1st tactical squad, which they had held in reserve to keep the line. The terrific din of battle inside the large echoing terminal building made it almost impossible to hear.

"The giant ones, they're tearing their way into the jetways and coming down the ramps from the gate areas!" roared Jarmo, his deep voice cutting through the clamor. "We should send half 1st tactical squad to deal with them!"

Droad nodded. "Take some of your men and join them," he said. He gave Jarmo a look, which the other immediately interpreted. Neither of them wanted Steinbach's men behind them and on their own.

"Good thinking, sir," said Jarmo, trotting off with his plasma cannon unslung.

The fighting went hard in the main terminal. Droad observed that his men had the numbers and the firepower, but they lacked the ferocity and discipline of the aliens, who were clearly oblivious to death and pain. When perhaps a third of the men were down, they fell back in disorder, taking more casualties as they broke ranks. The aliens, however, fought on without change although more than half of them had been destroyed.

Soon, every one of their snipers on the roof had been killed. The battle raged on, pushing the men back. At the second barricade in front of the doors of the security center and still holding the tops of the escalators, they held them. Using his sidearm to good advantage, Droad personally shot two of the hideous slug-like things that the flying horrors had vomited in the midst of his men.

A firm hand gripped his shoulder and pulled him around. He lifted his laser pistol reflexively, but it was only Sergeant Manstein.

"Things are going badly in the rear," Manstein shouted. "They can't stop those things at the gates. They'll be in here soon!"

Droad nodded. For a moment he stood panting, his face drawn and white with the stress of days of siege and battle. Then he ran to Steinbach, who was standing with Major Lee in the middle of a knot of men in body-shell. He relayed what Manstein had told him. Although Steinbach was reluctant, they were soon all heading for the gate area at a dead run.

Things were indeed going badly, thought Droad. Jun was killed, gored and trampled until his corpse was almost unrecognizable. Many men in black body-shell lay strewn about the scene. A dozen of the giant monsters were down, some of them only wounded. Trapped up on a catwalk in a construction area, Jarmo and the last of the men in body-shell were cornered and being stalked by the monstrous killers.

"Use concentrated fire to bring one of them down," said Droad

184

opening up on the leading monster. Surprised by this new attack, the rest pulled back into one of the gate areas, out of view.

Jarmo and his surviving men joined the others. Crouching behind a row of seats in the non-narcotic waiting area, a tense discussion began.

"Let's pull back. These things can't get us in the corridors," suggested Major Lee.

"We can't just let a pack of ten ton monsters roam around at our rear," returned Droad in exasperation.

"What did you do to my tactical squad?" Steinbach demanded of Jarmo, livid fury on his face. "This must be the most frustrating day of my life."

"We both took each other by surprise. I think they meant to sneak up on us while the other beasts hit us from the front, but that failed. Unfortunately, they did manage to ambush us."

"Ambush you? Ambush you? How can a pack of dinosaurs ambush anyone?" asked Steinbach, beating one gloved fist into another.

"It was a tactical error," admitted a Captain of the tactical squad, speaking up for the first time. "It was my error, not Jarmo's. From the description, we were expecting a herd of elephants, something like that, but these things are intelligent. They stayed back in the dark and then rushed us from either side. At first our body-shells saved us, but then they simply knocked us down, planted one of their huge feet on our guns and gored us."

Jarmo nodded in agreement. "They are faster than they look when charging."

Steinbach made a rude sound of disgust. He walked away from the circle of men. "I'm surrounded by incompetence," he muttered.

"What are they up to now?" asked Droad.

"They're holding back, waiting for reinforcements, perhaps, or new orders by radio," said Jarmo. Before he could say more, the sky outside brightened with an orange glare and the earth shook beneath their feet.

Droad looked at Jarmo and smiled. "The mechs."

As Droad expected, the battle for Grunstein International had been going well for the humans up until that point, but the arrival of the mechs decided it. They came out of their jump-webbing at a dead run, weapons blazing. Two flitters came down in front of the terminal, hitting the aliens there from the rear, while two more landed in the blast pans and a terrific struggle began with the monsters among the gates.

Cagey and wary, the juggers knew they were out-matched by the combined forces of the humans, but they didn't immediately attack in the berserk frenzy so common to the other types. These larger ones behaved more like hunters, more like men. They worked to sell their lives as dearly as possible. When it was all over, three of the mechs had been rendered inoperative.

Walking back to the security center through the smoking ruins of the terminal building, Droad noticed Jarmo, who came up and fell into step beside him.

"This is the time for caution, sir," said Jarmo in a hushed voice. His ever-vigilant eyes flicked over every moving thing around them.

Droad nodded vaguely, almost too tired to care if the militiamen assassinated him.

They made it all the way back to the center before Sergeant Manstein asked: "Hey, where did Steinbach go?"

Droad looked around, surprised. He had just been there a moment before, hadn't he? The last he could recall seeing him was sometime before the counterattack by the mechs. After that he had simply vanished.

"He couldn't have run out on us, where is there to go?" remarked Sergeant Manstein.

"Go find him, Jarmo," said Droad. "I don't trust the good General. From now on, it is your personal responsibility to keep an eye on him."

Jarmo walked away, smiling.

Eighteen

"Come on, you bastard! Come on," Ari hissed. He twisted the handle again, but the door wouldn't open. With an inarticulate sound of frustration he reinserted his identification card. He held his hands out before him, balled into fists, and pleaded with the locker door. "Don't be broken, oh please."

During the battles over the terminal building, the lockers had fared rather well, but they hadn't escaped damage completely. Several bullet-gouges and black laser-scorings marked the casement. The stainless steel finish of Ari's locker, in particular, was anything but stainless. A dark blotch of black and brown with a center of warped metal marked the heat of a deflected laser blast. The card-slot rejected his card again, spitting it out with a tiny electric whine.

"No, no, NO!" Ari howled. He pounded the locker around the hinges and the latch mechanism. Finally, something gave and the locker yawned open with dramatic slowness. His hand darted inside and drew out the satchel.

Placing the satchel delicately on the floor, he hunched over it like a hyena guarding its kill. Furtively, he flicked his eyes around the terminal building. No one seemed to be watching him. In fact, there was almost no one in sight of the locker area. A divider stood between him and the militia reservists who were taking roll and counting their dead in the main hall.

Careful to open the satchel with the precise movements that

187

were safe, and making doubly sure that the anti-theft systems were disabled with a hand-held snooper, he checked the contents. A great, beaming smile of relief relaxed his pinched features. The codekeys were there, undamaged and still in their protective cases. Everything was in order.

Ari closed the satchel, rearmed its defense and stepped around the divider. He reentered the ruined main hall of the terminal—and walked right into the wall-like chest of Jarmo. Ari made an involuntary, high-pitched sound of alarm.

"There you are, General," boomed Jarmo.

Ari grimaced. It seemed that the giant's eyes fell immediately to the satchel and remained glued there.

"Just going to the restroom," he explained weakly. He frowned and took a step back from the towering giant, trying to regain his composure.

"Sure," said Jarmo.

Ari nodded, then slid past the wall-like man and headed for the upper level. Twice, on his way to the unmoving escalators, Ari glanced back.

Jarmo hadn't moved. His eyes followed Ari's every step. Trying to be as casual as possible, Ari stopped along the way to the elevator rotunda several times, inquiring as to the health of various wounded militiamen. When he was quite sure that no one was following him, he slipped into the empty lobby and opened the outer doors with the yellow key from his satchel. Once inside he locked it again and went to work on the maintenance panel.

* * *

"There's someone in the space elevator sir, taking it up to the orbital station."

Droad's head snapped around. "I thought we took the elevators off-line. Use the emergency stop."

There was a momentary pause. "It won't work, sir. I'm trying to override with the manual backup. Nothing."

Droad strode across the room and leaned over the operator's shoulder, staring at his console intently. "Get me the interior of the elevator up on the holo-plate."

While the operator clittered at the keyboard, Droad called Jarmo and informed him of the situation.

"We can't allow alien infiltration onto the *Gladius*, sir," said Jarmo. "I'm on my way."

Droad continued to make the operator nervous, leaning over his shoulder while he typed. The main holo-plate flickered, then displayed a hunched form in a militia officer's uniform, working feverishly on the control panel.

"General Steinbach! What are you doing in that elevator? This spaceport is under quarantine!"

General Steinbach's head jerked up and shot a wide-eyed glance over his shoulder at the security camera. "Forgot, damn it," he muttered. He withdrew something from his satchel, a small object glittered a metallic red. He inserted it into the control panel and worked the keyboard for a few seconds.

"What's he doing?" demanded Droad.

"I don't know, sir. Wait," the operator's jaw sagged down. His console had gone blank.

With alarming rapidity, systems began to go down all around the security center. Steinbach's image on the holo-plate was one of the first to vanish.

"What's happening?" asked Droad, with the sinking feeling that he already knew the answer.

"I—he must have released a virus, sir. The whole system is going down. The security applications, the network, even the operating system itself has been corrupted. It'll take hours to reload and reboot."

Jarmo burst into the center, his sides heaving from running.

Droad glanced at him angrily. "It seems that General Steinbach has schemes of his own. He's now boarding the *Gladius*."

Jarmo flushed, his massive neck turning red first then his heavy face.

"I thought you were going to keep an eye on him."

Jarmo glowered, looking chagrinned. "He moved more quickly than I expected, sir. I underestimated him."

Droad nodded, accepting the apology. He doubted that Steinbach would fool Jarmo again. Not now that his professional pride was involved.

"With your permission, sir, I'll take a team up and retrieve him."

"No, no. For now he has escaped us. We have far more pressing problems."

"Yes," agreed Jarmo reluctantly. "What are we going to do about Fort Zimmerman?"

Droad sipped his hot caf, then set it down with a grimace. It had become cold caf. "We have to take it back. Has Dorman returned yet?"

"He's on his way. A few minutes ago he reported having shot down most of the enemy Stormbringers and having driven off the rest. He said there was heavy damage to the city."

"What about our own losses?"

"He only lost three planes in the engagement. According to him, the aliens are excellent instinctive pilots with inhumanly good reflexes, but they just don't know the planes as well as our pilots do. Not yet, at least."

Droad sipped a new mug of caf—a hot mug this time. It made sense that the alien pilots were naturals. It was beginning to seem that this bewildering variety of aliens were all of the same basic genetic stock, perhaps even the same species. "We aren't fighting an alliance of several alien races, Jarmo. We're fighting just one race, one very adaptable race."

"Your theory fits the facts, sir. Every time we meet a new type of alien, they seem to be experts at one part of warfare or another. Almost as if they were designed for it."

Droad touched his lips to his mug again, feeling the heat. It was with great trepidation that he asked the next question. "What's the situation in Grunstein?"

Jarmo turned and their eyes met. "Grim."

"The missile bombardment continues?"

Jarmo nodded.

"Then we haven't got time to wait. Get the men regrouped. As soon as Captain Dorman has rearmed his planes, we go on the offensive."

* * *

Standing in disgrace, the eldest nife presented his report with

190

drooping stalks. His cusps were mere slits, all but hiding his orbs from view. The Parent and her three young daughters sat on their individual birthing thrones, their tentacles moving in agitation.

"We should expel him from the nest," suggested one of the young parents. She clacked her mandibles contemptuously. "Without killbeasts to slaughter his prey and trachs to bring it to him, he'd starve within a week."

"You are far too lenient sister," admonished the second daughter. "I say we remove his genitals and send him into the field alongside the killbeasts. Let him lead the charge during the next slaughter he orchestrates."

The remaining daughter only grunted and warbled through her foodtube inarticulately. She was passing a particularly large larva and was beyond making sensible commentary. Behind her, a group of clattering hests reached anxiously for the new squirming form even before it had cleared her orifice and hit the chute. When she had passed it, she slumped over her birthing throne. "There, I have finished one replacement jugger for those you so stupidly squandered," she said.

"Yes, to have wasted so many of our precious juggers, that is his greatest crime to date," said her sister. "When I think of the agony I'll have to go through passing their huge bodies and those single thorn-like immature horns of theirs, I wish my chambers would just rupture fatally right now. It would be a relief."

"Those horns do almost invariably cause tearing," agreed the other daughter. "You are a most wretched mutation, commander."

Half-listening to her offspring, the eldest Parent, the one who had first invaded Garm, regarded the nife she had melded with so recently. How had such a genetically well-designed commander failed so miserably? Could there be a hidden flaw in his DNA? Could it be that he simply wasn't of good type? Something the checking enzymes hadn't picked up and repaired? A mutation of such magnitude would be a reflection on her own genetics. It made her shudder to think she could have produced something flawed from her own birthing orifice.

"No," she said aloud. Her daughters quieted immediately and the nife raised his stalks a fraction, hoping. "I won't accept that he is flawed. The only answer is that the enemy is of greater capability than we had previously assumed."

"But that oversight would still be his fault," the daughter to the Parent's left pointed out petulantly.

The Parent hesitated a moment, passing another larvae. It was only a hest and thus gave her no discomfort. With a liquid slapping sound, it rolled down the chute beneath and behind her. "I myself was as fully taken in as was he. I've reviewed the records of the battle transmissions; the bio-computers have sufficient capacity to track everything now. The enemy surprised us by adapting quickly to a new threat, then again by bringing in reinforcements from their great ship. Reinforcements that we had no prior knowledge of. All our software worms have been unable to penetrate the ship's systems."

"That's essentially correct," chimed in the nife. Already his stalks were on the rise. "In fact, every net on the planet surface has been penetrated and compromised. We've yet to get in viruses to disrupt them, but we have tapped them all. Every hour our knowledge of the enemy grows exponentially."

His stalks were nearly at full extension now, and he took the opportunity to stride up and down before his massive mistresses. Pausing in front of the youngest, he blinked his cusps twice in a conspiratorial and suggestive manner. She responded by sucking air through her foodtube, but didn't make any public complaints.

The nife continued to pace before them and speak with growing enthusiasm. "I'll take a chance, right here, right now, and say that victory is in sight for the Imperium. The planet is all but in our control—except for two pockets of real resistance. One is the united forces in the southern estate areas, where the enemy rulers seem to reside, the second is associated with the spaceport and the great ship itself.

"All we really need to do is take the ship. Besides giving us the high ground in this conflict and vast amounts of data concerning the highest technological achievements of the enemy, it will provide us an out if things should sour down here."

A chorus of blatting noises filled the throne chamber. The three daughters were voicing their displeasure by expelling air through their foodtubes. "Did I hear correctly? Not only does this buffoon fail us as a commander, but immediately he begins to plan for the failure of the entire campaign! What can be gained by planning for gross error?"

"But with one blow we could secure everything!" retorted the nife, excitedly. His mandibles worked the air like frenzied snakes. "We must seize the moment and mount a second, massive assault!"

Further rude noises greeted him.

The Parent slapped her tentacles against her throne, calling for order. Truly, things had been more orderly before she had birthed her daughters. Not for the first time, she considered sending them away with an umulk each to begin their own nests. Let them mature through hard labor and independence. However, she stayed this decision, telling herself that they were yet too young. Perhaps by tomorrow or the next day they would have matured sufficiently to run their own fledgling nests. Thoughtfully, she sat for a time, listening to her digesters and feeling her birthing chambers contract and expand.

"I have made my decisions," she said after a time during which the others had become increasingly restive. "You, eldest of my nife offspring, must gather all our strength in the polar region for one fatal thrust against the enemy. We will take the spaceport and the great ship."

"Oh, thank you, my Parent," cried the nife, his orbs wide and beaming. "You will not be disappointed, not in the least. I will—"

"See that I am not," said the Parent, overriding him. "Or else you will be both gelded and expelled from this nest."

The three daughters found this immensely amusing.

"I have further decided," continued the Parent, "that my daughters are quite ready to face the outside world alone. Tomorrow, with a small dowry of offspring, each of you will be transported to a strategic spot on the continent to begin new nests in secret."

It was the nife's turn to laugh. The daughters all but swooned at the idea of leaving the home nest, but the Parent remained adamant.

The nife then proceeded to flirt with them all in his customary, brash manner, winking his cusps and massaging their birthing thrones suggestively. When he finally exited, it was with a handsome flourish that left them all with their hormones flowing.

* * *

By nightfall, Droad and Jarmo were walking the walls of Fort Zimmerman, inspecting the damage. It had all gone with surprising ease. Taking complete leadership of the militia had been easy after Steinbach had run off. That single action, combined with the generally cowardly performance of the militia leadership during the battle had done wonders for Droad's popularity. The men were loyal to him now, he, his amazing mechs and his giants had saved them from the aliens.

Leaving the spaceport in the hands of Major Lee and a handful of his former staff, Droad and Jarmo led their small army against the fort. The assault on the fort itself had been little more than an exercise. It had been held only by a skeletal force of aliens, mostly the multi-armed, multi-eyed types that piloted the Stormbringers and the other vehicles they had captured. Captain Dorman had blown a hole in the outer fences and the rear wall of the fortress. Two lifters full of militiamen and mechs had stormed through the smoldering breach and slaughtered what resistance there was. The enemy had had only enough time to destroy the missile launchers before they were retaken.

"This easy victory doesn't make me feel much better," complained Droad, gesticulating at the fortress around them.

"At least we stopped the missile attacks on the city."

"Yes, that's excellent, but where are the enemy? There aren't even any corpses left behind except for those octopus pilots of theirs. Where are our dead militiamen from last night's banquet?"

"My initial investigation indicates that all the bodies have been removed and carried into the tunnels we found in the banquet hall."

"What do they want with all the bodies?"

"The social structure of these aliens reminds me somewhat of insects," said Jarmo, thoughtfully. A chill wind rippled his heavy coat. "The orderly way that they approach warfare and everything else; their lack of concern for their individual well-being. They are similar to ants, or termites. They even dig tunnels with fantastic speed."

Droad stopped walking and turned to Jarmo, listening carefully. The clouds had broken over the polar region and the sun could be seen, scudding along just above the horizon. Its light was welcome, but seemed to provide little heat.

194

"I can only surmise that after a battle they would eat our people and probably their own dead as well," concluded Jarmo.

"They eat their own dead?"

"Insects are very efficient."

"But these things aren't insects," argued Droad. "They're more like hot-blooded reptiles, like dinosaurs, than insects."

"Physically yes, but not socially."

Droad started walking again, and Jarmo fell in step beside him. He looked back toward the spaceport and the dark shaft of the space elevator that reached up into the sky, all the way to the orbital platform. It was like a metallic umbilical cord, stretching for miles right up into space.

"I still wonder why they pulled back. They must be regrouping, planning something big."

"I agree," said Jarmo. "They are probably massing in the mountains for a counterattack."

"Get the fort's battle computers online. I want them tracking all the appropriate radio frequencies. Find those aliens, Jarmo."

Jarmo smiled grimly. "They won't surprise us again."

Nineteen

The weird, table-like creatures carried Sarah and the others down into the tunnels. Sarah was wrapped in womb-like blackness. For seemingly an endless time she rode on the warm, undulating back of her beast.

Dazed by her recent experiences she stared upward, watching nothing but the colorful after-images that played on her retinas. The darkness didn't seem to bother the aliens; they apparently needed no help to guide themselves through their own tunnels.

Sarah began to feel a deep hopelessness, a pitiful despair that wasn't familiar to her. She tried to get herself out of this defeatist malaise, to tell herself there was always hope, but somehow the blackness and the odd stinks and sounds drove the hope out of her. It was as if grotesque minions of evil were carting her into the depths of hell.

An unwelcome addition to her discomfort was the terrible headache she had from having been drowned. Oxygen deprivation had sent a herd of galloping horses through her head, pounding down the gray matter with sharp hooves. She wondered vaguely if she had sustained any brain damage—and whether or not it would be possible for her to tell if she had.

Slipping in and out of consciousness, she slept.

* * *

Mom?

Mom, are you there?

Sarah reached up and touched her itching nose. The itch didn't go away however, as it was an alien stink, not really an itch.

"Mom?" asked a tiny voice from somewhere.

With a sudden intake of breath she came awake and sat up halfway. She only made it halfway because her head hit the roof of the tunnel that they still traveled within. "Bili?" she cried, ignoring the jolt of pain in her head. "Bili, where are you?"

"Here, Mom," said Bili, not so far away. From the sound of it, he was on the next animal up. She noticed something in her eyes, something that stung briefly. It was blood from her forehead.

Something came out of the darkness and touched her. It was an alien appendage of some kind, a hard horny thing like the claw of a crab. It touched her and pushed her firmly back down. She realized, swallowing a great scream, that it was only the beast she was riding on, pushing her flat for easy transport. Feeling like livestock on the way to the slaughterhouse, she let herself lie flat again.

"Bili, what's been going on? Are you okay?"

"You're alive," said Bili with intense relief in his voice. "The aliens haven't hurt me yet, but something's wrong with Daddy, he's breathing like a walker on a mountainside and won't talk to me. He just moans every once in awhile. I hope he dies, the fat bastard."

Sarah felt a sudden added weight on her shoulders. She had been so concerned about Bili that she had blanked out all the recent events with Mudface and Daddy. She shivered, although the air in the tunnel was surprisingly warm, even hot. She noticed that her clothes were still wet from the pool, which meant that she couldn't have slept too long. Now that she was more fully awake, she realized just how much pain she was in. Being murdered and then brought back to life played hell with your body. She felt like a bruised lump of overripe fruit.

"Daddy's here? What about Mudface?"

"They offed him," said Bili, sounding positively cheerful. "It was enough to make me cheer for their side. Almost."

Sarah was again taken by a wave of guilt. This whole situation was her fault. She had gone for the money by dealing with

197

Mudface and Daddy in the first place. She had even given the aliens her ticket for a ride down to the planet when they needed it. Worst of all, she had dragged Bili into all this with her, her own son.

"Oh, Bili," she said, her voice weak in the darkness. "I'm so sorry for getting you into this."

"It's okay, Mom. Besides, I'm the one you did it for. I guess I'll never get that regrow for my arm now."

In the blackness, Sarah let tears run down her face, but she didn't make a sound. It would only upset Bili.

After an unknowable length of time, during which Daddy made fitful mewling noises and breathed like a smithy's bellows, they reached an opening. Sarah could feel the wash of moving air, the different reflection of sound.

"We must be in some kind of big chamber," she said.

"You think this is where they're going to eat us?" asked Bili.

Sarah blinked rapidly in the darkness. "What are you talking about?"

"Well, why else would they drag us down here?" asked Bili reasonably. "These things are just like the bone-cutter ants down in the jungles around Bauru. They dig tunnels, attack everything that moves, carry food back to the nest on their backs."

Sarah could think of nothing to say. The boy was probably right.

After crossing the great chamber, which took long enough to convince Sarah that it was truly huge, they reentered a smaller side tunnel again. Soon they became aware of a growing glow of light from down the tunnel. Sarah raised her head and saw the dim outline of her son, crouching on the next animal up ahead.

The column stopped, and they were unceremoniously tossed into a shaft that branched off from the tunnel. Inside was a small, low chamber, perhaps thirty feet deep, six feet wide and three feet high. The room contained several people, in the midst of whom sat a tiny, portable glow-lamp, which was the source of the illumination.

They turned to look back at the beast of burden and were just in time to scramble out of the way as the massive form of Daddy rolled into the cramped chamber. At the entrance, one of the carrying types levered a heavy thickness of some kind of transparent material into the opening. Another type that they hadn't seen before, a small spidery creature with many eyes and appendages, squirted a substance around the border of the transparent material, sealing them in.

"Let me introduce myself," said a resonant, half-familiar voice behind her. "I'm—."

Sarah and Bili had turned around to face the speaker. They all three froze.

It was ex-Governor Rodney Zimmerman.

Before she knew what she was doing, Sarah had punched him in the face. His head jerked up, striking the roof of the low chamber. She followed up with a kick to the belly that probably hurt her sore body as much as it did Rodney, but the effect was gratifying. He rolled on the tunnel floor, groaning and trying to get away from her.

"Restrain her!" he shouted to the others, his nose bubbling blood. "She's a murderess, she and the brat. Killed a whole farming family and—Ow!"

Bili had produced a rock from somewhere and bounced it off the ex-Governor's tender nose. "The aliens got that family, you bastard!" shouted Bili. "The same way they got us now."

Muttering something about treason, Rodney withdrew to the rear of the chamber and squatted there.

Sarah and Bili pulled back from the rest of them, which was almost impossible in the cramped chamber. She did her best to avoid both Daddy and the ex-Governor. The other miserable-looking people in the chamber made no threatening moves against them.

Sarah, head still pounding, curled herself protectively around Bili, as she hadn't done since the accident when he had lost his arm. She watched the others closely. There were eight people in the chamber, including themselves, Daddy, Rodney Zimmerman and four others. She turned her attention to the ones she didn't know. There were two women, a little girl and a tall thin man with a pallid face and long limp hair that was so blond it was almost white. She noted the red streak across his face and knew him to be a skald, a member of a peculiar religious sect of Garmish origin.

The skald looked particularly distressed by his captivity. His body was frequently racked with spasms of twisting motion,

199

seemingly without purpose. His eyes were haunting holes of blackness. The others were doing their best to avoid him.

"I'm Sarah and this is my son, Bili," Sarah said experimentally, addressing the women. The women and the little girl huddled together, making no attempt to reply. They did turn their eyes on her, however, and the darkness she saw in them made her wonder what horrors they might have witnessed.

Sarah assumed they were related to one another. They were squat and strong-bodied New Manchurians, with the look of the land about them. Sarah was reminded of the farmer's wife, Sasha. A cloud passed over her face and she shivered in the sweaty cell, thinking about the bloody mess the aliens had left behind after attacking the farm. Could Sasha and Timmy still be alive down here somewhere? The thought cheered her a bit, although she didn't know why, given the grim situation.

Bili soon had had enough of her mothering and pulled away from her embrace, moving to the entrance. He circumnavigated Daddy and inspected the seal the aliens had made.

"It's like safety-glass," he said over his shoulder to Sarah. "Like inches-thick safety-glass."

Sarah joined him. "It's some kind of transparent resin. A polymer, I would imagine. It's quite amazing that they can secrete it from their bodies."

"It was only that special little one that could do it. The big table-like types just put the door into place."

Sarah pressed against the surface experimentally. It was as hard as rock, as unforgiving as iron.

"Well, I hope they don't let us suffocate down here."

Bili then raised his fist and pulled it back to pound on the surface.

"NO!" screeched someone behind them.

They turned to see the skald racing toward them on all fours, his thin arms and legs pumping like a scuttling crab running from the surf. Sarah almost screamed herself as she caught sight of his face. It was an image of extreme insanity. The mouth hung lax; spittle flew from the quivering lower lip. Odd croaking noises bubbled up from his throat. The eyes were the worst: two wild staring glints of blue inside a stripe of livid red skin.

Sarah pulled Bili back, away from the sealed entrance. She put her hand out to stop the skald in case he attacked them.

Seeing them move away from the entrance, his charge faltered, slowed, stopped. Aimlessly, he wandered to the nearest section of wall and propped himself against it. He slumped forward, resuming the same posture he taken before.

"Jeez," said Bili, frowning fiercely at the skald. "He's nutso."

Sarah only nodded, moving to a new spot from which she could watch everyone in the chamber and the entrance, too. It was clear to her now that these people had been stressed to their limits. They had stepped past the thin veneer of civilization and become barbarians. In the case of the skald, it seemed to have gone as far as insanity.

Time passed. She had almost dozed off when she realized that Bili had left her side to go exploring again. He was leaning over the prone bloated figure of Daddy and the sight of him, so near to those deadly hands that had strangled her just hours before, brought her instantly awake. She stiffened, but didn't want to just start screaming at him, in case the man was really asleep and not just laying for him, for her baby. She rose up into a cat-like crouch.

Bili noticed she was awake and crawled back to her. With intense relief, she gripped his shoulders. "Don't ever go near that man again, Bili," she whispered fiercely.

"Awe, come on, Mom. He's out cold. I think he's poisoned, too. One of those killer things cut off his some of his fingers, you know. I think they must have venom on their blades or something. He's sweating real bad and he stinks."

Sarah looked Bili over briefly, then looked toward Daddy's dark bulk. "Stay right here."

With infinite caution, she crept to where she could see his face. He did indeed resemble a victim of poisoning. He breathed in shallow gasps, his body was bathed in sweat and his arm was red and swollen. The stumps of his fingers had stopped bleeding, but were discolored and raw-looking.

"I think you're right. Still, you must promise me that you'll go no closer to him."

Bili nodded and promised.

A few more minutes passed during which the Asian women began to weep for some reason, speaking quietly among themselves.

201

"What have you all seen? Why have these monsters imprisoned us?" Sarah finally asked the group aloud, tired of moping in this dark hole. She was feeling better now and thoughts of escape were running through her mind.

It was Rodney Zimmerman who came forward to answer. He approached them warily, but smiled insipidly the entire time. Sarah was reminded strongly of a reptile. The stench of his clothes—she thought that he must have befouled himself—added to the image.

"You haven't been to the throne room then?" he asked, his eyes shifting from her to Bili and then back to her. He gazed frankly at her breasts, which were only partially covered due to her struggles with Mudface and Daddy.

Self-consciously, she shifted her clothing, but it did no good. Bili came to the rescue by placing his head back against her chest. She was grateful. Together they glared at the Governor of Garm. "We just got here, Zimmerman."

"Ah, please, call me Rodney," he said with a leer. "Then you haven't witnessed one of their feasts, yet?"

"No."

"They're quite a spectacle," he said, a shadow passing over him. He was silent for a few seconds, then coughed wetly. "They, the aliens, that is, have a big queen-mother alien. A whole group of them, actually. They seem to be the ones who lay the eggs, or whatever."

"Go on," said Sarah, intrigued despite her disgust with the source of information. She felt a desperate need to know what was going to happen to them.

"The trick to survival is to go unnoticed. I have been to the feasts three times, and still I return to my cell, unnoticed. Our fat smuggling friend over there," he nodded toward Daddy's limp form, "is currently my greatest hope. They seem to have an affinity for the fat ones, you see."

They followed his gaze. Sarah tried to find pity in her heart for Daddy, but couldn't. "So that's why all these people are cracking up. They've all been to a—feast?"

"Correct."

"Is that all they like, the fat ones?" asked Bili with hope in his dark eyes.

"No, they seem to like the young as well," he said with a

wicked smile, "and the females."

Bili seemed to shrink. "You're second in the fatso contest, you know," he said defiantly. Then he turned up to Sarah. "We got to get out of here, Mom."

"You really are a prick," Sarah told Rodney. "First you hand us over to killers, then you work hard to scare a little boy."

"Ah, please excuse me. My trips to the feasts have been very stressful. And as to the presumption of your guilt, all I can say is that I made a mistake. I thought you were murderers, you see. So when those wretched smugglers threatened to kill a lot of good people to capture you, well... I guess I made the wrong assumption," he gave her a winning smile that didn't quite cut through his greasy stench. She didn't believe him, but somehow just the possibility that it was all a mistake made her feel more trusting. After all, why would he lie now?

"So, how do we get out of here?"

As if he had been waiting for those exact words, Rodney came alive. "Now we are thinking along the same lines. I have a flitter, out in the forest not far from here."

Sarah narrowed her eyes. "How do you know where we are?"

"It has taken me some time to piece together our position from various sources, but after interviewing a lot of cellmates, I feel confident I know what part of the Polar Range we are under. What helped is that I keep a hunting lodge not far from here. That's where the flitter is stored."

"But where, exactly?"

A calculating expression came over his face. "Can you pilot a flitter?"

"Yes, of course."

"Of course," he echoed, smiling, wrapping his thin white arms around his knees and rocking back. "I've waited what seems like an eternity to hear those words. You are the first qualified pilot I've come across in three trips to the feasting room! I suspected it, of course, as you are a smuggler."

"So your plan is to break out somehow and get to the flitter and escape, right? Can you tell me where it is? How far it might be? I know these mountains well, I've flown over them a hundred times."

Rodney looked back at her with a crafty glint in his eye. "Ah,

203

but why would you take your worst enemy along with you on a jaunt into the wild blue? No, no, the location must remain a secret for now."

Try as she might, she could get no more out of him. She quickly began to see what kind of man he was and began to despise him even more deeply, now that he was familiar to her, than she had before when he had only been a cruel stranger.

* * *

Inside the dark, unknowable workings of Garth and Fryx's joint mind things had taken a turn for the worst. The stress of actually being captured by the Imperium and, horror of horrors, held prisoner inside an enemy nest, was simply too much for Fryx. His great age and natural reclusiveness didn't provide the mental structure he needed to face his worst nightmare.

Garth was caught in the middle. An insane thing was locked in his mind, threats no longer coerced it, and reasoning was pointless. It was all he could do to keep from attacking the other captives around him.

When the scuttling sound began again in the tunnels above them, only the faintest vibration came through to Garth's back and buttocks. He had placed himself completely against the resonant surface of the nest for precisely that reason, to be forewarned. His body rose up, twisting sinuously of its own accord, writhing like a headless snake in flames.

Fryx was frenzied, the enemy were returning, another feast had begun. Forcing his body to move in an organized fashion through sheer force of will, Garth crept toward the others.

* * *

Sarah shrank back from the bizarre skald's approach. He seemed to be forming a single word with his lips, straining mightily to get it out.

"Feast—" he slurred.

Sarah's blood went cold. Everyone in the cell fell quiet, even Daddy's gasps and warblings seemed to subside.

Then they could all hear it, feel it—the approach of churning feet on the nest floor.

"We must form a plan!" hissed Sarah to the others. "We must fight."

Rodney shook his head and snorted.

"We must do something!"

Rodney's shook his head more vigorously. "No. You must listen to me, you must trust me on this one point for I need you alive. You must not attract their attention in any way. To do so is usually fatal."

"Well at least it would be a clean death," retorted Sarah. She felt helpless and scared.

"What would your boy do then, eh? Do you want him to die alone down here? In the dark?"

"Bastard," she spat out.

The aliens had reached the opening by then and they removed the seal by squirting some kind of solvent around the edges, dissolving the earlier secretions. The humans, huddling, moaning, were dragged out and placed on the backs of the waiting transport creatures. Daddy was grabbed up first, and it seemed to Sarah there was some eagerness in the aliens that handled him. The thin skald fought them spastically, but was easily overpowered. The three Asians were spared for some reason, left behind on their own.

Soon they were moving through the black tunnels again to be dropped into a black pit in the midst of what felt like a very large chamber.

"It's always the same," Rodney hissed in her ear. She jumped, not having realized he was there. "We sit here in the dark, listen to them grunt and smack themselves, then finally they choose their first course and tentacles come down out of the blackness. Then comes the worst: listening to them feed."

"How have you survived three times?" she demanded, trying not to move, not to be noticed.

"Come with me, I have discovered an alcove that conceals most of my body from view. However their senses work, they seem to find me unpalatable in that position."

He took her hand and she almost jerked it back before controlling herself. She felt like she had been bitten.

Suddenly, new ghastly alien sounds erupted from above them.

205

Wet slappings, blatting noises, sudden warbling gasps. Sarah and Bili clutched at one another, trembling.

* * *

"A Tulk discovered amongst the food creatures?" gasped the Parent. "Do you have any idea how serious this is?" Her tentacles curled protectively around her foodtube in a gesture of fright.

"Well, I would suggest that we interrogate one of the food creatures," said the nife.

"Interrogate? How?"

"The bio-computers now have a thorough understanding of their sonic vibration-based speech patterns. If you could be troubled to grow a sound-producing organ for one of them, we could easily communicate," suggested the nife. The Parent noted that his orbs were riding very high indeed today. She suspected that he was after something special, perhaps he would even attempt to excite her enough to allow a second melding.

"A Tulk amongst our food-creatures," she repeated, still stunned by this monstrous concept. "The most hated enemy of the Imperium. How could we be so unfortunate? Are the food-creatures in league with them? Could it be that all of them are so infested? It's enough to make one retch."

"No, no. I doubt there are too many around, we would have discovered them before. Fortunately, we captured the creature alive. Now all we need to do is coerce a food-creature into communicating with it."

"So the food-creatures are telepathic?"

"The capability is latent in certain individuals."

"If they are telepaths, then I believe the presence of a Tulk in their brain-encasements could greatly enhance this capacity. Perhaps we could actually interrogate a Tulk, not just their slaves."

"A rare event indeed. Worthy, perhaps, of great rewards?" commented the nife. Nonchalantly, he eased nearer to her throne. For once the Parent tolerated his brash, overconfident manner. She even allowed him to caress her tentacle-tips.

"We will interrogate the food-creatures as you suggest," she said. "I will grow an appropriate organ, it will only take a few moments to construct the genes. We have a new set of food-creatures in the dish now. We shall interrogate and devour them presently."

* * *

"I don't understand it," said Rodney, his voice worried. "They always begin feasting by now. Why else would they have brought us here?"

Sarah shared his concern. If the aliens were deviating from their normal behavior on this occasion, what other deviations might occur? "Should we try to jump out of the pit?"

Rodney snorted softly. "It's been tried, believe me. One of my own bodyguards, the last to survive, tried it the first time I was in this pit. I decided—I mean he decided to do it, over my objections, of course."

"Of course."

"Anyway, he made it to the lip, about ten feet up. I heard him move around up there for about three seconds, then he dropped back down."

"Was he all right?"

"He was headless."

Sarah half expected Bili to say 'neato', but for once he didn't.

They waited there in the dark for a considerable length of time. Then, to everyone's surprise, a voice began to speak in the chamber above them.

"The food will answer the questions," it announced in a distorted warble. The phlegmatic voice rasped unevenly, like the voice of an old man with a cold.

None of them moved or spoke.

"Respond."

"What do you want?" asked Sarah. Rodney gripped her shoulder, pulling her back, but she shrugged him off.

"The food will answer the questions, or the food will be devoured immediately."

"Okay, I'll answer anything you want," said Sarah. She stepped out into the center of the pit, looking up into nothingness. Behind her, Rodney hissed in exasperation.

"Identify the specimen above the pit."

"I can't see anything."

There was a period of silence. Soon, the chamber was lit by a wan glow.

"Identify the specimen above the pit or a killbeast will damage you."

Sarah and the others were too busy gaping to even look at the specimen above the pit. All around them were hideous aliens. Pacing around the circumference of the pit was a creature with long stalks that appeared to contain his optical organs. The deadly soldier-types ringed the pit a pace or two back from the edge. Sarah immediately assumed that they were the killbeasts that the voice had been referring to. Further back, almost out of their sight, were huge dark shapes. Some of them had a single massive horn in the center of their heads while others appeared to be the digging types like the one she had first encountered. More grotesque than any was the bloated thing that perched on a chair or throne of some kind near the pit. The throne was built up of crude brown resins lumped together into an organic shape. Several more thrones were in the room, but they were empty.

Directly above them was suspended a transparent globe containing what resembled a small dollop of grayish jelly.

"Identify the specimen above the pit," the voice repeated. Sarah could locate it now. It came from a one of a cluster of tick-like things growing out of the roof of the nest. One of them had a mouth on it like a fleshy conch shell.

"Will you let us go if we can tell you what it is?" asked Sarah.

Rodney made a wordless hiss of warning. Sarah thought she saw the one with the eyestalks make a signal of some kind, but if there were any communications, they were silent. With amazing speed one of the killbeast guards leapt into the pit. Before the humans could do more than cower, the killbeast kicked at Sarah's head in a sweeping arc. The alien turned the blade flat at the last instant, knocking her to the floor rather than decapitating her. With easy grace it bounded back out of the pit.

"Food is not permitted to question the Parent or her offspring," warbled the translating conch shell.

Sarah climbed back to her feet, rubbing the back of her head and trying to moan softly. Bili came to her and embraced her.

Sarah waved the others forward. Rodney only huddled closer to the wall in his alcove while the skald merely ignored them. Odd tremors coursed through his body at random intervals. Daddy remained flat on his back in delirium.

"Help me look at this thing!" Sarah whispered to Rodney. "They might eat us if we don't identify it. It looks like some kind of sea creature."

Finally, Rodney shuffled forward. He held his hands curled to his chest and peered up into the gloom. "Some kind of jellyfish."

"We think it's some kind of jellyfish. A sea creature," answered Sarah loudly. "But we aren't sure."

There was a moment of silence while the leader aliens seemed to digest and discuss this.

"Food doesn't recognize the Tulk? They don't ride in your brain-encasements?"

For some reason the skald chose that moment to jerk spasmodically and topple to the floor of the pit. It seemed as if he was having some kind of fit.

Sarah looked at Rodney, baffled by the questions and the skald's behavior.

"It means our heads, we carry our brains in our skulls," he hissed back. He eyed his alcove longingly and rubbed his fingers together.

"No, they don't ride in our heads," Sarah said. "We don't know what a Tulk is."

This seemed to set off a debate, during which the smaller alien with the eyestalks marched up and down before the throne of the bigger one. There were many gestures, but few audible sounds other than occasional blatting noises, reminiscent of the calls of air-swimmers during mating season.

Finally, a decision was obviously reached. The smaller alien marched off out of sight, seemingly agitated. Then two killbeasts jumped down into the pit and tried to haul Daddy out of it. They had to get help from two trachs and another killbeast before they had him out.

Then began a most horrid feasting. Sarah held her hands over Bili's ears and turned his face to the wall of the pit, but that only left her ears open to the ghastly sounds. The Parent, which had to be the monstrous thing on the throne, ate Daddy by tearing him into little strips with her fast-working crab-like mandibles and sucking them up with a tube-like orifice. The ripping of flesh and the sucking noises filled the air.

Daddy regained consciousness briefly during the process. The other aliens easily constrained his thrashing. His desperate hoarse screams echoed through the nest. It seemed to Sarah that the Parent quivered a bit more excitedly as her food fought her.

When there was little left but exposed bone, the Parent sent more killbeasts into the pit. Rodney shoved Garth toward them and tried to wedge himself between Sarah and the wall of the pit. This did no good however, as he was taken next.

"How can it still be hungry?" asked Bili. He buried his face in her side, not expecting an answer.

"Stop them!" Rodney shouted down to Sarah as he was carried like a babe in the arms of a killbeast. "Stop them or your chances of survival are nil!"

"Tell me where the ship is! I can stop them!" Sarah shouted back.

The killbeasts ignored his ripping and biting at their tough bodies and pinned him in front of the towering mass of flesh on the throne. Sarah opened her mouth, deciding to try to save Rodney despite of his crimes and his deviousness, but before she could speak he was crying out the location of the secreted flitter.

"It's in the boatyard on Lake Axalp, on the south shore—" he broke off, shrieking as a pair of pincers sliced into his legs. "Do something!"

"I lied!" shouted Sarah, cupping her hands to direct the sound to the translating conch shell on the roof of the chamber. "I know what the specimen is. I've see the Tulk before."

There was no response for several seconds. Rodney continued screaming as a strip of his flesh was sucked down the Parent's foodtube.

Suddenly, the feast halted.

Sarah looked up expectantly, but the conch shell didn't speak. Instead, the majority of the killbeasts stiffened, as though they were receiving silent instructions, then raced off into the tunnels. The larger, horned shapes to the rear of the chamber stirred and trundled forward to surround the Parent in a protective ring of flesh. Rodney was rolled back into the pit where he lay in a heap, moaning.

"What's going on, Mom?" asked Bili.

Then she felt it. A tremor in the nest, then another. Soon, she heard it, and a few crumbling scraps of earth fell from the distant ceiling to dribble down on their heads.

Suddenly, the roof shook and sprayed them with loose earth. Several of the tick-like things fell into the pit with them, including the one with the conch shell mouth. They broke open and splattered them all with soupy flesh.

"Looks like brains, Mom," commented Bili as they scrambled for the alcove.

Sarah was only mildly surprised to find both Rodney and the skald had beaten her into the alcove. The four of them squeezed together; it was a tight fit.

"The nest is under attack," said Rodney fearfully.

Sarah nodded. "It's probably Stormbringers out of Fort Rodney. I hope they blow these aliens apart."

Then the light went out and there was no point in talking as the ear-splitting explosions began in earnest.

* * *

"This graphic clearly shows the location of the nest," said Mai Lee, pointing to the colorful mass of moving points of light that hovered over the holo-plate. "I've instructed the battle computers to display enemy movements by locating their radio emissions. You can see here that the central globe of the nest is buried between two peaks, in effect straddling the pass between Grunstein and the Slipape Counties. The larger of the two peaks is where you will land and set up your artillery, Zimmerman."

"How much resistance will we face?" asked Zimmerman, studying the graphic intently and rubbing his jowls.

"You can see for yourself that there are relatively few contacts up there, it's only a small outpost at most. You will land there, destroy any resistance, and begin firing on the nest immediately," boomed Mai Lee. The imposing head of her battlesuit swung to regard him.

"And what will you be doing?" asked young Zeel Zimmerman,

his face pinched in suspicion.

"While you bombard the nest, we will broadcast noise on the preferred alien communications frequencies. They will be under a heavy surprise attack with their communications jammed. Their command control will break down. We will wait for the nest to be breached. When the breach is wide enough, you will stop the bombardment while I will lead my troops into the nest and exterminate the queen."

Zimmerman's face took on an expression of great surprise. Even Zeel looked impressed. "You mean you personally will fight the aliens in their own nest?"

The battlesuit seemed to stand a bit more erect. "Correct."

The Zimmerman command walked out of the dome, muttering among themselves. They didn't like the plan, if only because Mai Lee had suggested it, but they couldn't come up with a better one.

After they had left and mounted their lifters to lead the assault on the peak, Mai Lee returned to the graphic she had just displayed. She pressed a key and the battlecomputer instantly displayed an altered image. A tight mass of tiny lights appeared, buried beneath the peak she had sent the Zimmermans to. A long conduit of lights led from the mass beneath the peak back to the central mass of the nest.

Inside her encasement of steel and collapsium, she chuckled.

The battle began exactly as planned. Smoothly, the blue-clad Zimmerman knights swooped down on the peak and brushed away the few killbeasts that were stationed there, tossing their blasted corpses from the cliffs. The weaponeers unlimbered their heaviest equipment and sighted on the innocent-looking patch of forest that covered the nest site. The first barrage ripped through the still air, sang for a moment, then broke apart into a hundred thunderclaps. Horkwoods a thousand years old split apart and disintegrated.

Simultaneously, the parabolic radio dishes mounted on her lifters focused on the nest and began broadcasting. She imagined the turmoil inside the fortress of her enemies and wriggled a bit in pleasure.

The bombardment and the jamming continued for several minutes when the nest was finally breached. The upper galleries vanished; the aliens caught near the surface were vaporized. Mai Lee ground her teeth, considering using the one or two tactical nukes she had hoarded and hidden from Nexus inspections for so long. In the end she forbear, they were too much like her own children—in fact, she considered them even more useful and dear. Spending them in this battle when more conventional weaponry could do the job seemed frivolous.

A twisting cloud of culus squadrons rose up from the blasted nest like a swarm of enraged bees. With alarming speed they flew to attack the source of the jamming, directly at Mai Lee's lifters. Gouts of plasma and long lines of tracer slugs leapt out to meet them. She ordered her lifter to beat a spiraling retreat. She didn't withdraw, but rather lengthened the time the enemy must suffer under her guns before closing.

Even while the culus horde approached, there was a slowdown in the bombardment. The firing slowed, became sporadic. Zimmerman called in a state of great distress.

"We must pull out!" he shouted at her, red-faced and sweating profusely. "There is a tunnel network beneath this peak. Aliens are sprouting out of the ground like fungus."

"You will hold your position at all costs," snapped Mai Lee, cutting off the connection abruptly. She wheeled the battlesuit and strode out onto the deck of her command lifter. The time for action had come.

With intense personal satisfaction, she called the commander of her helicopter gunships and ordered them to destroy the Zimmerman lifters.

She watched the graphics over the holo-plate tensely as the helicopters roared to the attack. Caught completely by surprise from behind, the Zimmerman lifters were blasted to fragments before they could get airborne. Only a few of the weaponeers even managed to return fire.

Mai Lee had been concerned that a few of the Zimmerman weaponeers would turn their artillery on her lifters, but she realized now that her fears had been groundless. Realizing that they were now trapped on the mountain peak, the Zimmermans fought a desperate struggle against the seemingly infinite number of aliens that now boiled from beneath the trees and boulders. They had no concern but for their survival. The fighting was hand to hand and to the death.

Before she could really savor the sweetness of having finally

213

ridded herself of an ancient enemy, the culus squadrons were among her lifters. Although greatly reduced in numbers, they still managed to wreak havoc, dropping shrades among the troops, slashing open weaker human flesh and crushing men inside their own armor. The pilot of one of the lifters was stricken by a shrade and the lifter sagged down into the forests. A great explosion shook the deck beneath Mai Lee's feet.

Soon, however, the attackers had been destroyed and with triumph Mai Lee's forces moved to assault the nest. Lifters set down in the cratered forestland, disgorging hundreds of heavy troopers in full battlegear. Mai Lee marched with them, but had the caution to hold back, entering the smoking hole only after the bulk of her forces had cleared the way. Her heavy metal claws sank into piles of blasted alien corpses.

* * *

The throne-chamber, located at the deepest point of the nest, was built to last. The upper galleries and tunnel networks were forced open like cracked mollusk-shells under the bombardment, but the roof of the throne-chamber held. Sixteen layers of complex polymers (incredibly long molecules built from chains of simple molecules) buckled and sagged downward, but didn't break. Thousands of pounds of explosives were spent in a few minutes. The hests had done their work well.

"Mom?" croaked Bili, his voice a gasp. He coughed up grit and inhaled more.

Sarah was lying on his chest, but at first she didn't hear him, and she didn't know he was there. The explosions had stopped, but in her head they rang on and on, with a sickening repetitiveness.

She simply rested her head on her son's hitching chest, aware only of the pressure and the texture of his dirty shirt. He put his arms around her neck awkwardly and hugged her.

She tried to raise her head, but a great weight pressed her back down. Shooting pains ran down her side. She stopped moving. Better.

Her movement elicited a reaction from Bili. He stopped hugging her and leaned forward, shouting something in her ear. "I

214

thought you were dead, Mom."

They rested for a time, their senses slowly returning.

Pain returned with her senses. Sarah found her voice after several minutes. "Bili, what's on top of me?"

There was a pause while she felt Bili's hand reaching above her, probing in the blackness. "An alien. A dead killbeast, I think. I'll try to get it off."

There was a pause, then a wrenching pain from her back. A great weight shifted, rolled away. "I got lucky," Bili shouted into her ear. "The damned thing shifted easy."

Sarah found she could move now, although movement wasn't without its cost in pain. She reached down and felt around with her right hand. Bruised, tender flesh met her probing fingers. She reached out with her left hand and bones grated in her wrist. She loosed a rasping scream. Fire ran up her arm. Clearly, her wrist was broken.

"What's wrong, Mom?"

"Bili, help me up," Sarah said, reaching for her son. Together, they managed to get her into a sitting position without causing more damage to her wrist. Bili rubbed blood back into his legs, which had been under her body and that of the killbeast's.

Suddenly, something came up and softly touched them both. A delicate hand brushed her cheek.

"Who is it?" whispered Bili.

Sarah reached out blind with her good hand and caught a handful of long fine hair. "The skald."

"The nutso?"

The skald moved away from them, then returned. He touched each of their cheeks in turn and moved away again.

"He wants us to follow him," said Sarah.

"Jeez, Mom. I don't know about this guy."

For some reason, she felt she could trust the skald to help them get out. He certainly didn't want to stay here, of that she was convinced. "Maybe he can help us get out. I may not be able to go far without help, Bili."

Grabbing hold of the skald's fluttering hand with her good one, she was quickly hauled erect and together they began climbing a shifting pile of rubble and bodies. The side of the pit had collapsed, allowing them to escape. She was surprised at the strength in the skald's wiry limbs. She leaned on him heavily.

Just as they reached the lip of the pit, they stumbled over Zimmerman. He was crawling on his belly, making his way out of the pit by inching along. His voice was bubbly, as though he spoke through a mouthful of blood. "Take me with you, or you'll never find the flitter."

"I know exactly where Lake Axalp is," Sarah told him coldly. It felt wonderful to be free of the man's controlling hand for once. "You have no hold over us."

"Wrong." he bubbled. He stopped, breaking off into a coughing fit.

"Come on, Mom. Let's get out of here before the aliens notice us," urged Bili.

Sarah hesitated. She nudged Zimmerman with her foot. "What do you mean, wrong?"

"I... I lied," he said, "only I know where the flitter really is."

Twenty

After many hours of vicious fighting in the black treacherous tunnels of the nest, Mai Lee's forces reached the throne room. Inside the battlesuit, she was sweating profusely, despite the continuous gush of cool air coming from the overtaxed air conditioning system. The suit was finally overheating due to the continuous one hundred and ten percent output she had demanded unrelentingly from the reactors. Her haggard eyes, dark with exhaustion, had pressed against the vision scopes until livid welts had almost swollen them shut. Salty perspiration burned her swollen tongue.

"This is it. This has to be it, we're at the bottom," she said, striding over a morass of stiffening corpses. The twisted form of a multi-legged hest entangled one of the suit's claws. Irritably, she shook it loose and flung it onto one of the empty thrones. She eyed the thrones disappointedly.

"Where are the queens? Are you sure there are no deeper levels?" she demanded of a nearby Captain.

The man shook his head, backing away from her in fear.

Her chest-guns tracked him on automatic, and she pondered the trigger lever with a sneer. Then she sighed. Another corpse would do little to help her now. Her troopers had been devastated in any case.

The situation was painfully clear. She had spent her strength against the nest in hopes of killing their queens and thereby breaking the back of her enemy. But the queens had vanished,

217

probably fleeing into deep escape shafts, the entrances buried and carefully hidden. She had broken her own back, not theirs. She had lost all but a few companies of troopers.

The aliens had won.

Rage and frustration took hold of her fully. With a booming roar of intense fury, she drove the battlesuit in great crashing bounds toward the four thrones. She opened fire on the largest of them, letting fly a blue gush of flame as she neared it. Chips and splinters of the throne exploded around the great chamber. Echoing reports rang from the walls with deafening volume. Under the fierce heat of the Gi's breath, the throne liquefied and ran like wax.

Bounding like a grasshopper, she pounced upon the largest of the thrones like a wolf leaping upon the back of its lumbering prey. Using the titanium claws, she ripped dark molten chunks of resin from it.

Then she saw the entrance to the larvae room. Pale squirming shapes turned their tubular eating orifices in her direction curiously. Inside her suit, a savage grin split her features. Clearly, the queens hadn't managed to save all their children.

Without hesitation, she strode into the nursery and commenced a most gruesome slaughter. Humping about in mindless panic, the larvae were blasted to fragments, withered by searing flames and ripped apart with merciless metal claws.

When it was over, she had regained some degree of calm. Exiting the nursery, she ordered her remaining troopers back to the lifters.

On the surface she was surprised to see it was dark, the sky lit only by the lurid glare of the smoky fires that still burned among the horkwoods. The condition of the lifters was another shock. During her absence shrades that had been deposited aboard the lifters during the suicidal attacks of the culus squadrons had burst from hiding and taken a grim toll. Most of the pilots and crews were dead. Many of the lifters were badly damaged and inoperable. She led her weary army onto those that were in the best repair and managed to get all her remaining forces airborne. A few squads of battered helicopter gunships joined them as an escort.

On her way into Grunstein, she paused only to circle around the peak where the Zimmermans had made their last stand. She was gratified to see nothing move other than the blue cloaks of dead men, stirred by the ceaseless mountain winds. The entire crown of the mountain was choked with bodies. The blackened muzzles of the artillery pieces pointed at the skies, like the sightless eyes of the dead.

She put the battlesuit into standby mode, letting the engines idle. The external vents opened, puffing out moist hot air and sucking in the fresh thin air of the night.

She smiled again to herself. She had lost this chance for victory, but her enemies had suffered greatly as well. Indeed, the Zimmermans had paid the ultimate price of obstructing her path.

"How should I set our course, Empress?" inquired the wing commander politely.

The chest guns snapped to target him, still on automatic. He stiffened, his ingratiating smile fading.

"We fly to the Grunstein Interplanetary Spaceport," answered Mai Lee. "It is time that we left Garm."

* * *

"I think he's getting heavier somehow," grumbled Bili, struggling to keep his corner of Zimmerman's makeshift stretcher aloft with his one good arm.

Sarah, taxed beyond making a reply, concentrated solely on putting her right foot ahead of her left. They progressed with agonizing slowness. Behind them walked the tall silent form of the skald, holding up the rear of the stretcher. She wondered what they would have done without his strange but strong presence.

Irritatingly, Zimmerman was awake and talkative, although reputedly unable to walk. "It's not much further now. If there's any way we can all pick up the pace here, our odds of surviving the night would be greatly increased."

Sarah halted. The others bumped to a stop. Her limbs trembled with exertion and anger. Turning her head, she glared down into Zimmerman's face. "We would all make a lot better time if we dropped you right here."

"Ah, but that wouldn't be prudent," said Zimmerman with a knowing smile. With an expression of sudden alarm, he raised up his head and peered into the dark forest that surrounded them.

219

"What was that?"

"What?" asked Bili, looking concerned. He eyed the forest with the distrust he had gained ever since seeing the digging alien after the crash.

"Could that have been a landshark?" asked Zimmerman. "They prowl this area all the time you know."

Sarah watched this fear-provoking performance with dull awe. How could the man be so relentlessly selfish and manipulative?

She leaned close, hissing into his face. "Knock it off or so help me, I'll drop you right here and you can crawl out. We may not make it, but you'll be dead for sure."

Zimmerman gasped and took on a look of great pain. He raised a hand weakly and closed his eyes. "Wait a moment, the hole that monster punched into my thigh is causing another spasm."

Sarah just glared at him, unimpressed even if his pain was real.

"Look now, everyone. I'm very sorry to be such a burden. I really regret every bite of excess food I've ever indulged in right now, believe me. But if we can pull together, if we can stick it out, we'll all survive."

"Save it," grunted Sarah, grimly taking a new grip on the pole and stumbling forward into the dark trees.

Zimmerman wisely fell silent for a time. Trudging forward, exhausted and injured, Sarah thought that this march had to be the worst experience of her life. Not for the first time, she reflected that the luck of her family had gone bad at the point of her husband's accident. It was as if she were in a deep well of bad luck, where she and Bili spiraled ever downward until now it seemed that the light at the top of the shaft had all but vanished entirely.

Utilizing reserves she didn't know she possessed, she eventually reached the outcropping of rocks that Zimmerman had said to keep an eye out for. At that point, he directed them to proceed downhill into a steep gully. The sides of the gully were wet and slick with moss. They almost lost hold of Zimmerman and pitched him squalling onto the rocks before reaching the bottom.

"Over there, under the tangle-bush. There should be a cave mouth," hissed Zimmerman, hushed now that their goal was so near. There was a genuine, feverish excitement in his voice.

They set down the stretcher and Sarah went forward to

investigate. Using a hand-held glow-lamp they had taken from a fallen trooper on the way out of the nest, she examined the walls of the gully closely. After a time she discovered the entrance.

"There's no way a flitter could fit inside that hole," she said, returning to Zimmerman. She directed the glow-lamp, set at its highest setting, into his sweating, dirty face.

He squinted and waved at the light in irritation. "Just take me inside. I'll show you."

Grudgingly, she obliged. Inside, the cave was quite a bit larger than it appeared. Although she saw no immediate signs of the flitter, she did see numerous familiar-looking bales of bluish reeds. Along one wall were stacked a dozen barrels of bluish dust.

"These barrels are full of blur dust. This is a smuggler's cache," she said, blinking in surprise.

"Of course. But fortunately, the former owners are beyond caring about this particular cache."

"How do you know that?"

"This was Mudface and Daddy's property," he explained, hauling himself into a sitting position. "Recall the feast."

Sarah shuddered. "I'd rather not."

"Didn't I tell you it was here?" demanded Zimmerman, beaming and looking for credit.

Bili gave him a wry glance. "Just tell us where the flitter is, fatso."

He waved his hand at the stack of barrels. "Look back there."

They did and found the flitter. It was a smaller model than Sarah had hoped for. It could hold six passengers in a pinch, four comfortably. She eyed the refined blur dust speculatively, licking her cracked lips. Any one of the barrels would bring a fortune on another system. She shook her head, as if to clear it. She was done with that kind of business. It had brought her nothing but trouble.

She noticed that the skald was eyeing the flitter curiously, running his pale thin hands over the stubby wings and the silvery landing skids.

Directly above the flitter was a camouflaged hole that leaked starlight. It would be a simple matter to leave the cave, except for one thing. "Where's the card-key, Zimmerman?" she demanded.

"Isn't it in the slot?" asked Zimmerman, smiling.

"No."

"Carry me into the flitter and I'll tell you where it is."

Sarah made no move. She glared at him. "You tell us now, or we leave you here for the killbeasts to sniff out."

"I don't want you to be tempted to leave me behind."

"I've never been more tempted to do anything in my life, but you will tell me now, before I carry your sorry ass another foot. I can hot-key a flitter, you know. As you continually point out, I am a smuggler."

Zimmerman looked concerned. "It would take longer."

Sarah only shrugged. Behind her, the skald had boarded the flitter and now sat quietly in the back.

Zimmerman chewed his lips and eyed her speculatively. "All right," he sighed at last. "The codekey is in the flare kit, attached to the back of the hatch."

Sarah snorted at the obviousness of the hiding place and went to retrieve the key. She stood there in the hatchway, looking back toward Zimmerman where he lay on the floor, still on the makeshift stretcher. He was doing his best to look pitiful. She moved to wave the skald forward to help carry Zimmerman again, when a heavy cough sounded outside the cave mouth.

"Landshark," hissed Bili, grabbing her arm and trying to pull her into the flitter. Sarah's mouth sagged. It must have tracked them, stalking them while they moved through the forests and following their spoor down into the gully. Wildly, she thought of the story of the boy who cried wolf once too often.

She stepped out of the hatchway, moving to help him, but she was too late. The landshark was already thrusting its snout into the cave mouth. A great bulbous head appeared, blocking the entrance almost entirely. Powerful forelimbs with six-inch curved claws made for digging followed.

"Let's go, Mom!" shouted Bili.

Zimmerman, terrified as deeply as he had been during the feasting, found the strength to struggle erect. Trembling with the effort to lift his bulk on one thin leg, he determinedly began to hop toward them, dragging his injured leg behind him. The landshark caught up with him in a sudden lunge, just as he reached the barrels full of blur dust. They went over with a crash, firing great clouds of bluish dust into the air.

In horror, Sarah slammed the hatch shut before the dust could reach them. There was no hope for Zimmerman now. Breathing in that much blur dust at once was definitely fatal. A few grains of the hallucinogen could keep you high for hours. Breathing in gouts of it was deadly. She doubted if even the landshark would survive.

With a great gulping motion, the landshark sucked the man into its toothy maw, making jerking motions as his legs vanished into its head.

Demonstrating its initial effects, the blur dust gave Zimmerman a sudden rush of inhuman vigor. Although he was already mortally wounded, he beat at the head of the monster with wild fury. Savage blows rained around its eyes and the sensitive olfactory regions, making it wince. Sarah thought that Zimmerman was probably breaking the bones in his hands, but he kept on striking it, even as his life's blood gushed out.

Then she managed to shove the codekey into the slot and hit the throttle for emergency lift. The flitter shot out of the shaft and into the open night air.

After a few minutes she managed to steady the wobbling craft and set a course for Grunstein Interplanetary.

Beneath them the treetops swept by with blinding speed. She hugged as close to the leafy canopy as she dared, hoping to avoid detection. None of them spoke about what they had left behind in the smuggler's cave.

* * *

Long after midnight, Drick was awake and back at his old desk. To his delight, he found his portable holoset and his flask of blur distillate were still there, although more than half of the moonshine had leaked out. The holoset was a disappointment as well, as all the net stations were out except for the automated ones that showed only the most dull comic reruns at this time of night. Not surprisingly, KXUT hadn't been heard from since the building had been bombed.

The vaporous distillate had lost none of its flavor however, and with a heavy contented sigh, Drick loosened his sash and leaned back in his self-contouring chair. Suddenly, he sat up with a brilliant idea. Keying in his account codes, he accessed the public net and coaxed the computers into providing him with a private viewing of last week's rayball game. He had been interrupted with the invasion at that point and had missed it. Damn the price, what did a few credits matter now?

He sipped his distillate and heaved another sigh as the holoset flickered, bringing the correct image up. Hot numbness washed over his mouth and took the edge off his tension. He had been tense for days now, he realized.

Bauru took an early lead in the game, scoring two goals from the third tier in the first period. The Dragon defense was hard-pressed to hold them, and when the Dragons finally got the puck, it took several minutes into the second period before they managed their first goal. Although his team was losing, Drick was happy. For the first time in a week he was comfortable and relaxed. He took another heavy slug of the drug, knowing it was too much, but wanting to do it anyway.

When the security plate glowed into life, it displayed what had to be the most unwelcome sight Drick had ever seen. It was a mechanical nightmare, a draconian battlesuit of some kind with a mouth that glowed with an unnatural blue radiance.

"Gi?" he questioned out loud, recalling vague memories of the thing from his great Aunt's estates. The distillate had dulled his wits. He took another drink, and was surprised to discover he had drained the flask. He was alarmed just a bit, realizing that he had taken too much, but then the feeling of alarm faded as the drug fell over him like a veil.

"I am bringing my army to the spaceport," she told him, her voice oddly disembodied from the alien image on the holo-plate.

"What do you want here, Gi?" asked Drick, his voice slurring slightly. He glanced down at the flat flask, but it was still sadly empty. With a studied concentration, he worked to replace the stopper. It seemed a difficult task.

"I'm not Gi, you idiot! I'm Mai Lee!" she boomed in irritation.

Drick squinted at the wavering holo-plate. He realized with a dull lack of concern that his vision had faded somewhat, a clear sign of a heavy blur dose. "Oh yes. How are you doing, Auntie?"

Mai Lee made a sound of infinite frustration. "Listen to me carefully, my drunken, imbecilic nephew. Tell me where Droad is."

"The Governor?"

"Yes," Mai Lee hissed through her teeth.

"He's at the fort."

"All right, good. I am bringing in several lifters and helicopter gunships. You must drop the security nets on the western side of the complex so that we can come in over the trees without detection."

Drick blinked at her in incomprehension. At length, she managed to get her message across. Accustomed to obeying his Aunt and almost beyond resistance in any case, he gave the appropriate orders to the handful of men who Droad had left in charge of the spaceport.

Having finished, he managed to key-off the pause button on his holoset and settled back to watch the remainder of the rayball game. The roar of arriving lifters and the heavy tramp of armored feet outside his office did little to interest him. It was the final period, and the Dragons had finally regained their fighting spirit. With two quick goals, they could still win the game. Drick was hardly able to make out the tiny figures on the holoset, his eyes were tearing up so badly. Streams of drying tears were cold on his cheeks.

There was a pounding on the door. He didn't respond until it crashed inward. A fantastic creature ducked its head as it entered. The tail twitched with the whining of servos, balancing the metal monster on top of the shattered door.

Behind the creature there was the flash and boom of gunfire. Men screamed and died. Drick struggled to grasp what was happening, but found it difficult to think.

"Follow me to the elevator."

Drick blinked dazedly. "Where are we going, Auntie?"

Mai Lee snorted. "To the *Gladius*, you moron. The clan is leaving this world. Will you attend me?"

Drick struggled to his feet. His thigh hit the corner of his desk, the flask and the holoset clattering to the floor. "Could you help me?"

Mai Lee looked at him for a moment, metal tail twitching. "You disgust me. If you can't make it to the elevator by yourself, you are best left behind."

Her claws left heavy scars in the broken door. Drick was left to

225

struggle to his feet alone. Feeling only the vaguest sense of urgency, Drick found the holoset with his groping hands. He reactivated it, relieved to find it still worked. For a time he forgot completely about Mai Lee, and sat on the floor, watching the end of the rayball game.

An unknowable time later he awoke to discover he was staring at a blank plate. Only a ghostly green nimbus shimmered over the set, the holo equivalent of static.

The intercom was beeping. That was what had finally sunk in. With infinite slowness and a mild feeling of annoyance, he answered the call.

"Major Lee?" said a voice. An image of a man's face stared out at him, but Drick couldn't make out who it was.

"Droad?" he guessed.

"Listen very carefully, Major Lee. You have to shut down the elevators immediately. The lifters coming in now aren't manned by Mai Lee's troopers, Jarmo tells me they are alien forces. They mustn't be allowed to board the *Gladius*."

"What?"

"Shut down the elevator, man! That is an order!" Droad boomed at him.

"Everyone's yelling tonight," muttered Drick. "I'm in charge of this installation, Droad. This is my post. I will not halt the elevator while my Auntie is using it." He sneered at Droad's wavering likeness in suspicion. The man thought he was God.

Droad fumed for a moment, then continued in a slow, gentle voice. "Listen, you must listen. The aliens are coming right in on you, I can't raise anyone else at the spaceport, and you've got to keep them from getting to the *Gladius*."

The man's kind demeanor didn't fool Drick. He was clearly just trying to get him into trouble with his Auntie. Drick was having none of it.

"You've got no authority with me, no matter what the identity computers say," said Drick, waving his empty flask at the image. He swung the flask at Droad, wacking the air where the holo shimmered. He stabbed the cut-off button and stood up. He almost fell again, but managed to keep up, pin wheeling his arms and staggering. He worked his way across his office, then pitched headlong over something in the doorway. His teeth cut into his lips

226

and blood ran down his chin. He felt about, more than half-blinded, discovering that he was lying on the smashed door. He lay there for a considerable time trying to gather his wits. Behind him the intercom beeped incessantly.

Then there was a crash down the hall, followed by the heavy thump of running feet. He tried to raise his head, gave up, set it back down again.

A dark shape ran by. Several more followed it. There was an odd stink in the air. Then there was another presence, coming up behind him. He struggled to turn his head. He felt the light touch of something rubbery and wet, probing against his back. He managed to turn his head to face it.

There was a shrade sitting on his back, staring at him. A quivering set of mandibles tasted his blood. A dozen sets of stubby legs suddenly stiffened, became sharp, stabbed into his flesh. Fiery pain raced through his dulled nervous system. The constriction began and his ribs crackled. Breathing became impossible. He struggled in silent, vague horror, unable to believe until the very end that what was happening to him was real.

* * *

"They're all aliens? You're sure?" asked Droad. He continued to stir his hot caf and blow into it, but it had long since grown cold.

"Absolutely. Not one of those flitters or escorting gunships is manned. They're all heading right in on the spaceport, dropping the troops and heading back to the forests for more. The radio emissions system I rigged up to detect the enemy is lit up like a star cluster," said Jarmo, his eyes never leaving his graphic projections. "We can't let any more of them get to the *Gladius*, sir. I believe the orbital station is already compromised."

Droad glanced at him and nodded. He looked out of Fort Zimmerman's north tower window toward the spaceport. Shooting up into the cloud layer was the ever-present shaft of shimmering metal that represented so much effort on the part of the colonists. Halfway up to the clouds, a large flock of air-swimmers serenely floated around it in a spiral pattern.

The elevator was Garm's greatest link to space, to the Nexus, and to the rest of humanity. By itself, it represented a great achievement of human technology, and was doubtless the most significant positive thing the people of Garm had ever created.

"Have we secured all the flitters capable of reaching orbit?"

"Yes sir, they have all been moved from the spaceport into the Fort compound. Others exist, however, around the colony."

"Tell Dorman to hit the elevator with his Stormbringers, but not to overdo it. He must at least break the shaft up until it is unserviceable," said Droad in a dull voice. He was uncharacteristically glum. His eyes were dark with fatigue and his face white and drawn. His first governorship was fast turning into one of the greatest disasters in human history. Even if the enemy could be stopped, the damage to the colony would take more than his lifetime to repair.

Jarmo relayed the orders and the two watched as the Stormbringers streaked to the attack. The planes themselves were invisible due to their great speed, of course, but the atmospheric conditions were right for contrails today, and so their progress could be tracked by the eye. Enemy aircraft rose up like angry wasps to meet them, but the shaft was really an indefensible target. Crimson explosions blossomed about the base of the shaft. The spaceport was quickly reduced to burning ruins.

"Now, we must decide our next move," said Droad. He tasted his hot caf, found it to be cold caf, and poured himself a fresh cup. He reflected that the sole thing he had enjoyed about this post so far was the excellent beverages that the tropical climate of Garm produced.

Jarmo sat back. "I would estimate that a fairly large number of the enemy has gotten aboard the *Gladius*. Mai Lee led the remains of her personal army up there as well, but I believe she will be sorely outnumbered."

"Even with the security forces on the ship?"

Jarmo made a wry face. "According to the mech Lieutenant's report, they are less than adequate to fight the aliens."

"So you recommend that we go to the aid of the *Gladius*? Or are you suggesting that we get aboard that ship and save our skins?"

Jarmo frowned, leaned forward. His serious eyes engaged the Governor. "Sir, I think it's time we faced certain realities. We are losing this war. It is clear that the aliens reproduce new warriors at a rate that we can't counter. We had the upper hand at first—"

Here Governor Droad interrupted with a snort. It did not seem to him that they had ever had the upper hand.

"—due to our superior numbers and firepower. However, the enemy have continued to grow in strength, coming back after each battle with greater forces. This is not just our experience, but from all the reports I have monitored around the planet."

"And while they grow stronger and use equipment captured from us, we have no more troops once we are fully mobilized."

"Yes, exactly. You see, if their numbers were to stop increasing right now, we could probably handle them. But of course, they will not. My calculations indicate that their numbers will double again in the next six days, even accounting for casualties."

"But if we can just get to the source of their reproduction, to their queens, we could stop them," argued Droad.

Jarmo nodded his huge head, but the frown didn't leave his face. "This is exactly what Mai Lee was attempting, and a good strategy it was. But according to the data I have gathered about the enemy movements, it's almost pointless. The alien numbers are now growing at several points around the planet, indicating they have many queens, and that they are breeding more even now."

The Governor put his hands behind his head and leaned back in his chair. He placed his heavy boots on the holo-plate and crossed his legs. Tipping his hat over his eyes, he thought hard. He always found thinking easier in a relaxed position.

"And there is another thing," Jarmo said.

"What?"

"Our supplies of ordinance and equipment are already dwindling."

Droad tipped the brim of his hat up to eye him.

"The main way we are keeping the aliens from overrunning us now is with greater firepower. But Garm has never planned for a long term conflict. The armories are well-stocked, but once the missiles are gone for the Stormbringers, for instance, there will be no more. Once we are down to hand-to-hand conditions, there can be no doubt which side will win."

Droad seemed to deflate somewhat. "You are telling me that

we are doomed. That we can't win."

Jarmo made no answer.

"Let's examine the options. Nuclear weapons?"

"Very few available. Even with the NCC proscription against them, there are a few on the planet, but all of tactical-level yield. Those that do exist are mostly hidden somewhere out of our reach on the Slipape County estates."

"Evacuation?"

"The *Gladius* is the only ship capable of carrying a large percentage of the colonists. Unfortunately, evacuation will take time, weeks at least, and I doubt the aliens will allow us that."

"All right, so what are they going to do?"

"I believe they will make an all out effort to take the *Gladius*. I believe they will leave the system at the first opportunity and carry their seeds to the rest of the Nexus."

Droad snapped up out of his chair. It fell back behind him with a clatter. He and Jarmo locked stares. The system operators around them, having listened in, watched them both intently.

"You're right," said Droad. He hadn't thought of the possible stakes involved. It was crystal clear to him now. These things were a threat to the entire Nexus, not just to Garm. "We have to move now."

Jarmo gave him a questioning look.

"We must take all our forces up to the *Gladius*."

As they turned to leave the observation room a messenger approached. It was the Hofstetten militia captain, the same one that had confronted Ari Steinbach and Major Drick Lee just before the assault at the spaceport. His red beard was frosty with flecks of melting snow.

"There's someone here to see you, Governor. She just flew a flitter into the compound and landed right in the courtyard. We almost blasted her out of the air."

"What does she want?" asked Droad hurriedly, pulling on his parka and donning a weapons harness. Jarmo busied himself with his plasma cannon, which he had stowed under the desk.

"She says she's been inside the alien nest, and she has important information about the enemy."

Droad waved for him to follow and Jarmo fell into step behind them. Jarmo watched the militia captain closely.

"She'll have to talk to me on the way up. She can ride up on my flitter. Get your men ready for an assault Captain. We leave in thirty minutes."

* * *

Jarmo and Droad rode in the forward cabin. Through the observation ports was a scene filled with gray clouds, as the nose was pointed upward at a steep angle. To their left was the silvery shaft of the space elevator, reaching up into the heavens like Jack's beanstalk.

Droad stopped talking strategy and turned to meet the tall, dark-haired woman who entered the cabin. He noted right away that she was an attractive woman, despite the fact that her face was streaked with scratches and her hair was a tangled maze. Her jumpersuit was fresh and clean, however, taken from Fort Zimmerman's ample supply rooms. Her eyes caught his full attention, they were quite shapely, but also haunted with dark visions at which he could only guess. Immediately, he believed her story of having escaped the alien nest.

"Come in and strap yourself into a crash-seat," he invited.

Behind her, two more figures came into the cabin. Everyone braced themselves against the acceleration of the flitter. At Droad's urging, all three of them sank gratefully into the crash-seats. Droad was surprised to see one of the others was a boy of perhaps twelve and the other was a skald. The absence of a left arm on the boy was his most noticeable feature, in addition to the fact that he was clearly related to the woman. They both had the same dark eyes and hair.

The skald was a different matter entirely. Droad had read about them, but had yet to encounter a member of their sect, which was the oddest religion on Garm. They were really a cult, a very mysterious one. According to his readings they were thought to focus their lives on achieving inner peace through meditation and wandering pilgrimages, but little hard data had ever been collected on them. It was known that they valued artwork, music and solitude. Sculptures created by the skalds of Garm were known and sought after throughout the Nexus, being one of the planet's more

231

successful exports.

In appearance the skald differed noticeably from the rest of them. He was tall and thin with long blond hair, so blond it was almost white. His sharp features and vacant, staring eyes made Droad wonder if he was the product of in-breeding or some other, more mysterious influence.

As they strapped themselves into their crash seats, Droad nodded to each of the visitors, as did Jarmo. The skald didn't respond, didn't even look at them. He merely stared out the observation reports at the metal shaft that led up into space.

"Hello, let me introduce myself," began Droad, smiling with real warmth. This was the first time he had the opportunity to meet some of the people of Garm who were neither military nor trying to kill him. "I'm Lucas Droad and this is my chief of staff, Jarmo Niska."

Sarah responded politely, eyeing the giant with unease. Pleasantries lasted only a few seconds, however, before the skald interrupted.

"Parent." he began. Everyone looked startled to hear him speak. He stared at Droad now with manic intensity. White flecks of spittle speckled his chin. His lips squirmed in an unnatural fashion, as if unaccustomed to speech. He stopped talking after this single word and appeared to have some kind of fit. He began thrashing violently in his seat, straining against the straps he himself had fastened over his thin pale body.

Droad pushed his hat back upon his head and watched the display with interest. Jarmo produced a pistol with a long black barrel from somewhere and directed it casually at the skald.

"What's with him?" asked Droad conversationally.

Bili answered him, speaking for the first time. "He's nutso. He's seen too many of the alien feasts."

"Feasts?" questioned Droad. He leaned forward and scrutinized the three. What could it have been like to be captured by aliens?

Sarah explained. By the time she had finished, the skald had lapsed into his previous, somnolent state.

"As far as we know, your experiences are unique, Sarah. We have had no other reports from anyone in close contact with the aliens, other than in battle. Your information could be useful, but you'll have to give it to me fast," said Droad. He turned to Jarmo,

232

whose pistol had disappeared to wherever it had come from. "How long until we hit the docking portals?"

"ETA twelve minutes."

Droad turned back to Sarah expectantly, and she began her story. The words came out of her in a torrent, making them ring truer to Droad. She began with her smuggling trip down, leaving out nothing, and ending with the death of Governor Zimmerman and their escape in the flitter. While she related her smuggling efforts, Droad and Jarmo exchanged amused glances. Here she was, confessing to a Nexus-level crime to the highest officers of law on the planet. She seemed blithely unaware of this facet, and as her story continued and became more and more an epic of horror and persecution, Droad could well understand why. He made no mention of her illegal occupation.

Droad steepled his hands and looked saddened. "I must personally apologize for the corrupt behavior of my predecessor. He brought a great deal of dishonor to my office. I find it difficult to grieve for him."

Bili snorted. "Good riddance. The bastard deserved it."

"Quite," agreed Droad.

Jarmo's phone beeped and he opened the link. He spoke loudly, his deep bass voice rumbling about the cabin like distant thunder. "We're leaving the Stormbringers behind in the atmospheric envelope. We're safe from enemy attack now until we reach the orbital station. I'm organizing the assault into thirds, sir. We'll hit all the open docking portals at once."

"Good. Let's just hope the ship's blast-doors are still open," said Droad. He turned back to the skald, who was now rocking himself, humming a soft melody. He frowned. "He did appear to be trying to tell us something. What was it he said? Parent?"

"Perhaps he meant one of the aliens. One of the ones we were questioned by, the big ones that did most of the—feasting. I believe the translating thing called it a Parent," said Sarah.

"One of their queens?" asked Droad.

"Yes."

Before they could continue a sudden lurch in the flitter's flight path indicated they were closing on the orbital station. They settled back in their seats while high-gee maneuvers were made. The flitter braked harshly, pressing them deep into the padding. Outside

233

the clouds were long since gone. They had been replaced by the blackness of space and the blazing glare of Garm's sun. Pinpoints of light marked the stars. Below was the wide blue-white disk of Garm.

Sarah became nervous. She wrapped both arms around her chest and squeezed. She put head back against the headrest and clenched her eyes tightly.

Droad watched in sympathy. "I can see that you have no desire to face the aliens again. If you like, you could stay with the flitters."

Sarah shook her head. Even though her hair was unkempt, Droad could not help but notice the pleasing way it fell about her face. "I'd feel better on the ship with you," she said. "The only safety from these things is having a gun in your hand."

Twenty-One

Everything went smoothly until they got to the orbital station. Beneath the massive shadow of the *Gladius*, the orbiter crouched like a beetle hugging the boots of a giant. The *Gladius* itself was a wonder to behold. Glowing modules rotated slowly about the central torus seemingly disconnected from it due to a trick of light and shadow. It grew as they approached until it filled the observation port, overflowed it, expanded to devour everything they could see. The tiny orbiter turned from a beetle into something the size of a large building. Open docking bays yawned to meet them.

"Sir, the *Gladius* is heating the power coils of its laser batteries."

Sarah looked alarmed. "I thought they weren't armed."

"The ship isn't a battlewagon, but they have enough armament to destroy flitters," said Jarmo.

"Do something before they fry us," Sarah hissed at Droad.

"Increase our velocity," ordered Droad. "Come in under full thrust."

Jarmo barked into his communicator. The flitter shook and lurched. Power rumbled through the deck. In the endless night around them the other flitters emitted tongues of flame.

Without warning, the flitter immediately ahead of them gushed violet light from the cockpit area, broke into two burning halves, exploded in a rush of silent heat.

The lurching and weaving of the flitter increased as the pilot mech jinked hard from side to side, presenting a more difficult target.

"There'll only be a few seconds before..." began Sarah, she trailed off as another invisible, stabbing laser beam incinerated a flitter at the edge of their formation.

"Let's pull out. Let's run," said Droad.

"No," said Jarmo, shaking his great head.

"He's right, we can't run now," added Sarah. Droad turned to regard her, feeling out of his element. Space battles were beyond his experience. "We're too late now," she explained. "They waited until we were right on top of them so that we couldn't run. The only thing to do is to try to close in and board."

"Transmit our identity codes to the ship," ordered Droad. "Perhaps they think we're aliens."

"We've been doing that since we launched, sir," replied Jarmo.

Another strike came out of the blackness. There was a reflection this time that came in through the viewport. A blinding radiance lit up the cabin for an instant, Droad swore he could see the bones of his hand like an x-ray image. Everyone was left blinking at after-images, purple blotches on their retinas. Somewhere behind them another flitter tore apart. Heated gases burnt out quickly; the hot bubbling flesh of the troops was transformed instantly into frozen foam by the void.

Then they reached the docking bays. Flitters crowded one another into the open doors like hungry air-swimmers jostling over a fruit-laden branch. Even as they reached the mouth of their designated bay, they noted that the doors were sliding shut.

"We aren't going to make it," said Bili with remarkable calm.

"We'll make it," Droad assured him. He wiped a droplet of sweat from his temple.

Seconds later, as they made their final approach, it became clear that they would make it, barring another laser attack. But at the final moment, just before they reached the yawning docking doors, there was a gut-wrenching burst of thrust. The flitter swerved off course and roared away from Garm and the orbiter, toward the imposing bulk of the *Gladius*. More flashbulb explosions came from behind them.

"What the hell's going on?" demanded Droad.

Jarmo was staring at his communicator in perplexity. "I'm out

236

of communication with the other flitters. The last report I received indicated that the orbiter itself was under laser attack."

"Well, get them back," snarled Droad.

"But why didn't we enter the docking bay?" asked Bili.

"Ask the pilot!" said Sarah. She busied herself fixing a vacuum-proof survival-bubble around herself. She handed another of the plastic bags to Bili, who worked it over his body with a grim professionalism that belied his years.

The flitter was now so close to the *Gladius* that they could have suited up and walked out. They braked hard and maneuvered between the stalks that led out from the central torus to the modules. The endless black expanse that was the hull of the central torus rushed to greet them.

"The pilot mech isn't answering the intercom," Jarmo informed them. He snapped off his harness and sped up the aisle between the seats, moving hand over hand between the plastic loops placed there for zero-gee travel. The door slid open and the pilot mech was visible from the rear.

Before Jarmo could enter the cockpit, however, the ship lurched violently again, braking and diving directly at the dark hull of the *Gladius*. Sarah gasped and Bili groaned aloud. When it seemed that impact was imminent, the observation ports suddenly blacked out entirely.

"We're inside one of the big airlocks," said Sarah in a hushed voice.

Soon, the flitter was brought to a rest on its skids. The centrifugal gravity of the *Gladius* took over and they felt the familiar pressure of weight again on their limbs. Sounds came through the walls of the flitter now that there was air to carry them. They heard the clanging of the air pumps, the grinding sounds of huge machinery in motion.

They rushed to the cockpit door, but the mech lieutenant beat them to the airlock. Jarmo had his black-barreled pistol out again, this time leveled on the mech's sensory array. While they confronted one another, they barely noticed the thin form of the skald as he slipped past them and exited the flitter.

"Report, Lieutenant," demanded Droad.

The mech turned to them and made an ushering motion with his massive bio-mechanical gripper. "I suggest we evacuate the flitter immediately, Governor. Whomever was operating the laser must know we're down here."

"Where is *down here?*" demanded Sarah.

"We're in the hold. I repeat: we should evacuate the ship."

Behind them the militia troops were already pouring out of the main cabin exits and taking up positions amongst the towering boxes, cartons and drums. The Governor and the others quickly joined them. While they took cover, the mech Lieutenant made his report.

"I realized at the last instant, sir, that entering the orbiter would not save us. The enemy made the mistake of firing on the orbiter before all of us had entered. This, in effect, tipped their hand."

"Did you signal your intentions to any of the other mechs?"

"Yes, but only I reacted in time and made it to safety."

"What about the rest of my men?" blurted Droad. "What about the flitters that made it into the orbiter?"

"I'm sorry, sir. Of course, you could not have seen what happened to the orbiter from the forward cabin. It was destroyed."

Droad stood stock still for a moment. The militiamen, Sarah and Bili looked equally shocked. The skald reappeared and stood behind the mech Lieutenant, looking at no one.

"You mean they're all dead?"

"Yes, sir."

"This is all we've got left to retake the ship with?" asked Droad, waving his arm at the others. He knew it was a mistake to sound so defeatist in front of them, but he couldn't help it. "We don't even have a full company here."

"Correct, sir. Now, I suggest we get moving."

Droad nodded dully and they all trooped after the mech. He seemed to be undisturbed by the loss that had stunned the humans. Only the skald seemed similarly unaffected. Droad noted that he was keeping quite close to the mech. Under different circumstances, he might have found the skald's new found loyalties amusing.

"But why didn't the other mechs figure it out?" Bili piped up.

It took Droad a moment to realize the boy was addressing him. "Eh? Oh, well, this mech is an officer. His capacity for independent thinking and acting on his own initiative despite his orders is greater than the others."

"So he's the smartest one, huh?"

"Right," said Droad vaguely. He sought out Jarmo. "No contact?"

Jarmo shook his head. There was another of the giants next to him, Droad was pleased to note. It was Gunther. At least he hadn't lost all of them. For perhaps the first time in his life, Droad felt the despair of harsh defeat.

"Our situation is critical," said Jarmo.

"To say the least," agreed Droad.

"We must shift our tactics from those of an assaulting army to those of a survival-oriented guerilla group. We must husband what resources we have left. We must bide our time."

Droad heard little of it. He eyed Sarah and Bili thoughtfully. Although they were just civilians, they seemed adept at survival. Still, it had been terribly arrogant of him to bring them along on this attack. He had placed them in mortal danger. He had failed them.

"Sir?"

"Eh?" said Droad, realizing that the others were staring at him. There had been a question asked, and he had missed it entirely. A moment of hot embarrassment flashed over him. He shook himself, ordered himself sternly to retake the reins of command. He still was responsible for the survivors. He looked up and contrived to appear confident. He threw back his shoulders and adopted a serious expression.

"For all we know the laser attack was fired by the crew," he said, addressing the others. "Perhaps they thought we were more aliens. Despite all our identity transmissions, they never did answer us. Then again, perhaps the laser was set up for auto-defense and attacked us while the crew was busy."

Some of the men seemed to take heart at this suggestion. He could tell that they had assumed that the aliens were firing at them, meaning that the aliens were in control of the ship. Even the slim hope that there was some other explanation, that it was all an accident, uplifted their morale.

Jarmo waited until the men were out of earshot before pointing out a critical flaw in Droad's theory. "This seems unlikely, given that the laser destroyed the orbiter at a critical point."

"Yes. Hmm." Droad glanced about to see if the men were

239

listening. "This whole situation does look like a set up, a trap. Either the aliens or Mai Lee ambushed us, I'll wager."

Jarmo agreed.

For a time they followed the mech through the vast maze of the hold. He seemed familiar with every aspect of it. They encountered no one, except for a few dead security men. The mech explained that they had died trying to keep his mech platoon in this hold. Droad made a wry face at the twisted bodies, and the mood of the men dampened again. It seemed unlikely that the crew of the *Gladius* would warmly receive anyone allied with the mechs. Reaching one of the distant walls of the hold, they found a blasted-open portal that led into a service duct. Trotting in single file, faces slick with nervous sweat and speaking little, they entered the bowels of the ship.

As they climbed up further into the heart of the great vessel, the signs of combat increased. Bulkheads were sealed and had to be forced. Automated cannon were set to ambush anyone ascending the decks, these had to be disarmed or circumvented. Dead crewmen and dead aliens lay strewn about the darkened corridors. The metal floors were pooled with blood and other inhuman and less identifiable body fluids.

The central galleries were huge airy chambers that normally operated as open marketplaces. Now, instead of being thronged with traders the chambers were vast mausoleums: dark, silent and stinking of death.

It was when they had reached the central galleries of the ship that the skald attempted to talk with Droad.

Droad was resting with his head in his hands. His sides were heaving slightly from the harsh march through the ship. He looked over toward Sarah and Bili, who seemed more tired than the others did. He would give them another minute.

"Feasting..." said an odd, croaking voice. Droad looked up to discover the long pale face of the skald looking down at him. He had approached silently and without warning. Droad found his stealth and bizarre behavior disconcerting. He frowned.

"What do you want?"

"The lines of the feasting..." said the skald. His face worked with fantastic concentration. His hands rose up slowly from his sides, white palms exposed and spread flat. Large blue eyes

240

seemed almost luminous in the center of a floating nimbus of flaxen hair.

"I don't understand you. Are you trying to tell me something?" asked Droad. He leaned forward, eyes narrowing. His curiosity was engaged. Could this lunatic help him?

"You must follow the lines to the feasting," replied the skald with great sincerity. He nodded to Droad slowly and smiled with relief, as if he had succeeded at an amazing effort of communication and imparted great knowledge. Still smiling vaguely, he began to step slowly from side to side, then to shuffle about in a circle. He hummed tonelessly. Droad thought of a corpse performing a strange flat-footed waltz.

It was clear that the man was utterly insane. Droad sighed, reseating himself. Had he sunk so low that he looked for answers for his problems from the deranged? He put his face back into his hands for a moment's rest. Quietly, the skald shuffled away.

"We have a contact, sir," interrupted Jarmo.

Droad's head snapped up. He reached for the phone, careful not to touch the transmit button. It wouldn't do for anyone to pinpoint them. He listened only. Unnoticed, the skald's pallid form slipped away, heading toward the entrance of the aft duct system.

"Sounds like that witch of a senator, Mai Lee," he commented. "All she's doing is requesting my response. Can you get me video?"

Jarmo presented another handset with a tiny screen on it. In flat 2D a face flickered into existence. It was a metallic head of some kind. For a moment, Droad believed this to be some new and terrifying variety of alien as yet undiscovered. Then he realized it was the stylized helmet of a hi-tech battlesuit.

He pursed his lips and grimaced in annoyance. "Where did she get that thing? Clearly against all Nexus proscriptions. Not that I'm surprised."

Jarmo looked on impassively. Droad knew he was patiently waiting for him to make his decision. Communicating with the woman could mean a dangerous enemy would pinpoint their positions. Or it could be an opportunity for the last remaining human forces on the ship to rejoin.

Droad rubbed his chin and lips, eyeing the tiny metallic image with distrust. "Just a recording repeating the same message. Have

241

you pinpointed her?"

"Bridge section," replied Jarmo.

Droad smiled grimly. "So she did fire the laser."

"Fire control could have been diverted at either the redundant bridge or the manual controls at the laser turret itself."

Droad frowned. "We need information."

Jarmo was silent.

"If we make a short transmission, can we be out of here quickly enough to avoid attack?"

"I don't know the layout of the ship well enough to judge. Let's consult the Lieutenant."

Droad agreed. He smiled slightly, noting that Jarmo, unlike everyone else in the group, always referred to the mechs by their ranks, never just as 'the mech' as the rest of the humans tended to do. He wondered if his lack of labeling had to do with his own genetic specializations. Although much less of a freak than a mech, some of the same technology, and hence the same stigma from normal humans, applied to Jarmo.

"If we maneuver down two decks using the aft conduit system, then double back into the primary filtration units, it is very unlikely any search party would be able to locate us," the mech informed them.

"Ready the team, then. In one minute I want everybody on their feet and ready to bolt into the ducts again."

Jarmo jumped up and everyone hurried after him and the mech. When he had them in position for a fast get away and had trotted back to the Governor's position, Droad opened a channel to the bridge.

The connection was made and the face of Mai Lee's battlesuit flickered into view again. This time it was a profile shot, however. The video pickup was limited, but Droad made out movement behind her. Large men in full body-shell passed back and forth with a sense of urgency. The dragon's head of Mai Lee's suit swung back to face him. He noted the eerie blue radiance that emanated from the jagged metal mouth.

"What is your status, Senator?" asked Droad. He endeavored to sound light and unconcerned. "Can we be of assistance?"

"You live, Droad!" boomed the hideous dragon's head. "I suspected as much. You're as hard to kill as these filthy aliens."

Droad's voice hardened. "So you're behind the slaughter of my forces? Why would you ambush us when we're coming to aid in keeping the *Gladius* out of alien hands?"

Mai Lee laughed. The amplified sound was so loud that the receiver's speakers distorted it into a shrieking squawk of noise at Droad's end. He adjusted the tiny volume knob in annoyance.

"The ship is in my hands now, Droad. You are only another contender for control of the only means out of this doomed system," she said. Droad looked surprised, and she snorted derisively. "Don't try to pretend that the thought of escaping this hell-hole governorship of yours had never crossed your mind, stripling. I won't believe that."

She broke off and shouted behind her. There was a commotion out of range of the video pick-up. Droad turned up the volume again and studied the image of the bridge intently, trying to figure out what was going on. She turned back to Droad and her amplified voice again overloaded the tiny handset. Droad twisted the knob downward again, grimacing at the noise.

"—Just to let you know what's coming: The waste will be spilling down to your deck within minutes. You've given me long enough to pinpoint your location. You're too far from your flitter to make it back in time. This entire conversation, by the way, was just to make sure you would have no opportunity to escape the radiation—" here she broke off again. There was the sound of gunfire behind her on the bridge. The connection fizzled and was cut off abruptly.

Jarmo was on hand, jerking the Governor to his feet and hustling him toward the ducts. The others were already gone.

"You must run faster, sir," said Jarmo.

Droad's every hurried step was painful. "The injury to my leg still hasn't healed completely," he said apologetically.

Without a word, Jarmo swept him up in his massive arms. Feeling the thick hard surfaces of Jarmo's biceps against his side, Droad was thinking too desperately to feel the humiliation of being carried like a baby. Jarmo picked up his pace to that of an Olympic sprinter and they vanished into the dark hole of the aft duct system.

"They're going to dump waste from the reactors, trying to kill us and the aliens, I imagine. Has the mech figured out a place to run to?"

Jarmo grunted as he ducked through a tight bulkhead. The metal opening skimmed by Droad's head at a dangerous speed, but it didn't so much as brush his sleeve. The giant had grace as well as speed and power. "The Lieutenant monitored the entire conversation. He has already selected a destination."

"Could she be bluffing? How could she have attained the security codes required to control the *Gladius* in every detail so quickly?"

"A problem I've been working on for some time now, sir. The only answer is that she must have had the proper override key."

"Like the one that Steinbach used to switch off the spaceport security and operate the space elevator with?"

"Exactly, sir. In fact, I think it likely that she has Steinbach and his bootleg set of keys in her possession. Such a technological piece of wizardry as those keys would be unlikely to have been duplicated successfully by two separate groups. If this theory is correct, I can only further lament my failure in regards to Steinbach's escape. If I had been more attentive with Steinbach, she may never have gained control of the laser, and therefore many lives would have been spared."

"Don't take it so hard, Jarmo," said Droad. He smacked the giant's massive chest. "You're too quick to judge yourself a failure, and I won't have that. Your performance is mine to judge, and I say you have done exceedingly well. Besides, your theory about Steinbach's codekeys has yet to be proven."

"I see no other logical alternative."

"Nor do I," admitted Droad. He sighed.

The conversation lapsed as Jarmo saved his breath for running. Droad attempted unsuccessfully to sit back and enjoy the ride.

* * *

The last of Mai Lee's simians were making a good accounting of themselves, but the aliens were too many, too fast and too vicious. Killbeast and culus squadrons charged the men in their body-shells, forming a wall with their dying bodies as explosive bullets shredded them. Almost too late, Mai Lee realized that they were all dying at a particular distance, in a line that crossed the bridge area diagonally.

"PULL BACK! PULL BACK NOW!" she boomed. Startled, intent on killing their attackers, only half of her men responded in time. Without warning, a hundred killbeasts vaulted the wall of quivering dead and rushed their lines in unison. The attack was lightning fast, there wasn't enough time to mow them down before they reached close range. Half of her remaining company were pulled down screaming and hacked to death.

"STEINBACH!" she grated at the cowering figure that crouched over the control boards. "HAVE YOU RELEASED THE RADIATION?"

"The controls are damaged, Empress," Ari said, wincing as she strode up and prodded his spine with her chest guns.

"YOU DARE TO DISSEMBLE NOW?" she demanded, incredulous. Her lust to see his lifeblood sprayed over the controls grew to an almost irresistible level.

Ari waved pathetically at the control boards. Numerous gouges and burn marks did indeed scar the surface. "The gunfire has damaged the master terminals. I am trying to access the engineering controls through the weapons section, but the codes don't seem to match. Besides, isn't it dangerous to release the radiation now, while the aliens are on us? They could pin us down for sometime yet."

Inside her battlesuit, Mai Lee's jaw sagged. Could this cretin truly be stalling to save his own skin? Did he not fear her more than a few thousand rads of gamma radiation?

She wasn't given any more time to threaten Ari, however, as at that point, new combatants entered the fray. Taking advantage of the turmoil, larger, more ominous shapes entered the room. Vast humping shadows towered over the wall of dead. Inside her dented and scored battlesuit, Mai Lee felt a thrill of fear. She had not yet encountered the enemy's juggers. She reformed her remaining troops on the main dais that surrounded the operators' chairs. She mounted the Captain's chair, which afforded her a clear line of fire. Dead crewmen, still strapped into their crash-seats where she had had them executed at their posts, surrounded her. She gave no commands to her troops; there was no need. She leveled her chest cannons and awaited the inevitable charge.

One of the juggers rose up to her full height. Astoundingly tall and massive, the others rose up after her and with a great reverberating cry of doom they charged the humans. The last survivors of the previous wave, a struggling knot of men and killbeasts, vanished beneath hundreds of tons of clawed feet. Carapaces and body-shell armor caved in, the victims squirming like crushed crabs beneath the treads of armored vehicles. The clangor of their charge across the short span of metal decking was enough to set everyone's teeth to aching.

In unison the humans squeezed their triggers and held them there, emptying their magazines into the onrushing hordes. The monsters were too big and full of vigor to die easily. Ripped apart and dead on their feet, many took another dozen steps before falling among the humans, too stubborn to realize their own deaths.

Once among the humans, the juggers set to their work with deadly efficiency, resembling a pack of tyrannosaurs slaughtering a herd of lesser creatures. Huge claws crushed the humans down, massive heads dipped, jaws ripped loose limbs, heads, entire torsos. The top of the operator's dais became a sea of flesh, a scene of wild confusion. Mai Lee fired her chest guns and gushed out her deadly blue breath, melting men, armor and aliens alike indiscriminately.

For a time, she lost herself to the slaughter. There was no thought of retreat or coordinated action of any kind. She and her battlesuit worked as a single entity, a deadly creature of living metal. Although the juggers were twice her size, she attacked them savagely, leaping onto their backs, clinging with steel teeth and titanium claws, firing her chest guns point-blank until the magazines were empty and still letting them rattle dryly long after. She tried to open the reserve magazines, but could not. There was a fault of some kind. The pink, blinking service-required light made her curse fluidly in Chinese.

She quickly gave up on her guns and attacked the enemy directly. Although they loomed over her battlesuit, Mai Lee tackled and pulled down alien after alien, ripping out throats, searing their bodies with radiation, and opening their bellies with long strokes of her claws.

Finally, she realized that the attack was over. She raised the bloodied, dented muzzle of her suit, swiveled the head. Carnage surrounded her. Dozens of aliens lay thrashing upon a bed of body-

246

shell-enclosed humans. There was no one else standing, neither human nor alien.

She looked down. In the grips of her great claws was the carcass of a jugger. The throat was tore open, the head tossed back. In her bloodlusting state, she had used her suit to claw and chew a great deal of the flesh from the creature's soft throat area. A hint of exposed brain glinted up at her in the florescent lights of the bridge.

Breathing hard, she tried to regain her composure, tried to think. Could she truly be alone?

She strode among the squirming bodies, casually delivering deathblows to mortally wounded humans and aliens alike. Mentally, she thanked the wisdom she had had to have this suit built and maintained for so many years. The suit's right foreclaw seemed damaged, it hung limply at her side, and the reserve magazines were decidedly jammed, but still in all, the suit had performed superbly.

Using the suit's sensory apparatus, she attempted to find a useful survivor. The suit's computer beeped, and a yellow indicator directed her to the door of the captain's ready room. Inside, she discovered General Ari Steinbach, just as he was cautiously crawling out from beneath the conference table.

He jumped and backpedaled involuntarily at the sight of her grotesque, gore-drenched battlesuit.

"Ah, General," she said. She was in a good mood now. Even his obvious cowardice in battle didn't offend her in the slightest. A warm glow of contentment had settled in her guts. She hadn't felt so relaxed, so sated in a very long time indeed, if ever. "You have again demonstrated your cat-like powers of survival."

"I am pleased to see that you have done the same, Empress," replied Steinbach with all the sincerity he could muster.

She chuckled. "I'm quite sure you had hoped I would perish even as I killed the last of the aliens, but you have not been quite so lucky."

"What of your troops?"

She shook the battlesuit's head. Ari took another step back, the human gesture, effected by the gross apparition of the battlesuit, clearly unnerved him.

"They are all dead. I am the last champion to exit the field."

She twisted the suit, gazing back at the carnage that was the bridge. Within a few days, she thought idly, the stink would be amazing. She snapped her head back. Steinbach tensed and she enjoyed his animal fear.

"I need your help," she told him. She explained about the jammed reserve magazines, and instructed him on how to open the external loading hatch. He followed her instructions with delicate precision, doing his best to avoid contact with the coating of slimy gore that encased the suit. While he worked, Mai Lee rested, closing her eyes and reclining somewhat in the cramped quarters. She wished now she could meditate peacefully in her castle, free of the loathsome discomfort of the suit, but the very idea of getting out of it was inconceivable now.

Suddenly, she was awakened from her reverie by a surprised squawk from Steinbach. There was a wild, scrabbling sound, which carried up through the body of the suit. With a snap and a clang, Steinbach closed the hatch. He stood before her, staring at the hatch and panting. Mai Lee regarded him with instant suspicion.

"What's wrong?"

"Nothing," said Steinbach, blinking and swallowing. "I just... I just about screwed up."

"What do you mean?"

"The magazine started moving, but some of the rounds were loose. I could have blown my hands off."

Mai Lee snorted in disgust. "Your cowardice is boundless. Did you fix the problem?"

"I'm not sure."

Mai Lee brought up the diagnostic screen. She clucked her tongue. The magazine was still listed as jammed. Experimentally, she aimed at one of the juggers and depressed the firing studs. There was a brief whirring sound and the clattering of dry firing.

"You have failed," she said sourly. The chest guns leveled on his face.

"Perhaps if you try the inside hatch. I wasn't able to reach all the way inside. The jam appeared quite easy to remedy, if you would only give it a little push."

With a sound of frustration, she released her harness straps and twisted the proper hatch release a half-turn. Then she stopped. She

248

looked at Steinbach through slitted eyes. She noted the way that his hands were fluttering over the tool he had been using.

"You seem to be sweating more profusely than before, General."

A smile flickered over Steinbach's face. He tried to look unconcerned. "You're scrutiny is quite imposing, Empress."

She gave a growl of distrust. Her hand slipped away from the hatch release. "What did you do? Slip a bomb in there?"

Steinbach looked offended. "Of course not, Empress. Check your diagnostics. Any dangerous weaponry would trip a dozen alarms, I'm sure."

Still distrustful, she did as he suggested. The diagnostics only found some kind of obstruction. No explosive devices were detected.

"So why don't you want to do it?"

"Empress, I am no technician. A man could lose a finger in there, with all that moving machinery. It would be so easy for you to reach the obstruction."

"You really are a coward," she said, snorting. Not liking him too close, in case something did go wrong, she marched the suit out into an open area of the bridge, between the line of dead aliens and the corpse strewn operator area.

She loosened her straps again and took a firm hold of the hatch release. With her other hand, she grabbed the ejection lever. She experienced only a moment of indecision. She chided herself for exhibiting cowardice akin to Steinbach himself. Had she not just bested an army of savage aliens? What could be wrong? The whole thing was ridiculous. Steinbach was a whimpering cretin.

She twisted the hatch release another half-turn and it popped open. Coiled up inside was the skinny, half-starved shrade that had hidden there since it had taken refuge in the suit while it was under maintenance beneath the castle.

Mai Lee's eyes bulged. She attempted to close the hatch again. It was a testimony to the weak state of the shrade that it was even a contest. Only the berserk fear of death gave her a chance. But slowly, relentlessly, the hatch was forced open.

She remembered the ejection lever too late, the shrade already had a loop of flesh around her calf and was winding its way up her body quickly. She pulled the lever anyway and the head of the

249

battlesuit popped off, landing on the deck of the bridge with a loud clang. She struggled to get out of the suit, got her head and shoulders into open air, then halted and began a pitiful wailing.

The dark, snake-like shape of muscle enveloped her. The ghastly sounds of feeding began.

* * *

"The door goes on three," said Jarmo. He counted off. On three, he depressed the firing stud on his plasma cannon. It took several seconds, but the blast doors finally burnt away. Jumping through the orange glowing ring of metal, a dozen militiamen entered the bridge.

Jarmo and the mech Lieutenant stood marveling at the mounds of dead when the Governor, Sarah and Jun followed them inside. Sarah clapped her hands over Bili's eyes, telling him to wait in the hall.

"It's too late, Mom. I've seen it," he said in a dead voice.

Droad watched them, frowning. Sarah looked as if she might cry. And well she might, he felt like crying himself. The carnage was awful. Tangled bodies lay strewn everywhere.

In the center of it all was Mai Lee, dead eyes staring forth from the top of her gore-encrusted battlesuit. The shrade that enveloped her was dead as well. The group naturally gravitated toward her.

"This must have been a fantastic battle," said Droad. "But who won?"

"I'd say that we did," said Sarah. She pointed to the blood trail of claw prints that traced the battlesuit's progress to its final resting point in the middle of the chamber. "It looks like she was on her way to walk out, when she opened the suit to maybe get a breath and that shrade got her. She wouldn't have done that if we hadn't won the battle."

"We, huh?"

Sarah frowned. "When it comes to these aliens, I would even claim kinship to this witch."

Droad nodded. Despite himself, he was impressed by the dead old woman. "She was the most vicious and cunning human we had to pit against the aliens. Even though she embodied the worst of our tendencies, I have to admit that she did a good job on them."

A few moments later, Jarmo walked up to make his report upon examining the room. "The good news is that the radiation was never released. It appears that the aliens attacked before they could manage it. The bad news is that there are still hordes of aliens on this ship according to the computers. And, well, look at this, sir," said Jarmo, holding up a leather bag of some kind.

Droad examined it. "Isn't that Steinbach's satchel?" he said after a moment.

Jarmo nodded his head. His jaw was tight, his face grim.

"Any sign of Steinbach among the dead? Or of the codekeys?"

This time Jarmo shook his head.

Droad looked him in the eye. "I'd like to give you your second chance at Steinbach, Jarmo. But the Mech is better for solo duty. Lieutenant?"

Lieutenant Rem-9 reported instantly for duty.

"Go retrieve the General, please."

Moving with sudden, unnatural speed, the mech raised his plasma cannon and vanished through the cooling ring of melted metal that had been the blast doors. Droad looked after him, wondering if he had done the right thing. He trusted Jarmo's judgment more, but without Jarmo at his side, things wouldn't have felt right.

Twenty-Two

Rem-9 moved swiftly through a hatch, down a long ladder of steel tubing and through a low-ceilinged chamber into a service elevator. The elevator hummed vaguely while he descended. He knocked out the overhead lighting with his plasma cannon. Standing tensely in the dark, he held his plasma rifle ready, muzzle directed at the elevator doors.

There were three possible destinations for Steinbach. He would definitely move to a spot where he could use his codekeys in private. Somewhere that would afford him a considerable amount of power. That meant either the laser turret, the engineering deck or the redundant bridge. The redundant bridge was a less elegant, smaller and more functional version of the bridge, located in the center of the ship. In case of a ship board disaster, navigational control could be diverted to that location. The mech headed for the redundant bridge first.

The elevator halted and the doors slid open. A long corridor stretched seemingly into infinity ahead, going right to the center of the ship and the redundant bridge. The corridor was choked with bodies, mostly of unarmed crewmen. Clearly, the aliens had slaughtered them. Rem-9 wondered if any of the crew or passengers aboard were still alive. He doubted it.

As he stepped out, he felt a deep, throaty rumble from somewhere inside the ship. If he had been able to smile, he would have. The primary engines were being stoked. He had guessed correctly. Someone was working the controls in the redundant bridge.

The slideway was not functioning. Nimbly vaulting the bodies, he raced up the corridor. Reaching an intersection, he slowed and caught a fluttering movement out of the corner of his eye. The culus was too close for his plasma cannon, so he smoothly grabbed it and destroyed it with his clicking, partially-metallic hands. He threw the destroyed alien over his shoulder, where it smashed into the bulkhead behind him. It slid to the floor and began to quiver and bulge. The shrade inside burst out of its guts, hissing and spraying vicious liquids about the corridor. The mech had his plasma cannon targeted and turned the shrade into molten, bubbling flesh. Satisfied both aliens were no longer a threat, Rem-9 set off down the corridor again at a dead run.

It wouldn't be long now before more aliens were on him, the sentinel had had long enough to communicate with its comrades. As he ran, Rem-9 couldn't help but wonder if the redundant bridge was in the hands of the aliens, if he was racing into a trap. Could they have learned enough of human technology to operate the *Gladius*? He couldn't be sure, of course, but he would put nothing past them.

He slowed as the entrance came near and approached with extreme caution. The security doors yawned wide. He listened for a moment, hearing movement inside. Then mumbled cursing.

The mech lieutenant quickly identified the source of the sounds. He rounded the corner and advanced on the militia General. Steinbach was bent over a control board, inserting his codekeys into the slots beneath the board and fiddled with the controls. He moved with quick, fluttering motions that displayed his state of high tension. The mech noted the bodies of several multi-tentacled aliens on the floor, a variety that he had not previously encountered. He wondered if they could be technicians, as they didn't look to be effective combatants. Perhaps these were the types that had flown the Stormbringers against the human forces.

When Steinbach looked up, it was into the dark muzzle of a huge plasma cannon. He squeaked, staggered back.

"You are away from your assigned post," Rem-9 said.

A rapid series of emotions flickered across Steinbach's face. Shock, rage, frustration, then calculation and finally a welcoming smile. "Lieutenant! You have survived! Excellent!"

The mech stared at him with fixated optics.

"I couldn't know if anyone was left alive in the wake of these aliens. I'm glad you're here, I need your help and your guns to fend off the aliens that are sure to try to retake this bridge."

"What happened up on the main bridge?" asked Rem-9.

Steinbach's face fell. "It was awful. A fierce struggle. Hundreds dead on both sides. I was one of the few survivors, knocked out and left for dead beneath a pile of aliens and Mai Lee's simians. Not, mind you," he added hurriedly, "that I was in any way working with that witch and her band of renegades. But when humans face aliens, one must choose one's own kind to stand with."

The mech was not able to nod, his neck being constructed of rigid materials. But he was capable of sarcasm. "The way you stood with the rest down at the spaceport?"

Steinbach blanched, but quickly recovered. "Look, I panicked. It's one thing to stand shoulder to shoulder against a normal, human foe. It's quite another to hold before an onslaught of vicious, seemingly invincible aliens."

For a fraction of a moment, Rem-9 was almost taken in. "But you have not operated like a man in a panic, General," he said quietly, nudging Steinbach in the chest with the muzzle of his weapon. "You operate like a man with a plan."

"I didn't say I lost my mind entirely," complained Steinbach, waving for him to remove his offending weapon. Rem-9 didn't budge. "Besides, all that is history now. All that matters is that we take over the ship and get rid of these damned aliens. I can be very useful there."

"Yes, the codekeys," said Rem-9, nodding to the slots at the base of the control boards.

Steinbach appeared startled. "Ah, yes. We must power up the ship and escape to warn the Nexus."

Rem-9 began to reply, but at that instant, there was a rustling sound out in the corridor. Without hesitation, the mech vaulted the control board. He crouched beside Steinbach, leveling his weapon on the entrance.

The aliens came in a rush. Rem-9 scattered the first wave of killbeasts with several powerful gushings of energy from his

254

weapon. The attack lulled somewhat. Occasionally, a culus dashed through the entrance and got in close. The mech obligingly tore them appart bare-handed.

"We will never take the *Gladius* back to the Nexus. I insist you direct the pistol you have concealed behind your back at the entrance and help me in defending this position."

"But don't you see?" Steinbach sputtered. "They're a genetically superior species. We can't win."

Rem-9 stopped firing for a moment, his optics swung up in honest surprise. "Why do you say that?"

"Isn't it obvious? They can rip us apart. Any one of their various types could kill any one of us."

"I reject your theory. I have slain many in hand-to-hand combat. Even if they could defeat me, I would not consider them genetically superior beings."

"But it's not just that," Steinbach sputtered. "It's their entire attack, their entire approach. No band of humans could drop onto a planet and just openly assault an indigenous species the way they have. They breed so fast, they are so technologically competent."

Rem-9 shrugged his massive shoulders. During their conversation, he had made good use of his weapon killing several more aliens. Those that got in close gave him a workout with his grippers. "Your arguments are absurd. Genetic superiority is determined solely by which species survives. No other determiner is worthy of consideration."

"That's just the point! There must be a hundred thousand of them left down there on the surface. Even if we kill all those on the ship, what are we to do with all those aliens down there?"

"Kill them," said the mech simply.

"But what if we can't kill them all?"

Again, Rem-9 looked at him in incomprehension and surprise. He attempted to explain the situation to Steinbach once again. "If there are a hundred thousand, and we kill only ninety-nine thousand of them, then we lose. On the other hand, if we kill them all, we've won. I suggest you continue firing your weapon."

Steinbach threw a few shots at the entrance, scoring no hits. "We must run. We must salvage what we can."

The aliens gathered themselves for a final suicidal assault, but couldn't overcome the mech's firepower, blinding speed and

255

strength. A heap of smoldering bodies choked the entrance.

"They seemed desperate."

Steinbach snorted. "Not as desperate as us. Come, let us ready the engines for flight while we have the time."

The mech brushed him away from the control boards and grabbed both the General's wrists in one, massive gripper. He plucked Steinbach's pistol from his hands like a father removing a dangerous tool from the hands of his young son. "You are not worthy of being armed. You are more likely to shoot me than the enemy."

Steinbach complained bitterly, but Rem-9 ignored him. He bent over the control board and began making adjustments. He reported his situation to the Governor.

"Things have not gone well here," Droad told him on the phone. "The aliens haven't let us rest. They now carry weapons from the crew. We have to do something before we're all killed."

"I suggest we flush the ship, as Mai Lee desired, but in such a way that we may survive," said the mech.

"No, no!" hissed Steinbach at his side. "If you release radiation while the core is hot you'll disable the ship! None of us will escape!"

Droad's tiny image smiled. "I overheard what the good General had to say. I think that is an excellent idea. This ship is the only way out of the system, and therefore the only threat to the rest of the Nexus."

"I agree."

"What is your plan, then?"

"I have been unable to gain control of the laser turret. The situation suggests that the aliens now have control of it. A heavy knot of their communications patterns are emanating from there as well."

"That makes sense. We have been unable to do anything with the laser from the main bridge, either. In fact, the skald has done little else but try to operate it, to our surprise. No one suspected him of such technical knowledge. For a time we tried to restrain him, but once we realized his task was futile, we let him try. I believe he has completely lost his mind."

"It leads one to wonder what horrors he endured during his stay in the nest," said Steinbach. "Horrors we should all be escaping

256

now."

"I believe we need to rejoin our forces," Rem-9 told the Governor. "Before releasing the radiation, I will seal off the connecting corridors between the bridge areas and the laser turret. We can meet there and retake the laser control center."

Droad nodded. "I believe the turret is relatively close to the hold."

Five minutes later, the mech made the final preparations for releasing a deadly blast of radiation into the ship. Steinbach was almost beyond self-control.

"I can't believe this! You're killing us both, you're killing everyone aboard the ship! This ship is the only way out! Can't you understand that, you great freak?"

"You would have me risk all the Nexus trillions, not to mention abandoning the millions down on Garm to save ourselves?"

Steinbach sputtered, unable to answer. His eyes roamed the room, searching for a weapon. Rem-9 was unconcerned. He had already made sure that nothing effective was available. He placed his gripper on the final execution switches. Doors all over the ship slid shut as a thousand bulkheads sealed themselves. A roiling cloud of superheated radioactive gases bubbled into the reserve ventilation tanks.

Steinbach uttered a sound of terror and threw himself at Rem-9. He wrapped himself around the giant's right arm. Rem-9 flicked his gripper in annoyance. Steinbach was sent staggering.

He closed the contacts, releasing the radiation. Alarms sounded, the control board lit up with lurid red and orange warning lights.

"You've killed us," croaked Steinbach in dismay. On unsteady feet, he headed for the open corridor. the mech followed.

After a moment's thought, he handed the General his pistol back. The man no longer had any call to use it on him.

For an instant, Steinbach eyed the sleek black barrel of the pistol with murderous intent.

"Fear has stolen your reasoning. You need me to survive, however slim that hope may now be," the mech told him gently.

Taking a deep breath, Steinbach ran after him down the corridor, seemingly resigned to his fate. Rem-9 was vaguely glad that he didn't have to kill the man. Enough humans had died, lately.

They rejoined with the governor in the corridors. Many of the remaining men were wounded, all of them were breathing hard. The aliens had not let them rest.

"So, we meet again, General," said Droad. "For once, we are all on the same side."

Steinbach said nothing. He gripped his pistol with both hands and watched the corridor intersections intently.

As they approached the laser turret, they were ambushed by a force of killbeasts with hand-cannons. The first rank of militiamen went down in a storm of gunfire. Rem-9 got in close with the killbeasts, smashing them down with his grippers. The things sprang back up, bouncing like rubber from the steel deck. Though the aliens' limbs were broken they fought on savagely. The mech finally snapped the last killbeast's carapace open across his knee. A sickening crunch sounded and the thing finally sagged down. The ambush had been repelled.

When they reached the correct side passage, Droad sent the mech Lieutenant into the contaminated regions to get the flitter and bring it back up to the external ports around the laser turret. It was time to abandon the ship after making sure the laser couldn't be used against the human forces on Garm. There was no more point to staying with the *Gladius*. She had become a deathtrap, a tomb for men and aliens alike.

To reach the turret control room they had to cross a maze of catwalks that encircled the huge laser apparatus itself. A flock of culus squadrons attacked them when they were most vulnerable. Two men were knocked from the catwalks and fell screaming to their deaths. The skald fell too, but managed to latch onto the safety webbing. Sarah and Bili pulled him back up.

Above their heads the coils crackled with vast energy stores. Static lifted their hair and their clothing. Hot breaths of air struck them from the cooling vents.

"They're readying the laser to fire," said Droad in a dead voice.

No one replied.

When they reached the control center, they leapt through the smoking hole Jarmo produced with his plasma cannon. There was no hesitation anymore, little caution. Most of them figured themselves as dead, they took what little joy there was left in life from hitting back at the enemy.

Inside the control center was a Parent, a team of arls working with the controls and two juggers. The three large aliens were crammed into the limited space. Despite their situation, the humans gasped at the ghastly sight of the Parent. Quivering polyps raised sensory organs in alarm at their approach. The two juggers then rushed them, roaring their battle cries. They fought with great physical power and skill, but couldn't face the combined firepower of the humans. Only Gunther was brought down, killed by a jugger's teeth that mauled his head.

It was Sarah who sidestepped the fighting juggers and raced to the Parent. She emptied her pistol and reloaded five times before the monster finally sagged down in death. The arls were coldly blown to fragments by the victorious humans.

All of them took a moment to catch their breaths and marvel at the grotesque Parent except for the skald. Coming from his habitual spot at the rear of the company, he sprang forward, pushing his way to the laser controls. His pallid limbs swung in great strides, his peculiar, rolling gait more pronounced than ever.

He attacked the control boards in wild abandon, working levers and clittering at keys feverishly. He hummed an odd tune as he worked, shuffling his feet from side to side. Flecks of saliva formed white dots on his face, sprayed the controls. Warning lights flared into life, a deep rumbling sounded in the equipment, signifying that the laser was refocusing.

"Hey, stop that lunatic!" ordered Droad in alarm. He rushed to the control boards.

Jarmo and Sarah beat him to it, however. Jarmo grappled with the man, and was immediately surprised with the supple, wiry strength in his skinny limbs. He tried to contain the thrashing, moaning skald. He became concerned that the man would break his bones in his struggles.

"He's trying to aim it," said Sarah, frowning at the controls. "How would he know how to aim a weapon like this?"

"I don't know," grunted Jarmo. He felt more than heard a snapping sound. The skald's arm had broken, but his struggles to get to the controls didn't slacken.

Sarah moved to face him. "What are you trying to do?"

The skald locked his eyes with hers. She saw a desperate need

259

to communicate there. His lips quivered and worked, his tongue rolled about slackly within his mouth. "Feasting." he whispered. "The lines of the Feasting."

"That's what he's been saying all along," remarked Droad, joining them. "The mech Lieutenant has reached the flitter. He should be here in ten minutes or so. Any idea what he's going on about?"

"He was with me in the nest. The Feasting was what the aliens did with us. The Parent and her commanders ate humans and other types of meat. The Feasting appeared to be some kind of ceremonial meal. They did a lot of it."

"So what does 'the lines of the Feasting' mean?" asked Droad.

The skald's struggles had subsided; he stood in Jarmo's implacable grip, eyes flicking from one of them to another.

"Perhaps he means the queens," suggested Jarmo. He loosened his grip a fraction, pitying the man. "Maybe he knows where the Parents are in their nests, and is trying to aim the laser at them."

Droad frowned. "But how could he know? They're all underground."

Sarah had been examining the skald's attempts at focusing the laser. She looked up at the others suddenly. "He's linked the guidance computer to track radio frequencies. If the Parents utilize a different frequency for command, it would be possible to isolate them and destroy them."

The three eyed one another in growing hope. Steinbach had joined them and was now listening intently. "The man's obviously a lunatic. We should get off the ship while we have the chance," he told the others. He looked at the skinny skald in contempt. "Nothing should delay our escape. I think we should be heading for the outlying islands in the tropics of Gopus. It will take years for the aliens to reach us there, if they ever do."

"We have some time. The radiation is killing the aliens, although they seem to be taking their time in dying, as one might expect," said Jarmo.

"Let's try it," said Sarah.

Everyone looked to the Governor. He nodded his head. "Let him go, Jarmo. Just watch that we know what we're aiming at before we let him pull the trigger."

They helped by using Steinbach's codekeys, much to the

General's disgust. The laser was quickly aligned and focused on an area in the foothills of the polar range.

"It could be the site of a nest," Jarmo admitted, reading the scanning reports. "Heavy radio traffic on the alien frequencies."

"How many contacts of this special type have the computers isolated?" asked Droad. He had found a source of hot caf somewhere, and looked better than he had in hours.

"We've located twenty, sir."

Droad rubbed his chin. "Destroy them all."

And so the laser fired. Then they aimed, focused, and fired again.

* * *

"I've lost contact with another of my daughters," said the Parent. She warbled her foodtube in despair. "They must have isolated our voices. They are all going so quickly."

"Hush, my love," comforted the high nife commander at her side. His orbs had sunk deeply within his cusps. It had all been so close. Another week and the world might have been theirs. "You mustn't speak. They may have yet to detect you."

The Parent rattled her tentacles, signifying a negative. She did, however, dampen her transmissions to a bare whisper. "It is too late. If they have any brains at all, and unfortunately it is apparent that they do, they would have discovered us all before beginning to fire."

"Then we must flee."

Again her tentacles rattled. She caressed his cusps idly, an unheard of familiarity which both exhilarated him sexually and depressed him at the same time. It was clear that she believed the end to be near. "The others have been trying. None have escaped. Their weaponry seems to be effective. Within minutes, all of us will be gone."

Even as she spoke these fateful words, the roof of the nest rumbled. Distant explosions rocked the stronghold. The surface was under bombardment of some kind.

Trees, earth and stones were vaporized by the first pulses of the laser. It continued to fire, blasting an ever widening wound in the

261

earth nearly as big around as the nest itself. A fountain of superheated gas and molten plasma rose up. Gouts of radiation were released, bombarding the Imperial warriors that rushed to defend the nest.

"The Imperium is defeated."

The nife commander knew sadness. He sidled close to the Parent, feeling the thrill of her touch. "We must meld during the last moments."

She agreed. As he mounted her throne for a final time, he reflected that this pod had been expunged, but that the Imperium must have had other survivors. The Imperium would go on elsewhere.

As they reached their moments of ecstasy, the roof of the chamber vanished and their bodies were melted to glowing slag along with the birthing throne they perched upon.

* * *

As the threat of the Imperium diminished, Fryx regained some of his sanity. It became possible again to threaten and coerce him. Garth lunged forward, ravenous for power inside his own body. His ambitions knew no bounds, he wanted nothing less than for Fryx to abandon his skull.

The battle raged for several minutes after the last Parent had been located and destroyed by the laser.

* * *

"What's wrong with him, Mom?" asked Bili. A concerned group ringed the skald, who lay on the steel deck of the redundant bridge, writhing and flailing in a pool of his own blood and mucus. An amazing amount of fluid was coming from his nostrils. The others looked on, at a loss as to what to do.

"He's having some kind of fit. Maybe we should try to restrain him, to keep him from hurting himself," said Sarah. She felt a pang of guilt, but couldn't bring herself to take hold of the skald. He was too alien; his demeanor during their acquaintance had never made him into a comrade.

The skald went from bad to worse. His nostrils flared grotesquely, and an incredible lump of translucent fleshy material seemed to be squeezing out of the absurdly small orifice.

"His brains are leaking out!" declared Bili with certainty.

No one contradicted him. When the spiny mass was half-way out of his body, Steinbach pulled a hand-cannon out and knelt beside the thrashing man. He placed the barrel against the man's temple. "It's clearly some kind of alien trick. He's infested with some kind of parasite. I told you the aliens wouldn't be so easily bested. We must kill him," he looked up to Jarmo and Droad for support.

The Governor appeared indecisive.

"We can't take any chances!" shouted Steinbach. "We must stop this new horror."

"Wait!" said Sarah, putting a hand on Steinbach's shoulder. "I know what it is."

She proceeded to explain about the jellyfish creature that the aliens had shown them in the nest. "It's called a *Tulk*. The aliens feared it."

Against Steinbach's loud protests, they decided to spare the skald. The Tulk was captured and placed in a plastic bag for safekeeping. Bili poked and prodded at the quivering form with a pencil until his mother shooed him away.

They did what they could for the skald, who seemed to be in a state of shock. Carrying the man and the Tulk who had ridden inside of him, they boarded the flitter and left the *Gladius*.

Epilogue

Droad sat on the verandah of Fort Zimmerman. His fist was placed against his chin, supporting it. His face was loose, his eyes distant. The final weeks of the alien invasion had gone well. Robbed of reinforcements and command control, the aliens had lost much of their effectiveness. As well, they had learned that the fighting varieties of aliens had exceedingly short life spans, often times they showed signs of old age in the first month of life. Without the constant supply of new offspring, the Imperium had been doomed.

He watched as fireworks went off in the central compound. Already repairs to the fort had begun. There were no longer any contenders for his rule, at least not for now. The people of Garm seemed sick of anarchy, and showed an uncharacteristic zeal for work on defense projects.

"What are you moping about?" Sarah asked him, coming up and putting a soft hand on his shoulder. "We've saved the world, let's celebrate!"

"I've nothing to be pleased about."

"Well, I certainly do. My son and I are alive and well. Bili's new regrown arm is looking very good indeed. You've even given me a commission in the Militia. Why not look at the bright side of things?"

"I've managed to lose nearly half the civilian population of Garm in the first two weeks of my rule. What kind of accomplishment is that?"

"Ah, but you've saved the other half. That's what you've got to be happy about. Better yet, you've halted an alien assault that could have carried on into the Nexus itself. You've held back perhaps the greatest threat humans have ever faced since we left Earth."

"But have we won the war, or just a battle?" asked Droad. "There's so much we don't yet know about the universe."

Sarah frowned, having no answer for that. Both of them gazed up at the stars with disquiet.

The End

More Books by B. V. Larson:

IMPERIUM SERIES
Mech Zero: The Dominant
Mech 1: The Parent
Mech 2: The Savant
Mech 3: The Empress
The Black Ship (Novella)

STAR FORCE SERIES
Swarm
Extinction
Rebellion
Conquest
Battle Station

Other Books by B. V. Larson
Technomancer
Velocity
Shifting

Visit BVLarson.com for more information.